The Wolves of Caledonia

A Novel of Post Roman Britain

Jason Kyle

Contents

Map of Britain

500 AD

Map of Southwest Britain

500 AD

Map of Caledonia

500 AD

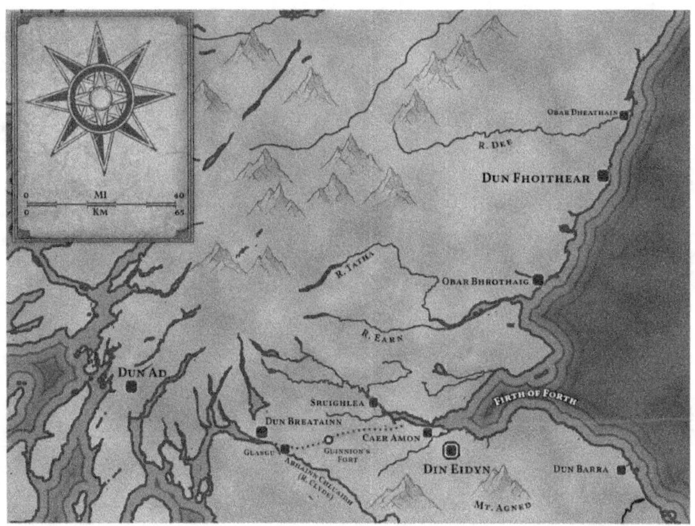

Prologue

Caer Gurcoc, Isle of Mona. 549 A.D.

PEREDUR RAN A HAND through his thin white hair and sighed happily. The fire crackled merrily, the meal his wife of many, many years had cooked not long ago still filled his belly. His lovely twelve-year-old granddaughter, Enid, was quick to refill his goblet with more mead the moment he drained it. That was his price for stories. Couldn't talk with a dry mouth after all, now, could he? He nearly jumped out of his chair when his two grandsons, eight-year-old Cadoc and Rhys, nine years old, knocked over his armor stand as they raced through the house. His armor and shield hit the wooden floorboards with a loud clatter.

"Boys!" Enid snapped. The noise almost made her spill the mead she was about to pour. "Settle down and stop behaving like barbarians."

"But Cadoc *is* a barbarian," Rhys protested, and pointed to smears of blue paint on the younger boy's face. "I'm King Arthur," he said, brandishing a wooden sword. "See? I've even got his sword, Caledfwlch."

"Arthur was the Duke of Battles, not 'King'," Enid corrected him.

"At least someone's been paying attention," Peredur chuckled.

"So do you want me to tell you a story or run around and play?" Peredur asked, nodding his thanks to Enid as she finished refilling his cup.

The two boys looked at each other, internally wrestling with the decision. A peal of thunder boomed outside, announcing a coming storm. Playing outside wouldn't be an option much longer then.

"Story," Cadoc answered for the two.

"First, why don't one of you boys close the window shutters, will you?" he asked. "Then I'll begin."

The boys got up and did as their grandfather bade them, then joined him at the large, round, wooden table.

"So... do you remember where we left off?" Peredur asked, thoughtfully stroking his beard.

"You were going to tell us about the Battle of the City of the Legion," Enid offered, taking a seat beside her grandfather.

"Ah. So I was," Peredur nodded. He took a sip of his mead and began.

"So, there we were, no lies. It was the seventeenth year of Emperor Anastasius' reign in the East... forty-two years ago now," he said after a pause. "My friends and I were tasked with scouting the Scoti raiding fleet on the coast of Hibernia, or Ériu's Land as they call it," old Peredur began his story, leaning forward in his chair.

"Some Scoti High king named Lugaid mac Loegairi had been causing a fuss along our eastern shores since shortly after we dealt with the Picts the previous year. We discovered that he had a massive fleet assembled — at least four dozen ships, and hundreds of men! Our kings concluded, thanks in part to information my own unit gathered, that King Lugaid was going to attack Caer Ligion, located on Powys' border, along the River Dyfrdwy."

"And King Arthur was sent to kill them?" Cadoc asked.

Rhys and Enid sighed, and planted their faces into their hands with audible slaps.

Peredur chuckled. "Well, High King Conanus tasked *Tribune* Arthur and the Red Dragons to assist King Cyngen of Powys in repelling the Scoti. Naturally, given his skills, our commander was given the position of Dux Bellorum, and therefore commander of all military forces in that region until the raiders were defeated."

Cadoc rolled his eyes at the correction. "So, tell us about the battle!" He pleaded.

"Well, Arthur assessed the situation and came up with quite the... welcoming party for the Scoti barbarians," Peredur smiled wolfishly. "Just driving them off wasn't enough. Not for our Tribune. He wanted us to *destroy* them..."

Chapter One

THE INHABITANTS OF CAER Ligion awoke to the shouts of the town watch and the clamor of a church bell. Less than two hundred paces down the river, the dark shapes of dozens of Scoti boats pierced through the surrounding fog in the soft light of the coming dawn on that Aprilis morning. Pale light glittered faintly off hundreds of oars as the raiders paddled towards us and we heard the bellows of their war horns announcing their presence.

Typically, when such raids occur, men are killed, women and children are carried away to become slaves, and homes are looted. If the townsfolk are able to react in time, everyone flees for the safety of the walls. Homes and shops between the walls of the town and the water's edge would still be looted, and a few would have been destroyed, but the townsfolk would be safe. This is the way of things.

This morning, however, it was the raiders who were in for a surprise. Once the raiders' target was determined, Tribune Arthur deployed his turma along with three others to the tarmac town, to bolster its defenses. Over one hundred and twenty of our men stood ready to greet the Scoti raiders upon their arrival, not to mention the additional three hundred or so men of fighting age who lived here. More turmae deployed to other towns on the off chance that the barbarians might change course and decide to attack some other target instead. Arthur was clever like that. Our tribune warned the people of the coming fleet and coordinated with the town's lord, along with King Cyngen in order to keep the people safe and to defend the town. Most commanders in his position would have been content with defending the walls of the fort at the expense of the outlying homes but ensuring that the people were safe and that the garrison suffered minimal casualties.

A more aggressive commander might have met the raiders on the shore and attacked them as they attempted to disembark. In that scenario, if the raiders decided they were at a disadvantage, they could simply break off the raid and row away, leaving them a threat to be dealt with another day. Or they might even attack somewhere else. That would have been good enough for most lords, but not for Arthur. He wanted to utterly crush these raiders and to do so in a way that sacrificed not a single woman, child, or home. During the night, we deployed throughout the unprotected homes closest to the shore and prepared a trap for the Scoti.

At the sound of the loud church bell, women scooped up their children and fled for the safety of the old Roman fort at the center of the town. Dogs barked at the commotion, but the people themselves moved about quietly and efficiently. As planned, men and older boys who were able to fight massed along the edge of the town, facing toward the shoreline with whatever weapons and armor they had, prepared to defend their homes and ensure their families' safe retreat into the fort.

"Wait for it," I said softly to the eight men of my section, or contubernium. We were all hiding behind a house a few hundred feet from the bank of the river. Across from me, behind another house, Decurion Owain hid with another section of our turma. He occasionally peeked out from behind his hiding spot to monitor the progress of the Scoti raiders as their fleet beached itself.

Our decurion was easy to pick out. Besides his plumed helm, Owain's white shield bore two red dragon heads, facing toward the central shield boss. Where the necks connected, toward the bottom of the shield, was the overlapping "X" and "P" of the Chi Rho. Everyone in our turma bore a white shield and a red Chi Rho upon its surface. Additional iconography of Michael the Archangel, and of course red dragons were also commonly displayed as well. My own shield also bore two dragon heads along the left half of it, and the Chi Rho on the right half.

As the sound of the women and children faded, we heard the faint voices of the raiders' leaders barking orders at their men as they disembarked. I glanced behind me at yet another house nearby. I couldn't see Decanus Sawyl's section, but I knew they were there, hiding, just as we were. There were nearly thirty of us in the turma. Three other turmae were dispersed throughout the town while the fourth, the tribune's, hid further back, in reserve.

We held our spears and shields at the ready, and our bodies tensed, ready to charge forward the moment Owain gave the word. It began to rain, and small droplets pinged off my helm, making it annoyingly hard to hear what was going on around me, so I kept my eyes glued to the decurion and adjusted my grip on the haft of my spear. Then the blaring of horns sounded, accompanied by unintelligible battle cries as the Scoti raiders charged into the shieldwall of the villagers. Iron weapons clanged against armor and wooden shields. Men cursed or shouted orders, while others screamed in pain.

Waiting there behind our house felt like an eternity, but finally the distinctive horn we used, called a lituus, blew, and small groups of townsfolk fell back in response.

"They're right behind us," a man yelled as he ran past us.

There was an edge of fear in his voice. I didn't blame him. He wasn't a soldier like me and the men I led, but just some farmer who'd been dragged from his field, had a spear and an old, beat-up shield shoved in his hands, and been told to fight. Maybe if the lord of Caer Ligion were smart, the farmers would have had a bit of training for precisely such events. Men in smaller towns and villages would have likely had combat experience, having dealt with raiders before. Towns the size of Caer Ligion were attacked far less frequently however, so when they got hit, they were generally less prepared.

My men and I, however, were not simple, levied militia. We were highly trained, very well-armed and armored, and most of us had seen combat at least once. Though not quite eighteen years old, I myself had already seen action several times, mostly fighting Picts in Caledonia less than two years ago. I'd helped defend my own home of Caer Gurcoc, on the western isle of Mona, against Scoti raiders last summer, along with my father, Lord Pelinor, and older brother, Lamorac. So when we heard the second blast of our old Roman horn, we didn't hesitate to spring into action.

"Now!" Owain ordered, raising his sword high overhead. My comrades and I rushed out from behind the house with excited yells, and in moments our turma was formed up in a small shieldwall, three ranks deep. My eight men were in the second rank behind Decanus Sawyl's section, with a third section, led by Decurion Owain, behind them. His second in command, Duplarius Cornelius, stood beside him with our brass-headed dragon banner. He cursed as its long red tail flapped about in his face. We positioned ourselves in the space between the two closest houses. Throughout the town, other groups of soldiers and townsfolk were doing the same thing.

Normally, we fought on horseback, of course, but Arthur wanted us to help ambush the raiders, and there wasn't enough good concealment for us within or even close to the town had we remained mounted. There wasn't enough adequate cover to hide our horses in the surrounding region so we corralled our horses within the fort and deployed as heavy infantry. Fortunately, we were as capable of fighting dismounted as mounted, as these barbarians were about to discover. We had the element of surprise, but the Scoti love a good fight, so our sudden appearance didn't deter them for more than a few moments, long enough for them to pause and reassess their situation.

A warrior I suspected was their leader bellowed to the men around him, and they threw themselves at us, howling their war cries. Unlike most of the men, he was one of the few in a polished iron helm and wore a coat of mail over his knee-length, colorful striped tunic. He also waved a sword about, high overhead. Like many of his companions, he wore no trousers under his tunic and sported a thick mustache and beard. For all I knew, this might have even been their king.

My heart raced as fear and excitement coursed through me in the face of imminent combat. With effort, I pushed those feelings aside in order to focus on the commands of my decurion and maintain awareness of the men in my section.

"Throw plumbatae!" Owain called out, and in well-drilled movements, my comrades and I switched our spears to our left hands and pulled darts out of their small rack on the inside of our shields or from small satchels at our hips. The darts had weighted iron balls near their tips and feathered ends, making them look a lot like short, fat arrows. Their size made them easier for us to throw while in a shieldwall than javelins were, and the weights on their shafts gave them a bit of extra punch, as well as making them easier to aim. Unless, of course, it was *me* throwing them. I consider myself an excellent spearman. I am competent with the javelin, sword, and even the bow and sling. But for some reason, I have always been embarrassingly bad with plumbatae. So, when Decurion Owain ordered us to throw, I wasn't very surprised when my dart flew at the man to the left of my intended target, who blocked the dart with his shield. Beside me, my friend Gilbert snickered. His grin was an odd contrast with the intimidating helm he wore, which hid the upper half of his face in the Germanic style, and made even his eyes all but invisible.

"Shut it, Gib," I growled.

"I didn't even say anything," he protested with a laugh.

This, in turn, caused a couple of others in my rank to laugh as well. Yes, even now, with a horde of hundreds of barbarians screaming and charging at us, my accursed comrades wouldn't ignore a chance to have a laugh at my expense. I sighed and hurled a second dart at Owain's shouted command.

Probably only a quarter of our plumbatae actually killed or seriously wounded an enemy, but it was something. More importantly it disrupted their charge, so they didn't hit our line as a single, unified force. Men stopped to hold their shields up or tripped over their dead or wounded comrades as they came at us, and come at us they did, howling and screaming. What they lacked in discipline, they made up for in ferocity.

The sound of shields and weapons clashing against each other rang out once again all along the town's perimeter. We skewered the most reckless of the Scoti on the tips of our spears. The rest, following behind, were more careful. First, they looked for openings in our lines. When they didn't find any obvious weaknesses, they decided to try their own ranged attacks. They backed away, leaving the ground strewn with their dead and wounded. Barbarians in front provided the cover of their own ragged shieldwall while those in the back prepared to hurl javelins at us. Some prepared slings. A few had bows.

Our decurions shouted warnings. "Incoming! Get your shields up!" We complied instinctively, raising our shields and hunching our heads down a bit. The men in the front ranks took a knee so that our shields could provide that much more protection. Moments later, the clatter of stones and arrows rained down on us. We blocked most of them with our shields, but grunts and screams of pain from within our formation made it clear that at least a few got through. Those whose shields were damaged by the javelins rotated to the rear rank of the formation.

Villagers behind our shieldwall threw their own javelins over our heads which also landed amongst the Scoti. One man even climbed up on the roof of the house to our right and loosed arrows at them with a bow. We added to the barrage throwing more plumbatae at the raiders. That was another advantage of the plumbatae over javelins. Each one of us carried four to six of those little darts. Most of the raiders only carried one or two throwing spears, in addition to whatever their primary weapon was, be it another spear, axe, or more rarely, a sword. I had enough time to wonder how long this back-and-forth would last when another series of blasts from our trumpeter sounded. It was the signal to charge.

"Last Hope!" We roared our numerus' battle cry in response to the horn blast and the turma at our center surged forward. Our shieldwall took on a sharply angled wedge formation, and at its tip was Decurion Galhault. He was a former mercenary from the region of Gaul and was a beast of a man who weighed nearly twice that of most men in our cavalry wing. There were at least a couple of men in our numerus who were taller than Galhault, including Arthur himself, but there were certainly none as broad, or as strong. If that weren't enough, Galhault wore a cloak trimmed with fur and a helmet with a tall, feathered crest jutting out, which had the effect of making him appear even larger still. Being in the turma to his left gave me a chance to see the Scoti instinctively cower before the giant as we rushed at them, then my attention shifted to the barbarians in front of me.

I batted aside the spear one man thrust at me, then slammed my weight into him from behind my shield. Unlike Galhault, I'm of average height, and was a bit leaner than most in my younger days. That being said, I know how to leverage my weight, so when I slammed into the Gael, he staggered back a bit, braced though he was. I followed it up by burying the tip of my spear into his face and drove him to the ground. Another barbarian stabbed at me, but Gib's shield was there, and he blocked it.

My world, and my awareness of how the battle progressed, condensed down to just the few feet around me. My cymbrogi and I worked our spears into the gaps of the barbarians' shieldwall, while using our shields to block their spears. They attempted to do the same to us. As spear shafts broke, or were lost, we drew our swords or axes and fought shield to shield. The light rain and our trampling feet soon turned the ground to mud.

I thrust my spear at the face of a man in the front rank, but he dodged aside. A barbarian in the second rank seized it below the blade, and yanked. I swore, and was pulled forward, caught off guard by the act. I let go of the spear, but not before a barbarian's spear hit my helmet and skittered off of it. The glancing blow still knocked me backwards. I staggered and slipped in the mud. I fell and cursed again, then yelped when another spear was thrust at me. I frantically blocked it with my shield. Gib stepped forward with his shield out and warded off another blow aimed at me, while someone behind me grabbed me by the baldric strapped across my chest and yanked me to my feet. I stepped back into formation, got my shield up, and drew my sword, then reengaged the enemy, targeting their spears with my blade in order to create openings for my comrades to exploit.

It didn't take long before a great clamor of voices shouted off to my right. The Scoti raiders ceased their attack, and their formation fell back. They squeezed together, attempting to keep their shieldwall intact. Those in front of me began looking around wildly. I could see the fear in their eyes, though I couldn't understand what their commanders were shouting. Then jubilant cries of "We've broken through" rippled through our own lines. Now I understood the barbarians' fear. Shieldwalls are a hard thing to break open if you can't flank around them, but once an enemy force does break through, it becomes easy for that enemy to pour in through that breach, isolate, and destroy the shieldwall in pieces. From the sound of things, and from the way the Scoti were behaving, somewhere in their formation, we had done just that. More than likely right in the center where Galhault was, if I were to guess.

I grinned and shouted encouragement to my own men. "Keep on them, lads! They're breaking!" I waved my sword overhead and my men surged forward, keeping in tight formation around me. To my left, I saw the snarling visage of our draco standard move up as well, causing the long, bright red tail to wave about. Decurion Owain led our turma, savagely laying about him with his blood-slicked sword and shield, shouting curses at the Scoti in one moment, and encouraging us in the next.

A spear jabbed out, aimed at the man to my right. I chopped down at it with my sword. The blow wasn't enough to break the spear's haft, but it certainly knocked it down and created an opening. The big man to my right, Marcus, exploited that opening by lashing out with his sword, stabbing the unarmored Scot through his shoulder. The barbarian fell back with a cry.

From somewhere far to my left, another horn blew, accompanied by the sound of hooves thundering across the battlefield. I risked a glance that way and saw a flash of spear tips and the distinctive white rectangle of cloth depicting a red dragon held by one of the men as they closed in on the Scoti formation's flank. I whooped for joy at the sight. Arthur had entered the fight!

While the bulk of our force were deployed within the town to bolster the townsfolk and fight the raiders shield to shield, Tribune Arthur had held his turma reserves, to be deployed as conditions developed. When the Scoti shield-wall slowly buckled and fractured, Arthur and his men emerged from behind us and smashed into the rear of the barbarians' right flank

In an instant, the left half of their shield wall shattered, and raiders in front of me turned and fled for their boats. The battle became a slaughter as we pursued, cutting them down as they ran. One of our men went down with an arrow buried in his chest. I looked up and saw that the first raiders to reach the boats had turned around and begun loosing arrows, hurling sling stones, or throwing spears at our men to cover the retreat of their comrades.

"Shields up," I shouted, and we slowed down in order to tighten up our formation. It had nearly dissolved as we chased down the raiders. Beside me, Gib had no sooner raised his shield to interlock with mine than a slender javelin slammed into and through it. Its metal tip halted an inch in front of my friend's face.

"*Skyt!*" Gib yelped in his native Frisian tongue. He looked wide-eyed at it, then over to me before the weight of the javelin forced him to discard his shield. Having a free hand now, he drew the long-bladed seax sheathed at his belt and gave me a quick nod, signaling that he was ready to continue. He made sure to make use of the cover provided by my shield and Marcus's beside me.

This pause allowed me to gain a broader perspective of the battlefield. Most of the barbarians were still fleeing and scrambling to get back into their boats. Some distance to my left, I saw one boat full of men had shoved off and was safely away. To my right, a cluster of raiders with a bit more courage than their fellows turned back to face us and formed up into a tight shieldwall. On the whole however, the battle had become absolute chaos. It began as two organized formations with a front of about seventy paces. Now it disintegrated into several clusters of raiders as they attempted to fall back to their boats. As our men caught up to them, they were forced to turn and fight or be cut down.

The Red Dragons easily adapted to the situation, organized into turmae of twenty to thirty men as we were. We fought the raiders in disciplined formations, even under these conditions. The raiders and the levied townsfolk, however, behaved closer to two riotous mobs, fighting and scurrying about, fleeing or swarming vulnerable targets of opportunity as they were presented to them.

On the left flank, Arthur and his mounted turma continued to chew up the enemy, though their momentum stalled amidst the swarm of the Scoti. Had the enemy been more consolidated, he would have disengaged and charged again, but in this mess of a battle, there was no point. I watched our tribune in awe for a moment. He was a blur of motion as he hacked, kicked, and shield-bashed barbarians with fierce determination. With his swirling red cloak, polished scale armor, and crested helmet, he looked like some kind of avenging angel, though the rain and spatters of mud and blood on him did tarnish the look a bit.

It was to my horror then when I saw Arthur's duplarius pulled from his horse. The white and red banner he'd been carrying flew through the air and was snatched by a filthy barbarian. Like the Romans of old, it was drilled into every cavalryman's head that along with never abandoning a fallen comrade, if possible, of equal value were our precious standards.

"The vexillum!" I yelled to my men, gesturing with my sword. "Save the vexillum!"

So frantic was I to retrieve the banner and so focused on the pagan bastard who now held it that I didn't even look to see who had heard or followed me as I charged into the chaotic melee. I slammed the boss of my shield into one barbarian's face and followed it up with a strike to his head with its rim, barely even slowing down. Behind me, I heard Gib's voice scream a battle cry before stabbing another Scot who rushed us from the right.

In another moment, several of us waded into the fight, and the ugly, bearded man clutching our banner was almost within reach! He had yet to notice me and my lads. Instead, his attention was divided between Arthur and his horsemen to his right, and glancing back to his rear, where men were still streaming into their boats.

A hairy, wild-eyed barbarian lunged in front of me, swinging an axe straight at my head! I brought my shield up with a startled yelp. His axe smashed into it, and at the same time, I lashed out with my left foot and kicked the barbarian in his shin. He staggered away, giving me the space to bury my sword into him. Someone stabbed my vulnerable right side then, and though my mail held, a wave of pain shot through my torso, and I doubled over with a grunt. I turned to face the new combatant, but Gib, ever at my side, was there in a flash. With a howl, he launched himself at the Gael, caving the man's skull in with his sword. Then he plunged his seax into a second barbarian. A spear thrust out from over my shoulder and killed yet another enemy in my path before I had a chance to engage him. Then the man trying to get away with our banner was there before me. I brought my left arm up and slammed my shield into his shoulder as he was turned sideways to me, still paying more attention to Arthur, also closing in on him, than on me. He stumbled, knocked off balance, and I dropped my shield, exchanging it for a hold on the wooden shaft of the banner.

"Get your filthy hands off our banner," I yelled as I yanked at it.

Despite the hit I'd given him, he didn't let go of it and we continued struggling for control of the sacred vexillum. His other hand came up with an axe. I had no shield, and as close as we were, I wasn't sure how effectively I could use my sword, so on impulse, I whipped my head forward and smashed my forehead into his face. I had the advantage of wearing an iron helm with a padded cap underneath. The barbarian wore no helmet, and my attack had the desired effect. He let go of the banner and fell backwards into the mud. I finished him off with a quick thrust of my sword into his unprotected torso.

I barely had time to celebrate my victory when yet another barbarian hit me in a diving tackle, and I was slammed to the ground. I'm ashamed to admit, both sword and banner fell from my grasp as I hit the ground. Stars exploded across my vision. Ears ringing, I squinted and blinked as the cobwebs in my head cleared, just as the dagger-wielding Scot straddling me tried to feed me his blade. I yanked my head to the side, and the dagger stabbed into the ground instead.

With raindrops falling upon my upturned face, I trapped the barbarian's arm with both hands, hooked my left heel around his leg, and prepared to roll him off of me, but before I could, a shield rim slammed into the side of his head, and he collapsed on top of me. I looked up, squinting, and saw a Chi Rho, encircled by an ornate red dragon on a field of white. While both symbols were common enough among the Red Dragons, I recognized this particular shield and looked up at its owner gratefully. I'd been saved by Arthur himself.

My tribune reached down and yanked the barbarian's body off of me, then offered me his hand. I glanced around long enough to see that our banner had apparently been picked up off the ground, so I snatched up my fallen sword, then grabbed his hand. He hoisted me up to my feet, looking me up and down while I spit away rain, blood, and dirt that had got into my mouth.

"You alright, lad?" he asked.

"I'm fine, Tribune," I gasped, though in truth I was a bit shaken. That final knife attack had come within a hair of killing me. He must have seen the fear still lingering in my eyes, for he clapped me on the shoulder as I wiped mud and rainwater from my face.

"Good job saving the vexillum," he said. "Chasing down these barbarians in their boats to retrieve it would have been quite the nuisance." His sea-green eyes glinted humorously.

With a start, I looked around, remembering my surroundings. Beside me, Gib now held the standard. All around, our men were wiping blades clean, checking each other over for injuries, and cheering. I saw no barbarians any-where on the riverbank. Instead, a few vessels were rowing away. Most of the boats were still beached and empty of occupants, giving me a good idea of how severely we'd beat the raiders.

"We won?" I asked, feeling a sense of profound relief washing over me.

Arthur flashed a grin at me. "Did you ever doubt we would?"

"None at all," I said, truthfully. "There were sure a couple moments where I didn't think I was going to live to see it though, Tribune."

Our commander laughed, then walked away, shouting for Decurions Owain, Galhault, and Drystan to join him.

"Contubernales!" I called out to the men of my section, "Assemble on me!"

Up and down the line, other decani were doing the same thing. We generally fought in tight enough formations that we rarely broke unit cohesion too badly, especially in more confined fights like this one had been.

As my men came over, I did a quick headcount. Gib was already here beside me. Marcus came over, supporting Taran, more often called Tor, who was limping slightly. Tor looked like a child compared to Marcus' burly frame. He'd lost his helmet and blood caked his mop of dark-brown hair. People often said Tor and I looked alike, though I didn't quite see it. He'd joined our turma a few months back, and was even from Mona, same as me. His family lived in Abberfraw though. Tall, blond Cadwal was right behind them, tugging an arrow out of his shield. Red-haired and freckled Euron came over. He had a nasty-looking cut on the side of his face but otherwise looked well. There was Dafydd, the shortest among us, already eying up the dead Scoti as he strolled over, looking for anything worth looting.

"Come on, Dafydd, get over here," I called out. "If these barbarians had anything valuable, they wouldn't have needed to risk their lives trying to loot this town, now, would they?"

The others laughed. Last came Kilydd and Quintus. My lads were all ac-counted for. I breathed a sigh of relief. I waited as Gilbert respectfully passed

Arthur's standard off to him, then searched out Owain. The members of my section followed me as we made our way over to him, gingerly stepping over the numerous bodies that littered the ground.

"Peredur," Owain nodded at me. There was a hard look in his eyes that set me on edge. "Do you have all your people?"

"I do, Decurion," I replied.

"You're lucky then. That was reckless, going after the banner the way you did."

I winced, understanding that there would be a longer conversation about that action later, when the other soldiers weren't around to hear it. For now, I nodded, then glanced around. There had been twenty-eight of us in total yesterday. We were short now. Before I could do my own head count, Owain continued. "I'm missing three. Sawyl is short one. Spread out, find our missing men. Nobody loots anything or goes to the rear until we find our men, unless you're in danger of bleeding out."

"We taking prisoners?" Marcus asked.

"If they look like they'll live? Yes. We can sell them," Owain replied. "Otherwise, finish them off. And be careful! Some of these barbarians might only be playing dead."

We nodded and began the gruesome task of recovering our dead and wounded. As we searched, the battlefield gradually filled with villagers and their family members who were doing the same thing. As was always the case following a battle, the sounds of the wounded and dying men tore at my heart. It didn't matter at this point whether the man moaning in agony was a Briton or Gael.

I loathed the sound of men suffering. The only sound that was worse was the weeping of the women when they found their loved ones on the field. That sound haunted me at night above all others. I'd once heard a depraved barbarian prisoner boast about relishing the destruction of his enemies and hearing the wailing of their women. The man had so disgusted me that I'd wanted to kill him then and there, prisoner or not. I'd been ordered to let him be, but I admit incidents such as that one had, in the past two years since joining the Red Dragons, made me understand, if not fully share, Decurion Owain's animosity towards the barbarians. Every time I had to assist our men in the search for fallen comrades and attend another burial, a bit more of my empathy was chipped away. I'd yet to even face Saxons on the field of battle, so I wasn't sure how I would feel towards them. I suspected I would feel less merciful towards them though, given that they were the people who'd killed my oldest brother.

We scoured the battlefield, hunting for our missing comrades. As we found one, we waved over a pair of stretcher bearers who would load the man up and haul him off to the field hospital our medicus, Tewdrig, had set up inside the walls of the town. The team would hurry over with a litter, load the man up, and take him away. When we encountered a dead member of our unit, we thrust a spear into the ground near their bodies so they could be removed from the field later. As we came upon mortally wounded Scots, we dispatched them. Just two years ago, I had found the task appalling and had to force myself to remember that we were, essentially, providing the mercy of a swift death to these men. I still disliked the task, but it had become far more bearable than it had been.

This dual task of identifying our casualties and finishing off the enemy took a couple of hours, thanks to the size of the battlefield. We found all of our missing cymbrogi, or countrymen. One was mortally wounded; the others had been slain. We gathered around the wounded man, Generys, in muted silence while Owain knelt beside him, holding his hand. Our priest, a big, strong young man named Derfel, prayed over him, then solemnly moved on to the others. A half dozen of our men died that day, with three times that number wounded.

We buried our soldiers, leaving the enemy to be buried by the townsfolk of Caer Ligion, then set up our tents outside of the walls, no longer needing to be concerned with Scoti raiders detecting our presence. I thanked God that today at least, our casualties had been light, and none had been close friends of mine. A vision of the rows of burial mounds behind the broken walls of Guinnion's Fort came unbidden, and I shuddered at the memory. We were lucky today. How long would that hold up?

"All who live by the sword, die by sword... eventually," I mumbled as I walked away.

Chapter Two

IN CAMP THAT NIGHT, the men sang ballads of the heroic deeds of our ancestors and drank toasts to fallen comrades in celebration of our victory. Many also gambled away some of the loot acquired from the battle. Rings, bracelets, and good-quality daggers exchanged hands more than once that night. More than a few also went into town in hopes of finding some female companionship for the night. Owain found me, sitting off to one side on a log.

"Good news!" He grinned. "That barbarian king, Lugid... Lugaid? Whatever his name was, he's dead now. Prisoners identified his body. Nobody knows exactly when he fell, not that it matters much. What does matter is that he's dead. We gave those Scoti bastards a beating they likely won't forget for a while."

"Good. They fought hard. I'd prefer not to have to face them again anytime soon," I grimaced.

Owain shrugged and took a pull from a wineskin I hadn't noticed until that moment. "No dice or drinking for you?" he asked.

"I had a cup of wine earlier, to toast our men," I said. "I'm not good enough at dice to bother with that."

"Nobody is good with dice. Some people just *think* they are." Owain smirked. "Unless the dice are loaded." He looked around and saw that nobody was paying us any attention, so he sat down next to me. His expression grew stern, and I braced myself.

He stared off into the camp for a few moments, then at last he said, "Your action this morning was reckless. You could have gotten men killed."

I didn't need to ask him what he was referring to. "Apologies, Decurion," I replied. "I saw the banner fall into the raiders' hands and acted on instinct."

"Our banners are important," Owain conceded. "But our men are more so. There isn't a man of the numerus that Arthur, or any decurion, would trade in exchange for a banner. You charged after it and pulled your contubernium out of formation with you. That weakened the formation of the turma. Had our turma broken, that would have put pressure on the other turmae. You're lucky that the barbarians were already disorganized by that point. Had we been fighting a more disciplined or determined foe, like the Saxons, that could have been disastrous for our entire formation."

My stomach turned in knots, envisioning the calamity that Owain described. *I only did what I thought was right*, I thought in horror. But the decurion wasn't done.

"Lucky for you, Arthur judges our actions based more on the actual results, rather than what might have happened. He and I talked about you earlier, and he pointed out that history is full of examples of bold moves men have made that could have ended badly. The important thing is that you make your gambles knowingly, with full appreciation of the risks involved and the consequences of failure. I think we both know that this morning, you took no time to consider the consequences."

"You're right," I conceded. My mind flashed again to the freshly dug graves of our men. The thought that my recklessness could have cost even more lives appalled me.

Owain clapped me on the shoulder. "Hey, don't let this incident cause you to become indecisive, either. You have good instincts. Arthur and I saw that in the Picti campaign, and you've done well with your contubernium since then. Even with today's action, it's important to balance out what might have happened with what did happen. None of your men died today which is, unfortunately, more than I or Sawyl can say, and you saved the vexillum. Remember, making bad decisions isn't the worst thing a leader can do."

I looked up at him, startled. "No?"

"No," he replied. "The worst decision a leader can make is to make no decision."

I nodded silently.

Owain stood up. "Learn from today, but don't stop trusting your instincts. You've the making of a good leader. And we all make mistakes, even Arthur."

I looked up at him. He must have seen the surprise on my face because he smiled. "I was a young decanus a few years ago when Arthur first led the Dragons into battle against the Angles. Ector was with him, as an advisor. How old are you, Peredur?"

"I'm seventeen, Decurion. I'll be eighteen in a few months."

"Seventeen, Owain echoed. "Well, Arthur took command of the Dragons when he was eighteen. Imagine being your age but being responsible for more than eight hundred men under your command instead of eight. And the Dragons' previous commander had been Ector Artorius, who was Uther's second in command when this unit was formed up in Armorica to fight the Goths. Yes, he made mistakes. You know we fought four engagements against the Angles along the River Dubglass?"

I nodded. "Those were a few years ago, but I remember the bards telling of Arthur's glorious victories there."

Owain chuckled dryly. "Peredur, ask yourself something. If Arthur's campaign against them had been so 'glorious', why do you suppose we had to battle them four times?"

My mouth hung slack. "Are you telling me the Dragons *lost* those battles?" I asked, incredulously.

"Eh, not lost, exactly," Owain hedged. "Mistakes were made, and the first three battles were... less than successful, shall we say. The important thing here is that Arthur learned from each fight and didn't repeat his mistakes. That allowed him to win a decisive victory the fourth time we met. But that was a costly campaign." His voice trailed off, and he stared off towards the river. I knew that look.

I sat with him in silence for a few more moments, then finally spoke up.

"With your permission, I'd like to go find Maithgemm," I excused myself.

"Certainly," Owain said with a wave. "Go on. I have things to do as well. Reflect on what I've told you, though."

"I will," I promised, and we both walked away.

I went through the tall, wooden gatehouse of Caer Ligion, wound my way past the shops and homes, and into a wide space where a large tent had been set up as our field hospital. I strolled in and found our medicus, Tewdrig, a heavyset, middle-aged man with shoulder-length gray hair sitting in a chair, eating a wedge of cheese and drinking from a wineskin. Beside him was Gemma, a young woman only a bit younger than I, and beautiful in spite of the dirt and blood that now streaked her face and clothing, as it did the older man beside her. Also in the tent was the towering, burly Gaelic warrior Digain and the plump, gray-haired woman, Madwen.

The previous spring, the auburn-haired Gemma and I had found each other in the woods of Caledonia. She'd presented herself as a runaway Picti slave when I first met her. While that had been mostly true, I found out later that she was also a niece of Domangart Reti, the king of Dal Riata. Despite that, following a decisive victory against the Picts at Guinnion's Fort, she'd chosen to come back south with us to Caer Lleon, rather than return to her family. She did at least write and had a message sent to her uncle, filling him in on her current whereabouts.

Faced with the choice of demanding her return — a long and dangerous journey for a young maiden to make, or allow her to remain in the care of the famous Tribune Arthur, a potential political ally, King Domangart decided to allow her to remain in place, at least for the time being and to send one of his household guard, Digain, to protect her. Madwen was sent to tend to her, and to safeguard her virtue, no doubt, while he decided what to do with her. Last winter, the three of them accompanied me back to Mona when I returned home for the winter. It had pleased me to no end to see my mother and Gemma get along so well. My father, Lord Pelinor approved of her as well.

When Gemma looked up and saw me, her face lit up into a broad smile. She bolted out of her chair and strode over to me, the hem of her dress fluttering about her. She planted her hands on her hips and made a show of inspecting me.

"You're safe," she exclaimed, then teasingly added, "About time you make it through a battle without needing to visit Master Tewdrig and I."

Tewdrig, who'd been in the act of taking a sip from his wineskin, sputtered and coughed.

"I don't get wounded that often," I muttered.

She arched an eyebrow. "Your scars say otherwise."

I opened my mouth to protest, then thought better of it. In the year and a half that I'd served with the Red Dragons, I'd already acquired a rather prominent scar on my right side as well as a smaller but still noticeable scar on my left shoulder, along with a couple of nicks from skirmishes I'd been in since then.

"How are you doing here?" I asked, changing the subject.

Gemma's eyes twinkled, clearly recognizing my effort. "Not as bad as at Guinnion's Fort. Only a few of our lads came through with anything serious." Then her expression darkened. "The locals got the worst of it. They don't have the armor or the training that the Red Dragons have. We spent all afternoon treating them, along with some of the more seriously wounded Scoti prisoners."

I nodded. "Care to walk with me?"

Though the sun had finally gone down, the clouds had dispersed and a bright moon illuminated the town well enough to get around.

Gemma glanced over at Tewdrig, who waved her off. "Go on, girl. I've no further need of you. Not until the morning when we pack up."

Gemma smiled and grabbed her light cloak, then followed me out of the tent. "I won't go far," she said, reassuring Digain when he made ready to follow us.

Digain, Madwen, and Gemma had a quick conversation in their lilting Gaelic language. I'd picked up a few phrases since beginning my friendship with Gemma, but they spoke too quickly for me to catch more than a couple of words.

"I shall accompany you," Madwen said primly, in heavily accented Brythonic, and the three of us strolled out of the hospital tent.

We stayed within the walls, being that it was night, and ambled along the streets, avoiding the muddiest ones. As always, it struck me as odd and a bit sad, seeing the old, Roman stone ruins mixed in amongst the wattle and daub structures that had grown up around them. Here and there, a family had even built up their home within some of the more intact Roman structures. It was much the same as in Caer Lleon and other towns I'd traveled through.

I gestured to one such building. Rainwater had cleared away some of the debris, and moonlight reflected off of some old tile flooring. "I wonder how long before all traces of Rome are gone from this place. How long before we re-learn some of the marvels lost with them?"

"Like what?" Gemma asked, curious.

"Some of these ruins have pipes under them. I've heard some old men say the Romans had a way to heat water, heat the floors of homes, and other such things with these pipes. Nobody has any idea how they did it. They had some kind of building material that was as hard as rock, but seamless. Same story with that. We've no idea how they made that anymore."

Gemma nodded. I noticed a distracted look in her eyes. "Am I boring you?" I teased.

She chuckled, and her hand played with the fastening strap of her belt pouch. "No, no. I love hearing you talk about how the Romans did this and that. It's just that..." Her hand fished out a scroll and held it under my nose before she continued. "A messenger came from Caer Lleon earlier this week, while you lot were preparing to fight the Scoti, so I didn't have a good time to give you the news... it's from King Domangart."

My stomach tightened into knots, suddenly more afraid of that scroll than any barbarian spear. "Are you being called home?" I asked.

"Apparently, my uncle has decided on a husband for me," she said, ignoring my question.

I stopped walking and felt my knees go weak. So soon? Gemma was an eligible maiden, but I'd hoped there'd be more time for me to woo her and maybe speak to her uncle at some point. I scrutinized her face, but when she wants to, Gemma is a master at hiding any emotion. It's a product of her years spent in slavery, I suspect.

"Wh — who are you supposed to marry? When?" I asked, feeling almost nauseous now. I didn't know if I loved Gemma, it felt too soon for all that, nor did I know if she loved me. At the same time, I thought that one day we might fall in love, and I didn't want her to be whisked off and married to some old nobleman!

"Some coastal merchant has been asking for my hand on behalf of his son these past few months, and finally met my uncle's bride price," she replied. The faintest smile played about the corner of her lips as she gave me this news, and she paused, staring intently into my face.

When I found no words would come to me, her lips twitched into a mischievous smirk before she continued, casually, as though she were discussing the latest current events.

"There's no date set, of course. Marriage itself could still be several months away. It's the betrothal, the declared intent to marry, that's important now. After all, you didn't think my uncle would be comfortable with me off traipsing around Britain with one of Arthur's men as an unmarried maiden, did you?"

My mind was racing. This was a disaster, but she appeared completely comfortable with the news. It made no sense. Then suddenly it did, as piece by piece, I started thinking about precisely what she was telling me. No way... Did she mean...?

"Wait a moment," I said slowly. "Are you telling me that your uncle and my father...? Are you betrothed to... *me?*"

Gemma, unable to contain herself any longer, burst out laughing.

"Yes." she exclaimed. Then she became serious and wagged the scroll in my face like a dagger. "Keep in mind that we're betrothed, not married! So don't go and get any ideas. I know how you men think."

I blinked and looked from the scroll in my face to her, then asked the first thing that came to mind. "How would you know that?"

She rolled her eyes. "I hear men talk. I see how men look at women when we walk by. When I was a slave, I could hear couples talking in their homes, among... other things. You aren't very complicated creatures, you know." Behind us, Madwen made a quiet noise that sounded suspiciously like a snicker.

On the surface, it might seem odd that a Scoti king would approve of a wayward niece living in a Romano-Briton community that frequently had to fend off Scoti raiders, as we'd just done. The Scoti clans, however, are no more of a unified people than anyone else. Our own kingdoms squabble and fight all too frequently, as do the Saxons, Angles, and Jutes, and the Picti tribes, though most of them were unified under the iron fist of King Drest II at the time. In the grand scheme of things, while we weren't of her own people, she was a well-placed line of communication that King Domangart Reti could use should he wish to connect with Arthur, or through him, the kings of Britain.

More directly, though not royalty, my family has always done well for itself, living as we do near the coast of Mona, dealing in the fishing trade, the selling of wheat, and our most prized commodity, horses. Gemma had accompanied me to my family's villa over the previous winter solstice, and my father broached the subject of writing to King Domangart, but we'd heard nothing since, until now.

We continued our stroll through the town, laughing and chatting — she did most of the chatting, and I mostly laughed. She did a number of impersonations of Tewdrig, which were spot on, as well as some of our companions. I didn't think her impersonation of me was particularly accurate, though.

It was so strange, I thought, even as I enjoyed my evening with her. It was like nothing changed between us, despite our official betrothal. In fact, the biggest, immediate change would be most felt by my father, who'd now gained a powerful new business partner in the King of Dal Riata. For his part, while he was on a higher social tier, being a king, Domangart gained access to a wider market. Ships would pass more frequently between Dal Riata and Mona, and from Mona to other parts of Britain and into Europe.

After half an hour or so, we made our way back to the edge of our camp. It was one thing for Gemma to socialize with the men during the day, but inappropriate for her to be in the camp after dark. So, we stopped, turned towards each other, and just stared in silence. We were only inches apart, and I could feel her hot breath upon me. I had never wanted to kiss someone so badly. The look Gemma gave me made me suspect she felt the same way. Then Gemma broke our gaze, giving Madwen a sidelong glance. I did too, and saw her, still a respectful distance away, but watching us like a hawk, hands folded across her chest. I sighed. Gemma giggled musically and turned to walk away. As she did, her hand reached out and brushed against my fingers. Her touch shot lightning up my arm, and my breath caught in my lungs as I watched her walk away.

"Some girl, eh?"

The voice caught me by surprise, and I almost jumped out of my shoes. I spun around, hand going to my sword. There, a few paces away, was one of our sentries. He wore a dark-colored cloak wrapped around his shoulders and a spear resting against one shoulder. He also had a big, stupid grin on his face.

"How long have you been standing there?" I grunted.

"Just walked up. I'm on roving guard. Saw you saying goodbye. That's Maithgemm, right? Tewdrig's apprentice?"

I nodded, still recovering my breath.

"Never had occasion to see her up close yet. I'm in Galhault's turma with your friend, Madog," the guard said conversationally. "Better be careful around her, though."

"Why's that?" I asked.

"One of our lads, Lucas, has been to the medicus before. Not from today's battle, mind you. He hurt himself playing some knife game with another fellow a few days ago. Anyway, Tewdrig wasn't in the tent, so Maithgemm offered to take care of him. Well, Lucas made a stupid remark that she decided she didn't like, and the way he tells it, she scooped up a pair of scissors off a table and smacked him right on the head with the handles before he had time to think. She told him, 'I'm a proper lady, not some camp follower or bathhouse worker, and you'll treat me as such!'"

The guard cackled and continued his story. "Well, Lucas isn't used to women being so tough, so he glared at her and started to chew her out for hitting him, but she stared right back, like she was daring him to say something improper again. He didn't know what to make of her, so he just apologized and shut his mouth. He let her bandage him up, too confused to say another word to her for the rest of the time he was in there."

"Lucas is the big one that always works out with your Decurion, isn't he?" I asked.

The guard laughed at that. "He sure enough is! Big as a bull, that one. That's what makes this so funny. Maithgemm scares the piss out of him now!"

I couldn't help but laugh, too, then I got serious. "To be clear," I told the guard, "Gemma is the niece of the King of Dal Riata, and as of this evening, she's my betrothed. I'm Decanus Peredur, in Owain's turma. Make sure the rest of your comrades know, too. If anyone causes her trouble in the future, they'll answer to me. She's been on missions with us and done well for herself. She's also helped patch up several of us, just as she's done for your lads. So, if anyone gives her grief, that person might find themselves dealing with my whole turma. Understand?"

The guard's eyes widened a bit, and he nodded. "Absolutely. I'll make sure the lads know. Just understand, Lucas didn't mean any harm. He'd never get rough with a woman without cause, least of all free Brittonic women."

I nodded, glad for the opportunity to smooth things out a bit and continued on to the large tent that sheltered my section. It was easy to find, even at night. I only had to listen for Gib's loud, erratic snores. Nobody in our turma snored as loudly as he did. In fact, I was pretty sure nobody in our entire numerus snored as loudly as he did. It's genuinely why Cornelius gave him the first shift on night watch whenever it was our turma's turn — it gave the rest of us a chance to get to sleep before he did. Tonight, I'd have to do my best, and after stripping out of my armor, outer tunic, trousers, and boots, I wrapped my cloak around my head to muffle the sound as I drifted off to sleep.

Chapter Three

TEN MONTHS AFTER THE battle at Cair Ligion, Owain first called us to his quarters one early, cold, Februarius morning. His quarters were the same size as the one my section and I shared, and like most of the buildings, was of wattle and daub construction, but this one was his alone, being a decurion. Like our shared room, his had an earthy smell to it, with a hint of the oil used to clean weapons and armor. His room, however, lacked the distinct, additional smell of old sweat found in our barracks.

In the room with me were Duplarius Cornelius and Sawyl, our turma's other decanus. All three men were in their mid to late twenties, though with his boyish features and curly blonde hair, Sawyl at least looked the same age as me.

"The Red Dragons are reorganizing," Owain told us, scratching at the light brown stubble on his jaw.

"Why? How?" Sawyl asked.

"We're currently still organized in the old Roman style, more or less," Owain answered. "The numerus equitum consists of thirty turmae, each one hosting twenty to thirty men. At least that's the goal. There are some turmae down to as few as fifteen men. As men retire, muster out due to injury, or die, we replace those casualties with new recruits from all over western Britain based on which turma needs men the most. This system worked fine forty years ago when our entire numerus would have been on duty throughout the year and mostly consolidated at a single fort. Over the years, however, the kings who finance us are able to provide less and less coin, and send us fewer head of livestock to sustain our numbers."

"Which is why we never have more than ten turmae activated and stationed here at Caer Leon at any given time," I chimed in.

"Correct," Owain nodded to me. "But now Arthur has decided that having every turma made up of men from all over Britain doesn't work efficiently. It makes it harder to activate a turma that's out of cycle, if we need the extra men for a campaign. So that's the first change that's coming. Our turmae will be reorganized so that they all consist of men from the same region. Secondly, for many years now, we've been losing men faster than we've replaced them. Our choice has always been that we either lower the standards of who we accept or allow the numerus to become smaller. Arthur will always prefer quality over quantity, and I and the rest of the decurions agree. In light of this problem, we will be reducing the number of turmae within the unit, from thirty down to twenty."

"That's going to make a lot of decurions and duplares very unhappy," Sawyl mused.

"Some will be," Owain agreed. "A few of the turmae being rolled up aren't even being led by decurions, though, but by their duplares. Others have a decurion but no duplares. But that doesn't matter as much, given that the entire numerus is being reorganized."

His brow furrowed, then he added, "Oh. There's one other change. From now on there are to be five turmae who will be permanently garrisoned here. Naturally, those will fall under the command of Tribune Arthur, Castellan Bedwyr, Vicarius Cai, and Decurion Caradoc, the training instructor. Their ranks and positions practically make them permanent fixtures around here anyway. The fifth decurion is yet to be determined. This way, only five of our remaining turmae will need to cycle through here on seasonal rotations."

***

The next few weeks were pure chaos as our entire unit was mustered for the first time since I'd joined. It was awe-inspiring to see over a thousand soldiers in Caer Lleon. I've been told that thousands of Romans once lived here. Many of the stone foundations of the barracks still remained. They had abandoned the fort ages ago, however, and the original structures, mostly made of wood, had collapsed and rotted away. Many of the smaller stone structures had been torn down and the stone used to repair walls, or other more important buildings, like the massive great hall at the center of the fort. In the years since the Red Dragons had reoccupied the old fort, we'd never needed to house so many troops as that of the legions, so the lack of barracks hadn't been an issue, until it was. Now, all available barracks were occupied, and field tents were set up once those were all filled up.

We all pitched in to help our cymbrogi settle in and enlarged our corral for the horses. Arthur, Cai, and Bedwyr sequestered themselves in the great hall as they dealt with the logistical nightmare of the task they had taken upon themselves. Meanwhile, we did what soldiers do when we aren't training. We drank, told exaggerated war stories, and played old games, or invented new ones. Sometimes those games resulted in fistfights. We also flooded the streets of the surrounding village, swarmed the merchants and especially the ale and bathhouses.

Our poor priest must have aged five years over this brief time, trying to keep us on the straight and narrow path of righteousness. It was probably about like herding cats. His sermons became more animated and more specific in the sins he denounced as particularly wicked, each Sun's Day at mass. A few of our lads took that as a challenge. Could they sin so spectacularly that it got the attention of Derfel and earn a mention at mass? If not, then clearly they hadn't tried hard enough.

Gemma, of course, assisted him in making sure I at least avoided getting into too much trouble. To my delight, however, she had enough of a mischievous nature to also have fun with. Case in point — after losing a game of tug of war against Drystan's turma, Gilbert came up with the idea of stealing their draco standard, in true, time-honored military tradition.

"That's always your go-to form of revenge," Gemma pointed out while we sat around our barracks following our defeat. "Somebody insults some-one, you steal their draco. Someone does better than you in some event, you steal their draco. You should be more creative."

"We could piss in their canteens," Marcus suggested.

"Or dump in their helmets," Gilbert chimed in.

Gemma looked at us, appalled. "Creative, I suppose, but gross! And excessive, I should think. All they did was wound your pride."

"You have a better idea?" I asked.

Gemma flashed me a wicked grin. "Of course. They embarrassed you? Embarrass them. Take their draco, sure. But as long as you're in their barracks, why not take their clothing, too? They'll be forced to come out to retrieve their belongings while wearing nothing but their sleeping blankets."

"That might work," Gilbert mused. "At least one or two of them prob-ably won't bat an eye at walking around camp naked though."

We all got a chuckle at that, appreciating the truth in Gilbert's argument.

"Then you put their belongings out where they'll be in full display, like at the great hall or something," Gemma countered.

The great hall was a massive building, one of the few buildings that was still mostly intact from when the Romans built this fort. It would be more accurate to regard the hall as two buildings, one in front of the other, and connected at the sides, creating a large, enclosed courtyard. The rearmost building was where the Red Dragons' officers conducted their business. The front of it, which had degraded the most since its construction, was little more than a gated entrance into the courtyard, which itself was used for communal meals by the fort's inhabitants.

"The courtyard would be a good place," I mused.

"They'd have to go right up to Headquarters. And there's always women and children running around the courtyard, preparing meals," Gilbert said, sharing Gemma's grin.

"Are we agreed then?" I asked, looking at the group around me.

"Agreed," they said.

We'd barely solidified our plan when we noticed a group of travelers riding along the main street of the fort and towards the great hall. In the lead was one elderly man with shoulder-length red hair streaked with white, as was his mustache and beard. He wore nice dark blue clothing that was of good quality but worn and faded. The woman next to him was some years younger than him, somewhere in her forties by my estimate. She was still attractive, though, with a voluptuous figure, and only had a bit of gray in her long, dark hair. These were Myrddin and Nimue. The young woman riding behind them, with long, flowing, fiery red hair, was unknown to me. Oddly, she had a bow and quiver of arrows slung from her saddle. She looked familiar, though, and I glanced at Gemma, noting a passing resemblance between them.

"Aunt Morgana," Gemma called out when she saw the trio of riders and raced over to them. For her part, when the red-haired woman saw Gemma, her own eyes widened, and she practically jumped to the ground. The two women squealed in delight and hugged each other.

"Morgana, you can catch up with your niece if you'd like," Myrddin spoke up. "Nimue and I will meet you at the great hall. Find us there, or at the alehouse in town later."

"Yes, Myrddin," Morgana acknowledged him with a slight bow, and the two older travelers continued onward.

"Gemma! It's been years since I saw you last." Morgana stepped back to look Gemma up and down. "Look at you now, all grown up."

"Yes. I'm even betrothed now," Gemma said, glancing over at me.

"My brother approved?" Morgana asked, looking over at me with a raised eyebrow.

"He did," Gemma said, waving me over. "Per, this is my aunt, Morgana. Morgana, Peredur of Caer Gurcoc. He's a decanus in Arthur's cavalry."

"Hmm. And he treats you well?" Morgana gave me a hard look that made me shiver, like she was peering into my very soul.

"Very," Gemma assured her aunt, slipping her hand in mind. On reflex, I glanced around, expecting Madwen to materialize and slap our hands away. Thankfully, she and Digain tended to give us a bit more space during the day, and while we were at the fort.

"You'd better," she said, looking at me. Then she smiled and turned back to her niece. "Well, he's a handsome lad, I'll give you that."

I blushed, and the two women giggled at me, which made me feel even more uncomfortable. Even worse, Gilbert and a few of the other lads were still present, snickering off to one side.

"I'm not going to hear the end of this for a while," I muttered. I'd fumbled and dropped my throwing spear in my first action with the Red Dragons, nearly two years ago. Only one or two of the men even saw me do it. Nevertheless, in an amazingly short time, everyone in the turma knew about it, and a few still brought it up from time to time.

"What brings you here?" Gemma asked Morgana. "You left Dal Riata so long ago! Have you been here this whole time?"

"I refused to let my father marry me off to some old goat of a noble," Morgana sneered. "And I never gave my brother the chance to even try. Better to live a simpler life of freedom than suffer that fate! So, I ran away. I lived with Arthur for a time, then left to live with Nimue. She and Myrddin have taught me much of herbs and medicine, and animal husbandry, among other things. As to why I'm here now, King Conanus has tasked Myrddin to meet with King Domangart to try and negotiate an alliance, or at least a non-aggression pact with him. Myrddin asked me to come along since I'm the king's younger sister."

Morgana's eyes widened suddenly. "You should come with us. I already told Myrddin I don't think I'll be as useful as he thinks, given that I've probably been disowned by Domangart. But you're his darling niece, who's done nothing wrong."

The two giggled again. "I'd love to go," Gemma admitted. "It's been years since I've seen Uncle Domangart, too. Nearly as long as it's been since I last saw you!" Her smile faded, and she looked back over at me. "But you're talking about a trip that could last for months. I don't know if I'd want to leave Per's side for so long. And I've been training as well. The fort's medicus, Tewdrig, has been teaching me medicine."

"Hmm. Could he come along?" Morgana looked from me to Gemma. It felt like she was asking Gemma if I could come with them, rather than asking me, which both amused and annoyed me.

"Maybe," Gemma agreed. "He'd need his decurion's permission, though."

Morgana rolled her eyes. "And this is why I live with Nimue. I do what I want, when I want, where I want, with no master or husband to tie me down."

"Sounds lonely," Gemma said.

"Not as much as you might think," Morgana replied with a sly glance toward the great hall. "The lake Nimue and I live at isn't too far from here."

The two talked and caught up for a bit. I'd heard of Morgana a few times, so it was interesting to finally see her in the flesh. She was taller than Gemma, closer to my own height, and had a sturdier build. Her breasts were smaller and her hips were narrower than Gemma's, though her femininity was unmistakable. Gemma's hair was more brown and generally worn in a braid. Morgana's face was heavily freckled, in contrast with Gemma's, and her eyes were gray, as opposed to Gemma's deep blue ones. It struck me that while the two women looked very similar, my impression was that Morgana appeared more like the wild, free barbarians we Britons had been in centuries past, and still were in the far north. Gemma, on the other hand, was calmer, quieter, and more... civilized.

A short time later, Morgana regretfully broke their conversation off, deciding to rejoin Myrddin and Nimue at the great hall. The rest of us went about business as usual until dinner time, then, like most of the inhabitants at the fort, we made our way to the courtyard where a group of the women who lived within its walls worked together to prepare and serve our meal. The spread laid out for us today was simple, but hearty, and consisted of pork, cheese, bread, and small purple carrots. This was all grown or raised from the farms in the village surrounding Caer Lleon and paid for by donatives from the various western kings of Britain in exchange for our military aid whenever they encountered problems with Scoti, Picti, or Saxon warbands. Arthur was adamant that we never involve ourselves in the many disputes between the Brittonic kingdoms.

We sat down at a wooden table together and dug in. Before long, however, another group of men at a nearby table drew our attention.

"Great. It's some of Drystan's wastrels," Gilbert grumbled, looking over at them.

"Ignore them," Gemma said, eating daintily at her food, in an amusing contrast to Gilbert, who already had sauce smeared onto the stubble on his cheek.

"Hey, look, it's Owain's girls!" one called out.

"Hey, Maithgemm, do they all bleed at the same time every month that you do? My mother and sisters back home do. So I was curious," another said. The men at their table all chuckled.

Gemma paused, swallowed her bite of food, then looked over at the group. Her eyes narrowed, and she singled out one of the hecklers. "Kynwas, do you still have a scar on the inside of your thigh from the battle at Caer Ligion last spring?"

"I do," Kynwas replied. "I took a spear to the leg."

"I was there, helping Tewdrig stitch you up that day," Gemma said. "We had to remove your trousers, you know. Seems to me that a lad of your... *size* shouldn't be so quick to mock another's manhood?" She held up her little finger and wiggled it for emphasis.

Gilbert, who'd been swigging some mead from his horn when Gemma started talking, suddenly gagged, and sprayed mead all over me and burst out laughing and coughing. The rest of the lads in my section, along with many of Kynwas' own mates, also howled with laughter.

"Hey! Watch it!" I cried, wiping mead off my tunic.

"Sorry," Gilbert said weakly, in between coughs.

Kynwas' face turned red as some of his friends paused in mocking us to wiggle their little fingers at him.

"And you, Eynon," Gemma said, addressing another heckler. "I know you, as well. You had a scratch on your arm when a few Saxons tried to rustle some cattle near the border, a couple of months ago, yes?"

The man Gemma singled out stopped laughing and gave her a baleful look. "It was quite a bit more than a scratch!" he protested.

"Pfff," Gemma scoffed. "Barely needed more than a few stitches. But you whimpered like a little girl." Gemma made an exaggerated look of fear and whimpered, looking away from her arm. "Please, be quick with it. I don't like needles," she said in deep-voiced impersonation of Eynon.

"That's not fair, bringing that up," Eynon grumbled.

"Then either stop running your mouth or be more of a man the next time you come to the medicus for stitches," Gemma snapped.

"I wonder how well you'd have done," Eynon protested, digging himself into a deeper hole.

"If I weren't a lady, I could show you my own scars. I was a slave once. And if I mouthed off, my mistress whipped me. Burned me a few times, too. Trust me, a few stitches are nothing!" Gemma sneered.

Seated beside her, I felt a jolt of horror. "You were whipped?" I asked quietly when she turned back towards her food.

She gave me an odd look. "I told you when I found you that night in the woods that I was occasionally mistreated. Yes, Per, I was beaten, whipped, and more rarely, they burned me. It's why I felt no particular concern for those wretches when I lit my master's house on fire." Her eyes widened, and she looked a little scared.

"My scars won't be a problem, will they?" She asked me in a quiet voice so that only I heard.

"A problem?" I asked, confused.

Gemma chewed her lip. "Someday we'll be married, Peredur," she said.

That got my attention. She had taken to calling me 'Per' over the years that we'd known each other, having heard it from my older brother, Lamorac, when she first visited my family. She only called me by my full name when she was really serious about something. Something was bothering her, but I was damned if I could understand what. When I said nothing, she blushed.

"Once we're married... you will see me naked," she whispered through gritted teeth, and gestured at herself for emphasis.

Involuntarily, I glanced down at her bosom and felt my body temperature rising. Gemma rolled her eyes and cuffed me on the side of my head.

"Peredur!" She hissed. Her eyes grew moist now. "I have scars on my back. I have more on my arms and shoulders. Please, tell me those won't cause you to turn away from me?"

Like being hit by lightning, I understood her fear once she spoke it plainly, but I was as confused as before. My brow furrowed. "Why would a few scars have any effect on me?" I asked. "You're a beautiful girl, inside and out. Anyway, as you've pointed out a few times, I'm starting to collect a few scars of my own."

Gemma wiped at her eyes. "You mean that? You won't reject me the first time you see me... fully?"

I sighed and took one of her hands in mine. "Gemma," I said, looking straight into her teary eyes. "I don't care about scars. I promise. When our wedding night finally arrives, believe me, your scars will be the absolute last thing on my mind," I said, trying not to be crass. I still couldn't fight the impulse to look down at her chest again. Fortunately, Gemma only giggled and sniffled. Then, before I knew it, she leaned forward, threw her arms around my neck, and kissed me.

A wave of pure bliss rolled over me, and I felt like I could just float away. Her lips were soft and tasted a bit like the mead she'd been drinking. I was dimly aware of the raucous cheers and whistles of the lads around us as I put my own hands on Gemma's waist. Then another's voice cut through my moment of bliss like a knife.

"My lady! Peredur! You're making a scene. In public," Madwen growled at us.

I hadn't realized she was even in the courtyard, though I should have known she would never be too far away. I felt like my very soul was being torn from my body when Gemma slowly pulled away from me, and I instantly ached for her to be back in my arms. Madwen was there, barely a few feet away, however, and glaring at us with her hands on her wide hips. Many of the men around us were either grinning and staring at us, or more discreetly glancing our way. There were a few women in the crowd with their husbands and children who looked absolutely shocked by our display. Gemma and I shrank in our seats, embarrassed by the attention our breach of propriety had earned us. I smiled, though, when I felt her foot bump against mine. I glanced at her, and she gave me an impish smile as we went back to eating.

The meal finished, we took our wooden bowls to a row of barrels full of water mixed with salt and vinegar and scrubbed them clean. Gemma and I said our goodbyes at the entrance to the great hall. She lived with Madwen in a small roundhouse in an area of the fort where many other officers' servants lived. I lived with my section in the barracks, along with all the rest of the soldiers, when we were serving out our seasonal duty at the fort. As we stood facing each other, we both glanced over to where Madwen stood watching, along with Digain now.

"Goodbye for now. I'll see you in the morning, I trust." Gemma chuckled. "Good luck with your little mission tonight."

I grinned back at her. "Maybe after we're done, I should swing by your house?

Gemma arched an eyebrow at me. "Just because I forgot myself momentarily and kissed you at dinner doesn't mean that I'm going to forsake my virtue entirely! We're betrothed, Per. Not married." Then she gave me a smoldering look full of promise and whispered, "Not yet."

I sighed and watched her go, then glanced over at a large old stone statue of Emperor Vespasian. It was chipped in places, and most of the paint that had originally adorned it was gone, but it was still a marvel to behold, no matter how many times I walked by it.

"That is one amazing girl," I told the statue, looking at it, but thinking again of our kiss. I continued to think on our evening together as I walked back to our barracks.

***

After attending to our weapons and kit, we settled down early for our "first sleep". Like most people, we of the numerus generally went to bed around sunset and often woke up for a bit in the middle of the night. Women often said this was the best time to conceive babies. Laborers used the time to catch up on chores, farmers sometimes checked on animals, and the like. Unless we were utterly exhausted while on campaign, we tended to use this time to quietly tell stories or drink a bit more mead or ale. Some lads might throw some dice for a bit.

That night, our plan was to raid Drystan's turma sometime during the "second sleep", so we bided our time. One by one, we woke up around the middle of the night. Those who were heavier sleepers and might have slept all the way through were nudged awake by the rest of us. We dressed in our darkest clothing and used the in-between period to hammer out details of our planned raid. Finally, we determined that most people were likely sleeping again, and so we quietly left our barracks.

The moon was full enough to see where we were going, and the sky wasn't so cloudy that the stars were hidden, either. We knew exactly which three barracks Drystan's turma slept in of the forty or so occupied structures, with each section filling up a building. Although decurions all lived in officers' homes located along the fort's main street, the duplares, who maintained the dragon standards, lived in the barracks like the rest of us.

As we approached, two of our lads stood by outside, pulling security to watch for anyone who might see us on their way to or from one of the cesspits around the edges of the fort. The rest of us quietly slipped into the first of the three barracks. We all stored our belongings in chests or sacks, along with our weapons and kit. Most of us only had a few sets of clothes and undergarments, so snatching up the belongings of the first section wasn't difficult. We scooped up and consolidated their clothing into as few sacks as we could for easier transport, then moved on to the second building.

I was in the middle of dumping one soldier's clothing into a sack when the soldier rolled over on his straw-filled mattress. It was Kynwas. My heart pounded as his face turned toward me, and I froze, staring intently at his eyes but saw that they were still closed. He let out a soft murmur and lay still. I continued to watch him until I had the last of his tunics and trousers stuffed into my sack before carefully opening the next soldier's chest. Gilbert, Tor, and the others filled their own sacks just as quickly and quietly. We moved on to the third building, and our plan went awry immediately. Just as I opened the door for the others, one of the men from inside was exiting. Marcus, first through the door, bumped face-first into the soldier, who hissed a curse, clutching at his nose.

"Watch it, bloody oaf," he hissed. Then he stopped and stared at us. "Hey, who are you lot?" His eyes widened in recognition, and he opened his mouth to wake his comrades. Gilbert was faster. He sidestepped behind the lad, wrapped one arm around his neck, the other behind his head, and he squeezed, choking the surprised soldier out. In moments, the soldier's eyes rolled to the back of his head, and after a few ragged gasps, he passed out. Gilbert immediately relaxed his hold and gently laid the man down. We were rivals, not enemies, after all.

"He'll wake up quick. What do we do with him?" Gib whispered to me.

I thought frantically. This little prank had just escalated far past our original intent. We couldn't leave him there. If we did, the moment he woke up, he'd sound the alarm.

"Gag him. Tie him up. We'll carry him with us to the courtyard with their stuff," I replied a moment later.

To their credit, my lads wasted no time whatsoever. They swarmed over the unconscious man binding and gagging him with the very clothing we'd taken from him and his mates.

"Put a tunic over his head, too," I told Gib as the man's eyes began to flutter. "There's a chance he hasn't recognized us yet."

Gilbert nodded and did so, just in time. The tied-up soldier began squirming around and moaning frantically until Marcus dropped a knee on the man's chest, pinning him to the ground. "Shut up and be a good lad, or we'll choke you out again," he whispered. "Don't worry, you won't be harmed. We only need you to hold on real good to your draco," he said, looking up at me with an evil grin.

I returned his grin, and while two of my lads stayed with the trussed-up soldier from Drystan's turma, the rest of us slipped into the final barracks and swiped their clothing. Lastly, as we left, I plucked their dragon banner from its stand, right next to their duplarius' bed. We took our plunder to the courtyard of the great hall, with Marcus, the strongest of us, carrying the kidnapped soldier over his shoulder.

I planted the banner in the grass in the dead center of the courtyard, wiggling it slightly to make sure it wouldn't fall over. Taking their banner was one thing. Disgracing it by letting it lay on the ground was an entirely different matter. Then Gilbert and a couple others set our kidnapped cymbrogi onto the ground next to his turma's dragon. We dropped the sacks of clothing all around, and on top of him, and left, laughing quietly as we returned to our own barracks.

Chapter Four

WE HELD A FORMATION the next morning for our entire numerus. There were so many turmae present that we formed up inside the old amphitheater located a short distance from the fort. The red tails of more than two dozen dragon banners fluttered in the morning breeze, and the rising sun glinted off their brass heads. A few turmae had lost their dragon standards, or they'd become so damaged that they were beyond use. As a replacement, they displayed simple cloth banners with images of dragons or the Chi Rho emblazoned upon them in red and white.

As I stood in formation with my men, I noticed that Drystan's turma had their own draco back. Some of my lads noticed too, and we exchanged a few grins. Word of our prank was already circulating throughout the fort, from a few people who had seen some of the soldiers moving about the barracks in their undergarments, demanding to know who had their standard.

"They look really angry," Gilbert mused, standing next to me. We both suppressed a laugh.

Arthur walked through the formation, flanked by tall Cai and the one-handed Bedwyr, distinctive in their crimson cloaks. They stood in the tiered seating area overlooking the field, and the decurions all called for us to shut up and stand at attention. Unlike us, who hadn't been required to wear full kit, Arthur and his two chief officers wore their armor and had their swords slung from their baldrics. The only item not worn was their helmets.

Once we'd all settled, Arthur began to speak. He already had a loud, clear voice. Being in the amphitheater allowed him to be heard by everyone present.

"I am thrilled to see our entire numerus equitum all assembled in one place, and humbled to be reminded that I command the greatest military force in all of Britain!" he proclaimed.

We all cheered loudly, filling the amphitheater with a deafening roar.

"All across this isle, would-be kings and tyrants fight to fill the void left by the Romans. The Red Dragons' legacy began in Gaul, as part of the force of Britons led by Ambrosius Aurelianus and my father, Uther, to fight the Visigoths there. We lost that campaign, and Rome itself fell to those barbarians a few years later," Arthur stated.

The mood sobered, as though our tribune were reminding us of a failure we ourselves had perpetrated, though that failed campaign had been over thirty years ago by this point. He continued.

"The Red Dragons persevered, however, and their leadership chose to return to Britain and continue the fight against the barbarians there. They saw this unit as the last hope of civilization. Within months of their return, they deposed the tyrant Vortigern. Within years, the Saxon forces under Hengist and his son Oisc were destroyed. Since then, although Britons have occasionally suffered losses at the hands of the Saxons, it has never been where the Red Dragons were present!" Arthur raised his voice as he spoke, shouting the last part.

"The Red Dragons have faced Anglian warbands in the east and defeated them. You have faced a massive Picti invasion far to the north, and defeated them. You have faced marauding Scots who thought to raid our western shores, and defeated them. I have no doubt you will continue to defeat every enemy that dares to face us on the field of battle for many years to come! We must, for we are Britain's last hope!" As he said this, Arthur smoothly drew his sword and raised it high in the air.

We responded by thrusting our fists into the air and echoed the Red Dragons' battle cry. "Last Hope!" we thundered. We chanted it several times as Arthur turned in a slow semi-circle so that he looked directly at each turma in the formation. I must admit, even as I chanted with the rest of the men, and my heart filled with pride in Arthur and in our unit, I also felt a small twinge of foreboding. Yes, the Red Dragons had been undefeated on the battlefield for many years up to this point. How long could Britain last, divided as it was? In spite of its proud legacy, the Red Dragons were shrinking in number year by year, as this very gathering emphasized, no matter how it was being presented.

Arthur spoke for a bit about how we were going to reorganize and condense down into fewer turmae, based more on the region we came from rather than filling them out in regimented units of twenty-five. Once he explained how things would operate going forward, Arthur, Bedwyr, and Cai departed. Other turmae were gradually dismissed from the amphitheater by their decurions. I realized as soon as Decurion Owain stepped up in front of us, flanked by Cornelius with our dragon standard, that something was seriously wrong. His lips were compressed into a tight grimace, and his brow was furrowed.

"Last night, someone raided some of our fellow Red Dragons' barracks. Those people took their belongings, their draco, and assaulted one of our brothers. It's been reported that members of this turma are the ones who did it," Owain spat out the words as he spoke, glaring at us.

Shock and fear washed over me. I thought we were just playing a prank, as soldiers often do to each other. Taking the banners of other turmae was one of the most common pranks. Clearly, Owain was not viewing last night's action this way. Gib and I glanced at each other.

"If someone doesn't confess very quickly, I swear I will flog every last one of you," he growled.

Gasps of astonishment rippled throughout the formation. I opened my mouth, but my throat caught, and no words came out. Then Marcus raised his hand. That spurred me into action. It was bad enough that I had apparently misjudged how our prank would be received. I would not compound that error by allowing one of my men to take the blame. Yes, technically it had been

Gemma and Gib's idea, but I had approved of it. Gemma wasn't even a member of our numerus, and I was our section's decanus, not Gib. My hand shot up, drawing attention away from Marcus, and I blurted out, "I did it, Decurion! It was my plan. Leave everyone else out of it."

At that, Gib whipped his head around to look at me, wide-eyed, then he too spoke up. "That's not true, Decurion. It was my plan! I was as involved as Peredur was."

"Sounds like you both want to be flogged together then," Owain snapped. "Anyone else want to admit to taking part?"

Again, everyone looked around. Marcus stepped up, looked over at me, then back to the Decurion. "I volunteered to go too. Seemed like a good idea at the time," he muttered.

"That's three then. Anyone else?" Owain said.

"No!" I said loudly, looking straight ahead. "Nobody else was involved. I apologize for my actions, Decurion. I thought it a harmless prank."

"A harmless prank?" Owain echoed. His face turned red. "Taking the draco by itself might have been forgiven. But then you planted it in the courtyard, for everyone to see. The first person to do so was none other than our Castellan, by the way, early this morning. So that got him involved. But you didn't leave it at taking their draco, did you? No!" He roared. "You stole the bloody clothing of Drystan's entire bloody turma!"

One of the other soldiers in the formation stifled a laugh, but not quickly enough. All eyes turned to that unfortunate soldier, and I sighed, seeing that it was Tor.

"Congratulations, Taran. You've now earned a place on the whipping post," Owain said coldly. "Anybody else think that stealing from your own brothers in arms is funny?"

It was deathly quiet.

"Good! So, you lot do have a bit of intelligence, at least," Owain said, throwing his hands up in the air. Then he brought them back down and continued.

"That was bad enough, but you didn't stop there, did you." He growled, boring holes into me with his eyes. "You assaulted one of Drystan's men as well. Choked him unconscious. How. Dare. You." Our decurion hissed through clenched teeth, balling his hands into fists. "Were anyone not of the numerus to assault one of our men in this way, that person would probably be flogged to within an inch of their life, then thrown in a cell for a while. The fact that it was a fellow Dragon who assaulted him is scarcely any better! So, Peredur, Gilbert, Marcus, and Taran, this afternoon you will each receive twenty lashes. You lot are dismissed. Get out of my bloody sight. Except you, Peredur. You stand fast."

"Yes, Decurion," I gulped, and watched as the rest of the turma scurried away. Now the whole amphitheater was empty except for me, Decurion Owain, and Duplarius Cornelius.

I stood before them, stiff and straight as a spear. I expected Owain to yell at me. He looked angry enough even to strike me. Instead, his reaction was much more devastating.

"You disappoint me, Peredur." He sighed and scratched at the stubble on his jaw. "You did a fantastic job in the Picti campaign. You did a good job against the Scoti. In the wake of this reorganization, you were being considered for duplarius. Now, this little act of immaturity is costing you not only that position, but you won't even be a decanus in your new turma."

Hearing and seeing Owain make that pronouncement made me wish he had simply struck me. I felt his words like a mule kick, straight to my soul. I barely even cared about the promotion I was being denied, though the demotion from decanus hurt my pride. Decanus offered no pay and was only a position, rather than a true rank, but I had grown accustomed to it over the past year. My stomach churned, and I felt my eyes burn.

I knew he wasn't the kind of man who liked hearing apologies, so instead, I cleared my throat and said, "I won't make a mistake like this again, Decurion. I won't disgrace the Red Dragons again."

"I'll hold you to that. Peredur, we've been getting reports of the West and South Saxons mustering forces and consolidating food stores in the region of Venta Belgarum. Arthur and the kings of Gwent and Ergyng suspect that an invasion is coming, maybe later this year. Caer Badon and some of the other likely targets of such an invasion are shoring up their own defenses as a result." Owain sighed, looking weary. "Peredur, we need every man, and we need them in fighting shape, physically and mentally. We can't afford the kind of shenanigans you pulled last night, causing or escalating tension between the turmae that could have negative effects on our combat readiness."

I had never felt so ashamed of myself in my life. I nodded. "I understand, Decurion."

"Good," he said. "Now, follow me. Let's get this done with."

I dreaded the whipping that I knew was coming but did my best to hide my fear and followed him without a word. I joined the other lads of my section who were to be punished. They'd been held by a trio of guards outside the entrance to the amphitheater. From there, we marched to a series of poles set up near the barracks. Our turma formed up, along with Drystan's. Glancing at their faces, I was at least a little relieved to see that they didn't look particularly thrilled to watch us as Gib, Marcus, Tor, and I removed our tunics, and our wrists were tied over our heads to four of the posts. Then Cornelius and the duplarius from Drystan's turma brought out long whips. Before they proceeded, they inserted sticks into our mouths for us to bite down on. Gib, lashed to a post across from me, spat his out.

"That tastes disgusting," he said with a wink at me.

The other turma's duplarius shrugged. "Suit yourself, man. Don't blame me if you bite your tongue off."

From behind me, Cornelius clapped a callused hand on my shoulder, causing me to flinch. "Be brave," he whispered. "Don't cry like a girl in front of all these men."

Not trusting myself to speak, I looked over my shoulder at him and nodded. Then I stared straight ahead, which meant looking at Gib, and tried to control my breathing.

For his part, the blond-haired Frisian broke out into a lewd drinking song. Then Cornelius and the other duplarius, behind Gilbert, commenced to whipping. I hissed in shock as the first stinging blow of the whip made contact with my back. I bit down hard on the stick Cornelius had put in my mouth, feeling my teeth sink into the wood. Then another wave of pain coursed through me, and another, and another after that. I groaned and whimpered, and my breathing came so hard and fast as I fought to keep from crying out that I grew lightheaded, and worried that I would pass out. That crazy Frisian bastard Gilbert actually continued to sing the whole time. Sure, he paused every time the whip hit his back, but then he went right on singing about that blond-haired beauty and her smooth, white thighs.

After what felt like an hour, the fresh waves of agony subsided, and I was left gasping and panting against the rough, wooden pole, with barely enough strength to stand, while Cornelius moved on to Tor. I had to listen to the whip smacking against his back, while Tor, a year older than me, yelped at first, then growled and whimpered into the stick clenched between his teeth. Marcus, tied up next to Gib, cried out once when it came his turn, and I saw tears stream down his cheeks.

I didn't know how bad my back looked, but I saw splatters of blood on the ground and on the sides of the wagon around me. I tried not to look over as Tor received his whipping. Finally, when all four of us had received our lashes, we were untied, and our comrades helped us to the medicus. Marcus managed a weak laugh when he saw that it required three men to help take him to the hospital, rather than the one or two the rest of us needed.

"Lose some weight, would you?" One of the three grunted.

"Muscle weighs a lot," Marcus panted.

Tewdrig was there, waiting for us, as was Gemma. Her eyes were red, as though she'd been crying recently. As we were helped into the hospital, she gave me a look of sympathy and understanding, and I remembered that she had endured whippings herself.

"Lay them down here, face down on these tables," Tewdrig said to our companions.

They did, and then the pair came over, dipping sponges into a bowl of what smelled like vinegar. Gemma confirmed this a moment later.

"This vinegar mixture will sting at first, but it will help clean your wounds," she said in a kindly tone. "After we'll apply some honey, mixed with other things, to help with the pain and healing," she explained. The sponge hit my back, and the throbbing pain flared up again as she applied the concoction, causing me to gasp.

In contrast to Gemma's soft, calming manner, Tewdrig was almost dismissive toward us. "Suck it up. Drink plenty of water over the next few days and you'll be fine. You lot hardly bled. Mostly welts and bruises. Unless you'll be needing to wear your armor much over the next week, you should be fit as can be within a few days. Long enough to think about how you screwed up, but not so long that you'll be getting out of work for too long."

The two applied the honey mixture and bandages to our backs, then we gingerly donned our tunics and shuffled back to the barracks. Quintus greeted us and offered us water after we eased onto our bunks.

"Owain made me the new decanus," he said sheepishly. "It doesn't feel right. I was on that raid, too. I should have been whipped, right alongside you lot."

"Nonsense," I grunted. "It should have been just me. I allowed it to happen. The only reason these fools were whipped with me was because they couldn't keep their mouths shut."

"Gib couldn't shut his pie hole even while we were being whipped," Marcus said, with an expression on his face that was part grin, part grimace.

"Just wanted to give you lads something to take your mind off the suffering," Gilbert said with a weak grin. "What better way than with my sweet, sweet voice?"

"Sweet?" Tor barked a laugh, then winced. "You sounded like a cat I once heard that fell into the river. Your singing was a distraction, alright. It was worse torture than the lash!"

We all got a laugh at that. Gib was unphased. "So you're saying my distraction worked. You having no ear for music is no fault of mine."

We got another laugh, then Quintus cut in. "While you were with the medicus, Owain stopped by. The reorganization of the numerus begins in the morning. We need to have our belongings packed up and ready to move to a different building before we go to sleep tonight."

"So you might not be decanus for more than today," Tor laughed.

"Maybe," Quintus acknowledged. "I mentioned that when he gave me the position. Owain said they intend to allow as many people as possible to retain their current positions. That will be easier with the decanii than it will be for the decurions or duplares. Even though we're cutting down the number of turmae, the number of contubernia within each turma will depend entirely on where we all come from. I'm Dumnonii. There's a lot of my tribe within the numerus, so our turma will be one of the larger ones."

"No surprise there," Marcus chimed in. "Arthur himself is supposed to be a major landowner in Dumnonia, at Din Tagel, I believe."

"I believe you're right," Quintus agreed.

"How do you not know?" Gib asked, surprised.

"Why would I?" Quintus countered. "Do you think I know every Dumnonii? Do you know everyone in whatever town or little kingdom you call home?"

"I know everyone worth knowing in Caer Badon," Gilbert said with a smirk.

"Can't wait to see how many contubernia they can make out of the Ordovices," Tor said dryly.

"More than you might think," I replied. Tor hadn't been out of Mona as long as I had, and so wasn't as well-traveled.

"The kingdom of Gwynedd is bigger than our little island. Granted, we aren't as big as Dumnonia," I said with a nod to Quintus. Dumnonia consisted of not just the Dumnonii but the Durotriges as well. "I'd wager we should be good for at least one, maybe two turmae Especially considering that influx of northern Britons that moved in when they helped us drive the Scoti out of the region back in our fathers' day."

***

Later that afternoon, Gilbert, Gemma, and I visited the alehouse only a few hundred paces out of the main entrance into Caer Lleon. Digain accompanied Gemma in place of Madwen, though he was nearly as bad as her at making sure I behaved properly around Gemma. Not that I aimed to misbehave... most of the time.

The alehouse wasn't anything fancy. Aside from the broom hanging above the door frame to denote its function, the building looked like most other shops in town. It was a single-level building with a large serving room full of tables and chairs. It was mid-afternoon, so most of the occupants were either soldiers like ourselves or older men who'd once been Red Dragons and had served under the Pendragon.

Within a few moments, the diminutive alewife, Brittia, came over to serve us. She was somewhere in her late thirties or early forties by my reckoning, cheerful, and had red-brown hair with only a hint of gray. Despite having one milky, sightless eye from some infection years ago, she was a pleasant, attractive woman.

"Gemma! Good to see you again," She greeted my betrothed cheerfully. Gemma smiled and returned the greeting. When Brittia, or Brit as she liked to be called, looked our way, her smile slipped a little.

"You lads alright? You look a bit stiff."

Gemma answered for us. "They got a whipping today. Pulled a prank on some wastrels in another turma, but the prank got... carried away a bit."

Brit flashed us a sympathetic look. "So, you'll be needing some ale then. You two holding up alright?"

"We'll live," I replied.

"Hopefully a bit wiser," a man's gruff voice said.

I knew the voice and immediately responded. "Absolutely, sir. I hate repeating mistakes." I glanced over and nodded a greeting at Nicholas, Brit's husband.

Nicholas was a heavyset man in his fifties, with short, thinning brown hair. He was originally an Eastern Empire man who'd migrated west and found his way into the Red Dragons as Uther and Ambrosius were rebuilding the unit in preparation for their return to Britain. In the following campaign against the tyrant Vortigern and his allies, Nicholas rose to the rank of Decurion before retiring and opening this alehouse with Brit. He'd lost a leg in the wars, but he had different stories regarding how exactly it happened. When he was sober, he'd say it was against Oisc's Saxons. When he was drunk, he swore he'd been swarmed by a pack of revenants, of all things, and that his leg had to be amputated when it had been bitten by one, lest he become one of the undead fiends. For her part, Brit never confirmed or denied either version.

"Every action should have a discussion afterwards, to properly determine what went right and wrong. Let's hear it," Nicholas said when his wife returned with our ales. She ruffled my hair like my own mother used to do as she set my ale down, earning a sheepish smile from me.

I told him, with Gilbert chipping in from time to time. Nicholas listened and said little. He smirked or shook his head periodically.

"Boy, when you make mistakes, you really go all out," he finally chuckled. "You should have tucked tail and ran as soon as that lad woke up."

"I didn't give him much chance," Gib admitted.

"At the very least, you should have done a better job not getting caught," another man's voice cut in.

We turned and saw that it was another old-timer named Damon. This friendly, gray-haired man was one of the most interesting of the regulars here, as he wasn't a Red Dragon, past or present. In fact, he had served Vortigern as a scout and spy. In that capacity, he'd become friends with many of Uther's officers and remained so throughout the war, right up until Vortigern's death. It's normally easy to dislike people in such professions, so it should say quite a lot about Damon's likeability that, when his occupation had been revealed to Uther, neither the Pendragon himself nor most of the other decurions took it personally. Instead, they had admired his bravery, loyalty, and resourcefulness. Then Uther promptly put Damon to work for him. Though closing in on sixty, being generous, I wouldn't have put it past the cunning old man to still be in the intelligence gathering business at some level.

If all that wasn't interesting enough, at some point during or shortly after Uther and Ambrosius' siege of Vortigern's fortress, Damon had acquired a large sum of old Roman gold coins. He now lived in the nicest house in the town around Caer Lleon, outwardly living the life of a scholar, and collecting books. He was often seen around town accompanied by a beautiful, dark-haired, exotic-looking woman, and always better dressed than any of its other inhabitants.

"We can't all be elite spymasters," I said, smiling at the cunning old man.

He grinned back, raising a finely carved drinking horn in my direction. We sat and drank and laughed. Between hearing of Vortigern's War from Nicholas' perspective as decurion of the Red Dragons, and Damon's as one of Vortigern's most active spies, it made quite an entertaining story.

"By the way," Damon commented between sips. "I've been digging into what happened with your brother, like you asked me to a while back."

That got my immediate attention. My oldest brother, Aglofael, had died fighting with the Red Dragons years ago, but my family and I had never gotten the details of his death or where he'd been buried.

"Based on the timing and a little process of elimination, I think he was part of a small group that was all killed in some fighting around Portus Adurni. Arthur had a lot of small groups stirring up trouble all along the Saxon Shore, behind enemy lines, while he conducted his first campaign against them around the River Glein. Arthur had men scattered out all over the place in that campaign, so it's been hard tracking down people who know about your brother's fate. I think I've found who his decurion was, though."

I nodded. "I know I speak for my parents as well as myself when I tell you that my family is deeply appreciative of your efforts and will be sure to reward you if you can find his resting place."

Damon smiled. "Don't sweat it, son. You're a Red Dragon. So was your brother. I'm glad to help with this matter."

I looked outside as a new patron came in and realized how late in the day it was getting. Like many buildings, the alehouse only had two small windows to let in light, making it easy to shutter them in cold weather. I glanced over at Digain, who returned the nod in an unspoken exchange.

"Listening to your tales has been thoroughly entertaining," I told the two older men, "But it's getting late, so we should probably get going."

Alehouses were acceptable for young ladies, particularly this one, but only to a point. Afternoons were fine, but the later it became, the less appropriate a place it became, at least for women of Gemma's status. Gilbert elected to stay behind and chat with Damon about something, in Germanic. That was another thing about that old man. He spoke Germanic, Latin, and others besides. I heard him speaking in some other language with Nicholas once that might have been Greek.

I wished the group a good night, left a few old copper coins on our table to pay for the ales, then I departed with Gemma, followed by the hulking figure of Digain. Once we passed through the gate of Caer Lleon, I parted ways with her, trusting her Scoti guardian to escort her to the servants' quarters, and I returned to my barracks. Exhaustion hit me hard when I sat down on my straw-filled mattress, aided by the ale. I kicked off my shoes and thin woolen socks and slithered out of my trousers. My linen tunic could stay on, I decided, dreading the arm and shoulder motions I would have to go through to pull that off. So I left it on, gently lay down onto my side, pulled my thick blanket up around me, and let myself doze off to sleep.

Chapter Five

Following a standard morning formation, everyone brought our belongings out of the barracks to begin forming our new turmae. Gib, Tor, and I however, were instructed to report to Arthur in the great hall. I felt my stomach churning and my heart skipped a beat when I was informed of this. Had they decided to expel me from the Red Dragons after all?

I walked in silence, fighting both the urge to run to the great hall and get it over with, and to walk as slowly as possible, out of dread. Gilbert didn't to share my fear.

"Relax. Stop over-thinking things," he told me. "If they were going to kick you, or any of us out, I'm sure they'd have done it yesterday after we were whipped. This is surely just some other thing, like when we were called on to do that scouting mission along the coast to watch for those Scoti."

All too soon we passed by the life-sized statue of Emperor Vespasian, through the front section of the great hall where women were still preparing for our late morning's meal, through the courtyard, and into the rear area of the hall. It was easy enough to find Arthur's office. A number of muffled voices were talking from inside, distorted by the heavy wooden door. A servant stood outside. When he saw us, he rapped on the door, and the voices stopped.

"Let them in," Arthur's voice called out.

The servant opened the door, and we stepped through. The tribune was there, sitting behind a large desk. Seated around him were Cai, Myrddin, Morgana, and even his hound, Cavall. Myrddin smiled at us and Morgana eyed me skeptically. Cavall came over and sniffed at us, tail wagging. I absently held out my hands for him while Arthur looked up.

"Thank you for joining us," he said. "How are your backs this morning?"

"Fine," I lied.

In truth, it had felt mostly fine, until I made the mistake of hoisting my sack full of gear over my shoulder, where it had smacked into my back, causing a massive spike of pain. It was still throbbing a bit, but I didn't feel like admitting that. Arthur glanced at Gib and Tor, who nodded their agreement with me.

"Glad to hear it. I've a mission for you three, and some others to be determined later. I admit, your stunt the other night made my decision harder, but I am committed to it," he said with a glance to Morgana. "I'm sending a dozen of you as an escort detail for these two, plus Gemma, to Dal Riata. You'll likely be gone for a couple months."

"Who's in charge of the detail? Who are we reporting to, I mean?" I asked.

"Myrddin is in charge of this envoy, and of your detail. In his absence, you'll answer to Morgana," Arthur replied.

"You said a dozen of us? Who's the other nine?"

"We're still sorting that out," Arthur answered. "Before yesterday's situation, it was easier. You and your contubernium have done the most independent scouting missions over the past couple years. I would have put you in charge of the escort and allowed you to pick your men. Now I have to be more careful and handle this myself. To be honest, you're only going because you're Gemma's betrothed, and she's going in order to support the mission of establishing an alliance with Dal Riata. I have to do this while also overseeing the organization of the numerus."

Fresh shame coursed through me as I recognized the extra burden I'd put on my tribune. At least this envoy was also a new opportunity to redeem myself.

Arthur continued. "You three can stay here in the great hall for the time being. Use one of the empty rooms in the front portion of the hall and help the women prepare for breakfast. I'll be rounding up the rest of the detail today. "

"How will we be traveling?" Gib asked.

"By sea. This envoy has been in the works for a few months now. So we've arranged transport already."

"Will we be bringing our horses?" I asked, feeling a twinge of fear at the expected answer.

"You will not. I know, we're cavalry, and our horses are our friends as much as they are the mounts that carry us into battle."

"Never mind that securing a ship large enough to transport so many horses in this part of Britain is nearly impossible," Cai added. "Anyway, you shouldn't need to be mounted for this."

"Your mission will be to sail to Dal Riata, protect Myrddin, Morgana, and Gemma while they meet with King Domangart Reti, then return home," Arthur continued. "It may only take a month. It should take no longer than two."

I nodded, feeling a bit glum at being away from my beloved bay mare, Carys, for so long. Arthur must have read my expression and gave me a look of sympathy. The bond between cavalrymen and their horses was not taken lightly, but I conceded his point. We did what had to be done in order to accomplish the mission.

"I'm not sure I'd be able to get her onto a ship again anyway," I said. "That first trip she went on when I sailed here from Mona didn't go so smoothly. Carys has been particularly suspicious of boats ever since."

Arthur cracked a smile, then dismissed us. We made our way out to the front of the great hall and got to work cutting up meat, stirring pots, and whatever else the women needed us to do. Thankfully, we weren't the only lads helping out. This was a common enough punishment for small infractions, from being late to formation to missing a spot of rust on our armor during inspections.

A short time later, a tall man in his late twenties to early thirties, an officer by the look of him, approached us while we were finishing up cleaning. He was clean-shaven, with short dark brown hair.

"I'm looking for Peredur, Taran, Gilbert, and Elis," he declared as he looked us over.

My friends and I gathered around him when called our names, as did another lad who had been on cooking detail with us for leaving his dagger out in the training yard.

"I'm Duplarius Tyree. I'll be leading Myrddin's bodyguard. Once we get back, we'll all be in the same turma, since all of us are from Gwynedd."

"I'm not," Gilbert commented.

Duplarius Tyree shrugged. "So I've been told. You're one of the several soldiers we have from frontier towns that don't readily fit within any particular kingdom's territory. So you've been assigned to our turma for convenience.

"Duplarius...?" I mused. "You were a decurion in the Pict campaign, right?"

"I was. We took a lot of casualties. My turma was one of them that got merged in with another," Tyree answered grimly.

I nodded, and we went to the barracks, helping Tyree round up the other eight members of our detail. I was pleased to find out that Marcus was also on it, which made sense. He was originally from Caer Londin before joining the numerus, and so had no real home outside Caer Lleon anymore as his former home was firmly in the hands of the Saxons.

The other seven members were new to me, and as we came upon them, we shook hands and got to know one another. The rest were all from various parts of Gwynedd. One, Lewys, was even from Mona, specifically the city of Aberffraw, a few hours south of my own home in Caer Gurcoc.

We enjoyed one last night on our mattresses in Caer Lleon, then the next morning, we roused early, and prepared for our departure. Gemma joined us, with Digain and Madwen. Trailing them was a large, shaggy, tawny-colored hound. I'd come across her at the old Roman fort where we made our stand against the Picts two years ago. We'd befriended each other, then she'd bonded with Gemma, and followed us back south to Caer Lleon.

Gemma had a sort of pleading look on her face as she glanced down from Mel, the name I'd bestowed on the dog, and back to me.

"No, Gemma, we can't take Mel," I answered.

"Aw, why not? She'd be a great companion."

"Maybe, but our boat isn't that big. There's too much of a risk of her jumping or falling overboard. And that's assuming the crew would tolerate her roaming around pooping and peeing on their deck in the first place."

"But she could help, uh, protect us, yes?"

"If we were a small garrison or village peacekeepers? I might agree," I said. "But war dogs, like hunting dogs, aren't very good by themselves. You need a pack of them. And they have to be trained. Mel is by herself, and barely tame, let alone trained. If we brought her with us into combat, she would either run off and be useless, or worse, she'd rush at some enemy and get speared."

Gemma's face fell. "How will she get by without us?"

I laughed. "How does she get by now? She eats leftover scraps from our meals, the occasional rat or other critter, same as all the other dogs that roam around the fort. She'll be fine. We won't be gone that long. And by now plenty of other lads from our numerus know her on sight and toss her bits of food. Dogs are useful to have around. Nobody will let her starve."

"I suppose you're right," Gemma said and bent down to give Mel a last bit of attention, which the hound reciprocated by licking her face until she stood back up, giggling.

I helped her up into her saddle, then jumped up onto Carys. Once everyone else was also saddled up and ready to go, we headed out and rode southeast to the Mor Hafren. It was a pleasant ride, with Gemma beside me and I could actually ignore the ache in my back from the flogging.

In front of us rode Myrddin and Morgana. To my amusement and Gilbert's astonishment, the strange old man had with him a large raven, named Tethra.

"If Myrddin had only one eye, he could almost remind me of Wodin," my Frisian friend marveled.

For his part, Myrddin generally allowed Tethra to fly about and do as she liked. Sometimes the bird cozied up on the old man's shoulder, and they "talked" back and forth, with him acting as though he understood precisely what the large black bird was saying.

"Is that bird coming with us?" Tyree asked at one point.

Myrddin looked surprised by the question. "I've raised Tethra since she was a chick. Of course she's coming with us."

The duplarius shook his head then and left it alone. Feeding and keeping track of the creature wasn't our problem, after all.

"He gets his bird, but we can't take our hound," Gemma grumbled, riding beside me.

I grinned and replied, "Rank has its privileges."

The journey only took a few hours, and I enjoyed that time with my mare, whom I'd raised since she was a filly. I patted and scratched her neck periodically, treasuring the feel of her as she trotted along contentedly.

Our ship was already there, waiting for us as we rode up to the harbor, early that afternoon.

"Goodbye, girl," I whispered to Carys, pressing my forehead to hers and scratching at her jaw the way I knew she liked. "I'll miss you."

I reluctantly pulled my gear off my mare and trudged up the gangplank onto the small ship. Down on the shore, a dozen other soldiers took the reins of our horses, waved up at us, then departed back to Caer Lleon. As we stowed our gear, sailors moved about preparing for our departure. The ship was a two-master, with a single row of oarsmen. It was a bigger ship than the one I'd taken from Mona to Caerleon a bit over two years ago when I turned sixteen, but it was still a bit crowded for my liking.

***

The journey north took nearly a week. I handled the sea well enough, only growing mildly sick once when a storm came up around the time we passed by the isle of Manaw to our west. The sky was dark with rain clouds that morning, and with each passing hour they only grew thicker and darker. Wind picked up, and then came the thunder.

"Donar have mercy on us," Gilbert prayed, invoking the name of his pagan thunder god as he clutched his hammer pendent.

Soon, the waves picked up, slamming against our ship over and over. It rocked to and fro, and in short order we were drenched to the bone as rain pelted us and sea water sprayed us. My stomach grew queasy and added to the misery of being cold and soaking wet. Gemma curled up next to me in our space between the benches, fairing no better than I. From his own position, poor Gilbert sat cross-legged, hunched over a bucket and retching from time to time, literally sick to his stomach.

"Focus on the coastline," I told him, pointing toward the distant, wooded shoreline. "It helps... a little."

Gilbert looked balefully at me through bleary eyes. "I hate the sea, and I never want to sail again," he said flatly.

Thank God, by that evening, the storm blew over though the sky remained partially cloudy.

I breathed in the sea air and savored the sun shining down on us for a change. Gulls flew about, squawking. I didn't mind the sound so much, but the noise drove Gemma mad, likely more due to her lingering seasickness more so than the birds themselves. Those gulls were a bit more of a problem for Myrddin, who had to watch them carefully. He'd secured a cord around his raven's foot to keep her nearby, but he was ever nervous about some seagulls swooping down and picking a fight with his precious Tethra.

Along with birds, we frequently spotted dolphins swimming and playing and jumping alongside our vessel as well. A large whale swam near once. It didn't bother the sailors too much, but the rest of us were awestruck by the size of it, and I for one was profoundly relieved when it disappeared. It had been a massive, dark shape in the water, and many of our men made the sign of the cross and prayed for salvation from such sea monsters.

Numerous fishing vessels of various sizes also sailed up and down the sea. Those of us who'd fought the Scoti at Caer Ligion were pleased to not see any raiders on our journey, even at a narrow point between northern Britain and Hibernia. We were still on edge, passing through that area. In fact, Duplarius Tyree went so far as to have us don our helmets and stand by with various ranged weapons at the ready, in case of trouble. Thankfully, however, none came, and soon enough we began passing by the jagged coastline and islands that made up the western coast of Caledonia, and the kingdom of Dal Riata.

Morgana came over to Gemma and I, watching our approach on the bow of the ship.

"We'll be home soon," she said with a smile, though there was tension in her voice as well.

"Whatever happens, I'll stand with you, Aunt," Gemma said, slipping her hand into Morgana's.

"Not to such an extent that it jeopardizes your own standing with the King,' Morgana protested. "I'll not let you become an outcast as well, if that be my fate."

"So where is Dal Riata on a map?" Gilbert asked. Morgana had a basic map of the area and produced it, laying it flat on the deck of the ship. Gemma and I helped hold it down to ensure the wind didn't carry it off. Maps were very valuable, and not easy to replace.

"This inlet here is where Dun Ad is," she showed us.

"Ah, I see... heh. That stretch of land south of the hillfort looks like a man's twig and berries," he snickered.

"It... what?" I asked, blinking in confusion.

"See?" This long bit here looks like the head and shaft. That smaller, round island south of it is the —"

I cut him off, and he shrugged. "I didn't shape the land like that. Just pointing it out."

"Ha! You're right!" Morgana chortled, canting her head to see the coastline from Gilbert's point of view. "A goodly sized one too, if flaccid."

"Ye gods," Gemma groaned and slapped her hand to her forehead. "Thanks for that. I'll never be able to unsee that now."

Gilbert cackled in delight that Morgana saw things from his perspective and was greatly amused by my and Gemma's embarrassment.

I walked across the rows of benches of the ship to stand besides Duplarius Tyree who was leaning up against the ship's steering, or right side, watching the jagged northern coast as we sailed past. He glanced over at me. "How are we doing this evening?" he asked. "Make it through the storm without emptying your guts?"

I snorted. "I did. Gemma's hanging in there. So are Marcus and the others. Gilbert filled up a bucket. Ironic, given his Frisian blood."

Tyree grinned.

I idly picked at a sliver of wood along the railing of the ship, then blurted out, "Did Arthur tell you why you're in charge of Myrddin's bodyguard, and not me?"

The older man gave me another glance out of the corner of his eye. "He did. That bothering you?"

I flicked the sliver of wood into the waves. "The demotion isn't... not that much. The look in his and Owain's eyes when they demoted me. That still gets to me," I admitted.

Tyree waived a dismissive hand. "You're young, Peredur. You're going to make mistakes. We all do. Your prank was immature and very inappropriate. You have plenty of time to recover from that though, especially in the wake of this envoy combined with the organization of the Red Dragons. By the time we return to Caer Lleon, nobody will even remember it happened."

"I certainly will," I said.

"Good," Tyree said with a nod, then turned to look at me. "Years ago, I was more hot-headed than I am now. I got on Artorius's bad side. I had a similar conversation with Myrddin as you and I are having now. He told me that making good decisions comes from developing good judgement. I asked him, 'how do I gain good judgement?' You know what he told me?"

"What?" I asked.

"By making *bad* decisions," the duplarius laughed, and I joined him, looking over at Myrddin. Just then he was swearing loudly and swatting at his raven, which was cawing at him, with one hand. In his other hand he held a small loaf of bread, which the raven was clearly trying to get to.

"Shoo! Accursed creature," the old man snapped at the large bird. "I fed you already."

Tyree and I grinned at the scene, and sailed onward, chatting occasionally to pass the time. The landmass Gilbert had so crudely compared to a man's member took a day to sail past. Then we veered sharply eastward, toward one of the many rocky coves in this region. Morgana pointed.

"Dun Ad is about five miles from that shore," she explained. "There's a river that runs right by the hillfort, but it's too shallow for ships, and it only connects to the sea from further north, at Loch Craignish."

"Will we be able to get horses there?" Duplarius Tyree asked, coming over to join us.

"Not likely," Morgana snorted with barely suppressed laughter. "There's a few fishermen that live along the shoreline hereabouts, and further inland there's some sheep herders. You won't see many horses among them, though. Those will be found at Dun Ad. We'll have to walk."

We said nothing in response to that disappointing news, accepting our fate. Thankfully, five miles or so wasn't too far. We disembarked upon reaching land, and once again, Duplarius Tyree instructed us to don our kit.

"Five miles isn't a long journey," he told us. "But that's still enough of a stretch of land for thieves and other outlaws to try ambushing us. So we'll put

Myrddin, Morgana, Gemma, and her servant in the middle of the group. Digain, I want you with them as well," Tyree said to the tall Gaelic warrior. "You were entrusted with Gemma's safety anyway, so I won't try and give you orders that might conflict with your purpose." He turned back to us and said, "I'll walk up front with you, you and you," he gestured to me, Gilbert and Elis. He then assigned four men to walk to the left, four to the right, and four in the rear.

We maintained a constant lookout in all directions as we walked. We slung our shields across our backs, and carried our few possessions bundled up into our bedrolls. We carried these from the end of our spears and rested them across our shoulders, enabling us to quickly ground our excess gear in a moment should we encounter any threats along the way. Even Myrddin and Gemma carried spears. So did Digain, who was as well armed and armored as the rest of us. As for Morgana, she had a long bow and quiver of arrows slung across her back along with her bedroll and other things.

Two miles into our trek, the massive hill that Dun Ad was built upon came into view. About that same time, Myrddin pointed to another hill some distance off, along our line of travel.

"There's trouble that way. We should avoid it."

Duplarius Tyree peered out at the hill for a moment, turned, and looked back. "What makes you say that, old man? I see nothing."

Myrddin shrugged. "I have something of a gift."

"He's right," Morgana chimed in. "Listen to him."

Tyree looked again at the hill, and the smooth trail we followed that led past it. Then he scanned the countryside and sighed.

I understood his trepidation. For miles around either side of our winding trail, it was bogland. The terrain itself was a sea of mud and shallow water. The danger with going off the trail was that there was no way of knowing precisely how deep any given pool was. It could be a few inches deep or a few feet. In either case, the ground would be soft and muddy, and likely to hold us in place as we attempted to pass through it, or at least slow our progress to an exhausting crawl. Scrub brush dotted the landscape, broken up by scraggly patches of trees here and there. The hilltop Myrddin pointed out was blanketed with vegetation, too.

Tyree gestured around us. "Can you divine or conjure up a clear route through this? Who knows how deep some of this will get. If we leave the trail and end up waist deep in mud, and we are being watched, we'll only make an easier target. At least on the trail, we can fight if need be."

Myrddin frowned but nodded. "I understand. Be prepared then."

"Get your helmets on and weapons ready," Tyree ordered and we complied, pulling our shields around from behind our backs as well. We were as ready as we could be. Morgana pulled her bow from its loops that attached it to the quiver and strung it. She also withdrew a few arrows from the quiver and put them in her bow hand, making them easier to get to in a fight.

"You going to be any good with that?" Tyree asked, looking at the bow skeptically. "The draw weight on that doesn't look very high."

"It's not," Morgana agreed. "And it likely wouldn't do much against mail or a good helmet. But I can kill a bounding hare with this from thirty paces, or double that if it's sitting still."

The duplarius shrugged and said nothing else. For soldiers, slings were generally better. Archers and slingers both take a significant amount of training. Both weapons are good to about the same range, though arrows do tend to fly a bit more accurately, especially at longer range. Sling stones don't have quite the same penetrating power as arrows, of course, but the force of a well-aimed stone can kill a man or break a bone, even through armor that might stop an arrow.

The biggest advantage that slings have over bows is that slings can be easily made and repaired with basic materials. The same is true for its ammunition. This can not be said of either bows or arrows. They require specialized skills and materials that take a long time to produce. All that being said, no military leader would ever ignore the benefit of having archers in support if they're available.

I thought about this as we made final preparations for combat, envisioning how awesome it would be to have dozens or hundreds of archers that could rain down arrows upon the enemy. Then we started out again, and my mind snapped back to the present. We continued walking, and I noted the countryside around us. The ground itself was lousy and would make a terrible place for a fight. Even the path we tread on now was muddy. Those surrounding hills, on the other hand arose around us like islands and made good hiding positions. What worried me even more was that if we stayed on the path, the hill Myrddin had pointed out was on our right. I voiced my concern, and Tyree acknowledged it.

"If there are raiders between here and Dun Ad, you can bet that hill is as good a spot as any for them to be. So be ready. They'll more likely give us a volley of sling stones and javelins first, so have your shields up and ready."

As always, my heart started beating faster and my palms grew sweaty in anticipation of a fight. All was quiet, beyond the sound of our own footsteps and the rattling of our equipment. Distantly, a raven cawed and circled overhead. I tried telling myself that we were worrying over nothing. There were a dozen of us, and we were well armed and armored. In other words, we were anything but a soft target. Surely there wouldn't be many bandits who would want to tangle with us. Then, too, we were only a few miles from Dun Ad, where King Domangart Reti himself lived. Surely this area was safe, if anywhere was.

I was wrong. We marched up to the hill and were nearly passing it when a rock smacked into the top of one man's shield. A moment later, another rock splattered into the mud around us.

"Enemies to the right!" Tyree shouted.

Immediately, we spun to the right, brought our shields up, and our spears thrust out.

"Get down!" I shouted at the trio in the middle. Gemma reacted first, practically dragging Myrddin down to his knees. Morgana crouched down a bit, nocked an arrow and began scanning over our shoulders, looking for a target.

Another hail of stones came out of the bushes and trees at the top of the hill. They hit the ground around us, whizzed past our heads, and banged off our shields. One soldier off to my right screamed in pain and fell to the ground.

"I've got him!" Gemma shouted and sprinted away, still hunched over to make herself a smaller target.

I saw some of the slingers now. They were crafty bastards, wearing tattered, green woolen blankets that blended in with the surrounding foliage. Here and there, I saw the glint of a helmet, further in the grove, but otherwise, most of the men looked to have no armor of any kind. Morgana saw them too, and as one of the slingers started to duck back behind a bush, an arrow buried itself into the man's head, and he toppled over backwards.

The trees and brush where the slingers were hiding were a hundred paces away, much too far for us to effectively engage with our spears, and they were uphill from us, putting us at even further disadvantage. Tyree came to the same conclusion because he snapped out the order, "Shieldwall!" followed a moment later with "Advance."

We got moving, and I spared a quick glance over my shoulder to see how Myrddin and the women were doing. Madwen was curled up into a ball. Gemma was splinting the leg of the man who'd been injured. Digain crouched in front of them, protecting them as best as he could with his own body and large round shield. He held his spear ready for throwing and scanned left and right, watching for any enemies that might slip around us. Myrddin scrambled about, snagging up the packs of clothing we'd dropped and piling them up into a makeshift wall to use as cover. Morgana followed behind our formation, loosing arrows over our heads, though the hem of her dress was getting covered in mud, making it more difficult for her to move. Not that we were having a much easier time of things. Our feet were sinking into mud ankle deep, and we were stumbling and staggering as we advanced up the hill, trying to keep our shields tightly together and hide as much of our faces as possible.

"Quickly now, lads!" Tyree bellowed. "Get those sheep humpers!"

I heard the loud, metallic clang of something striking metal, followed by a grunt of pain. Our formation froze in place, and all eyes looked toward our center, where Tyree crumpled to the ground.

My mind blanked out in shock at the sight of our leader's lifeless body. I was close enough to him to see his wide eyes staring unblinking up into the sky. An egg-like rock was embedded in his forehead, held in place by the iron helmet he wore.

"What do we do now?" one man cried.

"We need to fall back! To Hell with this!" another said.

In an instant, my mind refocused. I looked back up the hill and saw two more of the bandits or whatever they were go down to Morgana's arrows.

"Keep moving!" I shouted at the top of my lungs. I trudged through the mud as fast as I could, moving to take Tyree's place at the center front of the ragged formation. "Those bastards killed our duplarius! Now avenge him!"

The group let out a furious roar, and we surged up the hill at a run. When we were twenty paces from the top, I halted the group.

"Throw spears!" I shouted, and almost in unison, ten spears were launched up at the hilltop's defenders.

Spears are bigger, slower projectiles than stones and arrows, and easier to see coming, so most of our spears landed harmlessly into the dirt or stuck into trees. I still saw at least two more of the enemy go down with screams of pain. That didn't matter as much. What did matter was that for a few precious moments, the bastards had to take cover to avoid getting skewered. That allowed us to break from our formation and charge them.

I rushed the closest of them, sword drawn back, ready to thrust at him, when an arrow zipped past my head and slammed into the man's face. He tumbled away, and another man came screaming at me from the left, an axe raised high overhead. I stepped forward, brought my left arm up, and smashed his face in with the rim of my shield. He went down, and I finished him off with a quick thrust of my sword into his throat. Around me, the rest of the lads were meeting equal success.

The melee ended almost as quickly as it began. Morgana killed at least four of them. We killed twice that number between our volley of spears and then our initial charge up the hill. It was hard to tell how many more there were, because the rest quickly turned and scattered in. Gilbert hurled his seax into the slowest of the lot, and the long dagger plunged into the man's back. He staggered and fell to the ground with a cry of pain, which ended abruptly as Gilbert rushed over to him and finished him off with his sword. The rest of the lads taunted the fleeing enemy by grabbing their crotches or wagging their middle fingers at them, accompanied by hoots and jeers.

I glanced over at Morgana, who hung back a little. "I'm surprised you didn't feather a few more of them," I said, wiping mud and blood from my face.

Morgana looked at the feathered end of one of her arrows. "I make these myself," she said. "No quick task. These fools are no longer a threat, and so not worth wasting my arrows on them."

I chuckled, then looked past her shoulder at the prone body of our decurion, and my smile disappeared. "Anyone else hurt or killed?" I asked, looking around. I counted nine men as they re-emerged from the woods and breathed a sigh of relief. Nobody else had been killed or seriously injured then.

Gilbert, Tor, Elis, and I each grabbed a limb and gently picked up Tyree's body and solemnly carried him up to the top of the hill. We were still miles from the hillfort, and the rest of the trek was becoming rockier, and uphill. Adding to that, it our wounded man, Ithael would be useless in any further fighting, so I decided to bury him there. Let him sleep forever in soil enriched with the blood of the men who'd slain him. Fortunately, the ground was soft and easy for us to dig a hole in. Before we lowered him into it, we stripped him of his mail, his weapons, a pendant of a simple, ivory cross, and an old silver ring. He also had a small coin purse

"We can take these back to Caer Lleon with us and give them to his kin," I said.

We piled rocks over the grave to keep animals from digging him up and disturbing his rest. When we were done, I said a short prayer for him, commending his soul to God. Then, slowly, we went back down to the hill, hoisted our belongings, and helped Ithael, to his feet. His shin bone was broken by the stone that smashed into it. During the fight, Gemma bandaged and splinted the leg and found a stick he could use for a crutch. We redistributed his gear, then formed back up, with me in the lead, and continued our trek to Dun Ad.

As we resumed our trek, I walked beside Myrddin and Morgana. I was still mentally reeling from how quickly everything had changed.

"How do we proceed from here, Myrddin?" I asked.

"As we're doing now. North. At a fast walk," Myrddin said. I glanced at Morgana, who smirked.

"That's, ah, not quite what I was referring to," I stammered. "Duplarius Tyree was in charge of your bodyguard. Now he's dead. Who do you want take command of us now?"

Myrddin stroked his beard for a moment before replying. "Who would you suggest?"

"Me?" I asked, and my mind quickly began sifting through everything I knew about my comrades.

"That would be a good choice by my estimation," Myrddin said with a nod.

I blinked. "Wait, what? You're selecting me?"

"No. I am not. Are you volunteering?" Myrddin asked, giving me an unreadable look.

I frowned, confused. What game was this old man playing? Whatever it was, I wasn't in the mood. "We just lost a comrade. I'm not in the mood for riddles," I grumbled.

"Nor am I," Myrddin replied. "Peredur, I am not a member of the *Draconum Rubrorum*. I am not even a warrior. If *I* must choose your new leader, then I would say that none of you are truly fit to lead."

I walked in silence for a few moments, pondering on that. "So... you want us to decide among ourselves?" I finally asked.

Myrddin cocked a bushy eyebrow at me. "Is that what you believe is appropriate here?"

I stifled a groan. Was this man incapable of giving a straight answer?

"We'll sort it out once we've had some time to talk after we get to Dun Ad," I finally said. "If it's acceptable to you, whoever we choose will report to you in the morning?"

Myrddin stroked his beard again. "That sounds like a good idea. I shall be interested to discover who your group elects."

"Good talk," I said with a nod and dropped back talk to the others.

Chapter Six

THE THREE REMAINING MILES to Dun Ad should have only taken an hour, but because of our wounded man, it took closer to two. The hillfort was massive, on par with Din Eidyn and Din Pendyrlaw. A scattering of farms dotted the landscape around the hillfort, with the roofs of many more homes and shops visible from outside its sturdy-looking walls.

The gate stood open, and people traveled in and out. A trio of guards wearing layered cloth armor, armed with spears and shields manned the gate. They eyed us warily as we approached.

"Who are you, and what's your business here?" one asked in heavily accented Brythonic.

"We are the envoy sent by the alliance of the western kings of Britain," Myrddin spoke for us. "I am Myrddin of Caer Fyrddin, and I have brought the ladies Morgana and Maithgemm, as well as a detachment of men from Tribune Arthur, commander of the Red Dragons."

This got a reaction from the guards. Their eyes widened as they looked from Morgana and Gemma to us.

"My lady," one guard with a gray beard said to Morgana with a respectful bow. "My name is Cathal. I served your father, Fergus, in years past. Though I've not laid eyes on you since you were a child, I'd know you in an instant. You look like him." The guard cringed as he suddenly considered how his words might be interpreted, and he stammered to correct himself.

Morgana cut him off with a laugh and patted the older man on the shoulder.

"Relax, Cathal. I've heard that sentiment many times. I take no offense. May we go up to the great hall now? We encountered bandits on the road, and one of our men was injured. He needs help."

The guards glanced over at Ithael, and the bloody wound to his shin, then Cathal nodded at Morgana. "You may come in. I'll bring you to the hall myself. We can drop this one off at our healer on the way."

"Is he competent?" Myrddin asked.

"He's as good as most," the old man said with a shrug.

Myrddin frowned. "Peredur," he said, looking over at me. I met his gaze. I'd never been so close to him before and was startled to see that his eyes had a distinct purple tint to them. "Have a couple of your men take your wounded companion to their healer. I want you and the rest of your soldiers to accompany us to the hall while we meet with King Domangart. We'll arrange quarters for you and the others, then I'll visit your wounded soldier myself and see how his leg looks."

"Thank you, my lord," I said.

I was grateful, not just that he was willing to personally check on Ithael, but that he referred to the rest of the detail as my men. He nodded at me, then followed the guard up the winding trail of the hillfort past the various homes and shops, through a second gate, and up to the top of the hill. There was another cluster of guards posted at the hall. Unlike the ones at the gate, these all wore coats of chainmail over padded tunics, along with iron helmets and large shields slung on their backs. Swords and daggers were belted at their waists. They watched us as we came up the hill, then spoke with Cathal in their own Gaelic language for a moment. They told us to wait outside, but Myrddin singled me out, and insisted that I be allowed to accompany them inside. Cathal agreed, gestured for us to follow him, and he led the way into the hall of King Domangart Reti.

The style and construction of the hall was similar to any other home, in most respects, except that it was much, much bigger. It was big enough to fit over a hundred men inside. It had a stone foundation with wooden walls and a thatched roof. Wooden pillars at the entrance were carved with intricate knotwork patterns, however. The hall was dimly lit by a few narrow windows and from a fire burning in the hearth, located in the center of the structure. The floor was wooden, rather than simply dirt. The heads of bears, wolves, and other animals were mounted on the walls, along with elaborately woven tapestries. The place smelled of mead, of wood and smoke.

Off to one side, a man sat quietly playing a stringed instrument. A pair of much older men who had the look of servants, stood nearby. Rows of tables were arranged along each side, with a wide walkway down the middle of the building which led to a dais. Two bodyguards, as well armed and armored as we were, stood on the dais, flanking a large man seated on a fur-covered throne. He wore gold jewels decorated with gemstones, and very fine-looking clothing. His wavy blond hair was shoulder-length, and he had a full beard, streaked with white.

"Greetings, King Dom —" Myrddin began to say as he went into a deep bow.

The large, bearded man on the throne cut him off with a booming voice that filled the hall. "By the gods! Morgana is that you?" he asked, coming off his chair and bounding over to us in long strides.

"Hello, brother," Morgana said cautiously. "Are you happy to see me?"

"Depends. Do you have a son somewhere that you feel should be king after me?" Domangart asked wryly.

Morgana chuckled. "No sons, or daughters either. A family of my own was never my fate," she answered, again tentatively.

Domangart's eyes rolled and he frowned. "You've not changed much these past few years."

Morgana smiled. "I left seven years ago, brother."

"Seven?" The Scoti king muttered. "Has it been so many? How time flies. And who's this then?" He stared hard at Gemma, who stepped forward when the king looked her way, and gave him a deep curtsy. "I'm Maithgemm, my king. Lord Hamish's daughter."

King Domangart's face lit up and he stepped over to her. "Stand up girl. Stand up and let me look at you," he exclaimed. "I've not seen you since you were a babe, nearly. I almost went to war with that bastard, Drest, when Hamish was slain, you know."

"Why didn't you, my king?" Gemma asked, surprising me with her directness.

If King Domangart was offended, he didn't show it. "I didn't know which village he took you and the other captives to," he sighed. His kingdom is vast, and the villages are spread out. Had I invaded his territory without knowledge of your exact location, Drest might have taken some measure of revenge out on you. I'm guessing that by me remaining here, he never had cause to pay any attention to you, specifically?"

"No, my king. He did not," Gemma replied.

Domangart nodded in satisfaction. Then his gaze turned to me, and the affectionate look he had been giving Gemma melted away into a more neutral expression.

"And you must be Peredur, son of Pelinor, of Caer Gurcoc, am I right?" he asked, looking me up and down.

I cleared my throat, suddenly very nervous. "I am, Great King. I am honored to meet you. Gem — Maithgemm has told me about you."

"Has she now? Well, I've heard about you from your father. He tells me you're an important man among Arthur's cavalry."

I hesitated, not wanting to lie to a bloody king, but afraid of how the truth would sound.

"He is indeed," Myrddin cut in smoothly.

God bless that old man, I thought gratefully.

"He's one of Arthur's youngest riders, but he's already a leader in charge of more than half a dozen men. He's acted independently as a scout on more than one occasion and took charge of these soldiers here when their ranking officer was killed by brigands, only two hours past."

There was a slight edge to Myrddin's tone as he mentioned that, and I glanced over at him. He had a backbone then, under that loose clothing and frail-looking frame.

He also got Domangart's attention. "Brigands you say? So close to Dun Ad? I'll have words with Comgall," he growled. "How are the rest of you?"

"One of the men was wounded by a sling stone. He's with your healer now. The rest of us are fine, thanks in no small part to young Peredur's decisive leadership," Myrddin said.

Well now, I hadn't felt like I'd done anything special, but under the circumstances, I certainly wasn't going to contradict Myrddin's version of events. His words also made me recall our conversation on the road. He hadn't called me the bodyguard's new leader then, but he was certainly indicating as much now, I mused.

Gemma looked from Myrddin, to me, to Domangart, and in a show of support, sidled over to me and slipped her small hand into mine.

"Well, maybe I've made a good match for you yet," the king said to her, and the corners of his mouth twitched into a faint smile. "If only other women in my family knew their place, as well," he said, shooting a pointed glance at Morgana.

Morgana met his gaze but said nothing and maintained a carefully neutral expression. The two stared at each other for a moment, then finally the king looked away, shifting back to Myrddin.

"So, the southern kings sent you to talk with me, did they? Well, we can do that tomorrow. I'll have one of my servants provide you with quarters, and tubs of water. You can relax for the rest of the day, bathe, and feast with me here, tonight. That will also give you time to check on your wounded man, eh?"

Myrddin bowed low before the king. "We are deeply appreciative of your hospitality, King Domangart, and accept, of course."

"You and I will talk some more, too, lad," the king said to me.

I bowed. "As you wish, Great King," I said, and tried to suppress the queasy feeling that suddenly came over me.

"Sister, would you mind talking with me a while longer?" Domangart asked.

Morgana nodded. "I am at your disposal, brother," she said politely.

"Unless it's to use you to strengthen the family's position through marriage," Domangart added with a grunt.

Morgana smiled. "Unless it's for that, yes. I have dedicated myself to the gods. It would not do for me to marry."

"Ah? Well, better that outcome than some others, I suppose."

The rest of us bowed again upon our dismissal, then one of the older men who'd been in the hall stepped forward and after introducing himself as Domangart's chamberlain, led us out. I resolved to talk to the men immediately, in order to sort out our new leader should be. Myrddin's speech to the king gave me the confidence to consider that, despite the prank at Caer Lleon, I would make a good leader of the group.

***

Myrddin, Morgana and Gemma were allotted a guest house near the king's hall, while I and the rest of the soldiers were put in tents adjacent to them. Digain was also put in a tent with us, while Madwen rejoined the other royal servants' quarters.

We didn't need to go and check on Ithael, as it happened. We'd barely finished grounding our gear when he came hobbling up the trail to us. His leg was splinted and bandaged, and he walked with the use of simple crutches. Another man walked along beside him, carrying his armor and equipment.

"Ithael! How are you feeling?" I asked, rushing to assist him.

He waved me off. "I'm fine. Leg hurts, but the healer gave me a belly full of strong ale and other medicine to take the edge off. I'm afraid I won't be of much use for a while."

"So, nothing changes," Gilbert called out with a grin.

Ithael wagged his middle finger at the Frisian, and both laughed.

After I made sure Ithael's needs had been seen to, then I got the section together.

"Lads, I know Duplarius Tyree was in charge, and with him… gone, we all technically fall under Myrddin. But we need someone to be in charge internally as well, who can organize guard rosters, report issues to him, and things like that."

I scratched the back of my head, feeling a bit unsure of how what I wanted to say next would be received. Thankfully, I didn't have to say anything.

"Let me guess, you're nominating yourself?" Gilbert cut in with a smile. "Suits me."

"Why him? I could lead us," Tor cut in.

"I didn't hear you take charge when Tyree was killed," one of the others said.

Heads nodded in agreement. Tor flushed. "I could have. I just needed a moment to assess the situation."

"Could have. But didn't," Gilbert pointed out. "The moment Tyree went down, and the rest of us were taking that moment to 'assess', Per here gave us a command. And it was the right one. I've served under him before. So have you, Tor. I'm fine with doing so again, now."

"If he's so great, how come he got busted down?" A fellow named Ythel asked. Ythel was a blond man with a long, drooping mustache, and one of the men who'd been unknown to me until he was put on Myrddin's security detail with the rest of us.

"That wasn't entirely his fault," Gilbert said, looking a bit guilty. "We planned out a prank on Decurion Drystan's lads, and the prank sort of got out of hand. Per was our decanus, so he received the greatest share of the blame."

"As I should," I chimed in. "Mistakes were made, but all within circumstances I helped to create through my own lapse of judgement. It won't happen again."

"I'm fine with you being in charge," a quiet young man named Nefydd said. One by one, the others agreed.

"I appreciate your vote of confidence," I told the group.

The first thing we did after storing our clothing and bedrolls was to clean the mud and blood from our armor and weapons. That included running lightly oiled rags over everything to help protect our kit from rusting. I reported to Myrdden, ensuring that he had nothing for us to do for a time, then we also went down to the nearby river, called the Ad. We changed out of our soiled clothing and cleaned them, along with ourselves. The water was cold, but once we got to splashing around a bit, it became tolerable. And, cold or not, it felt good to be clean.

Later that evening, a servant found us at our tents, rolling dice. I noticed Gilbert off to one side, absently carving a small phallus on one of our tent poles. He walked up to Tor, who was loudly cursing a bad roll.

"Are you Peredur, son of Pelinor?" he asked.

Tor looked up at the man, annoyed. "No, he is," he said, pointing to me. "Why do people always confuse us?"

The servant looked from him to me. "You two do both match the description I was given. I apologize for the confusion…"

I looked over at Tor. It was indeed a thing that had happened more than once since Tor had joined our numerus a year ago. "I don't see it," I shrugged.

Gilbert and Ythel scoffed.

"I do," Gilbert said. "You two could pass for brothers."

"Are you sure you're not?" Ythel asked. "You're both from that little island on the coast, right?"

"That doesn't mean we're all related," Tor groused.

"Master Peredur, I was told to bring you to the feast?" the servant interjected.

"Ah? Fine, fine. I don't need to leave my dagger, do I? I've never feasted in a king's hall before," I said.

"Not unless it's a dagger like his," the servant said, pointing to the long seax that Gilbert always wore at his belt.

Gilbert rolled his eyes dramatically. "Britons are always complaining about our seaxes. I get it. You are all jealous that our Germanic daggers are bigger than yours are. No need to be mean about it, though."

Ythel scoffed. "We aren't jealous. We know you goat humpers are over-compensating for your small —"

Gilbert cut him off by reaching over and smacking him hard between his legs, causing Ythel to curl up as he whimpered and cursed in pain.

We chuckled, and I showed my smaller, normal-sized dagger to the servant, who wasn't as amused by our antics. He looked at it and nodded. "That will be fine, sir. I can escort you there now, if you're ready?"

I nodded and stood to leave, then hesitated. It didn't feel right, leaving the lads here while I feasted in the king's great hall. We were all of roughly the same social class, so the only reason I could see why I should be invited and not any of them was because I was betrothed to Gemma. That didn't quite feel fair to me.

Gilbert saw my look and correctly guessed what was on my mind. "Get out of here," he waved. "We'll stay out of trouble. Just bring us back a plate of something, and a wineskin of the good stuff."

"In the meantime, I wonder how good the soldiers here are at dice," Tor grinned.

I had started to leave with the servant, but that stopped me. "No using loaded dice! And no fighting," I warned them.

"I have never used loaded dice," Tor said, looking hurt. Then he shrugged and grinned slyly. "Well, never against men in our own turma."

I shook my head and hurried after the servant so they didn't see my own grin. That in turn made me wonder — just how often did our own officers, even gruff Owain, use that same trick of acting emotionless or disapproving, then immediately walk away to hide the fact that they were secretly amused.

The servant talked as we walked. There was no special occasion for a feast, so the hall would mostly be empty, and only the king, his two sons, Comgall and Gabran, a few close family friends, and our group in attendance. "But don't worry, the food and wine will still be plentiful, and should be to your liking," he assured me.

Together, we passed the guards, different from the men who'd been on watch earlier in the day, I noticed, and into the hall. The smells of various meats, cheeses, bread, and wine hit me like a wave as I stepped through the door, and my mouth watered. My stomach rumbled. I hadn't realized until this moment how hungry I was.

Music played softly in the background, as a bard with brown hair and a short beard told the small audience with a tale of Fergus Mor, Domangart's father, and the first king of Dal Riata. I glanced his way as the servant led me to my seat at the long table. The crowd cheered and howled with laughter at the bard's antics as he acted out the story, aided by the music. He had had an amazing gift at changing his voice to portray different characters in the tale.

I was seated between Gemma and Myrddin himself. Gemma immediately helped load up a wooden plate with various meats slathered in sauce, bread, and other food.

"What story is this?" I leaned over and asked Gemma as I cut into a chunk of what looked like boar meat with my dagger.

"It's the story of Fergus and a fight he had with a bear when he was a young man," Gemma replied, barely loud enough for me to hear. The bear took his leg and apparently decided he tasted so good that from then on Fergus had to keep an eye out for it every time he left his fortress. Finally, he gathered some men and went out to settle things once and for all."

I smiled and laughed as the bard pranced about, imitating the bear, then shuddered as I remembered my own encounter with such a beast, in these northlands, two years ago. That bear had been truly terrifying — the biggest animal I had seen in my life. I looked around the table. Morgana sat beside

Gemma, and I was a bit surprised, and amused, to see her digging into a chicken leg dripping in sauce with all the grace of a soldier in the field. She saw me glancing at her, looked down at her very messy meal, then back at me, and flashed a wide grin. Sauce was smeared across her cheeks, making her mouth look inhumanly large. I laughed in return and continued to look around the room. I'd spent too much time on campaign to let my attention focus fully on any one thing for too long. It almost felt ingrained in me, in just a couple of short years, to always be watchful of barbarians, and if possible, to sit where I could see at least the main point of entry.

The king had no such issues. The feast was only scarcely beginning, but he emptied mugs of wine and mead like he was dying of thirst. A large platter of food was also laid out before him, and as the meal wore on, I noticed with some amazement that nearly every time I glanced his way and noted that he had a large goblet in one hand and a hunk of meat in the other. The two large men beside him, clearly his sons, were digging in nearly as well. I didn't understand how he did it. I was only on my second cup of mead and had to slow down, already feeling a bit foggy around the edges of my mind. Beside me, Gemma sipped daintily at her cup and ate little bites of her own meal. The contrast between her and Morgana was quite amusing, I decided.

The bard eventually concluded his tale of Fergus, and the audience applauded him as he bowed and stepped away.

"Myrddin! You're reputed to be something of a bard yourself, are you not?" King Domangart called out.

To my astonishment, the king's voice was only slightly slurred, despite his heavy drinking.

"I have a bit of the gift, yes, Great King. Though I would never profess to be better than that lad there," Myrddin nodded toward the younger man. The bard flashed a grin of appreciation to Myrddin and raised a wooden mug in salute.

"Oh nonsense," the king scoffed, then belched loudly. "The mere fact that I've heard of your bardic abilities way up here in the north contradicts your humble claim. Give us a tale!"

"Any tale?" Myrddin asked.

"Certainly. I've been hearing about my father all evening. Let's hear something new!"

The lean old man slowly stood, walked to the center of the hall, and began to regale the audience with a tale of Arthur. His voice took on a rich, deep tone that was immediately enthralling. Where the previous bard had been entertaining and comical, and had us all laughing and clapping, Myrddin caused the diners to settle down and focus entirely on him. It was several moments before I realized with a start that the tale he told was of the Battle of Guinnion's Fort! My attention shifted as I searched my memory, trying to remember if Myrddin had even been with us for that campaign. I was fairly certain he hadn't been.

I nearly broke out laughing when Gemma, almost as though she were reading my mind, leaned over and whispered, "Wasn't he at Caer Lleon when the Red Dragons came north?"

"I believe so," I agreed.

Myrddin, nevertheless, provided us with a spellbinding narrative of the dastardly barbarian king, Drest, and his tens of thousands of Picts who swarmed Guinnion's Fort, but were defeated when the Red Dragons swept into them. In the background, the younger bard quietly added a tune on his lyre to compliment Myrddin's tale.

"I didn't realize Drest had so many men," Gemma whispered in amusement.

"Definitely didn't look like more than two or three thousand to me," I agreed, taking a sip of wine. This was still an enormous army of course, but not the innumerable horde that Myrddin depicted.

Myrddin finally finished his gripping tale some time later. One guest was passed out across the table, presumably drunk. Everyone else burst into applause or pounded their mugs on the table in delight as the old man took his bows and returned to his seat beside us.

"It sure was a good thing Arthur was able to kill so many hundreds of barbarians all by himself," I snickered. "It's a wonder why we bothered assembling so large a force to oppose the Picts."

Myrddin grinned good-naturedly and took a long drink from his mug. Then, with a pat on my back, he winked and said, "Never let the facts, or lack thereof, get in the way of a great story. The point is that Arthur fought Drest's Picts at Guinnion's Fort. If the story's told right, people shall remember that battle for decades, even centuries to come. Maybe longer still. Details will get lost over time or muddled with others from less skillful bards. But if say, a thousand years from now, people still remember that a brave Briton named Arthur won a great victory at Guinnion's Fort, well, that's good enough for me! If I merely recited the basic facts, do you think anyone will remember it for longer than it takes for the next bard to come along with their story?"

"Probably not," I admitted.

"Exactly. Now stop nitpicking how I preserve Arthur's legacy, build up your own reputation... and hand me that loaf of bread over there."

I laughed and did as the crafty old man bade me.

Late into the night, the feast slowly dwindled down as guests trickled away to their beds. I stuck a few wineskins under my arms, and Gemma helped me load up a plate of bread, cheese, and meat for the men. Servants helped themselves to the leftovers. Near the hearth, Myrddin was deep in conversation with the young, amusing bard, who we learned was named Woru.

"Say hello to the lads when you give them the food," Gemma said with a smile as we prepared to head off to our respective quarters.

"I will. Good night, my lady," I said with a slight bow.

"And you, my lord," she smiled up at me. Then she leaned up, gave me a quick kiss on my cheek, and whirled away with a laugh.

"You know," a voice said from the shadows, startling me so badly I nearly dropped the platter of food. "If you ever hurt her, I'll kill you."

I spun around, barely keeping the food from spilling off of it, and saw Morgana leaning against the side of the great hall, staring at me.

"Morgana, don't startle me like that," I sighed.

She smirked at me. "You probably think I'm little better than a barbarian. I saw you looking at me during the feast. I don't let my family marry me off. I don't wear my hair all prettily the way women usually do, and I'm deadly with a bow. Don't underestimate me, though, Peredur," she said, her eyes boring into me.

"I've spent my life learning from the wise women of Dal Riata, from masters of lore, medicine, potions, and poisons from the likes of Myrddin and Nemue," she told me. "I care for Gemma, I can see you two care very much for each other, and that makes me glad. As long as it remains that way, you can always count on me to be as a sister to you. But, if you ever abandon or abuse her, trust me, I will kill you." There was no hostility in her voice. Instead, she delivered the threat in a very casual, conversational way, and I found that a little unnerving.

I considered what she said. "You are a very strange and slightly unsettling woman, Morgana. But your terms are acceptable. I would shake your hand, but mine are a bit full at the moment."

Morgana laughed, and her mood shifted in an instant. "Let me help you with that."

Together, we returned to the tents where my companions were staying.

"About time you got here with our food, serving wench!" Gilbert called out with a grin, hearing and probably smelling my approach. Then he saw Morgana, who probably thought he was addressing her. His eyes widened, and a guilty expression crossed his face. "I didn't mean you, Lady Morgana! Honestly. I was referring to Peredur."

Morgana looked from Gilbert to me and laughed. She took the wineskins from under my arms and tossed them to the eager men, then gestured towards them.

"You heard the man, serving wench. Your lads are hungry," she grinned.

The men swarmed me, and in moments, all the food that had been piled onto the platter was picked clean.

"You two care to join us at our dice game?" Tor asked, gesturing to an open space in the wide circle.

"Don't mind if I do," Morgana said and, to their astonishment, joined the group.

The invitation had been genuine, but nobody expected a lady, and one related to the king, to take them up on their offer. She smiled broadly as she looked around at their faces. "I answer to nobody and do as I like. And that includes tanning your hides at dice."

"If you do as you like, then maybe you'd like to share my tent later. We could have a lot more fun than throwing dice," Marcus suggested with a wink.

Morgana took the wooden dice that were offered to her and hefted them, feeling their weight. "You mistake me. I said I do as *I* want, not as every horny lad around me would like," she said with a wink, then tossed her dice with a clatter onto the shield being used as a table.

Men laughed at her joke and groaned at her dice rolls. The banter continued, and after a bit, I went to my small tent. Unlike the tents we used in the numerus, which were big enough for at least eight men, the ones these Gaels had provided us were of various sizes. The tent I slept in fit me, Gilbert, and Tor. A bigger tent, the one that the men now gambled outside of, housed six. The last two shared a smaller tent that was scarcely more than a large blanket tossed over a frame.

With my belly full of good food, my head swimming slightly from the wine and mead, and the pleasant sound of my men laughing and joking outside, I soon drifted off to sleep.

Chapter Seven

THE NEXT MORNING, I reported to Myrddin. "I was elected as the new leader of your bodyguard," I told him.

Myrddin smiled knowingly. "Were you now. I suspected you would be. So, how are your men? Do they need anything?"

"I'll check on Ithael later today. Otherwise, we're fine. We have food and adequate shelter. We'll stay nearby, in case you need us," I informed him.

Myrddin nodded and gave me a slap on my back, then he and Morgana went to visit King Domangart, leaving my men and I on our own for a bit. I decided to conduct a casual inspection of the men's kit, then we scrounged up some wooden practice weapons and did some sparring. Everyone wanted a chance at fighting Digain, who preferred fighting with two weapons rather than the standard one, paired with a shield. In one-on-one duels, it was an imposing style of fighting, and one after another, we went up against the large man. Our drills drew the attention of some of the locals, particularly from two men who watched us intently, both with arms folded across their chests. Both sported red hair and short beards. The taller of the two had a warrior's build, while the younger was a bit heavyset. I recognized the older of the two as one of the men who'd been present at the king's side yesterday.

When it was my turn to spar with Digain, I pressed my attack, trying to keep him on the defensive. I varied my strikes between high and low, and tried to use my shield as a weapon as much as the stick in my right hand. Digain sidestepped and parried gracefully, though my stick caught him once on his tree trunk of a thigh. He countered with a flurry of blows from his two wooden swords and it was all I could do to evade or deflect his attacks until, finally, he sidestepped around my shield and smacked me hard on the back of my thigh. My leg buckled and I dropped to one knee.

"I yield," I yelped.

The large Scoti smiled, helped me to my feet, then took a quick drink of water from a large cup off to one side of our training area as Marcus stepped up. He was nearly a head taller, and definitely larger, than the rest of us. Pound for pound, if anyone was going to give Digain a challenge, it should be him.

"Good luck," I told him as I limped away.

Gemma was there waiting for me with a cup of water, which I took gratefully.

"Who are those two?" I asked in between gulps.

"That's Comgall and Gabran, the king's sons," she answered.

"More cousins of yours then?"

Gemma laughed. "All Scoti are my cousins in one way or another."

I looked over and, meeting Comgall's gaze, gave him a friendly nod. He returned it with a neutral look. Then both of us looked over as Marcus fell to the ground with a curse. Digain loomed over him, chuckling.

"Your turn, Tor," Marcus panted and came over. He had a cut on his forehead and was sweating profusely.

"Oh, let me see that," Gemma exclaimed. "Here, come sit down."

As she started to lead Marcus away, the man she'd identified as Gabran barked out a laugh.

"I thought these Red Dragons were supposed to be fierce warriors. Our man, Digain, appears to be better than all of them."

I glanced over and, ignoring the tone in Gabran's voice, flashed him a wry grin.

"We typically fight on horseback and in formation. I'm glad for Digain's company. We'll be the better for it."

"Do you and your men lack in skill when you have to fight one-on-one, then?" Comgall asked.

I shrugged. "We aren't as good as some, but the important thing is that we win our battles, so we're good enough, in our way."

Comgall nodded thoughtfully. Gabran, however, frowned and stared over at where Gemma was tending to Marcus' wound. He said something to a young woman beside him, and she, too, looked over at the pair in disgust.

"Is something wrong?" I asked the two.

"Yes. My friend and I were trying to clarify something. My cousin, Gemma, is your betrothed, is she not?" Gabran asked. "Or is Peredur that one over there, who's bleeding all over her like a stuck pig?"

I glanced over and saw that Gemma was cleaning the blood from Marcus' head and applying a salve. He hadn't bled too badly, given that it was a head wound. The mocking tone in Gabran's question was uncalled for. I gritted my teeth but tried to be polite. "I am Peredur. Gemma is indeed betrothed to me."

Gabran scowled. "And yet you have no problem letting her put her hands all over other men?"

"She's being trained by our medicus — our healer. She's saved several lives, including a few of my friends. So no, I don't have a problem with that," I replied.

"She helps your healer treat battlefield injuries?" The woman beside Gabran asked in shock. "So, she's put her hands on men while they're undressed?"

I saw the issue they were having and understood their shock. My own family had been uncomfortable with Gemma's choice when they'd met her. It wasn't especially unusual for women to assist in treating their own husbands and sons, and of course, women regularly helped other women, especially with things like birthing babies, but this was something else.

By now, Gemma had finished with Marcus and came over, hearing our conversation.

"When possible, our senior medicus, Tewdrig, deals with those sorts of injuries," she began, but the other woman cut Gemma off with a sneer.

"When possible? So not always? You're a disgrace to your family. I'd say you sound little better than a camp follower, or some slu —"

Slap!

Before either Gabran or I had time to register the move, Gemma closed the distance with the other woman and slapped her so hard across the face that the woman staggered back, almost to her knees.

"I honor Peredur and let no one challenge my virtue!" Gemma snapped.

"How dare you," Gabran growled. "Your time with the Picts and then these Britons has made you forget yourself, cousin." He stepped forward to grab at her, but this time my own hand flashed out, and I brought the blade of my hand down hard on his wrist, knocking it away.

By this point, the men of my section, having heard Gemma's slap, had paused in their sparring and came over to stand beside us. I noted that even Digain stood with us, though further back. Comgall also hung back, still watching this incident unfold as though it were a dramatic play being performed on a stage.

"You bastard! You hit me!" Gabran snarled. "You share my cousin with all of your filthy companions, and now you hit me?" His face turned crimson with rage and I noticed a few local men gathering around us too, drawn by the confrontation.

"It's not like that, you fat sheep humper!" Gilbert cut in. "She is a lady, and we treat her like one. More than that, she is a good healer, and for that, there isn't a man in the numerus who does not give her the same respect we give to Medicus Tewdrig or to one of our own brothers. Do not disrespect her again."

Marcus, Tor, and the others nodded their agreement, glaring at Gabran and the woman with him.

"You lot talk so tough," Gabran sneered. "I just watched one of our men whip all of you." He glanced around at several rough-looking men who'd emerged from the bystanders to stand beside him.

"Let's teach these Briton dogs a lesson!" the husky prince cried and lunged at me.

I barely had time to think as I ducked under his swing and slammed my right fist into his stomach. I followed that up with a blow to his jaw from my left. I saw Gilbert reach for the seax, ever present at his belt.

"No killing!" I shouted as my lads and the Scoti surged at each other. Then Gabran launched himself at me and drove me to the ground. I brought my arms up, protecting my face from the flurry of blows Gabran delivered. The moment an opportunity arose, I snagged my foot around his, trapped his arm against my chest, and rolled him over, so that I was on top of him.

"My turn, barbarian," I grunted and punched him in the nose, causing it to erupt in a spray of blood. I followed that up with a strike that connected with his ear. Another Scoti rushed over, grabbed me around my neck and ripped me off Gabran. I clawed at his thumb and forced him to release his hold, then spun around to face my new attacker as Gilbert flew at him with a howl. He punched the Scoti hard with a hook to the jaw, and the man staggered away.

At that moment, Gabran staggered to his feet and cocked his fist back. I slipped to one side, and his punch missed. My own didn't, and he stumbled backward, then fell onto his rump. I used the opportunity to glance around, and through puffy lips, I couldn't help but grin at the sight before me. The men of my section had formed into a tight circle. Gilbert, Ythel and Marcus were on the ground grappling with their opponents. The rest were on their feet, punching, kicking, and headbutting. Three Scoti were on the ground, bloodied and dazed, another was curled up in the fetal position, clutching at his groin and gasping in pain.

I broke away from Gabran and tried to haul Gilbert back into our circle as well. He struck my hand away and spun to face me with a wild look in his eyes. With a flash of recognition, he grinned broadly at me, and followed me back to rejoin our cymbrogi, only pausing to kick a man in the head who'd been rising from the ground.

Howling, the Scoti surged at us. I brought my knee up into one man's groin, then doubled over as another punched me in my stomach. Marcus grabbed the man by his beard, then punched him twice in the face before shoving him aside. I stood up, still wheezing for breath, and wiped blood from my eyes, with no idea whose it was. A fist came at me and blocked it with my left arm. My right jabbed him in the throat. He collapsed to the ground, retching. I kicked him into the next man who tripped and sprawled onto the ground. Gilbert bent down and struck him in the kidney, then went sprawling himself as someone punched him in the side of the head. Tor grabbed that man by his long hair, yanking him away from Gilbert. As another opponent charged us, Tor pushed the man towards him, causing them both to trip and fall.

Another Scot came at me, but he stopped a pace away, gasping for breath. I swung at him, and although my punch connected, it lacked any real power, and although the man reeled back a step, he kept on his feet. Beside me, Gilbert and his newest opponent actually broke out into laughter in between gasps for air. They were in a clinch, both hunched over and grabbing onto the other's neck, but were too exhausted to do anything more.

The fight dragged on a bit longer until finally, exhausted, the Scoti pulled away from us. We held our circle, standing shoulder to shoulder. We were all bleeding and soaked in sweat, and dirty as beggars. As ragged as we looked, I noted with smug pride that the Scoti looked worse. Our men stood firm, fists up, ready to continue the fight, while the barbarians surrounding us bent over, resting their hands on their knees as they gasped for breath — blood dripping from broken noses and split lips. More than one man, I noted, had bloody patches of skin visible, where hair had been ripped from their scalps.

"Last Hope!" I roared and pumped my fist into the air.

"Last Hope!" The rest cried in response.

A large, hairy Gael let out a yell and charged at us, swinging wildly at Gilbert. With a laugh, he leaned back, letting the Scot's fist fly harmlessly by him, then countered with two quick jabs to the man's stomach. He followed up by almost casually kicking the man in the chest. The man fell to the ground onto his back with a low moan.

"That's enough!" Comgall finally called out. I noted that Digain stood beside him. "Brother, help your friends to their feet and go get cleaned up." Then he turned to me and looked us over. "Peredur, you and your men fight better than I'd have thought. Maybe the Red Dragons' reputation hasn't been exaggerated. I suppose my cousin could do worse than marry a man like you." The prince smiled and nodded at me with a subtle sign of respect.

I hesitated a moment, then returned his nod. Had this entire altercation been a way to test me and my men? I turned back to my companions.

"Alright, cymbrogi, sparring is done for the day. Let's go wash up, then get our clothing fixed up."

Conveniently, the River Ad, from which the hillfort got its name, was nearby, so after pausing only long enough to go back to our tents for fresh tunics, trousers, and undergarments, we went down to the river and bathed, as well as washed the dirt and blood from the clothing we'd been wearing. The water felt frigid this time of year, and being this far north, but it was either endure it or be filthy, so we gritted our teeth and plunged in, determined not to show how uncomfortable we were in front of the Scoti men nearby who were doing the same thing. Besides, the cold water felt good on our cut and swollen faces.

"Heh. I wasn't sure these barbarians bathed," Marcus commented to me in Latin as he glanced over at the Scoti.

"They probably assumed the same about us," I chuckled, also in Latin.

We cleaned up, washed our soiled clothing, and idly bantered a bit with the Scoti. By the time we returned back up the hill to the upper portion of Dun Ad, we were laughing and chatting away about women, boasting about the largest boars we'd slain, and victories won against our shared enemy, the Picts.

Comgall and Gabran came over to the tents where my men and I were staying a short while later.

"I hope there's no hard feelings," Comgall said with a smile. "Father wanted us to see what sort of man you are. And all of us wanted to see how good you

Red Dragons were in a fight. My brother and I decided to settle both questions at once."

"By provoking us into a fight?" I asked carefully. My mouth was pretty sore from the hits I'd taken.

Comgall chuckled, and Gabran smirked a little. "Well, to be honest, we didn't plan it out that thoroughly. If you know anything about my family, though, we do love a good scrap. Supposedly, our grandfather, Fergus, considered fighting to be the absolute best way to really get to know someone. It's said that nobody could outdrink or outfight him. So, no hard feelings?"

He thrust out his hand, and I shook it, grinning back. I couldn't help it. The mirth in Comgall's eyes made me unable to respond otherwise. Gabran held out his hand as well, though when I took his hand, he attempted to squeeze mine to get a reaction. Well, my brothers and I used to do that to each other back home all the time, and the physical conditioning we did regularly back at Caer Lleon kept me strong, so I smiled as I looked him in the eyes and squeezed right back.

We stood like that for a few moments, each staring at the other with a tight-lipped smile until finally I heard an exasperated sigh from off to one side.

"Will you two give it up already?" Gemma groaned.

I looked over at her, then back at Gabran, who chuckled and grinned at me. We released each other's hands, then shared another laugh as we both immediately began wiggling and flexing our fingers.

"You'll do," Gabran said, slapping me on the back.

We relaxed for the rest of the day. A few of the men meandered around and socializing with the locals, which I was fine with, as long as they didn't leave the top level of the hillfort. I stayed at our tents, and Gemma kept me company. Myrddin and Morgana came by later that afternoon, asking me about the ruckus we'd been in earlier. When I told them, Morgana laughed. "Comgall is right!" She exclaimed. "Fighting is in our blood. I should have known something like this would happen. Glad you earned their approval though," she chortled.

"I'm glad this didn't turn into a serious incident," Myrddin said, but Morgana waved him off. "Nah! This sort of thing is normal with us. It's fine. In fact," she mused, "since the men did well, it might make Domangart more disposed to agree to some sort of treaty."

"If only he would just agree to help us with the Saxons first," Myrddin grumbled.

"The Saxons will take longer to defeat," Morgana argued. "It makes sense for my brother to want the Britons to come aid him up here in the north first."

The two continued their discussion, clearly picking up from an earlier one, so Gemma and I headed over to the great hall. From the smells that were drifting through the camp, I guessed that the slaves there were getting started on supper.

When we showed up at the hall, the bard Woru was there, singing another of his sagas and making full use of his uncanny ability to alter his voice to reflect various characters within it. King Domangart Reti was there, already drinking heavily. His sons, Comgall and Gabran, sat beside him. A few other nobles sat around, snacking and drinking as they chattered and listened to the bard. They nodded at us as Gemma and I strolled in, but kept their attention on Woru.

We sat down next to each other, enjoying the pleasant ambiance of the hall and its muted light, the smell of wine and cooked meat, and the sounds of the bard's voice accompanied by occasional cheers and laughs of the growing audience as more people showed up. By some small coincidence, I'm sure, Myrddin and Morgana appeared just as servants and slaves began laying out great platters of duck and roasted pigs, bread and cheese, and other delicious foods. The pair were given seats at the king's table, and Domangart greeted his sister particularly warmly, I noticed.

"I guess those two smoothed things out between them, I commented to Gemma.

"Good," Gemma beamed as she sliced off a strip of pork and bit into it, rolling her eyes in pleasure.

As we ate, Gemma playfully rubbed her foot against my leg and gave me a coy smile when I looked over at her. I took that as an invitation and casually rested my hand on her thigh. Her smile slipped, and she arched an eyebrow at me while giving me a side-eyed stare. I got the message and pulled my hand away. Her smile reappeared, and just that quickly, our wordless conversation was over, and we casually continued eating.

I noticed Woru chatting up Morgana at one point in a break between performances. I couldn't hear the conversation, but he seemed to be flirting with her. I was a bit surprised to see Morgana laughing and smiling back at him just as flirtatiously. I'd been under the impression she was spoken for by our tribune, but maybe I was mistaken? Then again, she behaved scandalously flirtatious as a general rule from what I'd observed, though she never actually slept with anyone, so far as I knew. She placed her hand over his once, and for a moment, I thought I saw a glimpse of white, like a small scroll, pass between her hand and his. Then Woru withdrew his hand and it disappeared under the table. Morgana squealed and giggled. I shrugged, and decided I must have been imagining things, or at the very least, none of my business.

We enjoyed ourselves the rest of the evening, though likely not as well as Domangart, who enjoyed himself so much that I suspect he must have drank an entire barrel of wine all by himself, and he still managed to leave the table of his own accord late in the night, if only barely. I felt a bit tipsy after a few mugs myself and decided to return to the tents before I drank too much. I felt bad, feasting in the great hall purely due to my connection with Gemma, so I scooped up a platter of food to bring to my companions as we left. Gemma allowed me to kiss her hand in farewell, then we parted ways. She returned to the quarters she shared with Morgana, accompanied by a serving girl.

The first sleep had already passed, close to the middle of the night, by this point, so a couple of the lads were still sleeping. Many others were awake, enjoying a bit more mead or ale and talking quietly in the moonlight when I showed up, so the food was a welcome treat for them.

"Well, spill it already," Gilbert prodded. "Did you find out anything more about how much longer we'll likely be here?"

"Where were any beautiful serving girls?" Marcus asked with a grin.

"We didn't talk business at the feast — at least none that I was able to hear," I answered. "I wasn't at the king's table with Myrddin." I turned to look at him. "There was one woman who was your type, I think. Easy enough on the eyes. Large bosom. She was probably old enough to be your mother, though."

Marcus shrugged. "What do I care about that? Just means she probably knows what she's doing!" He grinned.

I laughed. "Well, if you hang about outside the hall, I'm sure you'll catch her helping clean up once a few more of the guests leave."

"Lads, it's been a pleasure. Don't be surprised if I don't come back tonight," Marcus said and sprang to his feet, then strode away towards the great hall as Tor and some of the others laughingly wished him well on his quest.

I was too tired from the wine and mead I'd consumed to stay up and chat for very long, so I wished my friends a good night, crawled into my tent, and barely stayed awake long enough to strip off my shoes and socks before I fell asleep. I woke once to go to the edge of camp and relieve myself. There was some small commotion going on at the great hall, and were it not so late at night, I might have been curious enough to go investigate. But the sounds of men talking and scurrying about did not suggest any kind of physical threat, nor did my gut warn me of trouble. In the past two years, I'd learned to rely heavily on that intuitive sense for danger. So I shrugged off the unusually late activity at the hall, deciding that if it was of any importance to me or my men, someone would surely come and get us. I pulled my pants up, yawned, and quickly returned to my bedroll. It was chilly outside on this cloudy Martius night in these highlands.

***

In the morning, we were roused from our slumber by cries of alarm. My men and I hurriedly got dressed and armed ourselves. We made our way over to Morganna and Gemma, standing with a number of others outside the great hall.

"What's going on?" I asked the two of them. "Where's Myrddin?"

"He's inside," Morganna said, wiping at her eyes. They were red with tears I noticed. "My brother is... dead."

"Dead?" I echoed. "How? When?"

"He woke up last night with severe stomach pain," Gemma answered, putting a comforting arm around Morganna's shoulders. "A young woman who'd been sharing his bed rushed to get the healer. He brought Myrddin to the king. By then he was vomiting and suffering bowel movements. He broke out into a fever as well. They couldn't save him."

Morgana buried her face in her hands, sobbing, and Gemma sniffled, wiping at her own eyes. "He died not long after sunrise," she said. "His oldest son, my cousin Comgall mac Domangart, is to be crowned the new king of Dal Riata."

"Will you be alright?" I asked. "Is this going to cause trouble?"

Morgana wiped at her eyes and shook her head. "Myrddin believes he died of corrupted food, or possibly drinking too much. I agree, as does the healer living here."

I fished out a wineskin from my tent and handed it to her. She took it gratefully and took a long pull. As she did, my men gathered around her.

"What's Comgall like?" Gilbert asked.

Gemma shrugged. "I haven't seen him since I was a child." She looked to Morgana.

"I honestly don't know him that well, either," Morgana said. "I left Dal Riata seven years ago. We were children together. He was proud, a bit arrogant maybe. But he trained hard with weapons and was a good hunter. Him, his brother, and I represent the first generation born here to have almost no connection to Ériu's land — what you call Hibernia. Dal Riata is our homeland. That makes the Picts our biggest threat. I know there's no love between Gaels and

Britons, but I think Comgall will be more willing to deal with Myrddin than Domangart would have. With enough incentive, he may even be willing to agree to a full alliance with the kings of Britain, despite the tension between us and our southern neighbors in Alt Clut."

I nodded, taking it all in. "So my men and I don't need to worry about Comgall sending his guards to come kill us or anything?"

Morgana's full lips curled into a slight smile. "No, I should say not."

Well, that was a relief, anyway. If there was one thing I'd learned from history, it was that even the most stable kingdoms generally had a weak point when it came to transitions of power.

We talked a bit longer, then Morgana excused herself. There were funeral arrangements to be made for Domangart Reti, and a coronation to prepare for Comgall. My men and I spent the day more or less trying to simply stay out of people's way and being inconspicuous during all of this.

Over the next couple of days, Domangart's body was placed in a wagon and escorted to a freshly prepared tomb in the side of a hill. There, his body, dressed in fine clothing and gold jewelry, was buried, surrounded by his favorite weapons, a shield, and other various tools and such that a man would need in daily life, as was the pagan way. Though I am a Christian, there were many pagans within the ranks of the numerus, and the villages throughout Britain, so I wasn't overly uncomfortable with the ritual, though I did worry a bit over Domangart's soul, with no priest to commend his spirit properly to the one true God.

The day after that was Comgall's coronation, such as it was. The new king knelt upon a large stone block, which Morgana told me had come to Dal Riata with Fergus Mor from Ériu's land. An old man placed a simple, golden crown about Comgall's head — the same one that had belonged to Domangart and blessed him in the name of several gods whose names I didn't recognize. And just like that, Dal Riata had a new king.

Unlike the small feast three days prior, Dun Ad hosted a massive one in honor of both Domangart Reti and Comgall. Everyone at the hillfort took part, and even farmers from nearby villages came to pay their respects and enjoy the feast, paid for by Comgall, as a show of generosity to his people. Barrels and barrels of ale, mead, and wine were consumed, and more chickens and pigs were slaughtered and eaten than I cared to count. No matter where one roamed throughout the hillfort was the scent of cooking meat and the sounds of music and people laughing. I was disappointed to notice that the talented Woru was absent and commented on it.

"I talked to him after the feast the other night," Morgana said. "He'd already stayed here several days, and wanted to return south. He left three days ago."

Three days ago, I mused. So he left the same day King Domangart died. I considered the strangeness of it, but decided it likely meant nothing. Instead, I focused on the present, enjoying the music and festive atmosphere as Morgana and Gemma chatted. Once, I saw Gilbert walking by with a girl clutching his arm. The pair was giggling and acted quite cozy. They each had a mug in their free hands.

I grinned and nodded to him. "Don't do anything you might regret next year, Gib!" I called out.

Gilbert grinned back at me and reached down to squeeze the girl's rump, eliciting a squeal from her. "Just spreading our culture around a little," he laughed.

"Is that all you're spreading?" Morgana wiggled her eyebrows at the pair. They laughed.

"Morgana! You're terrible," Gemma gasped, looking shocked.

Morgana looked at her niece and laughed so hard that tears sprang to her eyes. "Oh, sweetheart, if you think that was terrible, you'd absolutely die of shock if you knew some of the things I've been up to." She paused to catch her breath. "I may be named in honor of the goddess Morrigan, but I find myself on much common ground with Flidais," she said at last, with a sultry smirk. "And I'm not referring to her love of animal husbandry."

Gemma's jaw dropped and she glanced over to me, covering her mouth, looking absolutely scandalized.

"Something I should know about this goddess, Flidais?" I asked.

"No," Gemma said sharply as her cheeks flushed red. This elicited another burst of laughter from Morgana.

"Ah, there you are... all of you together. Good," came the deep, sonorous voice of Myrddin. We all looked over as he came and joined us on our bench. "Peredur, have your men ready to leave in the morning. Something serious has come up," he said without preamble.

Immediately, my contented feeling faded away, and my attention focused on the old diplomat. "What's going on? Trouble with Comgall?"

"No. Well, not serious trouble. I was talking with him about the continued negotiations with the other, Brittonic kings. He's interested, all right. He's even willing to fight other Gaels, though preferably not others of the Scoti people if it can be avoided. The problem is that his condition is that they, in turn, must help him crush the Picts."

"That's quite the demand," I mused. "The Picts are a nuisance in comparison to the Saxon threat, Drest's invasion two years ago notwithstanding."

"Your assessment is correct. Our spies believe that a Saxon invasion is likely coming within the next year or two. Three at the most. The only thing they haven't determined yet is the target. Which is why an alliance that included military support from Doman — Comgall's forces would be a great boon, if we could secure it," Myrddin said, correcting himself. "But his desire is in direct conflict with ours. And it gets worse. Much worse."

"How so?" I pressed. By now, Morgana and Gemma were leaning in, listening intently as well.

"A merchant arrived the other day, with news that a rebellion has broken out within the kingdom of the Gododdin."

I groaned. Gododdin had been the target of King Drest's invasion. Now they faced rebellion?

"That's not all," Myrddin continued. "Many of the nobles, including King Leudon's own son, Medraut, are questioning his competence and ability to rule. Not quite so vehemently that it could be construed as treasonous, but it is causing division within Leudon's court. Division he can ill afford at this time. So now, in the wake of an imminent Saxon invasion, one of our largest allied kingdoms is dealing with a competently led rebellion led by a ruthless warrior named Garwlwyd. The nobility is split on how best to deal with it, and King Leudon's support is weakening."

A jolt coursed through my body at the rebel leader's name, and I held my hand up. "Wait — did you say the rebel's name was *Garwlwyd*?"

Myrddin's brow furrowed. "Yes. He's said to be absolutely terrifying. Maybe even a cinbin, along with many of the men he leads, as if one demonic wolf-man wasn't bad enough."

I cracked a smile at that. "I know Garwlwyd, or at least I did. He was the commander of the levied infantry who fought beside us at Guinnion's Fort."

I thought back to that tall, grizzled warrior. "He used to wear a wolfskin cloak, with the head as a cowl. I hardly think that qualifies him as a cinbin." I almost laughed at the idea.

Myrddin shrugged. "According to the merchant, many in Gododdin believe it. So much so that it's causing quite a panic among the Christian clergymen. The talk about him is that he's so ruthless and bloodthirsty that he makes a point of killing at least one Briton every day of the week, except on Sun's Day, so he kills two on Saturn's Day."

I rolled my eyes at the obvious exaggeration of that claim. "So, we're going to go investigate the situation ourselves?" I asked.

"We are," Myrddin confirmed. "I'll also be sending a letter to High King Conanus and informing him of everything that's happened here. Hopefully, he'll agree to request that Arthur return to Gododdin, sort the situation out, and get back to Caer Lleon in time to help defend our lands from the Saxons."

"Forces from Alt Clut or even Rheged are closer," I pointed out.

"True. But they have few cavalry. Their forces would be mostly levied infantry. Even two hundred Red Dragons, heading north from Caer Lleon, would be a swifter and more reliable response to this threat than five hundred levy infantry from Alt Clut or Rheged. Bryneich and Deira, south of the Gododdin, are Anglian kingdoms in all but name. They'll certainly be of no use."

Myrddin sighed and leaned back in his chair wearily. "We'll get horses from Comgall if he'll part with some and ride to Gododdin. From there, I can get a better understanding of precisely how bad the situation is and how we can resolve it as quickly as possible. We're going to need Gododdin's men, likely as not, to sort out the Saxons."

"I might be able to help with that," I said. "My father, Pelinor, breeds horses on Mona. If King Comgall is reluctant to part with horses for us, I might be able to persuade Father to sell some colts to him at a discounted price. There will still be the matter of acquiring a ship to transport them, though..."

"And if that doesn't work," Morgana chimed in, nibbling on the last bit of meat from a chicken leg bone, "I can always threaten to curse him with an affliction that will leave his manhood useless for the rest of his life."

She said it so casually and matter-of-factly that I could do nothing but stare at her, not sure if I should be horrified, impressed, or simply disgusted at her willingness to embrace witchcraft so openly. Gemma looked uncomfortable as well.

"That might be a bit hard to bluff him with," Myrddin mused.

"Only a slight exaggeration," Morgana smiled mischievously. "But even he knows I'm sometimes called *the Fey*. What good is that silly name if I don't make use of it from time to time?"

The two shared a smile. "Alright, Morgana, Peredur, you shall accompany me when we speak to the king about acquiring horses. Much as I want to go now, he's busy with his own people at present. We'll try approaching him this evening, or perhaps tomorrow morning. We need him in a good mood and not overly busy. So stay where I can find you, and stay reasonably sober from here on out."

I was surprised when Myrddin addressed that last comment to Morgana.

Chapter Eight

Acquiring twelve horses, saddles and bridles for them, two mules, and a wagon took a combination of all three of our tactics. Myrddin was able to acquire the mules and a wagon for himself and Morgana with some old Roman silver and gold coins. To make the travel more comfortable, he also acquired some thick furs to lay across the seat as a bit of padding.

I tentatively offered King Comgall a few of my father's colts, as long as he would provide the transport for them. For good measure, Morgana had casually let slip a remark that she could ensure Comgall was never able to perform with a woman again should he bargain too hard. And the gods disapproved of miserly kings, anyway. As a result, my men and I left Dun Ad on good, if not great horses, as did Gemma and Digain. It was decided that Madwen would be allowed to remain at the hillfort, along with Ithael. Myrddin added another few gold coins for his care and for his place on the next ship that headed south towards Caer Lleon. We couldn't take him with us, after all, not with that broken shin. Nor would it have been safe to allow a lone man to travel either to Din Eidyn, where we were heading, or the much further distance to Caer Lleon, over land.

"Comgall must have decided to trust you," Morgana teased me from her seat on the wagon behind us as we rode out of the gate. "You're likely all but married, in his mind. That's probably why he agreed to the horse trade, too."

"Or he trusts you to keep an eye on us in Madwen's place," I countered.

Morgana snorted with laughter. "If that were his plan, that would make him a terrible judge of character! I'd be less likely to keep the two of you apart and *more* likely to slip something in Gemma's drink that would make her want to positively ravish you, if only for the amusement I'd get out of it."

Gemma's face turned bright red, and she hung back for a spell, too embarrassed to look at either of us.

As he was riding near the front with me, I noticed Gilbert kept looking wistfully back towards the fort.

"Did you forget something back there?" I asked.

Again, Morgana laughed from her seat on the wagon as she too looked toward our Frisian friend.

"He's pining over a girl. I'd know that look anywhere," she said. "Is it the one we saw you with yesterday?" she asked him.

Gilbert sighed and nodded. "Her name is Eithne. Per, I think I'm in love."

I gaped at him. "Gib, you literally just met her."

"Ah, but he also literally just bed her, I'm guessing," Morgana smirked. "Was she your first, Gib?"

That elicited some chuckles from the other men, riding in a long column in front and behind Myrddin's wagon.

Gilbert shook his head, looking indignant. "I've been with others. But this *frou* is different!"

"The others were brunettes, and this one is blond? Or did this one have bigger...?" Morgana laughed, grabbing her own breasts for emphasis.

Gilbert actually blushed. "She did, but that's not what makes her special!" He protested. Again, we all laughed in glee. It felt nice to have someone besides me finally be the butt of the jokes where women were concerned. Not for the first time, it struck me as fascinating just how different Morgana and Gemma were.

"Not to spoil the mood," I finally cut in, "But remember, we were attacked by thieves on the way to Dun Ad. So stay alert, lads. We're back on the open road."

The men acknowledged, and though we continued our bantering, it was kept light and more subdued. Myrddin allowed his raven to fly about freely, hunting and exploring at her pleasure. "She knows where her home is. She always comes back to me," he said confidently.

"Yes, you're a very good mother to her," Morgana said drolly.

Conversations came and went as the miles wore on. The countryside east of Dun Ad was very rough, and because it was also marshy, we had to stick to the high ground. This winding path we were forced to take added miles to our journey and unnerved me and my companions. Typically, walking and especially riding along ridgelines was a huge mistake from a tactical standpoint. It silhouetted us against the skyline to anyone observing the area from a lower elevation, and made us feel highly vulnerable and on edge. When we could, we rode along the side of the hills rather than on their ridges, but that proved tricky as well, now that we had a wagon. Had it been my decision, I'd have not taken it, preferring to travel light and fast, per my cavalryman's instincts. Myrddin, however, had insisted on it.

"A wagon seat will be hard enough. I'm too old to be riding a horse for days on end. There are a dozen of you, and I have the Sight. We'll be fine," he'd insisted.

I asked Morgana what he'd meant by that as we prepared our horses.

"He can see things before they happen," she told me.

I had my doubts about that, particularly given that Myrddin was, as far as I could tell, a pagan. All true power came from God, as far as I was concerned. I said nothing to either of them, though, out of respect. They were as entitled to their beliefs as I was to mine, I reasoned.

Now, riding along the countryside, I hoped Myrddin's 'Sight' was real. Not only were we sky-lining ourselves far too often for my liking, but that cursed wagon made far too much of a racket. It creaked and rumbled along, especially anytime a wheel ran over a rock. Adding to that, Myrddin himself periodically cursed or yelped when that happened, and noise carries farther than most people think. I told my men to stay alert and keep a javelin ready.

That was yet another thing that troubled me. Had we been on our own mounts, with our own kit, each rider would have had a case of half a dozen small javelins slung from our horses. Additionally, each rider would have carried a long, sturdy spear with a large spearhead, used for our initial charge against an enemy. But the Scoti we'd purchased these horses and saddlebags from at Dun Ad had no such cases. Instead, each of us had a medium-length, light spear with a small head that could be used in melee combat or be thrown. These were the preferred spears of the Scoti and the Picts, too, for that matter. Given the choice, if I couldn't have our own spears, I'd have rather had those new heavy spears the Saxons were starting to use, with the large, wide heads and the wing-like bars that flared out at the base of the blade. But there was no point wishing for things we didn't have, and we Britons had been making do with what was available for quite some time now.

***

We traveled northeast for two days, being forced to go around areas of the jagged, Caledonian coastline where the sea carved its way deeply into the land, then eventually angled southeast, during our third day. Although it made the trail muddy and us a bit miserable, I was partially thankful that, as usual, clouds rolled in and began pouring down rain upon us. The darker sky and decreased visibility offered a bit more protection from potential scouting parties. This was particularly important since the further we got from Dun Ad, the more the land fell under Picti control. There was no definitive point on a map, of course, no clear border where we could acknowledge that here was Scoti land and there was Picti land. Who controlled what village or port or river crossing fluctuated constantly and was entirely dependent on how much effort any given warlord, tyrant, or so-called "king" was willing to exert in order to actively protect the area in question.

Thanks to the wagon Myrddin had insisted we bring along, we had a bundle of small tents barely big enough for two men each that we could pitch to shelter us from the storm once daylight began to wane. The old man broke through my reverie with a gesture to the dark gray skies and the rain pouring down around us.

"You see, young Peredur? This is another reason I insisted on having a wagon." He was quite pleased with himself as we set up camp within the sparse cover of a grove of scraggly trees.

I acknowledged his wisdom, though I still worried about the noise and the slower speed of our travels that the wagon cost us in exchange for the comforts it provided. The small tents weren't perfect shelters against bad weather like what we endured that night, by themselves. They proved adequate at least, when combined with the additional protection of the grove of trees we made camp in. We did the best we could at keeping our horses and two mules comfortable and dry as well. At least they wouldn't be lacking for grass to graze on or water to drink.

Once camp was established, I signaled for the men to assemble. They gathered around me, the hoods of oiled cloaks pulled up to ward off the rain.

"We need to be on high alert from this point onward," I told them. "Morgana says we're on the edge of Dal Riata's territory, and frankly," I glanced around, ensuring that her, Digain, and Gemma were out of earshot before I continued. "I think we can all agree that the Scoti aren't very good at securing even the area they do claim as theirs. Beginning tonight, we need to consider ourselves in Picti territory. That means we don't speak too loudly, we watch out for how big we make our fires at night..." I paused and looked balefully up at the sky before adding, "That won't be a problem on nights like this, but we still need noise and light discipline from this point onward. We have a two-day journey, maybe three, heading southeast before we reach the River Clud, which is supposed to be the southern border of Picti lands."

"Their boundary was set at the River Forth," Gilbert corrected me. His brow furrowed in thought. "If the line created by that river were to continue westward, it would essentially be that Roman dirt wall, but the main feature used in Arthur and Drest's treaty was the Forth."

Like me, Gilbert had been present at the battlefield when Drest's forces had been defeated, and he'd heard the terms given to Drest as well as I had, along with most of the Red Dragons who'd fought at Guinnion's Fort.

"Fair point," I acknowledged. "So theoretically, if we cut east using the old Roman road that runs east-west on the southern side of Antonine's Wall, we'll be able to move faster, and should be safe from Picts. As I recall, from Guinnion's Fort, it's a day or two's ride to Din Eidyn."

"Assuming, of course, that the Picts who don't fall under King Drest's control respect the border, and don't feel like doing a bit of cattle thieving or raiding across the border for slaves," Gilbert added.

"And you know the Dragons' view on making assumptions," I agreed. "We don't make any assumptions that we don't have to. Which is why, although we'll ease up a bit on noise and light discipline once we cross onto the southern side of the Wall, we'll still maintain a night watch. Two men up, wearing full kit in two-hour shifts, from sunset to sunrise. We won't be sitting on our arses, either. That will be two hours of walking around the camp, listening for people approaching, and watching for movement."

The group around me nodded, and we established the night's roster. There was no fire that night, so everyone ate a portion of bread, cheese, and some dried meat within the shelter of our own small tents, then went to bed. Tonight, Gilbert and I had the last shift of the night, and it felt like I'd barely dozed off when Tor whispered my name. My eyes sprang open. Gilbert, rolled up in his blanket next to me, was similarly woken up.

We pulled our clothes and armor on in a few moments, then crawled out of our tent.

"Anything happen so far?" I asked and yawned as I pulled my hood up. It was still raining, I noticed.

"Nothing to report," Tor said.

"Not like we could see or hear much, with this wind and rain," his partner, Nefydd, added.

Gilbert looked around and swore in his native Germanic tongue, pulling his cloak tight around himself. At least I presumed he was swearing. His people's language was so harsh to my ears that I'm pretty sure a love poem would still sound threatening.

"At least it's not likely any bad men are likely to be moving about in this, either," I said, patting my friend on the shoulder.

Having been relieved, Tor and Nefydd went back to their tent. Gilbert and I watched and patrolled our camp as the eastern sky slowly lit up with a pale gray hue. The rain died down, and the sky shifted to a pinkish color as the sun peeked out over the horizon, Gilbert began scrutinizing something to the north.

"What do you see, Gib?" I asked, looking from him to the rugged landscape before us.

Gilbert pointed. "You see that hill down there? The one with a rock outcropping on its eastern face?"

I cast my eyes about and saw the hill he was pointing at. It was several hundred paces away, and like ours, dotted with trees. We had a good view of it, being on higher ground.

I nodded.

"Look about ten paces to the left of those rocks. What does that look like to you?" He asked me, speaking softly.

I did and saw a vaguely triangular shape. I focused on it, and then abruptly saw it for what it was — a tent. It was nearly invisible with the foliage of the hillside behind it, but the faint bit of sunlight that was beginning to shine was hitting the flat, east-facing side of the tent, making it easier to spot. Having seen the one tent, I scanned the area around it and spotted several more. Including a single horse, picketed next to a tree.

I described what I saw to Gilbert, who nodded, seeing it too.

"Who do you suppose they are?" He asked.

"In this region, they're likely Picts. The worst-case scenario is that they're scouts for King Drest's forces. They could attack and kill us here and have no fear of consequences. Our bodies would probably never be found, and even if we were, we're north of the Antonine Wall. We're in their lands. Let's rouse the others and get moving."

We made our way from tent to tent, whispering their names or shaking their feet if they were sleeping too soundly. As they woke, Gilbert and I warned them to keep their voices down. We informed them of the tents off in the distance. Morgana and Gemma took a look, and both agreed that the cluster of tents likely belonged to raiders or thieves, rather than sheep or goat herders. "I neither see nor hear any flock," Gemma pointed out. "There are at least half a dozen men on that hill. The only possibility for them being herders would be if they were finding strays. That would not require so many men."

We broke camp smoothly and quietly and were soon on our way south. I'd hoped to evade the Picts, but we weren't so lucky. It was still early in the morning and as we were riding, Myrddin lifted one arm and pointed ahead to where his raven was circling, some distance in front of us.

"There is something out there," he said, looking over to me.

I peered ahead, but saw nothing. "Any idea what?" I asked.

"I am not certain." Myrddin shrugged. "But we should be wary."

This warning was annoyingly vague, but I recalled his warning in Dal Riata, and decided to loosen the spatha in my scabbard then I turned to the rest of the group.

"Be ready for trouble lads," I told them, "And keep a close eye on our surroundings."

They responded, and also made ready, unslinging shields and putting on their helmets. Beside Myrddin on the seat of their wagon, Morgana strung her bow and pulled a few arrows out of her quiver.

A short time later, we crested a low hill along the path, and I gasped. In an unseen gully, a band of Picts, three times our number, were arrayed before us — presumably the Picts we'd seen encamped the night before. Three of them were mounted and held spears. The rest either had spears and shields, or slings at the ready. Two more, hanging back a bit, had bows with arrows already nocked. Many of them with visible blue markings on their faces and exposed skin.

Options began flashing through my mind. None of them looked good. We could charge them, but as ready as they were, we had a high likelihood of taking casualties. God help us if Myrddin or either of the women were among them. Fleeing in any direction was likely to result in the same outcome, especially considering how cumbersome Myrddin's damned wagon was. I swore softly to myself and licked my lips. I had to make a decision, fast.

One of the riders walked his horse a step toward us, and pointed at us, barking something in his barbarian dialect. His blond hair was unkempt and he sported a large mustache. I also noted that he was one of the few men wearing armor — a coat of mail no less. A sword and dagger were belted at his waist. He seemed to want a fight, but I couldn't understand much else, so I glanced over to Gemma. "You get all that?" I asked her with a raised eyebrow.

"He says we're trespassing on Maeatae lands, and that by rights they should kill us all," Gemma said. Her hand slowly crept toward a pouch of throwing darts that she kept attached to her saddle.

"Tell him we we're only passing through, but if he indeed expects to *kill us all*, he'd better make his peace with his pagan gods, for we won't die easily," I told her, then turned my gaze back to the large Pict who was apparently their leader. I did my absolute best to present a calm, confident demeanor, despite the fact that my heart was beginning to race at what I expected to happen in the next few moments.

Gemma translated my words, and the Pict grinned at me. He drew his sword, followed almost instantly by us, and we formed up instinctively on line without my having to give any command to do so.

Just as it appeared that both our groups were about the rush each other, Myrddin stood up in the wagon and pointed dramatically up into the sky, then bellowed something in sounded like Greek. His raven promptly dove down and landed on the old man's outstretched arm and squawked as it looked around at all of us.

The Picts reacted in astonishment, looking wide-eyed to one another, and to the raven. Myrddin stared sternly at them, and made several dramatic gestures with his free hand, speaking to the Picti warband in the kind of voice our priest uses at Mass.

"He says the raven is a sign from the gods," Gemma translated for us in a low tone. "There should be no battle this day. Rather, we should honor the old ways, and allow a single champion from both parties fight. The losing side should give up its valuables and leave this place."

At Myrddin's pronouncement, the Picts began arguing and gesturing wildly.

"We should charge them now," Tor muttered from off to my right. "While they're distracted,"

"No! Stand fast," I snapped. I wasn't overly thrilled with Myrddin's plan, but it offered us better odds than charging into them, particularly given that their slingers and archers were still standing back, watching us, and ready for just such a move from us.

The Picti barbarians' jabbering soon gave way to a single word.

"Gartnait! Gartnait! Gartnait!" The Picts chanted.

The big man who'd confronted us turned back to the men and grinned broadly, then dismounted gracefully and faced us. He spoke loudly, thumping his chest as he did. I picked up the repeated use of the name 'Gartnait'. I turned to look at Gemma and Myrddin, expectantly.

Myrddin translated for us. "This young man says he is Gartnait, son of Girom. He will fight for the honor of his warband and of the Maeatae."

As Myrddin spoke, the Picti warrior growled, drew his sword, and smacked it against his shield upon hearing his name.

"This *hōrning swīn* is mine!" Gilbert snarled and made to jump down from his horse.

The instant he started talking, I knew his intent however and as he was next to me, my hand snaked out, grabbing the neckline of his mail.

"No," I barked. "Are you daft? Look at him. He's got too much reach on you. He'd skewer you before you could get in close enough.

"Who then? Not *you* I hope." Gilbert asked, still staring the Pict down. "You'd have the same problem."

I had in fact been tempted to accept the challenge. I was the group's leader after all. I was the most appropriate challenger... at least for the sake of pride. But I didn't have the luxury of thinking purely as a warrior. I was a leader of men in the Red Dragons. I needed to be strategic. I had one chance of resolving this danger with minimal bloodshed.

"Marcus," I snapped.

"Yes, Decanus," Marcus replied instantly, using my former rank.

"Think you can take this big bastard?"

"Me?" Marcus asked, surprised.

"Yes, you," I replied. "You're big, like he is. And you're as well-trained as any of us. I need you to kick his arse."

Marcus glanced from me then to the Pict, who rolled his shoulders and yawned loudly. He seemed uncertain, until the big man thrust his sword into the ground, pulled his clothing aside, and relieved himself — facing us all the while. The men beside me stirred, and behind me, I heard a woman snicker — Morgana if I had to guess.

"I want a whole barrel of wine for this," Marcus said jumping down from his horse and passing his reins to Tor.

"Don't kill him, if you can help it," I instructed him.

Marcus shot me a confused, frustrated glance but this was neither the time nor place to have a discussion about that, so he pressed his lips tightly together and nodded at me. Then he drew his sword and strode over to the large Pict.

"I am Marcus, son of Paulus, of Caer Londin and an *eques* of the Red Dragons." He spat. "I accept your challenge, *canis cinaede.*"

Our lads hooted and jeered at Marcu's insult as the barbarian tucked himself back into his trousers, let the hem of his mail fall, and retrieved his sword — flicking the edge of the blade up as he did so, sending a clod of dirt flying toward Marcus' face. Our big Romano-Briton simply lifted his large, oval shield and deflected it.

The Pict, Gartnait, leapt at Marcus with a loud roar, thrusting his sword at my cymbrog and kicking a leg out backward at the same time. Had the blow struck, even if Marcus blocked it, the sheer force of it might have knocked Marcus to the ground. Instead, Marcus jumped aside, then darted forward himself and punched the rim of his shield into Gartnait's head.

Were it not for the bronze helm the barbarian wore, that might have ended the fight then and there. Instead, while it rocked him backwards, Gartnait quickly fell back into a defensive crouch, with his shield and sword up and ready for Marcus' next attack. When it came, the two chopped and stabbed at each other in a flurry of blows — both were surprisingly fast for their size. Once, he managed to strike what might have been a fatal blow at the back of Marcus' neck, but the small, flared guard of his iron helmet saved him, and the blade deflected away, though the force of the blow caused Marcus to stagger away.

The two circled, and made a few feints and light jabs at each other. Both were breathing heavily and sweating profusely. Marcus looked to be the more tired of the two, but it was Gartnait who made the first mistake. He jabbed at Marcus' exposed face, which Marcus blocked, then swiftly countered with a low swipe at Gartnait's leg. Like most Picts, this warrior had a small, square shield, and the tip of our cymbrog's blade sliced into the barbarian's left leg, just above the knee.

He grunted in pain and clumsily leapt away, slashing a wide arc through the air with this own sword, expecting Marcus to press in.

Instead, Marcus circled the Pict, feinting once or twice, forcing the wounded barbarian to circle with him. Meanwhile blood flowed from the injured man's leg. Once, Gartnait lunged forward on his good right leg, thrusting at Marcus. That was his next mistake. His arm jutted out too far for him to properly protect, and Marcus neatly stepped back and slashed at the Pict's extended arm, cutting him again.

The Pict growled in frustration and smacked his sword against his shield.

In response, Marcus merely waved the tip of his sword at the barbarian's face, letting him see the blood there. Gartnait roared in fury and charged, swinging with his sword and jabbing with the rim of his shield. Marcus successfully blocked the sword strike, but the rim of the Pict's shield smashed into Marcus' forehead, and he staggered back, momentarily stunned. Blood dribbled down from a cut, caused by the rim of his helmet.

A loud cheer erupted from the onlooking Picts as our group gasped. Gartnait took advantage of the moment as Marcus's shield went wide and he thrust his sword at our cymbrog's chest. Marcus twisted away at the last moment and, God be praised, his mail did its job. Gartnait's blade deflected off the riveted iron rings rather than running him through. Marcus countered with a shield strike of his own. Again, the rim of his large shield struck the side of Gartnait's helmeted head, and Gartnait staggered away. This put too much weight on his wounded leg though, and Gartnait stumbled, nearly falling altogether. Marcus' sword snaked out, causing yet another deep cut to the Pict's sword arm. This time it was the Picts who gasped and cried out anxiously, and our group that cheered.

Although Marcus was sweating heavily now, he launched a flurry of powerful strikes at the Pict, who frantically blocked with his shield. The wood splintered and a sliver of it fell away. Marcus' breath came in ragged gasps and he slowly began circling again, just out of reach of the Pict's blade. The trampled earth around Gartnait was splattered with blood now, and he was clearly feeling the effects. He maintained a strong defensive posture, but his face revealed the struggle and effort it was taking.

"Yield," Marcus finally stated. Behind him, Myrddin translated his demand for the Picts. The barbarians howled and jeered in response, and Gartnait spat defiantly.

Marcus shrugged then dashed to the Pict's wounded side. Gartnait pivoted to face him, but he slammed the boss of his shield into the Pict. This time he was knocked fully to the ground. He crawled backwards, raising his sword in a feeble effort to defend himself as Marcus stalked toward him. I heard a cry of outrage from off to my left and whipped my head toward the sound. There was a flurry young Pict, possibly even younger than myself, raising his spear in a reverse grip, as though he intended to throw it.

With little time to respond, I spurred my mount forward, and the horse slammed into the Pict, knocking him backward. I drew my sword and pointed it at the lad, shaking my head. He scrambled to his feet and looked ready to fight me, but two of his comrades grabbed him by the arms and seemed to chastise him, for he backed away, and returned his attention to the duel. After a moment, I did too as I turned my horse back to rejoin the rest of my comrades.

The fight was over. Gartnait was up, but only on one knee. His left leg was too weak to stand on, and Marcus had kicked his shield away. The wound to his right arm was clearly causing him a lot of pain, and he'd been forced to switch his sword to his left hand. Still, he refused to concede.

Marcus sighed in frustration, standing just out of the big Pict's reach, and called out to Myrddin. "Can you please get this stupid bastard to surrender so I don't have to kill him?"

My companions chuckled a little at that, though I suspect that they, like I, had quickly grown a great deal of respect for this Picti warrior who appeared to be determined to die rather than yield. From his perch on the wagon, Myrddin began speaking to the warrior, and to his men beyond him. Gemma eased up beside me and translated.

"Your champion fought valiantly," she said. "Our man, Marcus, has won. The gods have made their will known. To continue this duel would not only dishonor them but also cost the life of a brave man — who deserves to live. Let us depart, peacefully this day, and hope never again to meet as enemies."

"Fat chance of that," Gilbert muttered nearby. His hand still on the pommel of his sword.

Gemma ignored his remark and continued translating. "This man deserves a long life, and to die in bed with a woman beside him..." her voice trailed off and she blushed deeply. "I'm not saying the rest."

This drew grins from our men, and hearty laughs and whoops from the Picts. Even Gartnait cracked a smile. The din faded back into a tense silence; all eyes turned to the wounded Pict champion. At last, he closed his eyes, and nodded with a deep sigh. He licked his bleeding lips, and spoke something, looking from Marcus to Myrddin.

Myrddin nodded and turned to us. "He concedes the duel to our champion, and acknowledges our right, before the gods, to leave here in peace."

"Aren't we supposed to also take all of their possessions?" Gilbert grumbled. "Those were the terms of the agreement, *ja*?"

"Let's not press our luck," I replied. "Lads," I called out. "I want to be at least fifteen miles from here by the time we make camp tonight."

As the men reformed, and Marcus turned away sheathing his sword, I saw Gartnait helped to his feet by the same young man who'd nearly inserted himself into the duel.

"Marcus," he said, and our comrade turned back toward the Pict.

Gartnait pulled a gleaming, if bloody silver torc necklace from his neck and handed to Marcus with a respectful dip of his head.

Marcus looked from it to Gartnait, then slowly took the torc. He stood motionless for a moment, as though unsure what to do next, then put it around his own neck.

"Good fight, Gartnait, son of Girom," he said, and offered his hand.

The Pict smiled at that, and took Marcus' hand, shaking it briefly. Then the two parted. The younger Pict helped Gartnait to sit down while two others began tending to his injuries. Marcus walked back to his horse and gingerly remounted.

"Are you good to ride?" I asked.

"I am," Marcus sighed. "But you owe that barrel!"

"I'll see what I can do," I chuckled, then signaled the column to resume our journey south.

Chapter Nine

A LITTLE OVER FIVE days after leaving Dal Riata, we reached the long berm that made up the Antonine border wall.

"Not much to look at, is it?" Tor asked. He was one of the few people in our group who'd never traveled through here. "You lads actually fought a Pict army along this wall?"

"Well, not on this exact spot," I chuckled. "Guinnion's Fort is another twenty-odd miles east of us."

"We'll probably go past it tomorrow, though," Gemma added.

We traveled most of that day, stopping for the night at one of the many small forts that lined the wall every few miles. There was almost nothing standing, of course. The ground was flatter, and there was a series of low, stone walls that had been the foundations of the original Roman buildings. Some of them had small trees growing inside of them now. Regardless of their present condition, the level ground and remaining walls still made the fortlet a useful campsite. Though overcast, there was no rain, so we built a fire inside one of the ruins and cooked some of our rations.

I was finishing up the last bit of cheese when I noticed Myrddin, reclining against a portion of a wall. His head was tilted back a bit, and to my shock, it looked as though his eyes were white!

"What's wrong with him, Morgana?" I asked, moving over to him.

Morgana peered over at him. "He's fine. He's in a trance. He does that sometimes."

"Is he seeing through his raven or something?" Gilbert asked, gesturing to the large black bird that flew about overhead. Marcus and Tor also came over to look.

Morgana shrugged. "Maybe? As I've said before, he has the Sight. It's said that he foresaw the war between Britons and Saxons when he was a child. He's supposed to have stood before Vortigern himself and warned him of the Red Dragon and White Dragon battling."

"Whaat?" Marcus exclaimed, acting shocked. "Myrddin predicted that a large, semi-hostile immigration of barbarians into Britain would end in warfare with our people? What wisdom he must have possessed to foresee such an unlikely event!"

I laughed with Marcus, then I noticed something. As I'd been talking, I was also looking closely at Myrddin's face and saw a sliver of his iris become visible. So his eyes hadn't gone white; rather, they were just rolled up. Leaning closer, I thought I heard an occasional snore, as well.

"He's not in a trance," I finally determined. "He's just an old man, sleeping."

"Doesn't look like he's sleeping to me," Tor argued dubiously.

"Gib, you remember Aylmer, right?" I asked.

Gilbert nodded, slowly. "Of course. He was our decanus for a while. Got killed at Guinnion's Fort." he pointed off to the east.

I felt a twinge at that but continued on. "Aylmer used to do the same thing. He'd be fast asleep, but his eyes would be cracked open sometimes. When he did that, his eyes rolled up some. Like how Myrddin is doing now."

"Maybe," Gilbert acknowledged, though he looked doubtful.

Myrddin's raven swooped down, landed on his shoulder, and let out a loud croaking noise. The old man's eyelids fluttered, and a moment later, he peered around at us.

"Trouble!" he blurted out, huskily.

"No, no trouble, old man," I reassured him.

Myrddin shook his head. "No, I mean there will be trouble. On the road ahead."

"What kind of trouble?" I asked, feeling a sense of unease crawl over me. "When?"

Myrddin scowled and glanced over at his bird. His bushy eyebrows hid his purple-tinted eyes for a moment, then he shook his head.

"I'm not sure," he admitted. "I just sense that we'll be in danger if we stay on this road."

"You don't say," I muttered. "Picts are roaming the region, there's always a risk of raiders, and King Leudon's kingdom is in rebellion."

"Maybe we should find another route?" Gilbert suggested.

"You want to get off the road and travel through the woods? With that wagon? Or maybe find a boat from somewhere, abandon the horses, and sail down the Forth?" I scoffed at the idea.

Gilbert shrugged. "What do you suggest?" He asked Myrddin. "Did your vision offer any clues at all?"

I rolled my eyes at his reference to a "vision" but turned to hear what Myrddin would say. He was ultimately in charge of us, after all. The rest of the group slowly turned to look as well.

Myrddin looked down the road, towards the east. "I think you're right, Peredur," he finally sighed. "Leaving the road and cutting through the wilderness will not only take longer but also be much more difficult with our wagon. Attempting to travel onward to Din Eidyn by sea is equally impractical, maybe impossible. So please, be alert when we set off again."

I did my best to hide what I thought of that comment and simply nodded respectfully. I also considered that he had warned us of trouble once before, and we were indeed ambushed. We'd had no functional alternative then, either. I assigned guard shifts for the night as we finished our evening meal. We let the fire die down, and everyone set up their tents within the ruins and went to sleep.

***

The next afternoon, six days since we'd left Dun Ad, we passed by Guinnion's Fort. I didn't know how I would feel, returning to a battlefield where a few of my friends, and many other Red Dragons I'd not known by name, were buried. As we approached, however, my jaw went slack. The large wooden fort that we'd restored to a functional level two years before had been burned to the ground.

We rode past in silence. I'd not have been surprised to see a few timbers torn loose to be used by locals, either for firewood or building materials. With the Picts presumably pacified, the fort wasn't that important anymore, and it had been a question even two years ago whether or not any sort of garrison would be left to man it. But the fact that the fort had been burned presented an entirely new situation.

Ythel sniffed loudly. "I can still smell smoke. This was recent. No more than a week ago, I'd wager."

I nodded in agreement and scanned the wooded hills around us, on edge. I couldn't imagine the fire starting on its own, nor could I see any reason for the locals to burn the fort down. That only left the Picts. I reined my horse in until I was alongside Myrddin and Morgana.

Gesturing at the fort, I asked them, "What do you think? Drest wouldn't be stupid enough to renew hostilities with us, would he?"

Myrddin stroked his beard thoughtfully as he looked around. "He might," the old man said at last. "His core reasoning for invading the Gododdin in the first place still exists. He's still facing the growing threat of Dal Riata to his west, and the only options available to him are to bend the knee to them, fight them, or invade the Gododdin. He's been losing his battles against the Scoti..."

Morgana shrugged. "Picts and Gaels have been raiding each other's lands across the sea for longer than anyone can remember. We're just finally turning the tide."

"So you are," Myrddin agreed. "And now Drest is responding to that in the best way he sees fit. This," he pointed at the fort, "is probably the Picts' doing. But whether it's simply a petty, isolated act of defiance or a prelude to something more nefarious isn't clear, unfortunately."

We continued riding for a short while longer, then, from off to my right, I heard Gilbert start swearing furiously. He broke off from our column and galloped away towards a section of the woodline a hundred paces behind the fort. It was the area the Red Dragons had set up our camp in, and more importantly, where we'd buried our dead. A feeling of dread came over me, and I turned my mount to follow him.

Once I'd joined Gilbert, I saw why he was snarling and cursing in such anger. The simple, wooden markers that had been placed at the head of their burial mounds had been hacked apart and ripped from the earth. Many of the graves had been dug up, and the bodies dragged up to the surface. They were, of course, little more than skeletons, but the horror of the level that their remains had been desecrated was nothing short of an outrage.

My own hands clenched into fists, and I shouted for the rest of the men to come join me. As they did, they too cried out in a mix of horror and shock. A couple, who'd also been at the battle, fell to their knees and wept bitterly. I wiped a tear from my own eye. Some of these skeletons could have belonged to my friends. All of them had been fellow Red Dragons.

"We need to rebury them," I said. The others agreed and we set about carefully picking up bones where they'd been thrown or dragged and gnawed on by animals and replacing them in their graves. Gemma came up to me and put a comforting hand on my shoulder. She didn't say anything, but she didn't need to. She'd been here too, helping tend to the wounded with our medicus, Tewdrig. We stood together for a moment, then joined the rest of the group. Even Morgana helped.

As we went about the task, my anger for the Picts grew. When I first joined the Red Dragons, I'd hoped to face off against the Saxons, to avenge my brother

Aglofael's death. He died several years ago, in Arthur's first campaign. Given the chaos of that prolonged campaign that had consisted of a series of attacks deep into Saxon territory, the soldier who'd given my family the news of his death had been unable to provide any specific details of my brother's death, and he'd been buried where he'd fallen. I'd looked forward to facing the Saxons in battle, though that hadn't happened as of yet.

Now, I felt my anger at them rivaled by the rage I felt at the Picts. How dare they do this to our dead, I thought. I could forgive them for burning the fort. That was simply a strategic matter, not to mention the symbolic value. But Arthur had dealt fairly with them when we stopped their invasion here, far more so than most kings would have done in his shoes. And this was how he was repaid. From the clenched jaws and furrowed brows of my companions as we worked in grim silence, I knew I wasn't the only one feeling the way I did.

By the time we'd buried the scattered remains back in their graves and piled rocks over them again, it was too late in the day to bother continuing on, so we decided to make camp there against the edge of the woods, in the same location our numerus had made camp during the campaign.

Still seething, I walked off into the woods to clear my head. I always found it easier to sort myself out when I was by myself than around other people. I did miss my mare, Carys, though. I took out my sling and started picking up whatever rocks were lying around and hurled them at a tree stump some thirty feet away, vaguely enjoying the 'thwack' the rocks made as they smashed into the wood.

"Is that tree stump a Pict?" a soft voice asked from behind me.

I turned, startled, and saw Gemma standing a few feet away, softly illuminated by the glow of our campfire further back towards the edge of the woods.

"Maybe," I chuckled humorlessly.

"How are you feeling?"

"Angry. And worried."

"Worried about what?" She found a fallen tree and sat down.

I sighed. "When I first joined the numerus, I was angry with the Saxons. I spent several years hating them for killing my older brother. And then I met Gilbert. It gave me some perspective. So did Decurion Owain. It's strange. Owain and I talked once, and he simultaneously defended the Saxons and other barbarians as simply being people trying to survive in their own way. At the same time, he freely admitted that were he in charge of the Red Dragons rather than Arthur, he would deal with them far more ruthlessly. I was appalled at the time. I argued that if we acted barbarically towards them, what made us any different?"

"What did he tell you?" Gemma asked.

"He said we aren't. We're like them, a people trying to survive. And his opinion is that by being more savage and ruthless than our enemies, we increase the odds of our survival. I didn't agree with him then. But then we fought the Picts, and I saw what the raiders had been doing to the townsfolk here. Arthur treated them as mercifully as he could have when we defeated them. And this..." I hissed through clenched teeth, "This is how his kindness was repaid." I gestured to a skull I'd found while slinging rocks. Probably it had been one of our men, and we'd missed it when we reburied the remains of our fallen.

"And now you think you were wrong, and Owain is right?" she prodded me.

"Maybe. And I hate the idea. I hate that I'm so angry. I hate that the Picts are making me feel the way I do. I felt ashamed of myself for hating the Saxons as a whole after I came to know Gilbert. But now a part of me wishes we could ride north and kill every one of those filthy, heathen Picts. Don't you hate them? After they took you as a slave and mistreated you so badly?" I asked.

"No. I do not. I was angry, even furious, with some of the people of that village. But I also understand that slavery is a fact of life, and that there are good and bad people everywhere," Gemma said. "And the people who mistreated me have probably paid for their cruelty."

I shook my head in mild amazement.

"You sound like my father. He adheres to an old philosophy called Stoicism — it dictates the control of emotion in favor of logic."

Gemma cocked her head. "I don't try to control all emotions. Only negative ones. On the contrary, I hold positive emotion in very high regard — love most of all. Even your Holy scriptures that the priest, Derfel, reads from at mass agree with that. Think of all the great deeds that heroes have done in the bards' tales as well. I think love is the chief motivation behind nearly all of them."

We stood in silence for a moment, then she continued. "Tell me, Per, why do you fight? Do you enjoy it, as Gib does?"

"I don't mind it too much, once I get past the fear," I replied.

"Hmm. But what do you seek to gain from it? Land? Wealth? Slaves?"

"I mean, I will probably need to acquire land of my own. My brother, Lamorac, will be inheriting Father's estate someday, as things stand."

"You could have worked to expand your father's horse breeding, or found a position on a merchant ship. I know your mother hoped you would go down that path," she pointed out.

"And as I did that, I would have to go about my life knowing that the Saxons were progressively taking over our land, and barbarians would keep raiding it for plunder and slaves."

"So you sought a career that could earn the land and wealth you need, but also that would help put an end to that problem, yes?"

"Maybe I do like to fight?" I mused.

"Possible. But there are better ways to earn coin if that were your goal," she argued. "You've mentioned the Eastern Empire, for example. If they're still as strong and powerful as you lot say the West was, once upon a time, could you not have traveled there and joined their army?"

"I could have," I agreed. "Such a move would make it incredibly hard to ever see my family again, though."

"Which is another thing you value highly — family," Gemma said with a nod. "Per, you're a defender by nature. You're an instrument of war, but not like a sword or spear. You're more like a shield. When you grow angry with people, like the Saxons or the Picts, it's not because you're a hateful person, but because you care deeply for people they've harmed. The fact that you worry so much about becoming blindly hateful of them is proof enough that you have a good heart. It's why I fell in love with you," she smiled at me.

"And here I thought it was for my good looks," I grinned back at her.

"I might have said that before you started trying to grow that beard," she teased me.

I touched the stubble on my jaw. "I thought it was coming in nicely."

"Sorry, but no, it's not," Gemma chuckled.

I let her lead me back into camp then, where the rest of the group was eating dinner around the fire.

Chapter Ten

Our seventh day on the road began peacefully enough. Although it was late in the month of Martius, the morning air was still chilly, and a light wind blew, causing our cloaks to flap about as we rode. At least rain today seemed unlikely, I thought. Particularly in this region, there was always the possibility of it though, of course. We passed by a few hovels along the way. At one such cluster of no more than half a dozen homes, a boy hopped on a mule and trotted down the road heading east.

"He was in a hurry," Gilbert commented, riding beside me.

"Yes," I mused. I glanced around, noting that a few other men had stopped working their fields to watch us. Something about the atmosphere gave me an uneasy feeling, though I couldn't explain why. After a few moments, I decided it was likely from the simple fact that we were a dozen armed men, traveling with a pair of women. Of course, we would draw some attention.

A couple of miles past the hovels, we trotted past three badly decomposed bodies dangling from a tree. The women gasped, and the mood became somber as we rode past them. There was no shred of clothing on the corpses, so I guessed they'd been stripped naked. Their hands were tied behind their backs, and hair still clung to their shriveled bodies, letting us at least know that they'd been men.

"Criminals?" Gilbert asked, looking around at the rest of us.

"Probably," I said. But something felt off. By themselves, the bodies swinging from the tree branch weren't all that unusual. Criminals often met fates such as this, and worse sometimes. But it was more than that. It was the bodies, combined with the oddity of the boy taking off down the road as we approached the hamlet, combined with the unfriendly, suspicious looks the farmers had given us as we rode by that were putting me on edge.

"Don't forget," Myrddin added when I mentioned all this, "The messenger at Dal Riata did say that there is some rebellion occurring here. Typically, these sorts of things end up becoming a matter of people in rural areas, like this, rising up against the centers of power in urban areas. So the people here could very well be rebels."

"Meaning those dead men could as easily be King Leudon's men as criminals," I said.

Myrddin nodded, and a shiver went down my spine.

"Wonderful," Tor muttered from behind us. "And with our armor and horses, we probably look like the King's men, making us a nice flashy target for any nearby rebels."

Again, I started to wish Myrddin hadn't insisted on his wagon. Without it, we could have diverted off the road and taken a less conspicuous route to Din Eidyn. Instead, we continued to follow the old Roman road as it led east, and by that afternoon, we found ourselves riding alongside with the Firth of Forth to our left. In other circumstances, the smell of the sea in the air, and the feeling of the wind lightly blowing would have been quite enjoyable. Now, however, I found myself simply wondering if the sea would be a blessing that helped prevent possible enemies from ambushing us, or a curse that would leave us with one less avenue of escape in such an event.

With the regular movement of the birds flying about, I initially missed the small, distant group of people near the water's edge. Marcus pointed them out. There were only about four of them, and once we saw them, we could tell that they were men and had shields slung on their backs. They stood there by a cluster of trees, watching us. One turned his back, giving us a good glimpse of his shield.

"Those are Picts!" Gemma exclaimed.

I gritted my teeth and looked over to Myrddin. "Do we go after them?"

Myrddin squinted and stared at the group, shading his face with one wrinkled hand.

"No," he sighed. "They're on foot, but close to the water. I suspect that they're moving about by boat. And since they're already observing us, if we started after them, even at a gallop, they'd have plenty of time to get out to sea."

I reluctantly nodded in agreement. "This is more evidence that the Picts are violating their terms of surrender," I pointed out. "Will you send a message of this to Tribune Arthur, or the Council of the Kings? They should probably know."

"I will," Myrddin assured me. "What troubles me the most is that the Picts might try and use this rebellion as a chance to launch a new invasion."

"Arthur should have destroyed them when he had the chance," Morgana said coldly. "He had King Drest in his grasp!"

"He was hoping to establish peace by showing mercy," Gemma argued.

"And look where that's gotten us." Morgana swept her hand toward the distant cluster of Picts. "If the Gaels and Britons of the Gododdin could unite, we would crush the Picts between us."

"That's the argument Comgall made," Myrddin mused. "I shall, of course, make the offer to King Leudon when we meet with him. I hold out little hope for such an agreement, however."

"Because of this rebellion?" Morgana asked.

"Because of that, and because, quite frankly, I doubt he will want to trust the Gaels to share a border with the Gododdin any more than he trusts the Picts. The Scoti have shown plenty of interest in expanding their own territory at every opportunity, after all."

Morgana shrugged. "Everyone expands their territory when the land is available, if their neighbors are too weak to control it. And why not? If a land has weak rulers, then raiders and thieves spring up like weeds. Those troublemakers can then begin causing problems in lands that do have strong rulers."

Myrddin stroked his beard and winced. "You're not entirely wrong, girl. Of course, that results in too many kings looking at their neighbors and deciding that as long as they are stronger, they're justified in expanding. The result is that kingdoms now rise and fall almost too fast to bother keeping track of."

I certainly couldn't argue the old man's point. My own homeland of Gwynedd, formed in the past thirty years or so, was a perfect example. Before Cunedda Wledig retook it for the Britons, it belonged to the Gaels. Before the Gaels seized the region, it was one of the provinces under the control of a Roman governor. All this occurred in less than a century.

The two continued their debate as we kept riding. I kept an eye on the Picti scouting party, who remained where they were until we eventually lost sight of them. That evening, we stayed on the road until not a single hovel was in sight, which had become harder to do the closer we got to Din Eidyn. None of us felt comfortable camping too near to other people in the area, however, given the volatile situation the region was in. This time, it was Morgana who chose our campsite for the night.

I set up a watch rotation, and we quickly went to sleep for the night. We removed our shoes and sword belts, but slept in our clothing and armor, with our helms and shields close to hand. The mood in the camp was subdued and a bit on edge, as everyone sensed that the closer we came to Din Eidyn, the more danger we were in.

I slept fitfully throughout the first sleep and prowled around the camp for a bit as everyone started waking up. I checked on the guards. Tor and Marcus were on watch. They'd neither seen nor heard anything unusual. I checked on the horses and mules, picketed together beside the wagon. They were dozing and grazing comfortably, appearing to be more relaxed than we were. I looked around. The moon was full, though clouds blotted out most of the stars, reducing our visibility.

After conducting my checks, I decided to walk out to the edge of camp to relieve myself. Somewhere out in the woods a wolf howled. Another responded, and I frowned. They didn't sound all that far away. Once I finished, I turned back towards the camp, then cocked my head, hearing a faint *whirring* noise. My eyes widened in shock as I recognized the sound, and instinctively dove to the ground. Much too late. Pain exploded in the back of my head. It felt as though I were spinning in circles, and something wet trickled down my cheek. I faintly heard the sound of shouts, more howling, and what sounded like a battle, then I faded out of consciousness.

***

Even before my eyelids fluttered open, I felt a throbbing, overwhelming pain in the back of my head. I groaned, and brought a hand up to my head. I had a large, painful lump there, and my hair was matted with dried blood. My mouth felt dry. I squinted and blearily at my fingers, straining to focus. After a moment, my vision cleared and I could see my hand clearly. There were traces of blood on my fingertips. I dropped my arm, feeling weak, and looked around at what was visible from where I lay. I was on my stomach on the ground. The trees around me were little more than dark silhouettes, but the eastern sky was beginning to glow. Dawn wasn't far away then. Birds chirped and flitted around, deeper in the surrounding woods, but I heard no other sounds, at first. As I concentrated, I detected the sound of shallow, raspy breathing from somewhere nearby. I knew the sound. Someone was dying, likely as not.

I slowly pushed myself up to my hands and knees, and a wave of nausea hit me so hard that I retched. It still felt like the world was spinning around me, as it did on the rare occasion when I let my cymbrogi talk me into drinking too much, and I closed my eyes. Gradually, the dizziness faded, though the throbbing headache did not. I cautiously got to my feet and for a few moments, though I felt like I was back on a ship. To be safe, I squatted down on one knee, then noticed patches of dried blood at my feet. My brain felt fuzzy, again as though I had drunk too heavily. I frowned, trying to think. I hadn't drunk recently, had I? I was fairly certain I hadn't. So what had happened? It was hard to think with my head pounding the way it was. My ears rang faintly, like an insect was hovering around my head. This was most noticeable when the surrounding birds went silent. Somehow, my mail was gone. I'd been wearing it last night. All of us had been wearing our armor, I remembered. Whoever had struck me must have assumed I was dead and stripped me of it, though I still wore the rest of my clothing, to include my padded tunic.

I looked around slowly, and as the shock hit me, clarity slowly returned. The horses and wagon were gone. One of the tents was still standing, the rest had been knocked to the ground. And there were bodies — bodies of my comrades. I gasped in horror and staggered over to the nearest one. It was Lewys, and he was dead. I moved from body to body. Ythel was still in his bedroll and had a spear pinning him to the ground. Not far away was Nefydd. Tears streamed down my face. I moved about our campsite, and my heart broke anew with each dead comrade I came upon. There were five in all. Gilbert, Marcus, Elis, and Tor were missing, along with Gemma, Myrddin, Morgana, and Digain. I was still hearing the faint, ragged breath of at least one person, though, and I kept searching the area. I found numerous bloodstains that couldn't be readily identified as belonging to any of my dead comrades, so I had to assume they were either from some that were still missing, or from our attackers, and their bodies had been taken away.

A few moments later, I found the source of the breathing. Digain was slumped against a tree, covered in blood from a dozen wounds. When I approached, he squinted up at me from his one good eye.

"Per... they took... Gemma," he wheezed. "...tried to stop them."

I dropped down beside him, assessing his wounds. "Who took her? Where? What about the others?" I asked. Frothy blood was coming from his mouth as he spoke, so I knew from experience that he was beyond saving. I took his hand, offering what meager comfort I could.

"Cinbin," Digain replied. "...took her, and some others... I fought them. I failed, Peredur... I didn't protect her."

Cinbin? I thought. The dog-headed creatures said to live in the deep woods? Surely we were too close to civilization for an encounter with them.

"You did the best you could," I assured the dying warrior. "You gave your life to protect her. No man could ever fault your effort." I squeezed his hand, and he squeezed mine back briefly.

His good eye focused intently on me. "Get her back... Promise me..."

"I will. I swear by all that is Holy that I will see Gemma safe again. And the others, if I can, if they still live. Go before God with pride, Digain."

Digain nodded.

"Do you have any idea where they took her?" I tried asking again.

The warrior gestured toward the east, then his arm fell limply to his side. For a moment, I thought he was dead, but his eyelids fluttered and chest continued to rise and fall, though very faintly.

I slipped away and scrounged around the destroyed camp for some water and found my canteen. I drank several long gulps as I returned to Digain. I offered him some water. He nodded weakly, and I carefully poured a trickle of water into his mouth. The corners of his mouth twitched into a faint smile, then he nodded at me, and died.

"Rest in peace," I said softly — closing his eyes and making the sign of the cross.

I wanted desperately to sort out which way Gemma and the others had been taken, but I was in no shape to go traipsing off down the road in God only knew what direction. And supposing I did catch up to whoever, or whatever, abducted my companions, what then? I was certainly not up for a fight in my current state. And then there were my dead comrades. The idea of leaving them to rot, exposed to scavengers, was abhorrent. But six bodies would take a long time to bury. Even without my head injury, it would likely take all day.

I considered my dilemma while I rummaged around the ruined camp. Clothing and bits of equipment lay strewn about everywhere. I had my canteen and found my cloak and shoes. My armor and weapons were gone, as was almost everyone else's. I did at least find Gilbert's seax and slid it into my belt. My own beloved spatha, handed down to me by my father, was also missing, of course.

In the course of looking for anything useful, I saw the tracks of our horses and wagon, so now at least I knew my companions had been taken northeast. I decided that the best plan I could come up with, under the circumstances, was to follow the trail. I would take a risk and stop at the first home I came to and ask the family there to come bury my dead cymbrogi. Many people in this area were Christians and should be favorably disposed to the Red Dragons for our victory against the Picti invasion. If I could make them believe I was a Red Dragon and not one of King Leudon's men, those two facts should buy me enough goodwill that whoever I ran into would be willing to assist me in the matter. Maybe, if God were particularly gracious, I might even gain some knowledge as to where my companions had been taken, and who took them.

The moment I saw that our attackers had taken the horses and wagons, and that their tracks led to a road, I decided that *cinbin* were not likely to blame, regardless of Digain's assertion. Cinbin were beasts, by all accounts. Had they attacked us, I couldn't imagine they would think to bother taking a wagon, and was certain they would not have left by road. They would return to the wilderness. For that matter, I wasn't sure I even believed that cinbin existed as anything more than ancient, Pagan superstition. Unless they were some sort of demon. Those exist, of course.

With a mix of heartache over the death of my companions and determination to find the remaining ones, I set off down the road. The pounding in my head made thinking, not to mention walking, hard, and I had to take frequent breaks. By that evening, I'd probably only traveled a few miles. Once, I saw a column of riders traveling northwest, at least a half mile ahead of me. From that distance, I couldn't identify whose men they were, so I peeled off the road and hid for a bit until they were out of sight. Memories of my flight from the Picti warband as they pursued Gemma and I from Guinnion's Fort to Din Eidyn two years ago sprang to mind, and I realized through my pain-induced brain fog that I was in the same area as I'd been back then. At least then Arthur and our numerus had been nearby, and I'd had my beloved horse, Carys to speed me along.

***

The sun was only beginning to touch the horizon when a cluster of round-houses and animal pens came into view from behind a wooded area as I rounded a bend in the road. A trio of dogs saw me and began barking as I approached, but they backed off when a man came out of the nearest hovel and threw a dirt clod at them.

We sized each other up. He was a lean man with short dark hair and a beard and looked to have just finished working in the fields for the day. I could only imagine how I must look to him. I winced. I was dirty and didn't have water to spare to clean the blood off my face. The man spoke first.

"Looks like you've had a rough day, stranger."

"I have. Raiders attacked my comrades and me last night. I'm Peredur, of Caer Gurcoc. I'm one of Tribune Arthur's riders. Please, good sir, I could use your aid."

The man stood where he was, at the entrance of his home. "I'm Ris. You're one of Arthur's men, you say? We know of him. Are the Red Dragons here again?"

I hesitated, unsure of what the safest answer would be. In the end, I defaulted to honesty and put my faith in the Lord that I would be rewarded for it.

"The Red Dragons as a numerus are still back at Caer Lleon. I came north with a bodyguard detachment for an envoy. We got attacked. Some of my men were killed. Their bodies are still back down the road a few miles," I gestured behind me. "They need to be buried. The people we were protecting were, I believe, taken hostage."

Ris frowned thoughtfully and folded his arms across his chest. He looked ready to turn me away when a freckled woman with reddish brown hair appeared from behind the house. Two slim young girls who looked like small versions of their mother trailed after, along with a blond-haired boy.

"Ris, I hope you're not planning on turning this young man away," The woman said sternly. "Look at him. He obviously needs help."

Ris winced and turned to what I presumed was his wife. "Luned, we shouldn't trust him. Who really knows who these 'raiders' were? This man could be one of Leudon's."

The freckled woman's large eyes narrowed, and she rested her hands on her hips. "It doesn't matter. He's barely more than a boy."

I cringed inwardly at that remark, but as she seemed to be in favor of helping me, I kept my mouth shut.

"He's injured," the woman, Luned, continued. "Whatever the situation now, Arthur's Red Dragons spared us in the past. You yourself fought beside them against the Picts, did you not?"

"I did, but it's different now," Ris protested. "Helping him under the current circumstances could draw... them to us."

I didn't know for sure who 'they' were, but I suspected that Ris was referring to the rebels. While they argued, the oldest girl, who looked about twelve, pointed up at me.

"What happened to you?" she asked.

"I think I got hit by a sling stone."

"You don't know?"

"I sure don't. I was in camp last night with my friends. I think I remember hearing a sling being spun around, and then I woke up this morning in a lot of pain."

"It looks like it hurts."

At that moment, Ris glanced over. "Eilidh, leave the man alone."

"She's no bother, and I'd never harm a child," I assured him.

Ris sighed. "Fine. I'll help you. I'll talk to our head man about getting some folks out to your campsite to bury your friends. You can stay with my family for a day or two until you're fit to travel. I'll ask that you hand over that blade though while you're with us."

I agreed to the man's condition, albeit reluctantly, and gave Ris the seax. "I'll expect that back when I leave," I said.

"Of course," he agreed. "I'll take good care of it. Now, why don't you let my wife take you out back? She has a bucket of fresh water handy and can tend to your head wound. Then, before you go to sleep, you can go down to the river and bathe."

"I appreciate your hospitality." I smiled wearily.

Luned smiled and gestured for me to follow her. I did so, and saw that she'd apparently been taking advantage of the pleasantly warm weather to wash some clothes, for a row of damp, clean clothing fluttering in the breeze from a line of rope. I squatted down by her bucket, and she took a cloth from the line, dunked it in the water, and gently got to work wiping the blood from my head while her children watched in rapt fascination. I bit my lip to keep from crying out in pain from her ministrations, gentle though she was being.

"So, you were part of an envoy?" She asked as she worked.

"I was," I said, trying to keep my voice steady.

"To King Leudon?"

"Yes."

"Regarding the Fisher King's rebellion, I assume?"

I hesitated. There was a fine line between casual conversation and inter-rogation. "Yes. Our envoy was led by a very wise man named Myrddin. He hoped he might find a way to end the rebellion peacefully. We need the men of Gododdin in the south," I finally answered.

"Oh? What's going on down there?" Luned asked, dunking the cloth in the bucket. The water turned pink with my blood.

"The Saxons are acting up. We think something big is coming. Having the men of Gododdin able to march south to help us, the way we came north to fight the Picts would be a great boon."

Now it was Luned's turn to be silent for a few moments. Finally, she asked, "These raiders who attacked you — did you see what they looked like?"

"I did not," I answered. "They ambushed us in our camp, took our horses, wagon, and presumably a half dozen of my companions as hostages, including Myrddin himself."

"Were there a couple of women in your group as well as the old man?" Ris's voice sounded from behind me.

I jumped, not realizing he'd been there, and whipped my head around to face him. That was a mistake. The sudden movement caused a massive spike of pain, and my vision dimmed and everything around me blurred momentarily when a wave of lightheadedness hit me.

"Easy there," Ris said in a calm tone.

"Are you alright?" The girl, Eilidh, asked, pausing in her playing to look at me.

"I will be," I told her with a grimace. I turned slowly toward Ris as my vision cleared. "You saw the raiders? The ones who attacked us?"

"Yes. It was some of the Fisher King's warband. They rode past here earlier today," the man replied. "Which is why I've been questioning my decision in offering you our roof for the night. If we're seen offering aid to enemies of his, it could go badly for my family."

"The women with them, did they look harmed?" I asked, trying to keep my fear in check and remain calm.

"I didn't see them up close. I was working in the field when they rode past," he answered.

"I don't know who this *Fisher King* is, but if he's terrorizing this area, I can leave now, if you're afraid my presence will incur his wrath. I'd not want to cause you or your family any harm. Anyway, I need to track him down," I said. My guts churned at the thought of what state Gemma and the rest of my friends could be in, right then, in the hands of those barbarians.

"The Fisher King himself probably wouldn't harm my family, or the women of your group he captured. He's made it known that he doesn't approve of harming women or children in particular. Many of his supporters, on the other hand, don't really care who they hurt, if they're Leudon's supporters or their kin."

I nodded, thinking through my options. "I'll stay for this one night and leave first thing in the morning. Would you mind at least telling me how I might contact this Fisher King? I need to discover what he's done with my companions. One of the women..." I cleared my throat, buying myself a moment to push down all the things I feared might be happening to Gemma, "One of them is my betrothed."

Luned put her hand to her mouth. "Oh, I'm so sorry," she said, then looked over to Ris questioningly.

Ris looked away, watching his children not far away, laughing and playing amongst themselves without a care in the world. He sighed heavily. "I won't betray Garwlwyd by sharing his location with you, but I'll have someone pass a message on to him. I should go talk to the neighbors anyway regarding the burial of your other companions."

"Garwlwyd?" I echoed in shock. "He's..." My mind flashed back to the lean, grizzled warrior I'd met two years ago at Guinnion's Fort. I recalled his love of fishing. "...the Fisher King." I finished, putting the pieces together. At Dun Ad, we'd heard that Garwlwyd had begun a rebellion against King Leudon. I hadn't heard the title of "Fisher King" until today, however. I stared at Ris, who stared back, giving me an odd look. "You're telling me that the raiding party who abducted my friends was led by Garwlwyd — your Fisher King?" I demanded.

"Not him directly. But they were his men, yes... this is important to you for some reason?" Ris asked cautiously.

"Yes! I know him. Well, I've talked with and fought beside him. God's blood, Gemma even stitched him up when he was wounded at Guinnion's Fort."

"You were there too?" Ris asked in surprise.

"Yes. I was in the column with Arthur when we broke up that first attack the Picts made on the fort. Then that night, I was stuck inside the fort. I fought on the north wall."

Ris shook his head in amazement, and a smile slowly spread across his face. "I'll be buggered. I was there too. Most of the men hereabouts were."

"Then you'll help me?" I implored Ris. "I bet if I could meet with Garwlwyd, I could get him to remember me. Surely, we could sort this out face to face."

"Calm down, Peredur. I already told you I would. This bit of information could certainly work in your favor. I'll be sure to pass your name along, if you'd like."

"Yes, please." My previous fears regarding Gemma's fate were at least dampened a bit, with the understanding that it had been Garwlwyd who'd taken her. Then I recalled that it had also therefore been his men who'd killed my six companions, and my moment of relief was snuffed out, replaced by my previous anxiety.

Luned finished cleaning the blood from my scalp and assured me that, although I had bled quite a bit, the cut itself wasn't bad. I walked over to the river, just outside the village, and bathed. I washed my clothes while I was at it. Thankfully, there was enough moon and starlight to make the trail visible in the dark. Ris was seated at a small table, illuminated by a small oil lamp, waiting for me. The three children were already tucked into bed together in a low loft. Luned was in her and Ris' bed underneath it.

"You can sleep on these furs here, for the night," he said, gesturing to a spot on the opposite side of the room from where he and his family slept. "I asked one of the men hereabouts who knows where the Fisher King can be found to relay our message. His men occupy a couple of fortified villages, but he moves around quite a bit. We should get a response sometime in the morning. You're welcome to stay with us until then."

"Thank you again for your hospitality and your aid," I said with a grateful nod.

Ris returned my nod and slid a small wooden platter with bread and cheese on it over to me. He gave me a cup of ale as well. Then he stood up, bid me good night, and slipped into bed beside his wife. I savored the fresh cheese, slightly older bread, and the ale. Memories of Garwlwyd flashed through my mind. I'd admired him back during the Picti invasion. He was a good leader and a powerful warrior. I recalled his preference for wearing a wolfskin cloak into battle, and pondered if that had been the source of him being rumored to be a dog-headed cinbin. It was hard to reconcile how I should feel towards him. I respected him as a warrior and former ally against the Picts on the one hand. On the other hand, his people had taken companions of mine as hostages, and killed others. The former could be rectified by an exchange of some sort, so long as they'd not been mistreated. As to the latter, well, that was a different story. I finished my ale, snuffed out the lamp, stripped down to my long under-tunic, then went to bed. As I lay in bed, staring up at the barely visible thatched ceiling, I regretfully determined that I likely needed to consider Garwlwyd an enemy now.

Chapter Eleven

DESPITE MY CONCERN FOR my friends' welfare, I slept soundly. I woke with only a mild headache with the rising sun, though the lump on my head was still extremely sensitive to the touch. The children still lay curled up in their blankets, though Luned was up and about.

"Ris already left with some other men to go recover your friends. They should be back in a few hours. We'll bury them here, in our own graveyard."

"Thank you," I said. "I should have gone with him. They're *my* cymbrogi."

Luned waved her hand dismissively. "You needed your rest, after the wound you got. And now you need to eat. I've some porridge on the table for you. And some ale."

I thanked her again and pulled on my clothes while she went outside. Once I ate, I decided I couldn't just sit around doing nothing, so to repay the family's charity and because I was restless, I chopped some wood for them as I waited for the men to return. The activity caused my headache to increase, however, so it was slow going.

A bit past noon, Ris and a half dozen other men returned, walking beside two wagons pulled by donkeys containing the bodies of my comrades. I followed them out to a clearing on the outskirts of the village where a number of modest headstones stood, and took turns helping to dig a large, deep hole where we buried my six companions together. There was no priest, for the village was too small for that. Many of them were pagans anyway. Instead, once the men were done, I stood over the burial mound and said a quiet prayer over the fallen.

When I turned away, I saw a man on horseback riding slowly towards us. The rider wore mail, a simple bronze helmet, and was armed with a sword. His face looked familiar, and I squinted up at him.

"I recognize you, friend, though I can't place your name."

The rider looked down at me with a wry smile. "I should say you do. I was your warband's guide when your chief took you up north to scout the Picti camp two years ago. I'm Brynn."

My eyebrows raised as a memory of the name came to me then. "Oh yes! I should have known. How are —" I paused as the significance of his appearance fell into place.

"You're Garwlwyd's messenger, I take it?"

"I am," Brynn nodded. "He'll be at Caer Amon tonight. I can take you there now, and you can wait for him."

"As your prisoner?" I asked warily.

A strained look passed over Brynn's face momentarily, then he replied. "No, as our guest. You have my word — you'll not be harmed."

"Before I go with you, may I know of the condition of my friends, whom you captured the other night?"

"They are being treated well," Brynn answered. "The Fisher King protects the women by keeping them in a house of their own. All of your comrades are allowed to walk about a bit during the day, and we feed them regularly. We wish them no harm, nor you, Peredur."

"The six men we just buried suggest otherwise," I pointed out, trying to suppress the flash of anger that had lit within me.

Brynn grimaced. "That had not been our intent. We sought to capture your group, bloodlessly. We'd hoped to capture and subdue you all as you slept, but of course, you had too many pickets posted, and so fighting broke out. Your six men were killed, fighting bravely."

Well, that wasn't quite true, I knew, given at least one had been killed while still lying in his blankets, but whether Brynn was mistaken or lying, I couldn't say.

"A couple of others were wounded," Brynn continued. "We took your people to Caer Amon, then allowed Gemma and the old man to take care of the men who were wounded." He looked around briefly, then asked, "Have you a horse?"

"I do not," I replied.

He nodded. "I'll speak to the head man here and borrow a horse or donkey that can be spared. You may as well come with me, unless you have anything to retrieve from your host's home?"

"I've a couple of things there. But not much. You and your friends saw to that," I responded, unable to keep the edge from my voice this time.

Brynn gave me a sheepish look, then gestured to the village elder's home. "I'll head over and talk to him about getting a horse for you. Meet me there when you're ready to leave."

I nodded and walked briskly away, back to Ris's home to retrieve Gilbert's seax and conceal it under my cloak. Brynn or one of the other rebels might end up searching me and take it from me eventually, but there was no reason to make it obvious that I was armed, I reasoned. Luned was there with her children, and she gave me a loaf of bread to take with me. I thanked her for her wonderful generosity, then left and walked through the village to rejoin Brynn at the village elder's home.

The weathered old man acted only too happy to loan Brynn and me one of his few horses, albeit an old mare whose best days were long behind her, once Brynn identified himself. With that issue taken care of, I followed the rebel warrior out of the village. From the river, I knew Din Eidyn was only about ten miles away, and I felt a swell of bitterness rise up. We'd been so close to reaching our goal, and then it had all gone so, so wrong. Now, instead of riding those last few miles east to Din Eidyn, we veered northeast, following the river, which Brynn called the Amon, and within two hours we reached a sprawling village, one that, like so many others, had clearly begun as a Roman fort. A few wattle and daub homes here and there were built atop the stone foundations of what had been barracks in a similar fashion to what had occurred at Caer Lleon and Ligion. A number of animal pens even made use of what had once clearly been either buildings or parts of outer walls.

The core of the fort remained intact and was clearly being used as the Fisher King's stronghold. I recalled that Arthur had briefly made his own headquarters here two years ago, when my turma, under Decurion Owain, had been deployed further west and built up our wooden fort along the Antonine Wall. Garwlwyd, Brynn, and so many other levied infantry had been there with us. And now Garwlwyd was being called the 'Fisher King', was in rebellion against King Leudon, and apparently set up his own headquarters here. How quickly things changed, I marveled grimly.

A wooden guard tower had been erected on the edge of the fortified village, and guards wearing mail and helmets manned it. We rode past, after Brynn checked in with the guards, and continued through the main street and up to the small fort on the edge of the village. Its western wall was up against the river, I noted, and although I couldn't see it from our position, I suspected that its northern wall was equally protected by the River Forth.

"You and your men are well-equipped," I commented as casually as I could.

Brynn nodded. "We are. Our rebellion goes much higher than the Fisher King."

"One of the noble families?"

"At least. Possibly the royal family," Brynn said. "At least, Garwlwyd thinks so. There are a lot of people in this kingdom who no longer have any faith in King Leudon."

"Who would you put in his place? Garwlwyd?"

Brynn chuckled. "No. He doesn't want the throne anyway. Don't read too heavily in his 'Fisher King' moniker. If we win this rebellion, our... benefactor will become king, and Garwlwyd will stay here and be the lord of Caer Amon with his family.

"Your benefactor?" I echoed. He'd paused in such a way when he said the word that I was struck with a realization. "You don't even know who you're fighting to put on the throne, do you?" I asked incredulously.

Brynn cleared his throat and adopted a neutral expression. "That's not for me to say, Peredur. If the Fisher King wants you to know that information, he can tell you."

"God's blood. You don't!" I exclaimed. The wheels in my head began churning. "That means your 'benefactor' is too afraid of revealing his identity publicly. If your rebellion fails, Garwlwyd will be seen as the leader, and the king's wrath will fall fully on him. But if it succeeds, he can simply reveal himself in the end, when there's no more risk."

"Like I said, all that's above my station," Brynn said with a grunt. "I keep my head down and do as Garwlwyd orders. He's done right by us so far."

We dismounted, secured our horses, and Brynn led me through the familiar front section of the great hall, the courtyard beyond it, and into the larger rear section. It almost felt like I was back in Caer Lleon. There was a small plaque carved into the stone above the entrance to the hall, but the lettering was too badly worn for me to read it.

As we entered, another thought hit me, and I mused aloud, "I wonder how your mysterious would-be-king will react if, assuming Garwlwyd does defeat King Leudon, the people assume he's the new king..."

A familiar, deep, gravelly voice spoke from inside the large chamber we were approaching, "I imagine our ally won't mind, as I've already given him my word that ownership of this village for me and my future kin is all I ask for. He will reveal himself soon enough anyway, I suspect."

"Or, he'll decide you're a dangerous rival who has a stronger claim to the peoples' loyalty than he, having done all the hard work to win this rebellion, and he'll dispose of you at his earliest convenience," I countered as I rounded the corner into the chamber, and stared up into the hard eyes of Garwlwyd himself.

It had only been two years since I'd seen him last, but he'd aged noticeably. I placed him in his mid-forties, but his coarse beard had become a lot grayer than when I'd last seen him. Creases on his face were more prominent, too. He still exuded a sense of strength and confidence, however, and I knew instantly that he was likely every bit as deadly of a warrior as I'd remembered him being. As he came toward me, however, I was startled to see that he walked with a pronounced limp. Then I recalled that he'd been wounded in the hip at Guinnion's Fort. He noticed my gaze and gave me a wry smile.

"If he decides to dispose of me, he may find that a harder task than he's prepared for, limp or no limp," Garwlwyd replied. "But I believe him to be an honorable man who will keep his word."

"So honorable that he orchestrated a rebellion while using you as its face, and betraying his king in the process," I prodded.

Garwlwyd scowled. "A king who cannot protect his kingdom and allows his lackeys to trample freely over his subjects is no legitimate king, but simply a tyrant."

"I cannot speak regarding your second charge, but as to the first, it's not uncommon for kings to need the help of allies against threats from time to time, especially in these dark days. The Red Dragons exist for that very purpose. Surely you hold no grudge against Tribune Arthur?"

"I do not," the Fisher King replied. "In fact, I regard him to be a more worthy man than our own king in every way. All the Gododdin sing praises of Arthur's heroics. It's not just the Picti invasion that I hold against Leudon. Not in itself. But he was completely unprepared for it. We've been dealing with Picti raids for generations, yet our 'king' has done nothing to seek a long-term solution to deal with them. And to add insult to injury, his tax collectors go to extreme lengths to take what precious little we have. One attempted to seize my own daughter, and threatened to sell her into slavery!" Garwlwyd snarled. His visage contorted into such a fearsome expression that it prompted me to recall the rumors that he and maybe some of his men were actually cinbin.

"Arthur's treaty was supposed to be that solution," I pointed out. "I am truly sorry to hear about your daughter, though. Is that why you rebelled?"

"Yes," the older warrior growled. "And it was our benefactor who returned her to me." Then his lip curled in disgust. "And how long did your Tribune's peace last?"

"It might have lasted longer if the Picts hadn't sensed King Leudon's weakness created by your rebellion." I countered heatedly.

"Grow up, boy. Drest was never going to keep the peace! Arthur fought bravely, and we of the Gododdin are in his debt for riding to our aid, but he was naive if he thought Drest was going to keep his word and stay north of the Forth. Our new king will ally with Dal Riata, and together we'll crush the Picts once and for all. What's more, he's offered to lend me a holy relic of the Christian God to aid my people in restoring the fish to the River Forth."

"I thought the Scoti are as fond of raiding cattle and slaves as the Picts?" I argued, ignoring his patronizing tone. "And what's this about a relic?"

"It's called the Grail. Leudon has it. It's a bowl that's supposed to have been used at supper by the Christ, or is connected with his death or something. Either way, it's said to have miraculous healing powers. Our benefactor has promised to lend it to me to at least attempt to bring the fish back to the Forth. There's been precious few fish for the past two years, ever since that late snow we had when the Picts invaded. The livelihood of many of the villages along the Forth, including my own former village, depended on those fish. It's why we fell behind in our taxes. And who knows. Maybe this Grail could even heal my hip."

The Fisher King sighed heavily. "As to the threat of the Scoti, yes. They have raided us in the past. And they probably will in the future. But our choice is to continue dealing with an ancient and assured enemy as well as a newer, more reasonable enemy, or just contend with the single, newer threat. Me and my kin prefer the second option."

I decided to change the subject then and address my more immediate concern. "The questions regarding this rebellion notwithstanding, I came here with Brynn because you captured some people who are important to me, including my betrothed. May I see them? Are they well?"

The Fisher King blinked at me, then nodded. "You may see them. I have treated my captives well. I have nothing against them. We hadn't wanted to kill any of your group, but your men fought back and died bravely." He paused and shrugged, then continued. "I only took them in order to obtain a ransom from Leudon. A messenger left for Din Pendyrlaw this morning with my demands. I've no reason to assume he won't pay for their release."

The big man ran a calloused hand through his long, dark hair. "I assume Gemma is your betrothed? Or is it that other woman?"

"It's Gemma. But I do care for the safety of all of them."

"Of course," Garwlwyd agreed. "Gemma and the other woman are in one house, the soldiers are in another. We treat them well." He paused, then gave me a warm look. "I'll give Gemma back to you. She stitched me up at Guinnion's Fort, along with many of my men."

An overwhelming sense of relief flooded through me, along with a bit of guilt that Gemma specifically was to be released, but I could do nothing for the others, yet. Something was better than nothing for the time being, at least, I decided. I thanked the Fisher King, and after a quick word, Brynn led me out of the great hall, and we walked over to a cluster of dwellings built up amongst the old ruins. Men weaved through them, all armed, making me feel even more like I was back in Caer Lleon, or at least a military compound. The men wore an odd mix of clothing and armor. Specifically, their stained, patched clothing was that of commoners, and yet many of them wore chainmail and had swords on their belts. All had at minimum the expected assortment of spears, axes, padded linen armor as well, of course. I'd noticed that at least some of the men's mail was second rate butted mail rather than riveted, and a few of them had tears in it, indicating that while someone had the resources to provide them with armor, they weren't necessarily able to repair it later on. Still, I could only assume that someone, likely their secret supporter, was providing them with the stuff, rather than it being obtained as battlefield loot, which must have cost a fortune. This, in turn, made me seriously wonder just how high up the social ladder their benefactor must be, to be capable of equipping so many men. Well, Brynn had mentioned the possibility of the man being a member of the royal family.

I was still pondering this when he led me to one house that had two guards idling nearby. A bar locked the door from the outside.

"The Fisher King gave me instructions to release the little red-headed one to this lad here," Brynn told one of the guards. "He's also being allowed to see the other prisoners."

The guard nodded and unbarred the door, then opened it. As light streamed in, I saw the figures of Morgana and Gemma sitting with their backs leaning against the wall, seated on the single mattress in the far back corner of the hovel. They turned toward the door, squinting.

"Meal time already?" Morgana asked.

"Per?" Gemma asked in surprise.

I didn't even have time to answer when Gemma sprang out of the building and threw herself at me, almost to the point of knocking me to the ground.

"I thought you were dead!" she sobbed, and her arms clutched tightly around my neck as she nestled her head against me.

I returned her embrace, reflecting that this might be the most intimate contact we'd ever had, and what a shame it was that it had to be under these circumstances.

I ran my fingers through her long, wavy hair and held her tightly.

"I'm alright. I got nicked by a sling stone and knocked out for a bit, but I'm fine now," I whispered to her.

"A sling stone?" Gemma asked in alarm, pulling away enough to look up at me. "Let me see." She put one hand on my chin as if to turn my head around and examine the injury, but I stopped her, clutching her hand.

"I'm fine," I insisted. "And you're free now. Garwlwyd's released you."

"Just me?" Gemma asked, confused.

"Just you, for now, as a courtesy," I emphasized. "He told me he's already sent a messenger demanding a ransom for the rest of you." I looked over at Morgana as I said that. I stopped when I got a good look at her face. She had bruising around her eye and a scab on her lip.

"What happened to you?" I gasped, releasing Gemma to come over to Morgana. "They hurt you?"

"I got knocked around a little the night we were captured," Morgana grumbled.

"After you nearly bit off Coel's finger!" the guard snapped from off to one side.

Morgana shrugged, and a sly smile spread across her face. "There is that," she smirked.

"But you haven't been mistreated since then?" I pressed.

"Beyond being fed stale bread every day and being cooped up in this hovel nearly all day with nothing to do? No. I'm fine," Morgana assured me. "Feel free to try and get this Fisher King of theirs to release me, too, though, hm?"

"I'll do what I can," I assured her. "If you'll excuse me, I'd like to check on the others?"

Morgana inclined her head. "Go ahead. I'll be here, slowly dying of boredom."

Brynn led Gemma and I over to another house, a short distance away, that was also under guard. He stepped up and spoke to the guard when we arrived at the next dwelling. The guard opened the door, and immediately a small rock flew out from inside, nearly hitting me in the head, as I'd been in the doorway at that moment.

I ducked to one side and swore from the fear, not to mention that the sudden movement had caused my head to throb with pain.

"Peredur!" a familiar voice called out in surprise.

"Yes, you idiot! And you nearly killed me," I snapped as I cautiously moved back to the doorway and looked in. Gilbert was there, having the decency to look embarrassed.

"How was I to know it was you? I thought it would be that *hōrbrēd* fool of a guard." Gilbert held up his hands defensively.

"You little turd!" the guard growled and reached for the axe in his belt, but Brynn stopped with a firm hand on his shoulder.

I, meanwhile, stared in shock at his face. There was a thick bandage wrapped around his head that covered most of the left side.

"Gib, what happened to your face?" I asked. "I mean, beyond your usual ugliness."

Gilbert grinned. "I took a sword cut the other night. The bastard who did it took off a bit of my ear, along with cutting my cheek open."

I gaped at him for a moment, then looked at the others as I asked, "How are the rest of you?"

Tor and Marcus were sitting against the wall. They looked fine and said as much. Myrddin sat on the mattress in the corner of the room by a small window. To my amusement, his raven was perched on the windowsill nearby. Then I realized there was one missing.

"Where's Elis?" I asked.

At first, only grim looks responded to my inquiry, then Tor responded. "He was wounded in the fight and died a few hours after we got here. Gemma and Myrddin were allowed to work on him, but they couldn't save him."

I gritted my teeth in anger. There were seven men now whose blood was on Garwlwyd's hands. Someday, he would answer for that, I swore to myself.

Brynn allowed us to visit for a bit. All were relieved and happy for us that Gemma at least had been freed by the Fisher King. A pair of guards came to relieve the ones who'd been on watch, and they brought bowls of barley porridge for my companions.

"You two aren't prisoners, so you can return with me to the great hall. There's more porridge available there. Rooms will be provided for you, or you can share a single one," Brynn informed us.

"We'll be grateful for separate rooms, thank you," Gemma replied for us. "Will I also be allowed to have my waist pouch returned, and Morgana's as well? There's medical supplies in them."

Brynn sighed. "I'll speak with Garwlwyd about it. In the meantime, if you please, come on and follow me back to the great hall."

I frowned as a sense of unease grew in the back of my mind. "Um, Brynn. Gemma and I are free, right?"

"Certainly," Brynn replied, looking back at me with a wolfish smile. "You're free to join the Fisher King at the great hall as his guests this evening."

So, that was how it was then. I shared a meaningful glance with Gemma and simply responded with "I see."

Brynn handed us off to an old man who took us to adjoining rooms in the front portion of the great hall. Mine had barrels of ale stacked up in one corner, Gemma's had a shelf of wood bowls and mugs in hers. But at least there were mattresses and some wool blankets in decent condition provided for us.

After being shown our quarters for the duration of our stay, however long that might be, the old man took us to the great hall and guided us to a small empty table. Another servant, a woman this time, served us with bowls of porridge a short time later. It was low-quality barley porridge, but as that was what they'd fed my companions, I was content with it. At least they gave us ale to drink. I couldn't help but notice that the dozen or so men who were also in the hall with us had porridge, but also had servings of cheese, dark bread, and hazelnuts. We were left alone to eat, though I noticed one or two men, armed with swords, were always in the area and generally keeping an eye on us.

"What should we do now?" Gemma murmured to me.

I glanced outside and saw that we had about a couple of hours of daylight left.

"Well," I said in between bites of my porridge, "It seems like, contrary to what we were told, we are in fact prisoners. That combined with the fact that they killed some of our people makes me feel like... leaving early would be a reasonable thing to do."

"Hasn't Garwlwyd already sent a messenger off to demand a ransom?" Gemma asked. "Morgana was sure he had. I suggested we might try and poison the guards to get away, but first she pointed out that most of the plants we would need are only just sprouting, this far north. She also said we'd be better off cooperating and not giving them any more reason to hurt us."

"Not an unreasonable plan, though it feels a bit... docile for Morgana," I mused.

"I thought so too," Gemma chuckled. "She's taken this whole thing far better than I'd have expected. Gilbert's the one who's been provoking the men at every opportunity."

"Why doesn't that surprise me," I smiled. "Yes, Garwlwyd has sent off his ransom demand already. I don't really care. He's a rebel now, Gemma. Whatever ransom he's given by the King will only strengthen him. Myrddin is a representative of Arthur and the southern kings, and you and Morgana are related to the king of Dal Riata. That will put a lot of pressure on King Leudon to either pay up quickly or mount a rescue. So yes, we probably could sit tight and let everyone be ransomed. If Arthur were in Leudon's position, I know without a doubt which option he'd take. But King Leudon probably won't go that route. So, it's up to us to leave and weaken the rebels' position a bit. Maybe we can even provide the king with information that will embolden him to rescue the others rather than pay for their release."

I was sure we were speaking low enough away not to be heard over the din of the other men's conversations, but I wanted to be cautious about precisely what I said. It was a pity that Gemma didn't speak enough Latin yet for us to converse that way.

"And leave our friends to their fate, here?" Gemma frowned.

"I suspect our own departure will be tricky enough. Getting to their separate dwellings, each with their own guards, and then leaving the fort with all of them undetected would be pushing our luck too far."

"That's what worries me," Gemma countered. "Myrddin and Morgana are valuable. They'd likely be safe enough. Gilbert, Tor, and Marcus would not only be even less valuable as hostages, but they could also be seen as a liability. Especially after we leave."

"Maybe normally," I agreed. "But we aren't just soldiers or simply members of some penteulu's household guard. We're equites in Arthur's numerus. Arthur is already practically a living legend, even up here in the north. The rebels have already killed five... six Red Dragons, not to mention Digain, but at least they died in battle. That will piss Arthur off, but that's forgivable to a degree. If Garwlwyd or his men kill even more after taking them prisoner?" I let out a long, low whistle. "That would set Arthur off. Even if he couldn't ride north in person, he would definitely send a turma or two up. Heads would roll for that! I'm fairly confident that Garwlwyd knows this, or honestly, I don't think he'd have taken anyone except you, Morgana, and Myrddin prisoner."

Gemma finished her own porridge in silence, then finally looked up at me.

"So what's the plan?" She asked.

I brought up a couple of ideas and backup plans in case things went wrong, as they tend to do. Finally, we hammered out what we figured were two solid plans that seemed the most likely to succeed.

"They could work," Gemma said with a slow nod. "What about our shadows?" She flicked a glance over to the men a few tables away who were clearly watching us.

I considered the problem. "I have Gib's seax. If we could lead them to the river once we're ready to leave, I should be able to kill them. Then we could hide their bodies along the shore." I paused, having a bad feeling about how Gemma would react to what I had to say next. "If you could distract them, I'd have an easier time ambushing them."

Gemma glared suspiciously at me. "What kind of 'distraction' do you have in mind?"

This conversation was becoming uncomfortably similar to an incident that had occurred two years ago, regarding some Picti sentries. Then, her 'distraction' had turned into her deciding to kill them herself with a sling.

"Chat with them?" I asked.

"Mm-hmm," Gemma murmured in her most skeptical tone. "We've only been prisoners for a couple of days, but we might be able to talk the guards into releasing Morgana so that she can accompany us to the river. Women need to bathe more often than men, especially when it's our time of the month. If we tell the guards that she's bleeding, they might let her come with us to the river. She could 'distract' the guards as you like to phrase it. I suspect she would even enjoy it. Assuming she'll help us, and not stick to the idea of behaving and waiting for the ransom to be paid. But if she is willing to help, then I could help you with the guards. You're good with a blade, Per. I'd never say otherwise. But could you really take out two men so quickly that they have no time to so much as cry out? We'll only have one chance at this."

I thought about it as I took another sip of my ale. "I've only the one dagger. While I'm taking out our first guard, how would you take out the second?"

"I've a dagger on me now," Gemma smirked.

"Wait, you have what? How? Where?" I asked, so startled I almost forgot to speak softly. We both glanced around the room, but none of the other occupants in the hall were paying us any attention, aside from the very guards we were discussing, of course. But they were sitting far enough away that they apparently hadn't heard me.

Gemma glared at me again before answering. "It's strapped to the inside of my thigh. I have a slit in my shift that allows me to reach it. I've gotten good at throwing it. I can do it... at close range. Thankfully, on the night we were taken, they only took my utility dagger I wore on my belt. They kept their hands off of me, more or less."

"Where did you get the idea to do that?" I asked incredulously.

"Morgana keeps a dagger on her thigh. So does Damon's mistress, Aurora. That old woman is far more than she or Damon ever lets on, you know. She's got as many tales as he does."

"Why do I feel like they've corrupted you?" I groaned.

Gemma smiled mischievously. "At least some of the tricks I've learned from them will probably get us out of here tonight. I learned a few other tricks from them that you'll have to wait until our wedding night to discover."

I gaped at her, completely at a loss for words.

Gemma gave me a quick wink, then stood up. "Come on. Let's go for that walk now."

I stood up and followed her out of the hall, and a servant or slave who'd been walking around filling cups for the men came by and scooped up our bowls. The two men who'd been casually keeping an eye on us also stood up and followed us out.

Chapter Twelve

We asked about regarding where we might find the Fisher King. After a few tries, one man acknowledged that he'd seen Garwlwyd go down to the river with his daughter with poles in their hands.

"He loves fishing with his family," the man chuckled. "That's how he came by his name, you know."

We thanked the man and went on our way.

It was a short walk from the great hall to the river and when we got there, we spotted the Fisher King easily. There was Garwlwyd, standing in the water up to his knees with a sapling in his hands. He wore only his under and outer tunics which hung down to just above the water level. Like laborers often do, he had stripped out of his trousers and shoes, which were on the river bank. A girl of about fourteen or fifteen sat there as well, on a blanket, and tearing bits from a loaf of bread in her hands. She noticed us first, and waved. We returned the gesture.

"Father, you have visitors," the girl called out the rebel leader.

Garwlwyd turned, saw us, and after pulling in his line, waded back to shore.

"You're interrupting my fishing. I hope it's for a good reason," he said sourly.

"If we're free, as you said earlier, I'd like our possessions back? Or at least Gemma's." I decided to be direct and see how 'free' we actually were. I pointedly ignored the armed men who'd trailed us there.

The Fisher King sighed, and took a slice of cheese his daughter offered him as he regarded me.

"As I see it, you're an enemy, or at least a potential enemy soldier in the middle of my fort. If I let you leave now, before we've heard Leudon's response to my ransom demand, you could go straight to him with whatever information you've gleaned since you've arrived. As for Gemma's things..." His brow furrowed thoughtfully as he bit into his cheese, then he resumed speaking. "Healers are knowledgeable of herbs. The same knowledge used to heal can also be used to poison, it seems to me."

He gave us a sharp look through narrow eyes at that, while I did my best to keep any emotion from my own face and meet his gaze. It was hard though. It almost felt like he could see right through us. That had, of course, been one of our plans.

"You have comfortable quarters, the freedom to move about the village, and eat in my hall like any of my men. But you may not leave, and you may not have your belongings until the matter of your friends' ransom has been concluded."

So there it was. We were prisoners. Well-treated prisoners, but still prisoners nonetheless.

"And what happens to us if Leudon refuses, or can't meet your demands?" I asked.

A flicker of something... uncertainty maybe, or discomfort, flashed across the Fisher King's face, but then it was gone just as quickly.

"He's a king, and Myrddin is famous for his value as an advisor and diplomat. Leudon has the means to pay, and he'd be a fool not to. I wouldn't worry about it. Enjoy the food my hall has to offer, relax here for awhile, and then you and your companions should be free to go."

"Even if everything you've said comes to pass, there's still the matter of your rebellion against King Leudon, and the very bad timing of it. What would it take for you to end this?" I asked, gesturing towards the fort.

The Fisher King smirked. "You trying to play the peacemaker in Myrddin's place?"

"I could never fill his shoes. But I would like to know how you think this is going to play out — or how you'd like it to."

"Simple," the man shrugged. "We continue to bleed Leudon's forces until his nobles remove him from power. My benefactor replaces him and restores justice. He lends the Grail to me and my kin to help restore the fish to the rivers, and crushes the Picts, with the Scoti's help. Which in turn puts the Gododdin in a better position to secure our southern border against the Angles — an enemy I assume you'll agree is worthy of our shared attention."

"They are," I agreed. "Though right now the Saxons are a more pressing concern. I doubt the Angles have recovered from the defeats they already suffered at Arthur's hands a few years ago."

"So maybe Arthur should ride up here and help us," the rebel leader said with a slight smile.

"Maybe you're not aware, but Queen Morgause is Arthur's sister. That makes the princes Gawain, Medraut, and Gareth his nephews. How do you suppose he'll respond if he decides they're all in danger?"

Garwlwyd frowned, but said nothing.

So, there was at least one thing about this situation that he hadn't appeared to be aware of, I thought with a bit of satisfaction.

Gemma spoke up then. "If we may, uh, Fisher King? I'd like to allow Morgana to accompany me so that we, or at least she, can bathe in the river tonight?"

"She and the others have only been in my custody for two days. She needs to bathe already?" Garwlwyd asked, raising one bushy eyebrow.

"We were on the road for several days before you took us hostage. On top of that..." Gemma's cheeks burned red and she cleared her throat. "She's ah... begun her monthly bleeding. So..." she trailed off, looking around sheepishly.

The Fisher King glanced at his daughter, then back to us, looking a bit flustered. "Ah. I understand. Between being married and having a daughter who's only... flowered recently herself, I do understand your request."

He glanced up at the sky. "It's getting late, and clouds are rolling in. We'll probably get a rain tonight. Typically, men of the village bathe in the river in the evenings after either training or working in their fields, and women bathe in the mornings. You can go then. My daughter can collect you at sunrise and take you both there."

My heart sank. That had been our primary plan. And now, for the time being at least, it had been ripped to shreds.

"Thank you," Gemma dipped her head courteously. "We'll leave you to your fishing now."

"Eh. We rarely catch anything these days anyway," Garwlwyd sighed. "Now I do it more out of habit, and I think more clearly here at the river."

"I'll see you in the morning I guess," the young girl said to Gemma with a wave. "My name is Rhian, by the way."

"Maithgemm, but you can call me Gemma."

We departed then, and went to the roundhouse where Morgana was kept. The guard didn't open the door this time but allowed us to talk through the small window. The women whispered together and Gemma explained what had been our plan.

"Well, at least I get to bathe tomorrow," Morgana mused. "Hopefully this Fisher King's daughter doesn't get suspicious if I don't look particularly messy. I told you we should have kept our heads down and waited for the ransom. I'm sure this whole thing will be over in a week or two."

I explained my reasoning for not wanting to wait until then.

"You make a good argument of course. And if your plan was able to include all of us, I might agree to it. But escaping with only a couple and leaving the rest behind seems too risky," Morgana argued.

I acknowledging her point. Inwardly though, I still felt my original choice was the correct one. We talked for a short while, then Gemma and I returned to the rooms we'd been given within the great hall and went to sleep.

Two weeks went by, and without Morgana to aid us in distracting the guards, we were unable to ambush them in order to affect our escape. Because of their tendency to hang back and not hover over us, we didn't have many opportunities to get very close to them. Even more frustrating was the fact that we didn't always have the same guards, so getting to know them and perhaps develop some sort of comradery with them that we could exploit proved exceedingly difficult. We did get the lay of the village pretty well though.

The great hall and the most important shops were all protected by a tall, stone wall roughly in the center of the fort. Surrounding it were all the homes and a number of small fields and animal pens that provided their food. These were mostly concentrated southwest of the great hall, as that had been built close to the river. The village itself was also built over and within what had clearly once been part of the original fort, but much of it had been dismantled, and the stones repurposed to strengthen the wall surrounding the great hall and the shops around it. It was still defended by earthworks though — specifically a berm with a wooden palisade built atop it. That provided a strong enough defense to thwart the few attempts King Leudon had made in retaking Caer Amon.

The one part of the village Gemma and I were allowed to go to that was outside the walls was to the river to fetch drinking water and to bathe in every week. We concluded that along the river would be the best place to ambush and kill our guards, if they ever gave us the chance. There were lots of trees and foliage in which we could hide their bodies and affect an escape, though only at night. During the day there were too many people using the river to try and catch fish or escorting livestock to it to drink.

One particular morning, Gemma and I arose early due to the great hall being a bit livelier than usual. We dressed and went outside. It was dawn, and Garwlwyd walked along in a procession led by an old man. With his off-white robe, long gray hair and beard, he had the look of a druid, or at least, as I imagined they would have looked. He carried an ornate spear with a white shaft, which had apparently been thrust into an animal recently, for the leaf-shaped spearhead glistened with blood, which trailed down the length of the shaft and onto the old man's hand. Other figures in undyed woolen robes trailed him, carrying simple, bronze candelabras, a round, silver platter with some twigs of mistletoe, and a small cauldron.

I'd seen this same procession once before, a week ago. Then as now, my hands fairly itched to get my hands on that cauldron! It wasn't a normal, bronze or iron thing for cooking, but an ornate pot that looked to have been made in gold, and on top of that it was decorated with amber, and other gems of blues and greens. I couldn't help but bite at my lower lip, imagining the fortune such a cauldron represented.

I was too cautious to ask anyone about the procession the first time I'd witnessed it the week prior. This time, glancing around, I noted Brynn and another man, Garwlwyd's son if I recalled correctly, standing not too far away, among a few other onlookers. I eased my way over to them, and after getting their attention, asked about it.

"It's a ritual, to attempt to entreat the gods into restoring fish to the river," the young man said.

I frowned. "The gods? You're performing a ritual to pagan gods? I thought Garwlwyd was Christian? He seeks the Holy Grail, after all."

Brynn smiled, and the younger man shrugged. "You Christians may be content with one god. We see things a bit differently. If praying to one god is good, more is better. We need the fish back, and don't especially care which god will answer our prayers, so long as one does. So today, we conduct a ritual to the old gods. Should we ever manage to get our hands on your cup of the Christ, we will pray to Him."

I wanted to shake my head and explain that it didn't work like that, but in the interest of not causing a scene, I pressed my lips together and stayed silent.

"I'm Dylan, by the way," the young man said, offering his hand. "Garwlwyd is my father."

I took his hand and shook it firmly. "I figured as much. You resemble him."

Dylan beamed, then grew serious. "You should know… it was me and my dogheads who attacked your men's camp, back on the trail."

My heart skipped a beat and anger filled me to my core. My hands clenched into fists, but I kept silent. Having Gemma gently put her hand on my shoulder helped. Dylan continued.

"I tell you this because I want you to understand — killing your men was not our intention. We meant to seize the lot of you, alive. That's why we attacked when and how we did. It was unfortunate that your sentries spotted us, and were able to put up a fight. Men died as a result. We had no anger towards the Red Dragons."

I still wanted to punch him, but instead, I let out a slow breath and put my hand over Gemma's to help calm myself down.

"Why do you call them 'dogheads'?" I decided to ask.

Dylan smiled. "Father's idea. After we decided to break away from Leudon's tyranny, we began putting on wolf or dog hide cloaks. He has us attack our enemies at dawn, or whenever it's particularly foggy. In bad light, it makes us look like cinbin. Scares the crap out of our enemies."

I nodded but said nothing. Dylan's smile slipped, and he sighed as we watched the procession round a bend and out of sight as they headed out towards the river. "We aren't the villains here, you know," he said.

I raised an eyebrow. "My dead comrades might disagree with you. The rest, including Gemma and I, living as *your hostages*, might as well."

"I told you, killing your men hadn't been our plan. Everyone respects Arthur and the Red Dragons, maybe as much as they do my father. They call him 'The Bear' in some stories, as a play on his name, Arth-ur. I've even heard some men boast about this or that warrior, only to have someone add 'but he's still no Arthur', as if Arthur is the truest measure of a war leader."

That made me smile, if a bit reluctantly. "As I understand it, he was named after a friend of his father's, whose name is Ector Artorius. So it's a variation of a Roman name. I've heard villagers even call him 'King Arthur', in a similar context to how your father is called the Fisher King."

"But he's not a king, right?" Dylan asked.

"No. He may as well be though, truth be told. He has a loyal army at his back, land, people to protect and who pay tribute. Arthur is a king in all but name, and there's more than one king in southwest Britain who doesn't particularly like Arthur but still walks very softly around him."

"And what would your commander do, if one day, your actual king came to Caer Lleon, demanded more taxes than Arthur could pay, and when we couldn't, the tax collector seized someone precious to him?"

I thought about Rhian, Garwlwyd's daughter, and figured I knew where Dylan was going with that question. "He'd likely do the same thing your father apparently did and fight back."

Dylan nodded. "Most men with the ability to do so would. And that's all my father did. Leudon, or maybe his lackeys, overreached and provoked a fight. You and your people, regrettably, got caught in the middle of it. That happens in war."

"Now let me ask you a question," I countered. "Suppose your father had sent out some of his valued friends to the south, say to investigate tensions between us and the Saxons. Then suppose that with no warnings or justification, Arthur seized them, slaughtered a few of them when they attempted to defend themselves, then held the rest as prisoners to be ransomed. How do you suppose Garwlwyd would respond, or at least want to respond?"

Dylan winced, and shot a glance over to Brynn, before turning back to me. "I suspect he'd not take it well."

I scoffed. "No, I wouldn't imagine so. And neither will Arthur. He regards each and every one of us as members of his own family. It's why the Red Dragons are so loyal to him. More than that, we regard our cymbrogi with the same loyalty that we share for Arthur," I stared hard at Dylan. "An attack against one of us, especially in the manner that you did, is an attack against all of us. If I were a gambling man, I would bet that pretty gold cauldron of yours that Arthur will rally the Dragons the moment he finds out what you and your father have done, and ride up here as fast as he can. And he won't have to ask for volunteers to come with him. He'll have to ask men to volunteer to stay back at the fort. Maybe King Leudon would pay your father's ransom. Arthur will surely not."

Dylan floundered for words, but I didn't stick around to hear whatever he might have said. I made my point. Instead, I took Gemma's hand, and together we walked away, back inside the great hall.

***

Three weeks later, our ransom was still unpaid, and we'd still found no opportunity to escape. We were taking a routine stroll around the village, in the first week of Maius, when Gemma deviated from the routine we'd developed. This particular day, she spent more time looking at the flowers coming into bloom. At one point, she paused to look towards the village, sighing heavily and stretching. I noticed that her gaze lingered on the guards, who as usual were a dozen paces behind us. They were talking and joking and paying us little attention however. For a moment I thought some cute animal or colorful bird had caught her eye or something. With a quick but casual motion, Gemma reached down and plucked a small plant from the ground, which then disappeared into the folds of her cloak, and she resumed walking. She didn't say a thing, but her posture was stiff and pensive, and I knew something was going on, though I'd no idea what.

"Care to share what that was all about?" I asked.

"Not here," Gemma replied with a whisper, looking straight ahead.

"Well, whatever you're up to, you might want to act less guilty," I whispered back. "You've picked up your pace and your posture is suspicious. Relax. Slow down. Want me to take... whatever that was you picked?"

"No!" She whispered tensely.

"All right," I said, raising my hands. "Like I said, relax."

"We need to get back to our rooms."

"So soon?" I asked. "We normally walk through the whole village."

"Yes. because I was looking for that plant."

Well now my curiosity was really piqued, but Gemma was clearly too stressed out over that twig she'd plucked for me to get anything more out of her. She didn't even seem to want to be next to me, which was definitely odd for her. So, I tried not to let her behavior get to me and I hooked my thumbs into my belt and chatted a bit as we walked back to our rooms.

From there, the guards typically hung out in the large dining area that connected to all of the various chambers, or in the central courtyard. It was still early evening, and servants were preparing food for Garwlwyd's retinue as usual. I followed Gemma into her room, and watched her produce the small plant from within her robe. She got to work plucking the leaves from it.

"What's that?" I asked.

"Foxglove," she replied without looking at me. "Make sure the guards don't come in, would you?"

I turned away and leaned against the door to her room, scanning the courtyard that all the rooms led into. As I'd expected, the two guards had taken seats on a broken, stone column and were only nominally paying attention to us.

It only took a few moments before Gemma rested her hand on my shoulder.

"I'm done. I've some leaves to put in their food tonight. It will make them sick for a while... or worse."

I sensed the hesitation in her tone, so I turned and took her hand in mine.

"Don't lose sleep over whatever happens to these men," I said softly. "Remember, they might very well have our comrades' blood on their hands. Do whatever you need to do to enable us to leave, and tell me what I can do to help."

"I need a distraction," Gemma said with a hint of a smile. "Just a few moments to drop in the leaves. They'll wilt in the stew and blend in with whatever other greens the cooks have added to it. As long as they aren't paying too much attention to the stew, they won't even notice a few bites that might taste funny."

"A distraction. Got it," I said.

"Once we feed them," Gemma continued, "the effects won't take long to set in, so we need to get them out to the river soon after."

"Otherwise, they'll get sick, or worse, and will simply get replaced by different guards," I realized.

"Exactly."

We stayed in her room planning our escape, and contingencies should those plans go wrong, and speculated a bit on precisely who could have large enough coffers to be funding Garwlwyd's rebellion.

"They don't trust their benefactor. Not fully," Gemma provided. "The other morning, when Morgana and I were bathing with the other women, Rhian was there of course. She gave us a few details that the Fisher King might have preferred we not know."

"Oh?" I asked, perking up.

Gemma nodded. "Apparently, this whole thing started a few months after the Pict invasion. The fish in the River Forth all but vanished over a season. That put the Fisher King's village in debt to King Leudon. His and nearly all the villagers sustain themselves through fishing. They pay their taxes with fish too. Debt grew, until finally, last summer, the king's tax collector decided to force the issue and attempted to seize Rhian as payment by deciding to sell her into slavery."

I felt my jaw go slack at the prospect. "That was about the stupidest thing a man can do to someone like Garwlwyd, attempting to take one of his children!"

Gemma nodded emphatically. "The Fisher King and some of the other villagers attacked the tax collector and his retinue and killed them. One soldier escaped though, with Rhian herself. She left out the specifics, but I think the guard uh, violated her," Gemma winced.

I whistled slowly, taking in the revelation. Dylan had hinted at something bad happening when we'd talked, two weeks ago, but I hadn't realized it was that bad. I said as much to Gemma.

"There's more," she added. "The Fisher King, Garwlwyd, mounted a rescue party, fully ready to burn Din Eidyn to the ground if it came to it, but before he could get to her, their benefactor saved her!"

"And then took advantage of Garwlwyd's gratitude and fury at the king's tax collector to get him to start a rebellion."

"Something like that," Gemma agreed. "There's still more to it though. This is the interesting part," she said leaning in and fixing me with an intense look. "Rhian told me while I was braiding her hair that the guard who abducted her acted as though he knew their rescuer! Like he tried to talk to the stranger just before the stranger killed him and took her back to her father."

"Any chance she gave you a description of him?" I asked.

Gemma grinned. "Yes. She says he's young, about our age. He has dark hair and blue eyes. He talks well and struck her as being very intelligent. Polite and gentle, too."

"Maybe he planned her abduction, and subsequent rescue," I mused.

"That's what her and her father suspect," Gemma nodded.

That got my attention. My eyebrows shot up and I sputtered, "They think that, and they're still risking everything to work with him? Why?"

Gemma shrugged again. "What else could he do? The Fisher King already became an outlaw by killing the tax collector and his bodyguards. If he breaks ties with the man then he has no support from anyone. As long as he works for this benefactor of his, there's at least a chance that everything will work out in the end. Morgana said as much, too."

I frowned. Gemma had learned a lot from Rhian, but it almost felt like something was off about Morgana as well. Was I being too suspicious? What was there to be suspicious of exactly? That she acted a little too cooperative and sympathetic with Garwlwyd? Maybe that just made her smarter than me, risking my life to escape when waiting a few more days might see me freed anyway. As for her sympathies, well God's blood, I was sympathetic to his situation now too. Especially after hearing more of what had led up to it.

By now the Fisher King's retinue and a few people who were likely family members had been walking through the courtyard and assembling in the feasting area of the great hall. We left her room and joined the trickle of bodies, and our two guards followed us in. There was no bard playing as there'd been at the feasts in Dun Ad, and the crowd here was smaller, but they made up for this by being noticeably more boisterous. I looked around, seeing the Fisher King seated at a small table on a raised platform at one end of the great hall with Rhian, Dylan, and a woman I assumed was his wife. Seated at the tables within the feasting area were about thirty men, plus some women. A few were probably the men's wives. Others, from their shockingly bold ways, were presumably there more for entertainment.

Gemma caught me staring at one woman, whose dress had slipped rather low over one of her shoulders and smacked me on the back of my head. I flinched and turned to look over at her. She glared at me.

"Keep your eyes in your head. Don't you dare be ogling the likes of them when I am right here."

"Yes, my lady," I muttered sheepishly.

She smiled at me. "Now, be a dear and get our guards to sit with us so I can do my thing."

I looked around and saw a serving woman carrying two large pitchers of ale. Thinking quickly, I stood up and intercepted her. "I'll take this off your hands for you," I smiled at her and smoothly relieved her of one of the pitchers, then walked over to our guards, who looked like they were about to go sit down with some of their friends where they could still keep an eye on us.

"You lads have to shadow Gemma and I constantly, and we've scarcely ever even spoken. Come, share some ale and eat with us. What are your names?" I asked, putting on my friendliest smile.

The two men paused and glanced at each other, then one of them shrugged and pulled out his drinking horn.

"I'm Etmic," said the taller and leaner of the two. "This toothless old man here is Tathal. We'll sit with you, for a bit."

"Splendid," I exclaimed with a grin.

I found us all a table as close to the exit as I could — even in Maius, most people tended to sit close to the hearth, where the servants were busy rotating a pair of chicken carcasses on a spit over the fire. Gemma sat down next to me, on my left. Tathal sat down in front of her, while Etmic sat across from me. I poured ale into their horns, then we began drinking and tearing into some bread that had been set on our table.

"So, were either of you men at Guinnion's Fort?" I asked after a bit of small talk.

"I was," Etmic acknowledged. "Old Tathal here had a broken leg that spring and had to stay back. He's still a useless gimp," Etmic smirked at his friend.

"Oh, sod off. We both know you barely did any fighting during all that, either."

Etmic shrugged. "The Red Dragons were better armed, armored, and mounted. So why not let them take the lead."

I smiled. "I fought dismounted once, during that night attack."

"Ah?" Etmic looked surprised.

"Yes. I got caught inside the gate when the attack started, so I ran up to the wall and fought with you ground-pounders," I nodded.

Etmic and I recounted some of what we'd seen — we were both there to witness Arthur fight King Drest in a one-on-one duel as it happened. Finally bowls of stew were distributed, and we began eating. Only a little while later, Gemma reached for her ale and accidentally knocked Tathal's stew bowl onto the floor. A pair of skinny hounds came scurrying over to lap up the mess.

"Oh, I'm so sorry!" Gemma exclaimed. "Here. You can have my bowl."

She slid her bowl of stew over to the guard, who begrudgingly nodded his thanks, and soon he was eating away, as though afraid that if he hesitated, the clumsy girl might knock that one over too.

It hit me suddenly that her switch had likely been very deliberate. What could be an easier way to poison someone than to poison your own food, then simply get someone to eat from it? The next thought that occurred to me was to wonder if she'd done the same to my own bowl! Was I supposed to switch my food with Etmic now?

Gemma must have read my mind because she patted me on the back and smiled. "Relax, Per, and eat up. I'll be more careful." She smiled and took a piece of bread, dunking it into my stew, since she'd sacrificed her own bowl.

I took her meaning and tucked into my stew. All the while I knew we needed to act fast. Presumably she'd just poisoned Tathal with that switch, but she still needed to get to Etmic.

"Hey Etmic, you have any dice?" I asked.

"I do, but you've nothing to gamble with, so what's the point?" He asked.

"I did have a pouch with some silver," I grumbled. "For all I know it was yourself and Tathal here who took it from me the night my companions were grabbed."

"Nah, I didn't get any silver." Tathal said. "Best I got was a new axe."

I glanced over at Gemma as I took another casual bite of stew. So at least one of them had been in on the attack that got several of our cymbrogi killed. Gemma met my gaze and I saw a subtle look in her eye. She was ready when I was, that look seemed to say.

"Fine, how about we arm wrestle? For bragging rights?" I grinned at Etmic.

Etmic scoffed. "You're barely more than a boy. What challenge would you be?"

"I'm stronger than you probably think. Come on. Surely, you're not scared of getting beat, are you? As you said, I'm barely a man." I propped my right arm up on the table, hand in the air. When he still hesitated, I couldn't help but add,

"Or do you only attack my people when they're asleep, and it's in the middle of the night?"

Etmic's eyes narrowed as he looked at me, and I thought I might have revealed something of my intentions, so I grinned and took a swig of ale. He followed suit, and after another moment he slowly planted his elbow next to mine and gripped my hand, then squeezed. From the look in his eye as he squared up to me, I anticipated this move and squeezed back. We stayed like that for a moment. His grip hurt, but I didn't show it. I know my own grip was hurting him too, and I saw his lips compress in response.

"Say when," I said in an even tone as I glanced at Tathal.

He started to reach his hand out, but Gemma beat him to it. She stood up and walked to the edge of the table, between the two of us and leaned over to put her hand over Etmic's and mine.

"Get ready... Begin!" She exclaimed and removed her hand.

Immediately Etmic's arm flexed and he began pushing my right arm down. I tensed, putting all of my strength into resisting him. My arm slowed, then stopped.

Etmic's eyebrow rose and he glanced over at me. "Heh. You are stronger than you look. I'll give you that." He flashed me a toothy grin then and pushed even harder. My arm began to move again.

"You're not strong enough though, boy." He laughed, and a moment later my knuckles hit the wood.

I glanced over at Gemma, who smiled sympathetically at me as she returned to her seat, rubbing her hands on the front of her dress. Looking back to the guard, I nodded to him. "Well done. I guess you're stronger than you look."

We both laughed, and got back to eating our stew for a bit. It was hard acting casual while also watching the two guards. I was sure Gemma had managed to poison them both, but I had no idea how long it took to affect them. For that matter, I knew nothing about what to even expect. I had to trust that Gemma knew what she was doing. Then, out of the corner of my eye I thought I noticed

Etmic's face scrunch up a bit as he took one particular bite. I casually looked over at Gemma as I took another drink of ale, and she took a bite of bread and nodded, as though appreciating the food.

The sun slowly sank over the horizon. Garwlwyd and his son remained at the table while his wife and daughter left. A few of the men who'd brought their wives also left. One man, seated against the wall, was already passed out, despite comrades around him laughing and poking at him. At another table, the woman whose dress revealed more of her shoulders and cleavage than was anything close to decent was sitting on a man's lap, laughing and drinking and kissing him. She wasn't the only woman acting that way either, now.

Men at another table laughed and broke out in drunken song. Our guards however, were careful to stay sober, to their credit, and my annoyance. I'd subtly encouraged them to drink, hoping to make our night go easier, but they were too disciplined to get drunk. The fact that the Fisher King was in the hall with us probably didn't help matters. Eventually though, something happened. Tathal began scowling and scratching a bit at his throat and stomach. Etmic began belching a bit more than I'd have expected, even under the present circumstances. He frowned and rubbed at his temples once, before also scratching lightly at his throat.

Gemma kicked me lightly. I ignored it at first, assuming it was an accident. She kicked me again a few moments later, harder this time. I glanced over at her and she flashed me a pensive look. I took her meaning and turned back to our guards with a smile.

"Well lads, I hope you weren't planning on drinking yourselves senseless tonight. I'm about full and ready to take a short walk for the evening," I said and stood up. Gemma followed my move.

"Oh come on, stay here and enjoy the food and the ale," Tathal protested, scratching again.

"That's just it," I said sheepishly. "I think I've already had too much ale. It's going through me quick. Let's go down to the river for a short walk, then we can return here, eh?"

Etmic sighed and Tathal rolled his eyes, but the pair stood up and followed us out as we strode out of the great hall and out towards the river.

It had begun raining while we were feasting — not quite a downpour, but definitely more than a drizzle, and we all pulled our cloaks up over our heads.

"Let's not be too long, alright?" Etmic grumbled. "My head is beginning to hurt."

"Maybe Peredur here isn't the only one who couldn't handle his ale," Tathal snickered, then he winced as he clutched at his stomach. "Uuugh. I think I ate too much."

We continued on in silence, walking through the streets that were rapidly emptying out and down the hill to the river. Lightning flashed, followed shortly by a peal of thunder. Almost immediately upon reaching the bank, Tathal scurried off to a tall thicket of brush.

"I need to empty my stomach. Watch them for me!" He hissed to Etmic as he went, removing his belt along the way.

Etmic didn't look so good either. He sat down nearby, scratching here and there, and wincing as though in pain.

"Is it just me? I'm starting to think there was something wrong with that stew," he groaned after a bit.

Gemma's demeanor changed then, in a way that I've rarely seen in all the years since. She calmly walked over to the man and crouched down on one knee so that she was looking straight into his eyes.

"There was," she replied in a flat tone that chilled me to my core. "I, Maithgemm, daughter of Hamish and granddaughter of Fergus Mor, the first King of Dal Riata, have slain you. Tell Digain that on your way to Hell, so that he may rest easy, knowing his murder has been avenged."

Etmic's eyes went wide, and he reached out to her, but she easily stood up and moved out of his reach. He doubled over and vomited. A short distance away, I heard Tathal doing the same. From the stench that filled the air, at least one of the two had apparently soiled themselves as well.

"We can go now" she said, her voice cracking a bit.

"We can just... leave them?" I asked.

"They're as good as dead," Gemma said, wiping quickly at her eyes. "I'm sure I put enough leaves in their stew to kill them quickly. Let's go."

I followed her south along the bank, sparing a single backwards glance at the guards. Tathal hadn't come out of the brush, which was now still, and Etmic lay on the ground, curled up and clutching his stomach. His breathing was already slowing down and sounded erratic. Even with her back turned, I knew from her posture that this had been hard on Gemma.

We headed south, following the river bank, but we didn't get very far before there was another flash of lightning. My heart lurched when I saw a trio of figures off to our left, barely ten paces from us!

Chapter Thirteen

I GRABBED GEMMA AND pulled her down, reflexively drawing the seax from my belt. There were no shouts of alarm and no thudding of feet rushing our way, so after a few moments, I let out a quiet sigh, determining that whoever the people were, they hadn't seen us. As the thunder died down, I heard voices.

"...hard to slip away. Gawain and his men are camped a bit south of here," a man's voice finished saying.

"Well, it's good to see you again, as always, my friend," a second voice said.

I recognized that rough voice, I realized with a start. It was Garwlwyd's.

"You're only saying that because whenever I come, it's to bring you iron or gold," the other voice said with a snort.

"You're not totally wrong," Garwlwyd said, sounding amused. "I do keep hoping that one of these days you'll come bearing the news that you've finally overthrown Leudon and are now king, though!"

The other man laughed as well. "That day may come sooner rather than later. My... king received your ransom demand. He is not keen to pay it, as I expected."

"He's in a bind no matter what though, of course," a woman mused. "Pay, and suffer the humiliation of the lost treasure, or let his invited guests be killed."

Gemma and I turned to each other. Her astonished, confused look must have mirrored my own.

"Morgana?" Gemma mouthed.

My brows furrowed. It certainly sounded like her, but with the rain, it was hard to be certain. Her voice didn't carry as loudly as the Fisher King's did.

"He may yet seek a third option," the man said. "He's sent Gawain and I out with a clutch of men to try and find out where you're keeping Myrddin and the others. Naturally I've done what I can to nudge him in the wrong way to the extent possible to stall. It's no secret though that your primary base is here."

"Must bother Leudon, knowing where my stronghold is, but not having enough men attack me directly," Garwlwyd chuckled. The other man and the woman joined in.

"I'm almost insulted that Leudon is so tight-fisted that he wasn't ready to cough up our ransom immediately," the woman said.

I stifled a gasp. She'd said 'our ransom'. Surely that had to be Morgana after all!

"We did make the price rather high," the unknown man snickered. "I suspect that no matter how he responds, this should prove to be the tipping point that will motivate the nobles to overthrow Leudon."

"And then you'll be king," the woman's voice said.

"Whoever you are," Garwlwyd growled.

"Patience," the other man soothed. "Let's talk some more in your hall. We can't stay overly long before we'll be missed, but I've enough time for some mulled wine and to give you a few more updates, along with this pouch of gold I brought for you."

Lightning flashed again, and this time I noticed more figures, further back. They were mounted, and the light reflected off helms. Horses snorted nervously in the storm.

"By the way," the woman said, putting a hand to the hooded figure's chest. "You owe me an explanation. It seems far too convenient that Domangart died as he did. He had no plans to ally with you. His son, Comgall, likely will. Was your pet bard there just to pass on information? Or did you task him with killing Domangart as well?"

Beside me, Gemma's breath caught, and she put her hand to her mouth. We both leaned forward from our hiding spot, desperately wanting to as much as we could, and to positively identify the two figures.

"My dear, I assure you, my reach is long, as you well know, but do you really think I'm powerful enough to have a king assassinated?" the man asked. "I actually find that a bit flattering…"

Thunder rolled again, maddeningly, so whatever answer she gave went unheard by Gemma or I. We heard the trampling hooves of the riders, and faintly saw the mysterious man mount up on his horse, then he and his men rode alongside the Fisher King and the woman as they headed off back toward the great hall of Caer Amon.

Once the trio were out of sight, Gemma and I continued our planned escape route.

"That man mentioned someone's camp south of here," Gemma said as she pushed a wet lock of hair away from her face. "Gawain I believe? Do you know the name?"

"I do," I nodded. "He's one of King Leudon's sons. So, if he's camped out somewhere around here, we need to link up with him."

We walked in silence for a time, both of us being too troubled by what we heard to want to talk. Eventually, Gemma spoke up.

"The Fisher King could have other hostages beyond just our group. He's been raiding all over Gododdin."

"It's possible," I admitted. It did make some sense. Seizing noble hostages for ransom back to their families was a profitable business as old as time, I suspected. Why wouldn't Garwlwyd do it as often as he could, in order to fund his rebellion? But the woman's voice had sounded too familiar, even muffled as it was through the rain. From the troubled look on Gemma's face, I was sure she felt the same, and my heart ached for her. I had come to regard Morgana as a friend. To Gemma she was *family*. I considered my tribune, too. I didn't know for sure, but I believed that Arthur had some sort of romantic relationship with

Morgana. And now it looked like she was colluding with Garwlwyd to remove Leudon as king.

"You think it was her though, don't you?" Gemma asked somberly.

I sighed and looked out across the river as we walked. "I'm sorry but yes, I think it was her."

Gemma slipped her hand in mind, and we kept walking.

***

We walked for probably three or four hours before I saw the soft glow of an oil lamp from within the inside of an open tent flap. Looking closer at the area, I noticed the outline of several other tents in the area, nestled up near a grove of trees. I gestured to them, and Gemma and I altered course, heading for them. It was still in the dead of night and although we were shivering from the cold by this point, I was still cautious. This camp could be Prince Gawain's, but it could just as easily be some cattle thieves, or a small group of Picti raiders. Of course, it could also simply be some goat herder any number of other possibilities. Even if it was Gawain's camp, approaching an armed camp at night unexpectedly was a good way to get killed by any sentries who happened to be on duty.

We got to within a hundred feet of the camp, and I did see an armed sentry then, sitting with his back to the fire. He looked too well armed to be an outlaw, but there was no way for sure to identify him, or the camp. I fretted over the problem, and we kept watch over the camp, suffering in silence. Better to be hungry, cold and wet than dead, after all.

We were still observing the camp as I tried to work out who the group was when we heard the sound of hooves approaching from behind us. I spun around and saw four shadowy figures riding along the same path we'd taken to get to the camp. I grabbed Gemma's hand and attempted to move into deeper cover, but someone shouted. They spotted us! I swore, and froze in place. To make further attempts at evasion now would almost certainly mean our death. So I stepped in front of Gemma and raised my hands.

"Don't hurt us! We're unarmed."

Well, that was sort of true. Daggers generally aren't considered weapons, after all.

"Who are you then? What's your business, lurking about out here in the dark?" A rough voice demanded.

"My name is Peredur. My betrothed here is Gemma." I hesitated, loath to say anything more, but my hand had been forced. What happened next was squarely in God's hands now. "I'm one of Tribune Arthur's cavalry and I'm seeking Prince Gawain."

One of the riders snorted and he urged his mount forward a couple steps until he was barely a foot in front of me. His hand rested on the pommel of a sword belted at his waist. "And what do you seek my brother for?"

"Your brother?" I asked, looking past the horse's head looming before me and up at the man riding it. His voice was frighteningly familiar. A hood shadowed much of his face but as close as I was to him, I could see that the man was about my own age, clean shaven, and had dark hair.

"This is Prince Medraut," one of the men spoke up. From his gruff voice, this was the man who'd spotted us a moment earlier. "Now answer the bloody question."

I realized, with dreadful clarity, Garwlwyd's benefactor must be none other than Leudon's own son, Medraut. My mouth went dry as I thought very carefully on how best to respond.

I decided to play dumb. I flashed the prince and his attack dog of a subordinate my most sheepish grin.

"Well, you see, I was part of a security detachment for the envoy of Myrddin, of Caer Fyrddin. Maithgemm here was also a part of that envoy, being a relative to the King of Dal Riata. We were attacked some time ago, and most of my group disappeared — either killed or captured or scattered while trying to escape.

That's what happened with Maithgemm and I. We've been lost as can be ever since. I was hoping to determine where my comrades were taken."

A look of doubt, or maybe suspicion, flashed across Medraut's visage, but he said nothing and allowed me to continue.

"A shepherd we ran into yesterday told us that Prince Gawain might be around here somewhere."

"Well, you managed to find his camp," Medraut replied, raising an eyebrow. "Come on, I'll take you to him. Wouldn't want you getting lost trying to find his tent."

Medraut's men chuckled, as did I, though mine was more from nervous relief. As he walked his mount alongside us, he looked down at Gemma with interest.

"So, you're related to King Domangart Reti... do you also happen to know Morgana?"

Gemma looked up at the prince. "Domangart was my uncle. He died recently though and his son, Comgall is now king. And yes, I know Morgana. She is my aunt. I'm a bit surprised that you know her."

Medraut nodded, and a slight smile tugged at his lips. That had to have been a test, I figured, considering that based on the conversation Gemma and I had overheard, he knew perfectly well that Domangart was dead. "She's a mutual friend of mine, through her close association with your commander and my uncle, Arthur.

The group casually surrounded us as they herded us toward the camp, and I tried not to show how incredibly uncomfortable that made me. As we walked, I noted that one of the men had a red deer stag draped over his saddle, with an arrow jutting out from behind its front foreleg.

"Nice, clean kill there," I commented to distract from my nerves.

"Thank you," Medraut smiled. "I brought him down a bit ago, just as he saw me and was about to flee."

"Well done," I said, genuinely impressed, though the sight of that stag troubled me a bit. Was the man I'd seen a bit ago Medraut? He'd certainly sounded like Medraut, and both the man I'd seen with the Fisher King and Medraut were wearing a dark-colored cloak, but at night, in the rain, I'd be lying to myself if I could confidently say I knew for fact that the two were wearing the same cloak. And just like that, I was no longer so confident that Medraut was in fact the man I'd seen. After all, what were the odds that he'd bagged a deer traveling to and from Caer Amon?

We reached the camp a little while later and Medraut announced himself to a pair of men on sentry duty, who were watching over the camp from the shelter of the large tent I'd spotted. The sides were rolled up, allowing the men to see in every direction.

"You two can sleep here for the rest of the night," Medraut informed Gemma and I. "It's not much, but it's dry. I'll have one of my men scrounge up a couple furs for you. We'll speak more in the morning."

"Thank you," I said with a short bow.

Medraut nodded to us, then strode away towards a large tent and ducked inside. Around us, his men took care of their horses before disappearing into other, smaller tents until Gemma and I were alone with the two guards. The gruff, bearded man who'd spoken to me earlier came back, carrying some large sheepskins.

"Here. You can have these for the night," he said, holding out his arm.

To my surprise, in his other hand, he produced a small round loaf of bread. "I thought you might be hungry as well."

We thanked him, and Gemma quickly tore off a piece of bread while I took the sheepskins from the soldier. Once he left, and Gemma and I wrapped ourselves up in the skins, I turned to one of the guards.

"So have you lot been on the road long?"

"A fair bit. We left Din Eidyn two weeks ago. Gawain and Medraut have had us riding up and down the countryside looking for you and your people, with no luck. It's like your group just disappeared."

"We didn't. Garwlwyd took us to Caer Amon."

"The cinbin? It's a wonder he didn't kill you all for sport," the second sentry remarked. "The stories people are saying about him is that he makes a point of killing a Briton every day of the week, and two on Saturn's Day, so he can rest on Sun's Day.

"He's no cinbin," I said, rolling my eyes. "He's just a man who wears a wolfskin cloak."

The guard shrugged, and I settled down near Gemma. We finished eating the bread, drank a bit of water offered by one of the men, then laid down and tried to sleep. Gemma fell asleep quickly, but it wasn't so easy for me. The sporadic crashing of thunder and flashes of lightning played a part, but I also worried that Medraut would come back and decide to take Gemma and I off to the woods and kill us as a precaution.

Eventually, I must have finally fallen asleep, despite my fears, because it seemed like in one moment, I was laying there wrapped up in the sheepskin listening to the rain pattering off the roof of our tent. In the next moment, someone was standing over me, lightly kicking my feet.

"Time to wake up, lad," a man's voice said. "Gawain and Medraut are ready to see you."

I blinked and rubbed at my eyes as I looked around. The sun was already visible against the eastern sky, and the rain had stopped, though the sky was still heavy with dark gray clouds. Beside me, Gemma yawned loudly. We each went off to the woodline, then returned to the guards' tent and allowed one of the men to take us to the largest tent in the camp. A purple banner depicting a stylized bird, in yellow and black, stood at the entrance. The tent's flaps were tied back and two men were seated at a small table inside. One I recognized immediately as Medraut. The other, I assumed, was Gawain.

Both wore fine daggers and swords at their belts and checkered cloaks of black and blue, fastened with gold and silver brooches. Medraut wore additional rings and other jewelry as well as an embroidered red tunic to go with his dark gray woolen trousers and leather shoes. Gawain on the other hand, dressed more simply in an off-white tunic, light brown trousers, and wore legwraps around his calves. He looked to be a bit older than Medraut and I, and had the same blue eyes his brother had, but whereas Medraut was clean shaven and had short black hair, this man had shoulder-length brown hair and a stubble. Where Medraut was reserved and gave Gemma and I an analytical gaze as he leaned back in his chair, the man across from him smiled warmly at me, prompting an instinctive smile from me.

"Welcome," the man said. "I'm Gawain, this is my brother, Medraut. I'm told you're Peredur, one of Tribune Arthur's men?"

"I am, sir. And this is my betrothed, Maithgemm of Dal Riata."

Gawain nodded to her. "Pleasure to meet you, lady."

We exchanged a few pleasantries and answered a few preliminary questions. Yes, a bit of food and wine would be wonderful. No, we did not require medical care. Then I quickly told of what my party and I had witnessed throughout our journey, specifically regarding the burned fort along the Antonine Wall, the desecration of our dead, the Picti scouts, and finally, I revealed how Gemma had been taken prisoner by Garwlwyd and I'd been allowed to see him at his fortress at Caer Amon. At that, Medraut's eyes narrowed, and his lips pursed tightly.

"You told me last night that the two of you had been wandering the countryside lost since your party had been attacked. You said nothing about Caer Amon."

"Didn't I?" I asked, acting as innocent as I could. "I must have been too tired to provide a clear report. My apologies."

Gawain waved a hand dismissively. "No matter. The important thing is that we know your friends are there." He turned to cast a frustrated look at Medraut.

"You see? I knew that's where the Fisher King would take them! But no, you were so sure they'd been taken to one of the other villages further south."

Medraut shrugged. "My men and I had heard reports from locals that they saw the rebels taking hostages south. I heard nothing to contradict that. My network is good, brother, but not infallible."

"Bah," Gawain huffed. "Well, the important thing is, we know where they are now. We should attempt to rescue them now so we don't have to empty the treasury paying that cinbin bastard's ransom."

"I hope you have more men than this," I interjected. By the size of the camp, I estimated that Gawain had no more than about twenty riders. "Garwlwyd's personal guard alone outnumbers this lot."

Gawain grinned wolfishly. "And how many men are awake and guarding the prisoners at any given time?"

I started to speak, then caught myself, considering the implication of his question. "Are you thinking of a nighttime rescue?" I asked, intrigued.

"I am, and you're right, we don't have enough men to attack Caer Amon directly. King Leudon has already sent riders with spare horses to Caer Lleon to request Arthur's aid for that. But, maybe we have enough men to infiltrate the fort, rescue Myrddin and your group, and get out."

Medraut growled at that. "He would grovel to Arthur to come save us, again? How does he think the nobles will react to that?"

"Better than if they were told Father handed over three hundred pounds of silver to ransom a handful of people who aren't even of our own noble families. And better than allowing the Fisher King to kill them and put their bodies on display."

"What?" Gemma and I asked together in shock.

Gawain winced. "I'm sorry if that comes as news to you, but that was the Fisher King's threat."

"Did he give a deadline?" I asked.

"Summer solstice. The message was very brief, and the messenger gave us a signet ring of Myrddin's as proof that they had him. Before the day was out, King Leudon sent riders to Arthur, and others to Dal Riata. We need help dealing with the Fisher King's rebellion, but maybe we can at least rescue his hostages on our own," the prince said.

"Imagine everyone's response if you try to mount a rescue effort and we fail," Medraut protested. "The hostages would die, *we* may die, or worse, get captured ourselves. Then Father loses a son or two, gets humiliated among the nobles, and Dal Riata will be outraged for getting a member of their royal family killed."

"Which is why we can't fail," Gawain said. "And anyway, I didn't think you would come with me on such a 'foolhardy mission'."

Medraut rolled his eyes. "Of course I'll still come. Yes, I believe the odds are against us, but what kind of brother would I be if I hung back and let you go and do something stupid without me watching your back? You'd fail for certain. And while I may be Mother's favorite, she would be furious with me if I let you go and get yourself killed."

Gawain chuckled, and even Medraut cracked a smile in response. "Sometimes I forget which of us is supposed to be the protective older brother here."

"Oh you are, no doubt," Medraut's smile widened and his eyes twinkled. "But I'm the smarter of the two of us."

"You might not be as smart as you think you are," Gawain grunted. Then he turned back to me. "Our messengers should have reached High King Conanus and Arthur about two weeks ago. Same with King Comgall."

"Our tribune would need a week or so to muster men and gather provisions, then another three to four weeks to arrive. That means the Red Dragons could be here in another... two or three weeks," I calculated.

Gawain nodded in agreement. "So, what can you tell me about Garwlwyd's forces at Caer Amon?

We talked for a bit, with Gemma adding in observations of her own from time to time. A servant came into the tent and set a platter of bread, cheese, and some dried pork on the table for us, and gave us more wine. Eventually, we hammered out a plan that even Medraut found no flaws in. Of course, for every part of the plan that we worked out, I had to secretly consider how Medraut could deliberately sabotage it. Neither Gemma nor I had enough evidence against him to accuse him to Gawain, his own brother.

"I'd like Gemma to come along with us," I said at one point.

Both men looked at me as though I were insane.

"Of course not," Gawain said, flatly. "Why on earth would you want to bring a woman, your own betrothed no less?"

Well, I wanted her along because she was the one person in this camp I knew I could trust to watch my back. Naturally, I couldn't say that. Instead, I held up my hand and began counting off reasons with my fingers.

"One, she's another pair of eyes. And she's been on scouting missions with me before. Two, she has medical training, probably more than any man who will be with us. Something I've learned during my time in the Red Dragons is that quick medical treatment in response to a serious injury can make all the difference between life and death. And three, she gives us more options. If we get spotted by a guard on the way in or out, she could simply pass as a villager and calm the guard down."

"This is unheard of," Gawain protested, shaking his head.

"Is it though?" I argued. "Women have helped serve as scouts, spies, and couriers for ages. Even the Holy scriptures describe times when the Israelites used women to pass messages and help spies infiltrate cities."

"We don't pay much attention to the Christian God up here in the north," Medraut frowned.

I rolled my eyes. "My argument is still valid. She's useful. I want her with me."

Gawain and Medraut exchanged looks. Clearly, they were unimpressed.

"Maybe Arthur is... odd enough to allow women on such missions," Gawain said with a scowl, "But I am not. She stays in the camp. We won't take long — If we leave this evening, we can be hidden outside of the fort by dusk. Once everyone goes to sleep, we'll go in. With any luck, we'll only need to kill a couple guards. Medraut is very good with a bow. We can kill them without them ever knowing we're there. So we'll slip in, rescue your group, and slip out. We'll be back by dawn," Gawain assured me.

"Fine," Gemma deadpanned. "I'll just wait here then. "Do any of you men have any needlework you'd like me to do while I wait?"

Now I recognized that tone of hers, and the frosty look she was giving Gawain, instantly. She'd given both to me on more than one occasion, usually when I'd made a plan that she didn't approve of, and thought of a better way to achieve the desired outcome. I tried to hide my smile when Gawain, not knowing Gemma as I did, took her at face value and simply replied with, "No. Not here. But you can aid the men staying back with cleaning and cooking up some of this stag my brother was good enough to hunt down."

"Certainly," Gemma smiled.

Oooh boy, I thought as I nearly burst out laughing. Poor Gawain had no idea what hole he was digging for himself. I was sure looking forward to seeing him find out though. I only prayed, for his sake, that he didn't get himself wounded that night.

To her credit, she did help skin and butcher the stag. Someone had already gutted it earlier that morning. In fact, to the amusement of everyone in the camp, Gemma became mildly annoyed with the man helping her and suggested she should do the job herself. The man handed over his cleaving knife and grumbled as he stomped away. Gemma paid him no heed and quickly went back to work on the deer. In a bit over two hours, she'd carved the carcass up, with minimal help from me, mostly to hold the legs or remove sections of meat once she'd carved it up.

"Impressive!" Gawain admitted, watching her work. "You didn't need to butcher the stag though. That kind of work is beneath your station —"

"I've spent the past two years learning medicine from Myrddin and Tewdrig, the numerus' medicus, and applying those lessons on the battlefield," she informed him cooly. "Before that, I was a slave for five years in a Picti village, and had to slaughter, dress, butcher, cook and serve livestock, among other things. This," she gestured to the stag as she wiped her bloody hands on some grass, "was easy."

Apparently, she'd also been learning God only knew what from that old spymaster and his mistress, I thought to myself.

"That is quite the unusual education," Medraut mused.

Gemma and I shared knowing smiles, but said nothing as she strode off to the river to wash the blood from her hands and forearms.

We spent the rest of the day preparing for our incursion into Caer Amon. They lent me a spare gelding, and found some weapons and armor for me to use. Nothing as good as what I was accustomed to of course, but anything was better than nothing. Medraut found a padded tunic for me to wear, and one of the men who was to remain behind lent me a small shield. Another gave me a spare axe, which I thrust into my belt.

The princes, of course, not only wore finely crafted, thick leather padded tunics, but very well-crafted armor as well. Gawain wore a long coat of shimmering riveted mail, split at the groin to allow for easier wear while mounted, with rows of brass rings at the neckline and hems. Medraut wore a thigh-length coat of sleeveless scale armor, called lorica squamata by the Romans. The scales were fastened to a leather tunic of crimson-dyed leather. It was similar to the armor worn by Arthur himself in fact, though the scales of Arthur's squamata were gilded with brass. Arthur even had an additional layer of scales around his shoulders. Medraut's squamata, by contrast, looked as functional, if not as flashy. His shoulders were also reinforced, but with simple hardened leather, dyed the same crimson as the undercoat. Instead of brass, the iron scales of his armor were nearly blackened.

The princes' retinue were also well armored, as good what the Red Dragons wore. They wore coats of mail over padded leather or cloth tunics, and all carried daggers and swords slung from baldrics. A few had axes looped through their belts as well. Four or five had slings looped through their belts. All three of the men who seemed to be Medraut's personal retinue wore quivers of arrows across their backs, along with wearing blackened mail, dark burgundy tunics, and black, hooded cloaks like their master. Perhaps it was simply my bias against Medraut himself, but the three men appeared to be shifty and unsavory, the kind of men who might follow someone into a dark alley, rob and murder him.

As we saddled up that evening and prepared to ride out, Gawain donned an iron and brass helm with a nasal as well as cheek plates. It was studded with gems, and the brow was reinforced for added protection. A stylized boar was fixed to the top of the helm. Medraut unstrung bow rested in a case that hung from his saddlebag, much like how we of the numerus equitum carried a case of javelins. He also wore a slightly more modest-looking helm than his brother's, not unlike the one I'd had myself until a few days ago, except his included a brass faceplate.

"Is that a Saxon helm?" I asked, curious.

"Not specifically," Medraut replied. His voice had an odd, tinny quality, from behind that somewhat human-like faceplate, and the eye slits were small enough so that behind them just looked black. I shivered at the inhuman effect it gave him. "A smith in Gododdin made it, but he did get the idea from our Anglian neighbors to the south. I appreciate the full protection it provides, regardless of where the design came from."

"Wouldn't want his pretty face to get messed up," Gawain chuckled from a few feet away.

"Some of us do care about our looks, yes," Medraut nodded agreeably.

"Oh, I care too," Gawain grinned. "Too many women would be devastated if I went and got my nose chopped off or some such thing. I protect my face by making sure it doesn't get hit in the first place. I find that approach works better than any faceplate."

"Until it doesn't." Medraut snickered.

I couldn't help but chuckle at their exchange. I was still pretty sure Medraut was a traitor, but I was beginning to hope I was wrong. He and Gawain clearly cared for each other, and I found myself drawn in by both of them. I also hoped I was wrong because, of course, if Medraut was in fact a traitor and working with Garwlwyd to dethrone King Leudon, tonight's planned rescue might go very, very badly.

Chapter Fourteen

The twenty men Gawain and Medraut chose to accompany us got underway as the sun disappeared behind the western horizon. We brought half a dozen extra saddled horses for my companions. The men whose horses we were bringing stayed at the camp with Gemma and the two servants. Within three hours, we arrived at the outskirts of Caer Amon. A few people moved about, as we'd arrived in between the first and second sleeping periods. We stayed hidden within the woods outside of the village until we were sure nobody was awake, then our group split up again at this point. Half stayed back with the horses, hidden among the trees. Those men were also all equipped with bows in order to provide us with ranged support, should we return with rebels on our heels. The rest pulled their cloaks up around their armor and helmets to minimize the risk of the moon reflecting off the metal as we quietly walked up to the low earthworks that had been dug around the village and up to the wooden palisade atop it. Medraut and three other men took a moment to string their bows, then the biggest of the men hunched down against the wall and locked his fingers together. One by one, beginning with Gawain and Medraut, the rest of us stepped up into his cupped hand and let him hoist us up and over the wall.

A dog started barking at us, and Medraut smoothly drew an arrow from his quiver, nocked, and loosed it in what looked like one fluid motion. The arrow struck the large dog in the head, and it collapsed to the ground, dead with barely more than a quick yelp. I flinched at the sight, repulsed by his action. *Maybe* it was necessary, for we couldn't afford to let that dog wake up the whole village, but I didn't have to like it.

We crept through the village without further issues and quickly came to the stone walls of the fort. A simple, one-man boost to the top wouldn't work for this wall — it was too tall, as I'd briefed the princes back at their camp. Medraut wordlessly pointed to a lean man who, like me, wore only padded linen armor. Around his chest, however, he carried a long, knotted rope. With amazing skill, he carefully scaled the rough stone wall. He paused briefly when he got to the top, looked left and right, then crawled over. A moment later, the rope snaked out from between the crenelations, and the end of it hit the ground. Medraut snatched it up and immediately climbed up, followed by his other two men. Gawain gestured for me to go up next. I was a bit awkward. I grew up climbing trees, and occasionally low walls, but rarely ropes, so I struggled a bit, my feet slipping a couple of times. The second time I did so, my knee banged into the stone, and I sucked in a sharp breath, fighting to keep quiet. I slowly exhaled, tuned out the pain, and kept climbing. Once I got to the top, Medraut and another man helped me over.

Next came Gawain and the other men. We'd barely taken the ramp that led off the earthen rampart and down onto the ground when we heard a guard yawning as he patrolled along the wall above us. As one, the ten of us flattened ourselves against the base of it. The guard paused. He must have been focusing all of his attention outside the wall, which was reasonable after all, because he didn't see us, and after a couple of moments, he continued walking past. One of Medraut's men raised his bow, intent on loosing an arrow into the guard's back, but Medraut put his hand on the man's arm, and pushed it down. We let the guard go.

Now that we were inside the fort, I took the lead and guided the group past the granary, some shops, and an armory that surrounded the great hall. I paused at the armory, looking over at Gawain. He nodded his consent, and I went inside. There was a small stack of padded cloth and leather armor on one shelf, and even a few coats of mail, but I ignored those. Donning mail took time, and I didn't have enough time to try each coat on, hoping one of them might happen to be mine, or that one would fit properly. I scanned the shelves, hoping I might see my helmet or shield at least. I didn't, but when I studied a rack of swords, my heart skipped a beat when I noticed a familiar, old-fashioned spatha with a nicked and worn ivory pommel and guard, with a decorative brass guard plate. I grinned in delight as I snatched it up, fighting the urge to pull the blade free of its scabbard just to cherish the familiar feel of its grip once again. Instead, I slung the baldric attached to the scabbard across my chest, then grabbed up a handful of other swords and axes that looked suitable for my companions, and rejoined Gawain, Medraut, and the others.

The brothers looked over my haul and nodded in appreciation, then we resumed our movement through the fort. We encountered another dog roaming about, but this one only growled and slunk away. Upon reaching the northwest corner of the great hall, I signaled for the group to halt and had everyone duck behind a building. People were probably sleeping on the other side of the wall, so I kept my voice low.

"The hovels where my companions are being imprisoned are around the corner. There's a pair of guards at each one. They'll likely spot as soon as we round that," I warned them.

Medraut nodded, and he and his three men nocked arrows, preparing to deal with the guards. Then there was a distant commotion coming from the southern side of the fort. Calls of "fire" rippled through the night. We all glanced that way and saw a faint, orange glow from the other side of the fort. I had a suspicion regarding its cause, but kept my thoughts to myself.

The guards noticed, too, and we heard them talking anxiously. One of them volunteered to go check it out. From inside the house we were hiding behind, we heard muffled voices, and a man yawning.

"Strike now," I said instead.

Medraut nodded again, and the men raised their bows as they rounded the corner. The consecutive sounds of bowstrings thrumming were heard, then Medraut's low voice came from around the corner.

"Clear."

The rest of us joined Medraut and his archers, and I saw the dead bodies of the three guards. I rushed up to the door and moved to lift the wooden beam barring it from the outside, then paused.

"Gib, it's me. Don't throw a bloody rock at my head this time!" I hissed and removed the beam.

Gilbert was indeed there, just inside the door, crouched and ready to pounce if he'd needed to. Behind him were Marcus and Tor, also standing, and looking sort of ready for a fight, but also a bit sleepy and confused. In the far back corner, Myrddin was still in the process of waking up.

"I come bearing gifts. Take these and let's go," I told the lads as I handed them the swords and axe I'd scooped up. "I salvaged this, too," I told Gilbert and pulled the seax out from behind my back and handed it to him.

Gilbert took it with a broad grin and thrust it into the sheath he still wore at his belt.

"Just swords? What about armor?" Marcus asked.

I rolled my eyes. "Some people..." I grumbled.

"Just no pleasing them," Gilbert agreed. "They'd complain if you hung them with a new rope."

We shared a subdued chuckle.

"What's going on outside?" Myrddin asked with a yawn.

"I've come with the Princes, Gawain and Medraut, to rescue you. Garwlwyd was going to kill you all if King Leudon couldn't pay your ransom," I told them. "I need to get to Morgana now." I paused and looked outside where the men were keeping watch for more potential threats. I whispered hurriedly to my companions, "Don't trust Medraut! Keep an eye on him. He's the one with the faceplate on his helm."

They nodded, though they gave me odd looks, and we filed out of the door. Medraut had already gone with his trio of bowmen and removed the bar from Morgana's hovel, and the two were talking in hushed tones as we came over to them. Morgana threw her arms around Myrddin and hugged him, then looked him over, as he did the same, with both asking if the other was alright. It would have been an endearing scene, reminiscent of a reunion between an elderly father and his loving daughter, were it not for the fact that I was also suspicious of Morgana.

Gawain interrupted them by walking over and gently, but firmly, putting his hand on Myrddin's shoulder.

"Come on, sir. We need to go now. A fire's started on the opposite side of the fort. We need to take advantage of that distraction and get out of here while we can."

Myrddin nodded, and Gawain started off, sword in hand. As with most forts, Roman or otherwise, the walls around this one had a north and south gatehouse, though the southern one was the larger, primary one. Our exit strategy hadn't specified which gate we would make for once we'd rescued Myrddin and my companions, as we hadn't known for sure which would be the easiest to get through at the time. Now, thanks to the fire in the southern side of the village, our choice was made for us. We headed toward the north wall of the fort, grateful to notice that the streets were empty. We ducked and hid once as a pair of men carrying buckets that splashed a bit of water as they headed south.

The small gatehouse loomed into view, along with a pair of bored-looking guards leaning against the wall. The head of one of them rested against his chest as though the man were dozing. The other guard, wearing a helmet, was more obviously awake. Medraut brought his bow up and loosed an arrow at a guard. The arrow zipped through the air and hit the stone wall beside the head of the guard in the helmet with a loud clacking noise, then bounced away.

He missed! I thought in surprise, then just as quickly realized he'd probably hit exactly where he was aiming for as all Hell broke loose. Both guards jumped and saw our large group in an instant. They began screaming their bloody heads off, and in moments, cries of alarm began echoing throughout the fort as guards posted around the walls responded.

"Run! Go! Go!" Gawain cried, and we rushed for the gate. I cursed Medraut in my head as we sprinted for the gate, even as the guards slammed it shut. Either they were very brave men determined to die well, or they were simply too slow, because neither one of them ran away, despite our numbers. They thrust their spears at us, but Tor grabbed the spear of one man while Gawain ran him through with his sword. Gilbert accounted for the second guard, knocking the spear out of the way with his axe and stabbing him with his dagger, held in his left hand. But in the few moments it took to get to the gate and kill the two guards, more arrived, rushing towards us from the ramparts. Two of Gawain's men were in the process of lifting the wooden beam that barred the door closed when one of them screamed and fell to the ground with a javelin buried in his back. Those of us with shields spun outwards and formed a shieldwall.

A raven, circling low overhead, cawed, and then Medraut swore and cried out in pain. I spun to look his way, absently noting that with his hood still up and hiding most of his helm, it gave him a very disconcerting impression of having a blank-eyed, metallic face. Now he was hunched over, and his left hand clutched at his right shoulder. The raven flapped away, still cawing noisily.

"Slingers!" Medraut hissed in warning.

I scanned around but only saw guards coming at us. More men, some wearing nothing more than their linen underwear and carrying weapons and shields, came rushing down the street towards us from the vicinity of the great hall. More spears and javelins were hurled at us from men on the ramparts as we finally got the gate open. A trio of men with javelins popped up from the thatched roof of a building nearby. They were smart enough to realize that attacking our group head-on, which now numbering about fifteen, would not have been conducive to a long life. Before any of us reacted, however, a rock streaked out from somewhere and hit one of the men. He yelped and disappeared from view.

The other two began looking around, trying to identify the new source of their troubles.

So, there was an unknown slinger out here. I didn't have time to search for that new source of mischief, however, as my companions were already streaming through the northern gate and running northwest towards the modest earthworks that protected the village surrounding the fort. I sprinted after them, and yelped in fright as an arrow zipped past my head and buried itself into the wall of a dwelling off to my right.

We had nearly reached the edge of the village, some hundred paces from the central fort, when a group of horsemen came galloping towards us from the village. Like the other group further back, these men were mostly half-naked, but they carried weapons. Only the one in the lead was fully dressed, to include a long coat of mail and a distinctive, wolfskin cloak. I swore.

"It's Garwlwyd," I shouted a warning as he charged at us.

Gilbert, Tor, Marcus, and I instinctively formed up in a loose half-circle, shielding Myrddin and Morgana, though it was a bit weakened with no shields in their hands. Gawain and Medraut's men also formed up, on our right, tying in their meager battle line with the earthworks. Another slingstone flew out from somewhere off to our left, and it smacked into the Fisher King's horse, who reared up, nearly throwing his rider. Gawain scrambled up onto the earthworks surrounding the village and struck at the rebel leader, who parried the blow. I didn't have time to watch any more of their fight, because then the rest of the horsemen were on us!

Two of them were killed before reaching us, felled by arrows loosed by the princes' men. Three more horsemen charged into Gawain's men, but were stopped by our shields and thrusting swords. Not all of the men had brought shields, however, and another three mounted rebels smashed into them. Two were knocked sideways, while one of them was trampled. Our mysterious slinger struck again, hitting one rider in the right hip. He yelped, and in that moment of distraction, one of Gawain's men ran him through, then yanked him to the ground where he was killed, and his terrified horse turned and galloped away. The other two rebels wheeled around, hacking and slashing at the men around them.

One horseman made the mistake of charging at Marcus and Tor. It was a mistake because as men of Tribune Arthur's numerus, we were nearly as proficient at fighting dismounted as mounted. And one of the drills we were trained in was repelling cavalry. Granted, we were at a distinct disadvantage by having neither spears nor even shields, except for me, but we could still handle a small number of horsemen at least. Tor and Marcus jumped aside, and then while Marcus engaged the rider from the right, Tor used his free hand, grabbed the rebel's shield, and jerked it aside before stabbing the man through the ribs. He fell to the ground dead. Marcus hopped up on the man's horse, and Tor grabbed his shield.

A man on foot came at me. He was shirtless and shoeless, having on only trousers. More importantly, though, he had a large round shield and a sword. He swung at me with it, and I brought my borrowed shield up, blocking the attack. The rebel followed that up immediately by punching me in the head with his shield's boss, and I staggered backwards. He brought his sword back for a thrust when Gilbert, on my left, lashed out with his seax, sinking his blade fully in the man's naked torso. He grunted and staggered backwards before collapsing to the ground, clutching at his stomach.

Gilbert reached down to snatch up the rebel's fallen shield when another man rushed up, thrusting a spear at him while he was crouched down and more vulnerable. I swung my shield out and batted the spear aside, then stepped forward and thrust my sword into him, under his armpit. As I withdrew my blade, a stone streaked past my head and smacked into the shield of yet another rebel who was coming at me with an axe raised overhead. The impact caused the man to pause and bring his shield up, giving me an opening at his exposed legs. I sliced at the side of his right knee, and he collapsed to the ground with a shriek of pain. Tor stepped forward and thrust his sword down into the man, killing him.

"I wish someone had brought me a sword," Morgana grumbled from behind us.

"Apologies. Didn't know you were proficient with one. I only knew you used a bow," I said with a glance over my shoulder at her.

"I'm not great with one, but I'd sure feel a lot better right now if I had one," she retorted.

One last horseman came at us, rushing straight at Gilbert, who flung his shield at the horse. The horse swerved sharply away, then reared up as he was struck. With his left hand now free, Gilbert rushed at the man, leapt, and grabbed a fistful of his hair, yanking him out of the saddle and slamming him to the ground. Before the rebel was able to recover from that, Gilbert brought his sword down and hacked at him several times, screaming as he did so. Like Marcus had done, Tor vaulted up onto the horse's back before it could run off, though it took him a few moments to get the frightened creature under control. I handed a shield up to him, then we got back into the fight.

All of us were locked in combat, fighting with Garwlwyd's men then. I spared a quick glance at the rebel leader and Gawain. They were still fighting, though they were dirtier and bloodier than they'd been a moment ago. Medraut and two others were up on the berm, loosing arrows at the Fisher King's men. I had a moment to survey the area around us and noticed several men scattered about, dead or wounded, with arrows in them. A number of additional men lay on the ground, clutching at wounds that had drawn little to no blood, having been caused by the impact of stones hurled at a high velocity from our hidden slinger. Most of the dead rebels, however, were at our feet. Close to two dozen dead and wounded lay around our formation, and the ground became stained red with their blood, but we were still surrounded by men as more kept streaming across the village to come deal with us. Many of the latecomers had patches of soot and smelled of smoke, which suggested that the fire that had provided our initial distraction had been put out, or at least contained. I also realized that this damned village had been housing more warriors than I'd have imagined.

I barely had time to catch my breath after killing a man who'd come at me with a pitchfork when a large bearded man wearing a bronze helm and a coat of mail came at me. Like Garwlwyd, he wore a wolfskin cloak, and in his hands, he carried a shield and sword. Beside me, Gilbert was battering away at another rebel, methodically hacking his shield apart with his axe and making thrusts with his seax when opportunity presented itself. Everyone around me was fighting their own assailants, so I was on my own with this towering brute.

He came at me with a roar, swinging downward towards my shoulder. I blocked with my shield and was alarmed to feel the shock of the blow all the way up my arm. I counter-attacked with my sword, which he took on his shield. Before I could strike again, he unleashed a flurry of attacks, striking high, low, and then high again. It was all I could do to block as he rained attacks down on me and had no chance at all to strike back for several moments. One of his slashes got past my guard and cut into my left calf. I gritted my teeth and pushed through the stinging pain.

When the opportunity presented itself, I retaliated, swiping at the big man's legs with my sword. He dropped his shield and blocked the attack, as I expected, and that gave me the opportunity to punch him in the face with the boss of my own now-battered shield. He staggered back a step, and I thrust at his head. He turned away enough so that the tip of my blade skittered off of his helmet rather than striking a fatal blow. I brought my sword up for another attack, but he deflected the blow at the last moment. I lashed out with my foot, kicking him in the side of his left knee.

The rebel warrior roared in pain as his knee buckled, and he swept his sword at my head. Seeing that he was off balance from the injury to his knee, I drove my shield into him, blocking his slash and knocking him backwards. He fell onto the ground, and I stabbed at him, trying to finish the fight before he could get back onto his feet. He kicked at me with his right leg, and I slashed it, eliciting another bellow of pain and rage from the man.

Still kneeling, the big man swung his sword up at me. I skipped backwards and out of the way, then bounded to my right and, while he was struggling to get up, I chopped my sword down at his exposed neck, a hair below the rim of his helmet. My blade sank in deep, and the big rebel warrior grunted. In quick succession, I hacked at him two more times before his lifeless body fell to the ground.

I looked around quickly and saw that the rest of my companions had been holding their own with equal success, and in fact, though we were still surrounded, the warriors had backed off, holding their shields before them and their weapons ready to strike. They slowly edged away from the berm, however. I spared a glance towards it and understood why. The men we'd left in the woods with our horses had heard the commotion and galloped up to the wall and were hacking the wall down from the other side. The rebels, seeing logs being chopped apart, understood that we were being reinforced, but couldn't see how many were there.

"Let's get out of here!" I called out. Immediately, Marcus, Tor, and Gilbert escorted Myrddin and Morgana to the wall and helped them squeeze through the newly created hole. The more injured men filed through next. At this point, a very familiar, female voice called out from a cluster of roundhouses some seventy feet away, "Wait for me!"

We all looked, and saw Gemma jumping down from the roof of one of the houses and ran over to us. I noticed a sling in her right hand. One of the rebels reflexively brought his spear up in a reverse grip, and I tensed, ready to charge at them, but the man didn't throw it, and within moments, Gemma was safely within our shieldwall and guided through the wall. I got to enjoy a brief look of astonishment and confusion that turned into a deep scowl from Gawain as Gemma squeezed past him. Before I withdrew, I quickly bent down and scooped up the sword of the large rebel warrior I'd killed.

To his credit, despite his own injuries, Gawain was the last to slip through the wall, which we on the other side had continued to tear down and widen the breach to expedite the withdrawal. One rebel stepped up to the hole in the wall a moment after Gawain joined us, but Gilbert threw a spear that he'd taken during the fighting. The spear slammed into the man's chest, and he fell backwards with a cry. Nobody else stepped up to the wall, and we were able to mount up and ride away.

I noted three empty saddles as we rode, which prompted me to conduct a quick scan of the group as we rode back towards our camp. Tor was cradling one bloody arm, but otherwise looked well. Gilbert and Marcus looked fine, as did Myrddin, Morgana, and Gemma. I breathed a sigh of relief.

Turning back to the front, I noticed Gawain looking around, doing the same thing as me.

"I'm sorry for the men you lost," I told him, when I saw the sour look on his face. He'd seen the empty saddles, just as I had.

Gawain looked over at me, pressed his lips into a firm line, and nodded sadly at me. He turned and looked straight ahead for a bit as we rode, then finally he said, still looking ahead, "I hope Arthur is able to come up here with enough men for us to storm Caer Amon. I've a score to settle with the Fisher King now. Dealing with him was already my duty. Now he owes me for the deaths of three good men. *My* men," he hissed.

"We will, brother," Medraut assured him as he pulled his helmet off and hung it from his saddle.

I wanted to draw my new sword and strike his head from his shoulders at that moment. How could a man be capable of such deceit and treachery? I fumed. My swords remained in place, however. So far, Medraut simply hadn't done anything I could use as evidence should I try and accuse him. As if the snake could sense my gaze on him, he turned in his saddle and gave me a faint smile.

"You and your men did well for themselves. I saw a bit of that fight you had with that big man at the end. Is that his sword?" He gestured to the new sword I had thrust into my belt.

"It is," I agreed, and drew the blade to admire in the moonlight. "It's a very well-crafted blade. Too good for some local villager to have purchased. Just like his armor. I'm guessing whoever's propping up these rebels must have supplied this stuff. I'd love to be able to look this man in the eye... whoever he is, to show him that now at least one of his expensive blades will be used against the rebellion."

I got the satisfaction of seeing Medraut's smile slip, if only for an instant, before it was back in place. "It is a nice blade, and an upgrade from that old spatha you have in that scabbard there, but it's not that nice."

We rode on for a bit. Occasionally we heard the deep cawing of a raven flying overhead, loosely parallel to our own course.

"What is with that accursed bird?" Medraut growled, looking up at the sky.

Myrddin chuckled when he looked up as well. "Oh, don't mind Tethra. She's only my pet raven.

"Your pet?" Medraut echoed skeptically. "That bird acted like it wanted to attack me back at the fort."

Myrddin waved a dismissive hand. "Nonsense. She's as friendly as can be."

He held out his outstretched arm and let out a series of whistles. The raven responded by circling down and landing on Myrddin. As if to make a lie of Myrddin's assurances, she then turned her head to stare at Medraut and began cawing and croaking in a distinctively unfriendly manner. Her head bobbed up and down a bit, and she puffed out her feathers. Finally, still cawing away, she launched back into the air straight at Medraut!

The prince swore and ducked out of the bird's path, cursing as Tethra flew up into the air and resumed her aerial course. Myrddin looked embarrassed and shrugged his shoulders when Medraut turned to glare at the old man.

"Friendly as can be, eh?" He grumbled.

Beside him, Gawain laughed uproariously at the incident, as did a few of the other men.

Gemma and I shared a look. Ravens were supposed to be smart creatures, and it struck both of us as further evidence that Medraut was surely a villain. Then she dropped back and signaled that I should do the same. I did, and we slowed down until we were in the rear of the column of riders.

"Nice work with that sling back there. I'm dying to know how you slipped away from camp and caught up to us in the fort in order to provide us cover from that rooftop," I said with a grin.

"That's not important right now," Gemma replied in a low tone and a cautious glance toward the head of the column, where Gawain and Medraut rode side-by-side.

"Medraut nearly killed Myrddin!"

My jaw went slack with disbelief. Surely, he wasn't that evil, was he? "What happened?" I asked.

"I barely had enough time to start slinging rocks at the rebels as they started attacking when I saw Medraut get behind Myrddin. He drew his sword, and I swear by the old gods and on Jesus the Christ that if I hadn't been able to shift my aim and loose a stone at him instead of the rebel I'd been about to target, he would have run the old man through."

She gestured up at the raven. "I might not have noticed it either, until that raven dove down at him."

I was at a loss for words. I wanted to deny it. Aiding a rebellion was one thing, but killing an old man... why? What would he have had to gain?

I must have muttered that part out loud because Gemma replied, "Remember that conversation we heard? King Leudon will lose respect among his nobles if he fails to pay Myrddin's ransom, and the old man is killed. Well, since we were in the middle of rescuing him, that plan was ruined. Medraut could have salvaged it by killing him during the rescue. None of you were looking at them.

He could have run Myrddin through, and in the confusion, it would have been assumed that a rebel had killed him."

I nodded as she spoke, seeing the logic of it. My anger towards Medraut burned even hotter. And once again, there was nothing we could do about it. If Gemma told Gawain what she'd seen his own brother do, why would he believe her? Medraut would simply deny it and say she'd misunderstood his intent. There was clearly a bond between the brothers. No way would Gawain believe Gemma over Medraut. I'd certainly need stronger evidence than Gemma's testimony had she made such an accusation against my own brother, Lamorac.

"We'll have to keep an eye on him. I'm sure he deliberately missed his chance at killing the guard as we tried to get out of the fort. That's what tipped them all off in the first place," I muttered.

"I saw that too," Gemma nodded.

"With most other archers, I might have dismissed it as bad luck. But he's shown himself to be very good with a bow. He shouldn't have missed."

"How's your leg?" I noticed that you got hurt. Again," Gemma pointed out, arching an eyebrow at me.

"It's fine. Just a scratch," I said, waving her concern aside.

"Aren't you supposed to be good enough at this sort of thing to not get cut? I thought that's the point of all the training you do."

"Ideally, yes," I admitted with a sigh. "The most important thing is that we can kill the other man and live to fight another day. I did."

"Hmm. Well as your physician, I suggest you work on not getting cut so much, regardless."

"Yes, Medicus," I said, matching her snarky tone.

Two hours later, we arrived at the princes' campsite. We dismounted, and Gemma and Myrddin started walking down the line, identifying who was injured, then sorting out who needed attention the most urgently.

Two of Gawain's men had bled heavily from serious injuries, and Myrddin began working on them while Gemma scurried about finding a needle and thread that another man had to repair clothing. She ripped up another man's blanket for bandages, then hunted about with Morgana for various plants and other things that Myrddin needed for poultices to aid in their healing.

Others, like me, had minor injuries that were able to be ignored until the two seriously injured men had been seen to. I was relieved to discover, upon rolling up the hem of my torn and bloody trousers, that the cut I'd received only needed a few stitches, unlike a nasty cut I'd taken to my side two years ago while fighting the Picts. I had a wicked-looking scar from that one.

After Gemma had personally stitched and bandaged a wound to Gawain's right forearm, the prince turned to me with a wry smile.

"I seem to have badly misjudged your lady, Peredur."

I chuckled. "Yes, you did. But fear not. You're far from the first man to have done that. There's some within the Red Dragons who are downright afraid of crossing her."

Gawain's smile widened. "Good to know. I'll be sure not to repeat that mistake. So, she's your betrothed?"

"She is," I replied with a smile.

Gawain nodded approvingly, then looked at the bandage on his arm. "We need to return to Pendyrlaw and report the situation to Father. He should be pleased. We bloodied the Fisher King's forces, and rescued Myrddin and your envoy right out from under his nose."

"How is the situation with the King and Queen?" I asked, recalling the bit of conversation Gemma and I had overheard the other night.

Gawain scowled. "Not good. Counselor Guinnion and a few others have been very vocal in their criticism of King Leudon's ability to rule. He's been in a tight spot for several months now. If he cracks down on the complaints too hard, it may cause people to riot or join the rebellion now that that's happened. On the other hand, if Father ignores them, it makes him look weak and emboldens the nobles already accusing him of exactly that."

"Will it help him or hurt him if or when Arthur brings up the Dragons in a few weeks?"

Gawain ran his hand through his hair and sighed heavily. "Probably both?" He finally answered. "With Arthur's help, we can deal with the Fisher King's rebellion, which will help settle people down. But it will also perpetuate the idea that he's too weak to rule, particularly among some of the ambitious nobles."

I saw an opening here and prodded at him a little. "Who do you think the nobles would replace him with, if they did decide to overthrow him? You or Medraut? Or someone else entirely?"

"There's our youngest brother, Gareth, too. He's a child, though," Gawain commented. "I don't quite know, though. That's one thing that's been puzzling us. A number of nobles seem convinced that someone else would be a more fit king than Father, but nobody is being named as a potential replacement. It's... peculiar."

I glanced around, not seeing Medraut nearby, so I pressed on. "The night Gemma and I escaped Caer Amon, we heard the Fisher King talking with a couple of people, a man and a woman. The man gave Garwlwyd some gold. He's been supplying them with weapons and armor, too. From what we could hear, he might even have been the man preparing to seize the throne in the event that King Leudon is overthrown."

Gawain turned to regard me with an intense stare. "And you're just now telling me this? Could you identify him?"

"I couldn't," I admitted reluctantly. "It was dark, and raining, and he wore a dark cloak with a hood up. I could only see the lower half of his face. He was clean-shaven and about my size."

Gawain scowled. "Could you at least recognize his voice if you heard it again? Or Maithgemm?"

I hesitated. Now I was walking a very thin line. I still wasn't comfortable enough to tell Gawain that I believe with near absolute certainty that the man working against his kingdom was his own younger brother. Not yet, at least. At the same time, I needed to watch what I said so as not to erode any validity in what we'd seen should the opportunity arise to identify Medraut at a later time.

"I might be able to. Especially if Gemma is with me to corroborate."

Gawain nodded slowly. "A clean-shaven man, about your height and build, and wearing a dark cloak, eh?"

"That's what we saw," I confirmed.

At that very moment, Medraut walked over and joined us, eating a strip of deer meat. "Well, the men have been tended to, courtesy of Myrddin and Gemma," he said with a smile and a nod to me. "They're doing their best to devour the deer I killed the other night. So, we should be good to eat a light meal in the morning, then make the ride back to Din Pendyrlaw. If we get an early start, we could even be home in time to sleep in our own beds... or in your case, in the bed of whichever mistress hasn't forgotten about you by now," Medraut grinned.

"Forgotten about me?" Gawain asked, raising his eyebrows. "We've only been gone for a couple weeks."

"Exactly," Medraut smirked.

Gawain flipped his brother the middle finger as Medraut strode away, laughing.

I watched him go, appreciating once again that convincing Gawain of Medraut's treachery was likely going to be a minor miracle. And with that thought, I bowed my head to thank God for the good fortune I'd had thus far, and to pray for His help and guidance in the coming challenges I was sure to face.

Chapter Fifteen

As planned, we woke up at the crack of dawn, much to Gemma's chagrin. She was often a bit cranky any time she had to wake up quite so early. Aside from her, we broke down the camp quickly and were on our way east before the sun had fully crested the eastern horizon.

We took a break by a stream to water the horses and eat later that morning. Tor spotted another group of men, on foot, about three hundred paces away to the north. Sunlight flashed off helmets, shield bosses, and spear tips that some of them wore and carried.

"Those look like Picts," one of the men said, squinting at them with his hand shading his brow. It was the gruff, angry-looking man who'd been with Medraut the night we first encountered him.

"They probably are," I said after walking over to stand beside him. I took a bite of bread and stared at the group, too. His eyes were better than mine, though. There looked to be six of them. Aside from their weapons and bits of armor, I could see that they wore cloaks, which flapped a bit in the morning breeze. At least one of them looked bare-chested, but I couldn't be sure.

"We could go after them," Marcus mused, overhearing our conversation.

"Too far away," I dismissed the notion.

"I don't like it. It's like they're baiting us," Medraut's man growled.

"They could be," I acknowledged. "We've seen them a few times, always from a distance, and always within a short distance of the water, where they could make a quick getaway. I've done enough scouting in the Red Dragons to recognize when we're being scouted."

Medraut's man scowled, spat in the distant figures' direction, and returned to sit with his master and the other two men who shadowed him wherever he went. I returned to my cymbrogi, who in turn were intermingled with Gawain's men, laughing and joking as we broke our fast. I told Gawain what we saw, and he simply nodded.

"Not surprising." He said between bites of bread and cheese. "We've been getting more and more sightings of Picts along the coast for the past few weeks. Father has speculated on whether they're simply emboldened by the Fisher King's rebellion, or worse, they may be coordinating with him. My own thought on the matter is that they're simply keeping an eye on our troop movements to determine how many men we have and what we're up to."

"Why's that?" I asked.

He ate his last bit of food and washed it down with some wine before answering. "The Fisher King seized Caer Amon last fall. He's been launching raids from there since then and has taken over several villages in the southwest region of the fort. If he were in league with the Picts, I'd have expected them to have thrown in with him by now. No..." he sighed. "I think they're simply being opportunistic. They're watching us fight amongst ourselves and determining where we're most vulnerable. When they're ready, I'm sure they'll strike."

I nodded glumly. His assessment made sense. Then a conversation I'd had with Garwlwyd weeks ago resurfaced suddenly. "The Fisher King said something about that when I first met him at his headquarters. At least a part of the reason he's supporting this... unknown patron... is that he believes a new king will ally with Dal Riata to crush the Picts."

Gawain rolled his eyes. "That would have been nice to know sooner. Any other useful conversations you'd care to share?"

I flinched and apologized to the prince. "This was over two weeks ago when I talked with him. A lot has happened since then. I assure you, I'm not withholding information deliberately."

Well, technically, I was. I wasn't telling Gawain that I was certain his own little brother was in fact the Fisher King's benefactor and likely had plans to usurp the throne and make himself king. But without some very strong, tangible evidence I suspected that bringing this little tidbit up would go very poorly for me.

To his credit, and my discomfort, Gawain seemed to detect my evasiveness, because he stared intently at me for a moment.

"You're a hard man to read, Peredur," he said. "You act simultaneously earnest and honest, but also so... guilty. I get the feeling you're hiding something from me, I just don't know what, or why."

"I'm just a bit anxious sometimes," I lied. "It gives people that impression sometimes." My heart beat faster as he continued to stare at me. I hated lying to him, truly. In fact, I hated lying in general. And in Gawain's case, I'd come to genuinely like and respect him in the short time I'd known him. It was easy to believe that he was Arthur's nephew. All that aside, I stuck to my decision to hold off on telling him about Medraut.

After another long moment filled with awkward silence, Gawain dismissed me. "Fine. Well, we need to get back on the road if we're to reach Din Pendyrlaw by nightfall."

We put away our extra food, saddled up, and headed out again. There were no further Pict sightings, if indeed the group of men we saw were Picts, and shortly after the sun went down, we reached the imposing hillfort of Din Pendyrlaw. I'd been here once before, two years ago with the Red Dragons. It had awed me then, and it awed me now.

The hill that the fort was built upon stood practically as tall as some of the mountains in my homelands, if only because the rest of the land around it was relatively flat. Like most hillforts, there was a great hall at its summit, and numerous earthworks and timber walls built to defend the fort and the sprawling village that surrounded it. The great hall itself, as well as the innermost defensive wall, even boasted stone foundations. The lights of numerous torches moved about along the walls from patrolling sentries. In the distance, past the hillfort, came the faint bleating of sheep and the lowing sound of cattle. This was the seat of power of the Gododdin, and the home of King Leudon and Queen Morgause. I'd only seen them briefly from a distance during my first visit here. The Red Dragons had encamped at the base of the tall hill, and only Arthur and senior officers had gone up to the top of the hill where the King's great hall stood.

This time around, my comrades and I followed Gawain and Medraut through the village and the first low wall around the outskirts. We wound our way up the hill, all the way to the top. The guards recognized the princes on sight, and the banner one of Gawain's men carried, and quickly opened the gates for them. Once we arrived at the uppermost level of the hillfort, my men and I were given quarters within one of the barracks, built against the wall. Morgana and Gemma were given another room with the princes' young sister, Teneu. Myrddin, of course, was provided with guest quarters, also within the great hall itself.

"I wonder if we might get the king to supply us with weapons and armor while we're here," Gilbert mused as we stuffed our new mattresses with fresh straw.

"It's not like he can't afford it," Tor agreed. "On the way up, I got a look at his herd out there. He must have hundreds of head of cattle and sheep! I've never seen so much livestock."

Marcus and I chuckled in agreement, then the four of us dragged our mattresses back over to our new billet and made ready for bed, not that any of us had much. Aside from the weapons I'd pilfered from the armory at Caer Amon, none of us had anything except the clothes on our backs and cloaks some of Gawain's men had charitably given to us. Gilbert finally, carefully, removed the bandage he'd had wrapped around his head the entire time since the night our camp had been ambushed, and I saw the extent of his injury. Before I could stop myself, I let out a long, low whistle. There was indeed a wicked cut from his left cheek that ran all the way along the side of his head. The upper tip of his ear was also gone. It looked clean and like it was healing well, though. Gemma and Myrddin had indeed done a good job in tending to him.

Gilbert saw me and the other two lads gawking at his injury and grinned. "Looks great, ja?"

I blinked in surprise. Most people would be horrified. "You haven't seen it yet, have you?" I asked.

Gilbert continued to grin. "Sure, I have. A few days after we were captured, we were allowed to go to the river and bathe. I saw it well enough in my reflection. It is a scar worthy of a true warrior! I almost don't even want to wear a helmet the next time we face an enemy. They will think 'If this man survived even that wound, what will I have to do to actually kill him?' *ja*?"

We laughed, and I shook my head, thoroughly amused.

"Maybe I should keep my hair short too, so they can see the scar better," Gilbert mused, tracing his finger lightly along the scab.

I should have known Gilbert, of all people, would be thrilled to have such a gruesome scar across his face.

The handful of other soldiers who lived in the barracks where we'd been quartered had also noticed Gilbert's injury, and one of them asked about its origin. The blond Frisian was, of course, only too happy to tell about the night we'd been attacked, and how he'd killed two of Garwlwyd's men with his seax before one of them had swiped at his head with a sword, nearly cleaving his head in half.

His mood became more somber when he recounted how seven of our comrades hadn't fared so well. The soldier who first approached us went and retrieved mugs and a large wineskin, and we drank a toast to our fallen comrades. My eyes moistened as we drank to each of our fallen. I recalled my oath to Digain, now fulfilled. Gemma was safe. His killers could still be out there, though. The man responsible for the raid certainly was. Then there was Medraut, who'd set this entire thing into motion, likely as not.

We shared a few more stories and a few more drinks until finally everyone began to blow out the oil lamps that lit our barracks and went to sleep.

***

Several days passed by as we waited for something to happen. Gawain assured us that his father was working on the matter, but that it was after all, one of several important issues the King was dealing with. Finally, on the morning of the second day of the second week of Maius, a middle-aged servant in a long, plain tunic and snug-fitting trousers, stylish leather shoes, and a cloak fastened around his shoulders with a nice-looking, silver brooch came to the barracks. I noted a roll of clothing in his hands, tied up in a leather strip.

In a surprisingly deep voice, the servant boomed, "Is one of you Peredur, of Caer Gurcoc?" His gaze began to settle on Tor, who was yawning loudly and sitting up in bed. I blinked in surprise at the comically mismatched voice the mild-looking servant possessed. The fact that he mistook Tor for me made me roll my eyes and I held my hand up to get his attention.

"I'm Peredur."

The man flashed me a puzzled look. "I expected someone a bit older... eh, no matter. Your presence is required in the great hall. The sooner, the better."

"Let me get dressed, and I'll be right there. Just me?"

"Just you. Your men can stay here and relax. Do you know the way?"

"I'll find it well enough."

"Very well. Prince Gawain said you probably needed these."

The servant gave me the bundle he'd brought over, nodded at me, and left.

"By Woden!" Gilbert exclaimed with a laugh, watching the servant go. "That little man's voice was that of a great warrior.

"It make you jealous?" I teased my friend as I laid the things out on my bed.

"A little," Gilbert agreed with a grin.

The leather strip binding the package together turned out to be a long belt. Included with that was a fresh, linen tunic and underpants, a light blue outer tunic, tan-colored wool trousers, legwraps, and socks, all made of soft, thin wool.

I hurriedly dressed, forgoing the wraps in order to save time, then headed out of the barracks and over to the great hall. I did wish I'd had a dagger for my belt, feeling a bit underdressed without one, and made a mental note to take care of that later.

Gawain, leaning against a large set of double doors, found me as I strode through the corridors of the great hall a short time later. He looked me up and down briefly with approval. "The clothing I sent you fits you well, I see."

"They do, thank you," I replied with a smile. "What's going on?"

"Your master, Myrddin, is meeting with my father and I, and a couple others. Myrddin requested your presence."

He led the way into King Leudon's audience chamber, such as it was. I'd never been in a king's... well, anything, really, so I didn't know precisely what to expect, but I'd envisioned something a bit grander. The days of Roman splendor and majesty were long gone, but I had always figured that if anyone could keep a sliver of that alive, it would be kings, right? Maybe somewhere, my vision of a king's royal chambers with a tall, intricately carved throne and a hall decorated with gold and ornate tapestries existed. I imagined the halls of men like our own High King Conanus or King Clovis over in Gaul, which some were beginning to call Frankia, looking like that. Maybe theirs did. King Leudon's hall certainly did not.

His hall was somewhat dimly lit for this time of morning, despite the fire blazing in the hearth and a few tall but narrow windows. Sure, he and his wife were indeed seated on tall chairs, which in turn were perched upon a dais, but it was all wood, and furs of various beasts that cushioned the chairs and decorated the walls, along with some of those beasts' skulls. Before the king was a long, rectangular table, littered with mugs, platters of bread and cheese, and a couple of small oil lamps. Two large hounds lay not far from the king's chair, sleeping.

King Leudon was a surprisingly unremarkable-looking man — stocky, though whether from fat or muscle was hard to say. Bare headed, he wore his light brown hair long despite a noticeably receding hairline. A long mustache and beard framed his face, both gone completely gray. Beside him, Queen Morgause was tall, slender, and moderately attractive in spite of her middle age. She had the same blue eyes her sons did, and the same nearly black hair that Medraut had also clearly inherited.

Gawain strode in and took a seat near the end of the table, closest to King Leudon. Medraut was there as well, seated across from him, closest to the queen. I saw an empty chair beside Myrddin and scurried over to it. He nodded at me before taking a swig from what smelled like wine but said nothing.

The king himself nodded to me but otherwise ignored my entrance and gestured toward another man at the table, a lean man in his fifties with white-blond hair. I recognized him and tried not to grimace. It was Lord Guinnion, the king's chief counselor, and the man who had taken nominal command of the levied forces that fought alongside us against the Picts. I neither saw him so much as draw his fine sword nor get even a little dirt or blood on the pristine, polished armor he'd worn. Worse yet, he never failed to demand to be addressed 'properly' as he paraded about the fort acting as though he alone were in charge of its defenses.

Needless to say, the men of our numerus equitum and even many of the levies had despised him, especially with Tribune Arthur, and at the time, Penteulu Garwlwyd showing everyone what true leaders were like. Someone had even gone so far as to carve phalluses, and a man meant to represent Guinnion, performing certain... depraved acts upon one of the large doors of the headquarters building where Guinnion stayed. The culprit was never identified, though for my silver, I'd have bet on Gilbert. He was known to be a whittler of some skill.

"As I was saying," Guinnion spoke up, "the rebels hit another granary last week, at a village not five miles south of here. They need to be stopped, yesterday!" He pounded on the table in emphasis, no doubt thinking it made him look firm and imposing, rather than the whiny, gutless bureaucrat he was in fact.

The king sighed. Clearly, this was not the first time this argument had been made. He didn't even deign to answer Guinnion's demand, and instead, gestured to Gawain, who nodded and stood.

"Our forces are doing what we can, and we are chipping away at his manpower, but he has pockets of men all over the region. Any move we make is seen and reported to the Fisher King. He knows the disposition of our forces at least as well as anyone in this room. If we send out soldiers in too small a column, he ambushes it. If we consolidate too many forces and try to move on one of his camps, he attacks us somewhere we aren't, like that village you mentioned, Counselor Guinnion," Gawain growled in frustration.

"What about infiltrating Caer Amon and assassinating him?" A fat lord seated beside Guinnion asked. "Wasn't that your suggestion, Medraut?"

"It was," Medraut replied, sounding as weary as King Leudon looked. "It's been tried. I've sent agents in on at least three occasions since he captured the town. They failed. The Fisher King is clever, and his men are veteran warriors, and very loyal to him."

Guinnion huffed. "My King, if you cannot stop this simple fisherman from carving out his own little kingdom right under your nose, why do I and the other lords of the Gododdin pay you taxes?"

At that, King Leudon's eyes flared open in anger, and his hands curled into fists.

Muscle, I decided. The king was big, but in the way that some strong men are. I suspected that he might be the strongest man in the room, including the powerfully built Gawain.

"Curb your tongue, Counselor," the King growled with unmistakable menace. "My sons and I are doing everything possible to put an end to this rebellion as swiftly as possible. Your taxes pay for the food, kit, and horses of those men. Men who are far more useful to me than you have been of late, I could add!"

"Calm yourselves, my lords," Medraut added smoothly. "In a few weeks, Arthur and his Red Dragons will be here. Some are already present, in fact," he raised a hand and gestured to me. "As before, Arthur will rid us of this nuisance, and things will be as they were."

If Medraut's words were meant to placate the men seated at the table, they had the opposite effect.

Guinnion leaned forward in his chair and slammed the table again in his anger.

Another of the lords shot up out of his seat, pointing accusingly at the king. "You're putting us in debt to Arthur and High King Conanus again? He's been hounding us for aid against the Saxons ever since he bade Arthur to come save us from King Drest's forces, and now you've gone crawling back to him as a beggar with hands out pleading for a crust of bread?"

King Leudon stood up too, as did his hounds beside him. "You will shut your filthy mouth and speak to me with due respect, or I will shut it for you, High Steward Clydno!" He roared.

The lord identified as the ruler of Din Eidyn paused and looked briefly at the other lords but stood his ground in the face of the king's wrath.

"Ha!" Clydno scoffed. "You aren't even able to put down the Fisher King, in Caer Amon. What chance would you have of forcing me to say, continue paying taxes, from within the walls of Din Eidyn? And why should I? I may as well cut you out of the process and just pay High King Conanus. All you are is a glorified middle-man."

"We at Eildon Hill would join you," another lord growled.

"You forget one small detail, Steward," the king said in a slow, calm tone that sent a shiver down my spine.

"Oh? And what is that?"

"You aren't *in* Din Eidyn at present."

The room went deadly quiet as the lords stewed over the very obvious threat that King Leudon had just issued with such a simple statement. Clydno sat down hard and folded his hands across his chest, still looking furious, but he did close his mouth. The other nobles followed suit.

I looked around the room and noticed Medraut had a very calm expression on his face, in stark contrast to everyone else in the room, who looked either angry or anxious. Then I also noted that cast frequent looks over to the end of the table where his mother, Queen Morgause, sat. She was the picture of serenity, as though nothing being said at the table was unusual. At one point, her hand even came up and hid her mouth as she rested her chin, but not before I saw the ghost of a smile playing at the corners of her lips. Startled, I looked back at Medraut and nearly jumped in surprise to see that he was studying *me*!

A shiver went down my spine, but I met his gaze and tried to calm my nerves by grabbing a mug that had been placed in front of my seat and took a sip. The act had the opposite effect of what I desired because I swallowed wrong and began coughing. That, in turn, drew everyone's attention, to include the king's.

"What's wrong, boy? Are you poisoned?" He demanded, staring in alarm at me.

Another man at the table who'd been taking a sip of his own wine, immediately spit it out and slammed the mug back down on the table. Others scooted back, looking at their mugs in horror.

I slammed my fist into my chest once, cleared my throat, and rasped, "No, Great King. Not poison! I'm sorry for the confusion. I um, just choked on my wine."

King Leudon stared at me, and slowly, every lord in the room did too. My cheeks burned, and I wanted nothing more than to disappear into the floor! I have never been so embarrassed in my life as I was in that moment.

Then Gawain burst out laughing — not a polite, mild laugh as when someone hears a good joke, but a full-on roar of laughter that filled the entire chamber and immediately caused his eyes to tear up. A moment later, Medraut sputtered into his own laughing fit after a failed attempt at stifling it. This, in turn, triggered a laughing fit from the rest of the lords at the table, to include Myrddin and the king himself, I noticed in absolute horror. Only Queen Morgause maintained her aloof, calm demeanor, though even she covered her mouth again after looking over and giving me a slight nod, with a distinct twinkle in her eye.

The laughter began to die down after what felt like an eternity. King Leudon, breathing heavily and wiping at his eyes, wheezed, "Young man that just put every fool I have ever seen, or will ever see, to absolute shame. I don't think I have ever laughed so hard in my entire life!"

"I'll attest to that," Medraut remarked dryly.

I sighed and slunk down in my seat as that elicited a fresh burst of laughter from the table. Like the king, every last one of them was red-faced, teary-eyed, and clutching their stomachs or pounding the table. Servants began cautiously popping their heads into the chamber's doorway with bewildered looks on their faces. Myrddin, wiping his eyes with one hand, clapped me hard on the shoulder.

"Don't let it get to you, boy," he chortled. "Laughter is good for the soul, and anyone who can provide it to others, no matter the cause, will always be thought fondly of."

I pressed my lips together and simply nodded, resigned to my fate of having been labeled the greatest fool ever by no less a person than the bloody King of Gododdin. I could only pray that my comrades would never, ever, hear of this tale.

"Well, now that this young lad has cooled the room down a bit," King Leudon said with a chuckle, "We do need a solution to this issue. Myrddin," he said, gesturing a meaty hand to the old man beside me. "We invited you here specifically because you are famous for your wisdom."

"I like to think the ladies of this fair isle might also know me for other reasons," Myrddin interjected with a droll smile and a sip of his wine.

The king grinned, as did some of the others.

Myrddin took another slow drink from his mug, and his brow furrowed thoughtfully.

"Peredur here has informed me that he is familiar with the Fisher King, that he knew him briefly when last the Red Dragons came to the Old North. As a result of that camaraderie, the Fisher King allowed him to go to Caer Amon, and he was treated hospitably, from what I gather."

I winced as the old man said that. He was right. I had been. And then Gemma and I had poisoned two of his men and escaped. I consoled myself by recalling that we shouldn't have needed to escape in the first place.

Myrddin continued. "It's come to my attention that, among other things, the Fisher King greatly desires the Grail, which I understand to be a holy relic of some significance. The offer of merely the use, not even ownership of the Grail, was one of the promises made by our true enemy, the man who persuaded Garwlwyd to rebel in the first place."

I glanced over at Medraut to see if he showed any reaction to that, but the slippery bastard was too good. His face didn't move a muscle that I could see. Until he turned to look at me. Then his eyes narrowed marginally, and his brow furrowed. For an instant, his eyes flickered over to his mother, then locked back onto me with a look I could easily imagine a wolf getting that is fixed on its prey.

"Perhaps," Myrddin continued, "If you were to offer the Fisher King the use of the Grail, along with maybe one or two other concessions, he would end the rebellion on his own."

"What other concessions?" the King asked, narrowing his eyes.

"Allowing him, his family, and his supporters a pardon, or at least allowing them to live in exile, might be considered?"

"So he can regroup, build his strength, and try again? Not bloody likely," King Leudon scoffed.

"What if he agreed to come south, to Gwent or Gwynedd, where he is far from Gododdin, and under Arthur's own watchful eye?"

The king paused, considering, and glanced around the room.

"That sounds reasonable to me," Gawain commented. Other heads nodded or murmured approval as well. Neither Medraut nor Queen Morgause gave any response to the suggestion.

"There is one problem with your proposal," King Leudon finally said to Myrddin. "We don't actually have possession of the Grail anymore."

My eyebrows rose in surprise, and Myrddin frowned.

"Interesting," he mused. Would you mind telling me where it is?"

"The Grail was brought here by Bishop Germanus more than fifty years ago and acquired by my family a short time later. My father gifted it to a chapel north of here, founded by Ninian, the Apostle to the Southern Picts. He had hoped, through that donation, to aid in their Christianization and form eventual peace with them." The king winced and shrugged. "You can see how well that plan worked out."

"Where is this chapel?" Myrddin asked.

"At a fort, along the eastern cliff of the North Sea, or Mare Germanicum if you prefer. It's called Dun Fhoithear. By land, it's a hundred and forty miles north of here."

Myrddin nodded along. "Well then, I propose we send a small group of men to take a boat across the Forth of Firth, up the coast, and retrieve the Grail. The journey should only take a few days, I would imagine. Then we can bargain with the Fisher King and put an end to his rebellion."

"And what of Arthur, who's likely already on his way here?" King Leudon asked.

"You also have a Picti problem," Myrddin pointed out. "With the rebellion ended, you can focus your efforts on identifying where they are massing, if they are, so that by the time Arthur arrives, likely within the next three weeks, you'll be ready to lead an incursion into their land and end that threat as well. These two victories, combined with regaining the Grail, should reassure any doubters within the kingdom that you are still a strong ruler and have God's blessing. How does that sound to you?"

"Bargaining with a rebel who has been terrorizing the land hardly projects strength," Queen Morgause finally spoke up. "And don't forget that many believe that he and his army aren't even men, but cinbin."

"It's certainly the quickest, most efficient approach that I see that will at least end the conflict, Queen Morgause," Myrddin insisted. "As to that rumor, it is almost certainly only that. As their prisoner, I certainly saw men wearing wolf skins, but nothing more."

"And what happens when this group you propose to send north can't find the Grail, which has probably been stolen and is now sitting on some barbarian chief's dining table somewhere in the Highlands?" Morgause continued. "As my husband has pointed out, nobody has laid eyes on the thing in fifty years."

Myrddin shrugged. "It would be a modestly sized expedition sent out, and at an even more modest cost. Low risk, high reward."

"Except to the men you would send out on this fool's errand," Morgause snorted derisively.

As quickly as she uttered the words, I saw a sly expression cross Myrddin's face, and his gaze turned towards me.

I swore up a storm in my head, getting a pretty bloody good idea why Myrddin gave me that look. A scripture from the book of the prophet, Isaiah, popped into my head.

...I heard the voice of the Lord, saying, Whom shall I send, and who will go for us? Then said I...

"Here I am. Send me," I sighed in resignation. Another lesson I'd learned in the Dragons — when you know you're about to be 'volun-told' for a mission, you may as well volunteer. You'll be thought better of that way. "I've no idea where this chapel or outpost or whatever this place is, though."

The king gave me an amused look. Queen Morgause and Medraut gave me not-so-amused looks.

"I will take you there. You have my sword," Gawain said immediately, raising his hand.

"And your bow?" I asked Medraut, doing my best to keep any hint of sarcasm from being detected.

"No," He replied flatly. "As Mother said, this is a fool's errand. A waste of time."

"He also gets seasick," Gawain smirked.

Medraut inclined his head towards Gawain in tacit acknowledgement of the point, but said nothing further.

"So, who else will we go north with?" I asked, glancing from Myrddin to Gawain.

"We can take your friends," Gawain said. "I assume they, like you, have done missions in small groups into hostile territory before?"

"Too many times at this point. May Gemma come along this time?"

"You want to bring a girl with you on this?" One of the lords asked in disbelief.

I gave Gawain a sideways glance and did my best to suppress a smirk.

Gawain saw it, returned my smile, and replied. "My lords, I have seen Peredur's lady dress a stag like an expert woodsman, use a sling to strike down rebels, and bind the wounds of our wounded after the fighting. Furthermore, I told her before infiltrating Caer Amon that she was not permitted to come, and yet the next time I saw her, she was inside the fort with us, making herself quite useful. Frankly, I'm not sure we could keep her from going north even if we ordered her not to come, short of locking her in a cell, in chains."

"Yes, and one of her errant stones struck me in the shoulder," Medraut grumbled.

"Or you got in the way of her target," I added, unable of course to clarify that he had, in fact, been her intended target.

"How did she get into the fort?" Queen Morgause asked.

"I asked her about that later. She told me she waited until she figured we were a couple of miles down the road, then slipped away from camp with one of the horses. She talked her way into the outer gate by telling the guards she was there to give the Fisher King's daughter some medicine for a feminine condition. Once she was through, she set fire to a house, then immediately raised the alarm."

"To draw people toward the fire and away from us?" Medraut mused.

"And because she didn't want anyone to be killed," I clarified. "From there, it was easy enough for her to pass through the inner gate as well and climb up onto the roof of another house once she heard the fighting break out."

"Resourceful," Queen Morgause acknowledged. "Well, if this young lady chooses to accompany you, and you are willing to risk your betrothed by allowing her to accompany you..." Morgause shrugged. "The consequences are yours to bear, I suppose."

"So we'll send Prince Gawain here, accompanied by Peredur and his... four companions to retrieve the Grail. How soon can you depart?" Myrddin asked Gawain.

The prince considered the question. "I suspect Peredur and his friends will need to be properly outfitted. That might take a bit of time, depending on what our armorer has on hand. Between that, acquiring provisions, and a few other details, I think we could be underway in three to four days."

"It's settled then?" Myrddin asked, looking around the room.

One by one, the lords nodded or voiced their approval of the plan, with varying degrees of enthusiasm or skepticism, and I was dismissed, to my relief. Gawain followed me out, and together we began making our plans as he walked with me to the barracks where the rest of my companions were lounging about.

"Get off your lazy backsides, lads," I called out as we approached. "We've a short boat ride ahead of us, and a holy relic to find that will hopefully put an end to this rebellion before the Tribune gets here."

"He'll love to hear that. Three weeks on the road, just to be told he's no longer needed," Gilbert snickered.

"We still need to sort the Picts out again, likely as not," I pointed out.

"And if we can do that decisively enough, and our subjects calm down enough, maybe we can muster some men and ride south to help you lot against the Saxons." Gawain smiled. "In the meantime, let's go and visit Cantrevs, our armorer, and get you lads properly kitted up before we go sneaking into Picti land."

"Well now, I like the sound of... most of that," Tor said with a lopsided grin.

The rest of us laughed appreciatively, sharing in Tor's sentiment, and made our way through the hillfort's more important, and therefore nicer shops, and over to the blacksmith and armorer. I felt rather excited to see what the shop would have available, and was generally warming up to the mission itself, right up until Marcus asked, "So how did that council meeting go? Anything interesting happen?"

Gawain laughed, and I swore inwardly. So much for that incident with the wine staying private.

Chapter Sixteen

WE GAVE OURSELVES TWO days to prepare for the trip. In that time, Gawain would arrange for a boat to be prepared for us on the coast, near the mouth of the east-flowing river that ran past Din Pendyrlaw. Our first stop was the armory. It was an impressively large shop and connected to the smithy. Weapons and armor were everywhere, hung up on the walls or resting upon shelves.

"Take what you need. I'll cover the costs," Gawain told us. "But consider these a loan. This bloody rebellion has been a drain on our supplies, so after we return with the Grail, you need to return whatever equipment you take. I'll cover the cost of anything that might become too damaged to return."

We were all a bit disappointed, but we also understood the situation. Good armor and weapons weren't cheap. It was generous of Gawain to lend us this stuff at all. Many other lords in his shoes might have just issued us heavily-used padded tunics, dented, rusty helmets, spears, shields, and a word of encouragement.

Tor, Gilbert, and I were all fitted out with new, short-sleeved coats of mail with hems that came down to mid-thigh. Gemma received an odd look from the large blacksmith and armorer when she too took a knee-length padded tunic. I saw the bald man give Gawain a curious look, to which the prince smiled and nodded. The smith shrugged and let Gemma be about her business.

To our amusement, Marcus had to make do with only a padded tunic as well, though it wasn't the weight of the mail that was the issue in his case, but rather, it was his weight. Marcus wasn't fat in the way that some lords or monks sometimes are, but he was certainly larger than most men, and as a result, none of the mail the armorer had on hand fit him.

"You need to eat less or run more, *myn dikke freon*," Gilbert teased the man.

"You calling me fat, you ugly little Saxon? I'm just too muscular for any of these coats," Marcus protested in annoyance. "And don't be speaking that barbarian language at me so I can't know what you're saying!"

Gilbert chortled. "Muscle, is it? I've never known a man whose muscles caused mail to be too tight around the midriff. Your stomach muscles must be truly impressive. I guess I just can't see them through all that..." Gilbert gestured to Marcus' gut and broke into laughter before he could finish his statement.

If looks could kill, the one Marcus gave Gilbert would surely have done the job.

"Eat dung," he growled in Latin.

Gilbert, who didn't speak Latin, merely smirked and went back to looking at armor.

Tor and I laughed as we selected daggers from a shelf and attached them to our belts, then selected helmets.

"That Fisher King owes me a good helm." Gilbert grumbled as he selected a simple bronze helm. "The one his men stole from me had nearly full head protection. And it was iron. Much better than this stuff."

"It's better than nothing," I offered, trying to console my friend.

The last thing we did at the armory was to select shields. Unlike the rest of the kit, the shields were ours to keep. I selected a plain one and resolved to paint a design on it later. Gawain took us to a couple of other shops and introduced us to some people who had other things we needed. By that evening, we each had an extra change of clothing, along with everything else we needed in order to make the trip to Dun Fhoithear and back. He also secured pouches of proper lead shot for our slings and a bow for me, as I was proficient with it, if not an expert archer.

We ate a good dinner, after which I carefully painted a large, red Chi Rho on my new shield. I wished I had the skill to paint a dragon on it as well, like my previous shield had, but I didn't, and neither did any of my comrades. There were probably a couple of artists in town who could have done the job, but I had neither the coin to pay them nor the time to wait on someone. I finished painting shortly before the sun went down. Gilbert paused in his dice game with Tor to give it a critical look before giving the shield and me a nod of approval.

The next day, I decided to visit the training yard and shake the rust off my archery skills, as it were. I hadn't used a bow much in some time, as the sling was generally more convenient. To round out the day, I worked with wooden swords against Gilbert and the others. I'm better with the sword than the bow anyway.

That evening, in preparation for our departure, I checked over my group's equipment one last time, if only out of habit than any real concern that we'd overlooked anything. Simply going through the routine of conducting inspections before a mission helped put me at ease and allowed me to rest easier. I went to bed later than some of the others, nonetheless. The mission itself appeared fairly straightforward and should be brief, but I'd learned the hard way not to trust in how easily things should go. And then there was Medraut. He worried me more than the Picts did. He had promptly disappeared after the council meeting yesterday morning, and in all the wandering about I'd done since then, I'd seen neither hide nor hair of him. With someone like him, that was more troublesome than if he'd been underfoot the entire time. I had a bad feeling he was up to something. Would he and some men ambush us on the journey? Rile up the rebels to attack in our absence? Or would he get ahead of us and maybe try to take the Grail before we could get there? There were a number of possibilities. The worst part of it was, I'd never been able to catch him doing anything that I could reveal to Gawain and reveal his treachery.

As I mentally gnawed at the problem, my eyes grew heavier. Lying on my mattress there in the dark, and listening to the rhythmic sounds of heavy breathing and the snores of the other men in the barracks, I slowly let myself drift off. The last conscious thought that crossed my mind was to marvel over how often I seemed to wind up in situations where I was either alone or in a small group of men, deep in hostile territory.

***

The next morning, our group, which consisted of Gawain and his three men, me and my three companions, and Gemma, ate a hearty, early breakfast, then left Din Pendyrlaw. Myrddin and Morgana came out to say goodbye and wish us good fortune. Gilbert and I shared amused glances that not one but two young women came to wish Gawain farewell.

"Do you suppose one of them is his sister or something?" Gilbert asked.

"None of them look related to me," I mused.

"Look at how they're interacting," Gemma cut in. "No, neither of those women is his sister. And no, Per, you may not have another woman, too."

My mouth hung open in confusion. Where had she gotten the idea I would even want two women? She was enough of a handful already!

Gilbert burst out laughing, and behind me, I heard Tor or Marcus cackling as well.

The seven of us traveled east, on horses borrowed from King Leudon's stables. Another nine men rode behind us and would take our horses back to the hillfort upon our arrival at the coast, five miles away. Naturally, clouds had rolled in during the night, and I glanced up at the sky periodically as we rode, half expecting it to start raining on us.

We made it to the coast of the northern sea in barely an hour and transferred our belongings from our horses' saddles and onto a long boat that a couple of other men had prepared for us. Gawain and his men took up the oars on one side of the boat, and my men and I took the other side. Gemma sat beside the sail and prepared to work it. Thankfully, I had a chance to teach her to work a sail with my section when we'd conducted our reconnaissance of the Scoti fleet a while back, and now she enjoyed sailing whenever opportunity arose.

If all went well, we would sail wide around the jagged coast for the better part of the day, beach our boat for the night somewhere to the north, then reach the fortress or monastery or whatever exactly Dun Fhoithear was sometime late the next day, if the winds favored us. We loaded enough supplies for close to a week. All we had to do was hope that the Grail was indeed still there, and that we would be able to find it, and that it would be intact. The more I thought about it, the more I couldn't help but see Medraut's argument that we were on a fool's errand. But as Myrddin had said, our mission, if it went according to plan, should have a low risk but a very high payoff should we succeed.

We rowed out of the small inlet and out onto the sea, finding our rhythm quickly. A short time later, Gemma raised the sail and caught a wind, and we lurched forward. There was little for us to do at that point but put away the oars and enjoy the wind at our backs and the wide-open sea around us. Only Gilbert acted uneasy at the sight, and queasy from the rocking of our boat upon the waves.

"I thought you Saxons were supposed to be good at sea," Marcus chortled. "You look like you're going to be sick. This isn't as bad as that storm we faced on the way up to Dal Riata."

"Saxons don't spend any more time at sea than most other people. They only had to be able to cross the sea once, to get from Germania to Britain. And my Frisian family made that crossing two generations ago," Gilbert countered. He did indeed look nearly ready to throw up, I noted with sympathy, but at least he felt well enough to correct Marcus's generalization of his heritage.

"I lived my entire life at Caer Badon," Gilbert continued. "That's more than twenty miles from the sea. What cause did I ever have to put myself through this misery? I've been at sea more times since joining Arthur's cavalry than I have my entire life."

I chuckled at the irony of Gilbert's situation.

Marcus laughed too. "I grew up in Caer Londin, until my father grew tired of living under Oisc's rule and moved our family west, to Gwent. So I've always lived close enough to the sea to piss in it nearly from my doorstep."

"I never want to spend another day at sea after this trip," Gilbert groaned.

I frowned, recalling something he'd told me once before. "I thought you Frisians all lived right along the coast of northern Germania. Didn't you tell me once that your people in particular were *rulers of the sea?*"

Gilbert shot me a baleful glare, then finally leaned over the edge of the boat and vomited. When he was done, he pulled out his canteen and rinsed his mouth out before turning back to me.

"I never said that," he grunted.

"I seem to recall that you did, too, "Gemma chipped in with a mischievous smile.

"Both of you can *swive* off," Gilbert muttered hoarsely, while the rest of us broke into laughter at his expense.

"Don't give them any ideas," Tor snickered, which caused Gemma to blush.

The weather worsened as the hours wore on. The waves became choppier, and the wind blew harder. God be praised, the wind stayed at our backs for the first part of the day, and we made good time. We sailed past the large island at the mouth of the Firth of Forth, but had trouble maintaining our heading as time wore on. Still, we continued on, to Gilbert's dismay.

By early that evening, it began to rain, and the wind shifted. We pushed on for another few hours until finally, Gawain decided to make for the shore.

"We would have needed to go ashore in the next couple of hours anyway," Gawain informed us, studying the dark clouds. "We may as well use this wind and veer west now."

We did so, and within the hour, we were approaching the coastline again. We saw the distant shapes of roundhouses and realized that we were heading roughly towards a small Picti village. From his seat in the front left side of the boat, Gawain gestured off to the left of it.

"I see trees in the distance," he called out to us, shouting to be heard over the rain, wind, and waves. "We'll beach there, carry our packs inland, and make camp in the cover of those woods."

We nodded or waved to let him know we heard him, then started working the oars, while Gemma brought the sail down. I saw at least one rock outcrop off to our right, some thirty paces away. I prayed silently to God that there weren't any more such rocks in our path, waiting to rip our boat to shreds. Our boat rose and fell with every wave as we got closer to shore with each passing moment. Every time our boat dropped, I felt myself tense up, afraid that it would be met by a submerged rock. I recited the Lord's prayer in my head and focused on rowing. On her own initiative, Gemma stood up, tightly clutching the mast, and chanted a song for us in a strong, clear voice. I didn't know the words, for she sang in her native Gaelic language, but the rhythm helped keep us in time with each other as we pulled on the oars. That gave me something else to focus on besides the threat of submerged rocks.

Before I knew it, we were at the beach, and Gawain hopped out, hitting the water with a loud splash. He grabbed the boat's bow and dragged it toward the shore. I quickly followed his lead, and together we hauled the boat onto the windswept shingle. Thunder rolled and lightning flashed once, a long way off. Everyone hopped out of the boat, quickly grabbed their packs, and shouldered them.

"What about the boat?" Marcus asked. "If the Picts see it in the morning, we could have a problem."

"Well, it's too big to carry off, especially with our packs." Gawain shrugged. "It's a chance we'll have to take."

Marcus nodded, and we set off into the woods, nearly a quarter of a mile inland, with Gawain in the lead. We found a good spot, safely hidden from the village, a short time later. As quietly as we could, we gathered or broke enough tree branches to weave a small, overhead shelter together, dug out a fire pit, and one of Gawain's men got a small fire going. Ideally, of course, being less than a mile or so from a Picti village overland and less than that by water, we'd not have risked a fire. Tonight, however, we were tired, cold, and soaked to the bone. A fire wasn't simply a good idea at the moment, but a borderline necessity. So we risked it, but did what we could to mitigate the risk of discovery. Everyone huddled around it for some time until we were at least tolerably dry.

We ate a bit of dried meat and some cheese while we dried off, then Gawain set up a watch. Two men on guard in two-hour shifts. He generously put me on the first shift, and himself on the second. And I do mean *generously*. I've heard bards tell stories of heroes who volunteered to take a first watch as if it were some grand gesture. It's not. First watch is the easiest. Everyone is already awake. Then once you do go to sleep, you have the entire rest of the night to sleep, uninterrupted. Even the last watch of a rotation isn't bad. Yes, you have to wake up earlier than the others, but once again, you get to sleep nearly all the way through the night. It's the middle watches that nobody wants, because then you're woken up, probably from a deep slumber, and have to force yourself to wake up and be alert for an hour or two. The middle of the night is also when it's usually the coldest, and a body most yearns to be bundled up in a nice warm blanket. And Gawain, a prince and the leader of our group, who by rights didn't even need to take a shift, had volunteered for that shift. My respect for the man went up several notches.

We went to sleep quickly, and it felt like I'd barely closed my eyes when Gawain was prodding my feet with his own. I looked up at him blearily and yawned.

"What's the situation look like this morning?" I asked and rubbed sand from my eyes.

"It's still stormy," he said quietly, looking down at me. "Rain stopped an hour ago at least. I've a feeling it will be like this all day, though. We may have to decide whether to wait it out or continue overland. We've crossed the Firth, which was the biggest obstacle in our way. We should only be twenty to thirty miles from Fhiothear."

I nodded and proceeded to pull my shoes on. We had all slept fully clothed aside from our shoes in order to get them fully dried out, and so we could be ready immediately in case of trouble. Unsurprisingly, only Gemma hadn't woken up. She still lay curled up in a thick wool blanket near the fire pit. I chuckled, noticing the thin trickle of drool that leaked from her mouth. Then I noticed, in the distance, the faint sound of sheep bleating.

Gawain noticed me cock my head up towards the village and nodded. "A bit after the rain stopped, someone moved a small flock of sheep into the clearing out there."

I nodded. "Will we be able to get to our boat without being seen? Where there's sheep, there's shepherds".

"Possibly. This weather will keep most people inside if they don't have to be out and about. If we move quickly enough, even if we are spotted, it will only likely be by one or two people. By the time they rouse anyone who might care enough to confront us, we could be back out to sea."

"I'd just as soon chance the sea," I said. "If we walk, never mind the added time, we'll be having to watch out for Picts the entire time. We're a lot safer if we can get back out on the water."

"It's settled then," Gawain decided. "We'll try to continue on. But we'll need to be ready to go back to shore if the weather gets any worse than it is now."

I agreed, appreciating the fact that he was even including me in the planning, rather than simply ordering me to simply follow his lead. Together we briefed our men, after I woke up Gemma, who groaned and gave me an evil glare upon first opening her eyes and muttered something at me in her native language. I didn't understand it, and decided I was probably better off not knowing anyway.

Once we were packed up and ready to go, we headed out. Myself and the two men Gawain brought who had bows now strung them so they were ready for quick use if needed, and we headed out to the beach at a brisk walk. Sheep were scattered about in small clusters, walking around and grazing on the tall, wet grass. There were several small lambs running around and playing too. These didn't shuffle away from us like the older sheep did.

We'd gone about two hundred paces when I saw the grass moving a few feet in front of me, and looked down to see a large adder slithering across my path. I yelped in surprise, and acting purely on reflex, I drew my sword, and swept it down onto the foul creature, cutting it in half. The two parts squirmed and slithered, causing me to leap away in revulsion.

I heard a high-pitched cry from off to my left. I spun to face the sound, as did my companions, and there, not ten paces away, was a small boy, wearing a long tunic and no trousers, staring at us in wide-eyed dismay. He pointed up at me and began blabbering something I couldn't understand. Gemma did.

"He thinks you killed one of his sheep," she growled.

"Forget the bloody sheep, we need to go!" Gawain snapped.

Then, from the closest house, a man and a woman emerged into the field. The woman wore a simple dress, while the man wore only a pair of checkered trousers. He had an axe in his hand, though. They saw us and began shouting. The woman looked to be yelling and gesturing for the boy to come to them, while the man brandished his axe and began to dash about, alerting the rest of the village.

Gawain swore, and without needing to be told, we picked up the pace. We still had a good three hundred paces to go over open ground before we reached the shore and our boat. I looked back, saw Gemma struggling to keep up, under the weight of her pack, and grabbed her hand, pulling her along with me.

We didn't make it. Half-dressed they may have been, but villagers poured from their houses armed with whatever they had within easy reach. In the short time it took us to reach the boats, gasping for breath, about thirty men and older boys were there, arranged before us, armed with axes, spears, and farming tools.

"We can cut this rabble down," Gilbert said, letting his large pack fall to the ground.

One by one, the others followed his lead. Owain barked something to the villagers in their own language. An older man stepped up to him, answering in equally harsh tones, pointing and gesturing at us, and then to the flock of sheep we'd just run past. More words were exchanged, and Gawain drew his blade, as did the rest of our men. I nocked an arrow but kept it held low and ready for use.

Then Gemma was there, pushing my arm down still lower, and she strode between our two groups. She also began speaking rapid-fire at the villagers and gestured to me. There was more talking, but whatever she was saying calmed them down.

"You understand her," Gawain asked quietly to me.

"No, sir," I admitted. "I've picked up a few phrases in their tongue, but mostly I've been teaching her Latin."

Switching to Latin himself, Gawain continued. "She's telling them you saved one of their lambs from that snake."

My eyebrows rose in surprise, which gave way to admiration at her quick thinking.

One of the villagers jogged away, heading back toward the woods where I'd killed the adder. Gemma continued to talk with them for a moment before turning to us.

"These people are Taexali. Some of them fought for King Drest. Some of them still do. But like a lot of other tribes, they aren't especially happy with him. Especially after he got so many killed two years ago. They're also Christian," she added with some emphasis. "The people of this village have been mostly Christianized from the work of the missionaries who came here years ago."

Again, my eyebrows rose in surprise. I looked over to Gawain, who was watching the villagers with increased interest. He also now held his sword down, almost casually. We were also still on edge until the villager came back. Eventually, he did, with the boy running along beside him, and the two halves of the adder in his hands. He was smiling broadly.

The Picts, Gemma, and Gawain started talking again, and Gawain turned to us. "Put your weapons away." He shook his head, clearly amused, and turned to me. "Peredur, you've just earned us the hospitality of these people," he chuckled. "Between you killing that snake and saving that lamb..." He gave Gemma a wry smile, "and the Chi Rho they saw on your shield, they see it as an omen of God triumphing over the Devil, or some such thing. They're saying it's a sign from God that Drest's reign will end, and Christianity will be able to thrive here again."

I grinned back. "I like the sound of that omen," I said as I put my handful of arrows back in my quiver. The tension of the moment eased, and everyone else put their own weapons away. The Picts did as well. They led us to the village, laughing and chattering, with Gemma and Gawain translating. They confirmed that the monastery we were looking for was thirty miles north of us. We built a large lean-to out of a spare sail from our boat against one wall of the village elder's home which was the largest in the village. Gawain paid him in silver for one of their pigs, as well, which we slaughtered and roasted. The wind picked up, blowing in a southern direction, making travel by sea completely impractical, so we settled in and prepared to stay the night at the village.

With nothing better to do while we waited out the storm, Gawain took advantage of this unexpected source of knowledge and questioned the village elder on the situation north of the Firth. It turned out, King Drest had indeed become very busy over the past year, recruiting young men, forcing villages all over to pay tribute, and boasting of how he was going to bleed the Gododdin dry, even if outright conquest may not be possible.

"How recently have you seen him?" Gawain asked between bites of his roasted pork.

"Last week," the elder replied, to the astonishment of our group.

"How many men does he have?" Gawain pressed him.

"Hundreds," the old man said after a moment.

Well now, that wasn't as bad as we'd feared it would be, but that still sounded like Drest had amassed quite a large force. There were kingdoms in the south that would crumble under the weight of that size of a force, especially if it were led by a competent leader, which Drest was.

Gawain frowned. "I don't understand how he's able to field such a force. The amount of weapons and armor needed, the food he would need in order to equip them, should have been nearly impossible to produce, especially so soon after his defeat at Guinnion's Fort."

Right then, I wished more than anything that I could provide that answer to him, but as always, there was the problem of how he would react should I accuse his own brother without any evidence to back it up. I filled my mouth with food to help resist telling Gawain what I knew, regardless of the risk. Thinking of Medraut also sapped me of a bit of the contentment I felt sitting here against the village elder's home, enjoying the juicy meat of the hog we'd butchered. I had a bad feeling that he was out here as well, somewhere.

The day wore on. Children came and gawked at us, particularly Gilbert, much to his amusement. He made faces and funny noises at them, which caused them to burst out into fits of giggles and laughter. It rained for a bit late in the afternoon, and everyone left us alone and went inside their own homes. When it stopped, towards sunset, I saw the elder and a man about my age, his son maybe, bring a black stallion with excellent muscle tone out into the field. I saw immediately that the horse didn't act fully tamed. He kept tugging and pulling at the lead and snorting.

When the young man tried mounting the stallion, and he sidestepped away, my suspicions were confirmed. To the growing interest and amusement of our group, the young man tried again and again to mount and then stay mounted on the stallion's back. On the rare occasion the horse allowed him to climb up, usually with the help and distraction of the elder, the young man didn't stay mounted for long. The stallion almost immediately bucked him off, or spun and pranced around in tight circles until he went tumbling.

"Look at those barbarians," Tor chuckled in Latin. "That's not how you train a new horse for riding."

"No, it's not," I sighed, responding in Brythonic. These Picts were skipping a whole lot of groundwork, where the horse being trained is led around first, then gets used to the weight of a saddle, and then finally came actually riding it. And that should have happened while the horse was younger than this one, as I did with Carys. My father would likely have a heart failure if he saw how these villagers were attempting to break in this stallion.

After what must have been nearly an hour, the two finally gave up and led the horse back to a corral attached to the rear portion of the large roundhouse. Gilbert and some of the others whistled and cheered their approval for the entertainment they'd been given. The young man flashed us a wry grin and waved at us as he limped away.

"I bet I could ride him," I mused quietly, though not quietly enough. Marcus heard me and cocked his head toward me. "You think so? How sure are you?"

"Pretty sure," I replied.

"Sure enough to place a wager on it?"

I laughed. "A wager? With what? I've no coin on me. Neither do you."

"We do back at Caer Lleon. I'll bet you wouldn't last to the count of... eight on that black devil's back."

"That's oddly specific," I smiled.

Marcus shrugged. "I just spit out a number. But I like it. Eight bits of silver if you can ride that stallion until a count of eight."

I glanced over at Gemma, who'd been close enough to hear the conversation. We weren't married yet, but I learned some time ago that she was much more frugal with coin than I was. By heeding her advice, the tidy sum of silver I'd earned from the loot I'd taken at Guinnion's Fort and the Caer Ligion had grown substantially over the past year and a half, so I practically regarded my small fortune as *ours*.

"Eight bits of silver?" She thought it over. "Are you sure you can do it, Per?"

"I am," I replied with growing confidence.

"Go for it then. We can afford the loss if you're wrong. And either way, it will be entertaining," she smiled at me.

"Well then," I said, returning her smile, "Why don't we go and see the village elder, shall we? Uh, did you get his name by any chance?"

Chapter Seventeen

THE VILLAGE ELDER, URADECH, was happy to allow me to try and ride his stallion when Gemma and I spoke with him in the morning. The young man, who I found out was indeed his son, was even more so. We didn't get into the details of how he'd acquired the horse in the first place. It was one of only three others in the village. What we did find out was that they'd been unable to tame him in the months that he'd been in their possession, and Uradech was even open to selling the beast if we were interested. In hindsight, that probably should have clued me in regarding how my morning was going to go, but I was confident in my abilities with horses and focused on the possibility of winning Marcus' silver. So while Gawain and the others refilled their canteens, ate some more of the boar we'd roasted last night, and made ready to return to our boat, I prepared to ride that stallion, with his consent.

"It's still pretty windy, and I don't like the look of those clouds out there. I'd prefer not to get back out on the water today," Gawain said. "So you have my blessing,"

"They've skipped a few steps, but I'd certainly like to try," I told him, and he wished me luck as he went back to packing.

For this occasion, I wore my helmet and padded tunic, along with my dagger. I left my coat of mail and sword baldric with Gemma. Uradech brought the horse out and I walked up to him, talking quietly and calming. They'd put a bridle on him, though he had no saddle. A fresh feeling of annoyance flared up. This poor horse should have already been used to a saddle before anyone ever tried riding him. I almost felt guilty at volunteering to try riding him myself, but I'd seen how rough the chief and his son had been with the stallion, and I hoped that maybe, if I were a bit more gentle, I could succeed where they had not. The real problem of course was that I had no idea how long they'd been treating this stallion the way they were.

The black stallion, who stood a solid thirteen hands tall, turned to regard me, ears forward as I approached. When I got within arm's reach of him, he sidestepped away. I continued to make soothing noises, and let the stallion get used to my scent, and the sound of my voice. After a bit, I nodded to the village elder who backed off a pace. I moved around to the stallion's flank, braced for anything, and jumped up onto his back and held onto the reins. He snorted and stomped the ground with his hooves.

My cymbrogi, lined up along the wooden fence, began pounding the railing rhythmically. "One. Two. Three..." they chanted. There was a moment of calm, and then I felt the stallion's muscles bunch before he began spinning around and jumping.

I clamped my legs around the stallion's flanks and held on for all I was worth until after what felt like scarcely more than the span of a couple of heartbeats, I was thrown clear. I hit the ground and rolled, then shakily got to my feet.

"You got to six. You almost made it," Marcus cheerfully called out.

I groaned. "We didn't specify how many attempts I could have," I pointed out.

Marcus scowled.

"You're right, you didn't," Gemma chimed in with a smug smile.

'Best out of three then?" Marcus asked.

"Agreed," I replied.

We shook hands, and then I walked back up to the stallion. Again, I stood in front of him and let him see and smell me, and hear my voice. Then I walked around to his side, grabbed a tuft of his mane, and leapt onto his back. There was no moment of calm this time. My backside made contact with his back and then he threw his hindquarters high into the air, and his head arched down. I went flying over his head and slammed to the ground, though I was experienced enough to at least roll as I landed.

As I lay there, trying to catch my breath, I heard Marcus' braying laughter, and that of the others watching. I groaned again, and probably whimpered a little as I slowly, painfully, got back up to my feet. I adjusted my clothing and shook it off, then strode back over to the stallion. This was my third, and final attempt.

"Eight," I whispered to myself. "I just need to stay on your back to the bloody count of eight..."

As I'd done the first two times, I walked up to the stallion, who flinched away and snorted at me. I stared into his eyes for a few moments and prayed. Then, for the third time, I circled around and jumped up onto his back. He pulled the same stunt on me that he did the previous time and kicked his hind legs high up into the air, but I was ready for that, and leaned back, squeezing his flanks with my legs as tight as I could.

The stallion's legs slammed back to earth, and then he began to spin, kicking and bucking intermittently. I felt like a dog's plaything, being shaken around violently every which way. But after a time, I've no idea how long, the stallion abruptly stopped. His flanks were heaving, and he was sweating. Around me, my comrades were staring wide-eyed and slack-jawed at me. I grinned at them, then looked at Marcus.

"How long have I been mounted this time?" I asked.

"Huh? Uh..." Marcus stammered.

"You made it," Gemma answered for him, and she beamed up at me.

My good, dear friend Gilbert let out a whoop of triumph at that, and the stallion bolted.

He took off so fast and so suddenly that I almost fell off. Almost. Instead, I gripped tightly to him with my legs and held onto the reins as he sped away. I tested his reaction to me tugging on the reins and of course got no response.

This stallion was too untrained to have been ready for a rider. I knew that but had tried anyway. Now I was stuck on a runaway horse's back who didn't give two figs what I wanted him to do.

At this point I had two choices as I saw it. I could find a soft patch of grass and take my chances in leaping off the horse, and probably injure myself in the process, or I could try to subtly steer him toward higher elevation to wear him out faster. I didn't particularly like either option, but to jump off meant I would be stranded somewhere, on foot, possibly injured, and without my sword. I let the stallion run and began to scan the terrain around me first to watch for any looming hills I could nudge the stallion towards, and second, to keep my bearings as to where we were. So far, it seemed that we were traveling north.

In record time, the stallion took me at least two to three miles before he slowed down. I made the mistake of trying to steer him a bit towards a hill I saw off the trail aways when he had done so. I guess he'd more or less forgotten I was even there until that point, because once I tried to guide him with the reins, as gentle as I was, that horse decided to try and buck me off of him again. He pulled his usual tricks and nearly threw me before he finally calmed down again. I made soft, comforting sounds and patted his neck, and sighed when he started running again. He wasn't going at a dead gallop this time, but close enough to it to not make much difference.

We traveled another three miles or so before that stallion and I finally reached an understanding in regards to who was in charge, and he was willing to let me guide him, most of the time. Unless I tried to guide him in a direction he didn't particularly want to go, then he ignored me. He kept going north though, which was potentially both good and bad for me. The stallion only fully stopped when we came to a river — well, more of a stream anyway, that crossed our path and flowed east toward the northern sea.

The stallion drank thirstily, and I took the opportunity to splash handfuls of water upon his flanks, partially to clean the sweat and grime from him, but also to test his reaction to the water. I considered my options again. By now I was roughly six miles north of the Picti village, by my estimate, and had been gone from the village for about half an hour. What would Gawain do in that time? Try to come after me, on foot? Wait for me to return? Or would he continue as planned and take our group north in the boat.

I decided to base my course of action on the stallion's. If he wouldn't cross this stream, then attempting to ride north with him would be problematic, in which case I was better off returning south, on foot. If the stallion was willing to carry me north to the fort, then I might make it there within a day or two. I let him graze for a bit, as I didn't have any food on me, then I slowly took his reins and walked around with him for a bit, leading him into the edge of the stream, to see how he'd react to the water. He hadn't been properly conditioned for a saddle, and definitely not for a rider, but at least he was comfortable enough being led, I noted. The same was true of the water. He enjoyed that, and pranced about, splashing me.

After a few moments, I grabbed a handful of his mane and hopped back up onto his back. The stallion reared up once, and jumped a couple times, but it seemed more of a formality for him, rather than a true desire to throw me, like his pride wouldn't let him tolerate me on his back without at least a gesture of resistance. But I was on to his tricks by now, and stayed mounted. I slowly took up the reins and guided him toward the far side of the stream and nudged his flanks with my heels. He sprang forward, as though he meant to run, but the water prevented him from speeding up as much as he might have done otherwise, as I'd hoped. The stream itself proved a perfect test for the stallion's tolerance for water, given that it was only a dozen paces wide and the water level barely came up to his chest. We crossed the stream in no time, and I decided to continue north, hoping that my disappearance wouldn't cause them to delay the mission by looking for me.

As the stallion took me closer to Dun Fhoithear with every passing hour, I considered my next move. I wore little in the way of armor, only my helm and padded tunic. Worse than that, the only weapon I had was my dagger, so even should I manage to arrive before Gawain and the others, I held no illusion that I would be able to accomplish very much on my own. Fortunately, God's grace and my unusual experiences within the Red Dragons had turned me into a rather competent scout, if I may say so. My potentially early arrival therefore might put me in a position where I could at least reconnoiter the fort, or monastery, or whatever Bishop Ninian had built, and provide Gawain with actionable information upon his arrival, presumably in the next day or two.

The black stallion was happy to set a fast pace, as though he'd forgotten how to merely walk, and as long he was still taking me north, I saw no reason to rein him in. I knew Dun Fhoithear was supposed to be along the coast, so I only had to make sure that I didn't venture too far inland and add extra miles to the journey.

We crossed over two or three more streams before coming to a particularly large river in the early afternoon. The stallion grazed and drank, while I took the time to unwind one of the legwraps I'd chosen to wear this morning and fashioned an improvised sling. Then I gathered up a handful of smooth stones along the shoreline and slipped them into the small pouch attached to my belt. Now I had a functional ranged weapon, should I run into any birds or hares.

This river was very wide, and the current looked strong, particularly after the recent rain. I decided, albeit reluctantly, that crossing so close to where the river fed into the sea was not a practical option, so I gently led the stallion west for awhile. About four miles into my detour, the river narrowed significantly, and I was able to safely cross, though I got wet again. Thank God the sun was out, for even in late Aprilis, that water was bloody cold!

Once across, we pushed on. I saw some deer once from a good distance off in between two large groves of trees. Birds flew overhead, squirrels chattered at me from the safety of tree branches as I rode past and once, I saw a brown, mountain hare, but by the time I'd loaded a stone into my sling, it had bounded away, almost as though it had sensed the imminent danger it was in. Finally, as the sun began to sink low over the horizon, we came to yet another river. The stallion nickered at me when I dismounted at the shore, looking across.

"Don't worry, boy," I said. "We aren't crossing this one. Not tonight. I want my clothing as dry as possible. Besides," I added, still looking across the slow-moving waters of this latest river, "You've probably carried me about twenty-five miles today. That's enough until tomorrow. You've earned your rest."

If Gawain's estimate was accurate, we should be at Bishop Ninian's chapel sometime later tomorrow. I needed food, I decided, so I found a spot in some trees that offered overhead shelter as well as a break from the wind and lashed the stallion's lead rope to a thin tree. With him secure, I pulled out the sling I made from my legwrap, loaded a stone into the pouch I'd fashioned, and strolled around.

The sun was getting lower and lower, and I started to worry that I wouldn't find anything before it was too dark to see when movement along a nearby tree trunk caught my eye. I looked over and saw a nice, large squirrel. Now squirrels wouldn't have been my preferred choice by any means. There's not a lot of meat on them, and what meat they do have is tough and has an odd flavor. But I hadn't eaten all day, and I still had another day of riding before I reached Fhoithear, with no idea what I would find once I got there, so I got my sling spinning. The squirrel paused in its climbing and looked straight over at me. I brought my arm forward and released the running end of my sling and the stone flew at the squirrel, killing it instantly.

I hurried over to it, then skinned and gutted it and brought the little carcass back to my campsite. In no time I had a fire pit dug out which I filled with twigs, followed by larger sticks, and then lit it with the iron striker and flint that I kept in my belt pouch. Finally, I spitted the squirrel on a long stick and cooked it up. As I'd expected, it wasn't particularly tasty, but it took the edge off my hunger. With any luck I would find a hare tomorrow, I thought. And if God decided to smile down on me, Gawain and the rest would already be at Dun Fhoithear by the time I got there, though I doubted it. The wind had been blowing hard all day, and only let up within the past hour or so. They likely wouldn't be able to get back out at sea until morning, I reasoned.

I didn't have my cloak with me that day, only my padded tunic, which did offer some comfort against the wind, but I still broke apart some tree branches and rigged up a crude shelter. Without some rope it wasn't perfect, but it was better than nothing. With nothing more to do until morning, I finally curled up near my fire pit as the flames slowly flickered out and went to sleep.

***

The clouds blew away during the chilly, Caledonian night, and I woke up shivering with cold, in spite of the sun actually being visible in the sky that was finally clear again. On top of that, my stomach growled with hunger. I also felt sore from head to toe thanks to the times that cursed stallion had bucked me off or tried his best to do so. Suffice to say, I did not begin the day in the best of moods. So rather than get back on the trail, I decided to hunt for some more food.

I kept my eye out for berries, and wasn't surprised when I didn't see many that were already ripe enough to eat. I did flush out a hare, God be praised, and once I'd dressed and cooked it, I devoured every scrap of meat I could sink my teeth into. By that time, the sun was fully over the eastern horizon, and it was warming up. I crouched down at the river's edge and scooped up handfuls of water until I was sated. Hopefully, back at that village, Gawain and the others were headed north. In the meantime, I sighed, I had yet another bloody river to get across.

That large river I'd camped beside ended up being the last major river I had to cross on my second day, though there were a couple more small streams. Those were narrow and shallow, however, and caused me no issues. The stallion was also more cooperative today. Sure, he whinnied and stamped his feet a bit when

I first hopped on his back, but he got into the rhythm of things quickly enough once we got going.

The sun was out and my clothing dried off quickly enough. We made good time, and by late that afternoon, as I rode north along the coast, I saw what had to be Bishop Ninian's chapel.

At first, it simply looked like a cluster of buildings, built on a headland that jutted out a bit further than the rest of the coast. But as I got closer, my eyes widened and I let out a low whistle in awe of the place.

Just as Gawain had described to us on our day at sea together, the chapel was built upon the most perfect, defensive ground imaginable. More than that, it was breathtaking. I halted my stallion simply to gaze up at what I could only regard as a colossal, God-sized boulder that absolutely dominated the entire landscape. It wasn't quite an island, for it did connect to the rest of the coastline by at least one narrow land bridge, but that was it, as far as I could see. Not only that, but the headland's sides were sheer rock and looked nearly impossible to scale. I imagined what a nightmare it would be to assault such a position, were it properly defended, then just as quickly, I prayed to the Christ that it was not, for the sake of my mission here.

I continued on toward Ninian's chapel on the headland and made out a cluster of buildings. One, further back and closer to the sea, looked to be stone. A little while later I found a narrow path leading up to the site. It dipped down sharply, almost to sea level, then back up. Even this path could have been easily defended, for a naturally formed, tall, narrow rock wall lined the right-hand side of it. At the far end, someone had built a large wooden gatehouse. The gates themselves were smashed in, and as I rode up, I saw a pair of skeletons in tattered, soiled clothing littering the ground beyond it. One of the skulls cloven almost in half.

I considered turning back then. I was in no shape for a fight, if this place was occupied, but considering the state of the gatehouse, I reasoned that it might be abandoned, so looking around shouldn't be a problem.

The entryway was tall enough that I was able to pass through it without dismounting, and the trail continued upward, though now it was cut deep into the ground, so that earthen walls lined the path. A shiver went down my spine as I imagined an attacking force attempting to breach this entry. They would be unable to form any formation whatsoever in this narrow corridor, and defenders would be able to line the walkway along both sides from above, loosing arrows, slingstones, or thrusting down with spears. In two spots, the trail went straight through tunnels that hid the walkway in shadow. I rode through the first of them with no issue, but at the second of them, the ground erupted into a flurry of movement and the sound of flapping wings as a small flock of birds, unseen due to the shadows, abruptly took to the sky at our approach.

The black stallion reared back, nearly throwing me. I swore and made the mistake of reflexively tightening my hold on his reins as I squeezed my legs around his flanks. He reared again and tried to turn around, but the narrow confines of the trail prevented him from doing so. Unable to flee the way we'd come, the stallion shot forward at a gallop. Now fear shot through me as well, for I had seen how small this landmass was, and how high over the shore it was. There was little space for a panicked horse to run up here, so the moment the entryway gave way to open ground I hastily made the sign of the cross, then leapt off his back. I landed hard, and rolled with the momentum, then sat up, momentarily dazed.

I watched the stallion race to the edge of the headland, then turn sharply away before continuing on, galloping in a wide loop around the clearing, which was surprisingly flat now that I'd reached the summit. I sighed, grateful that neither my brother Lamorac, nor my father, Lord Pelinor had been here to see me. Both would have undoubtedly been full of criticism in how I should have been better prepared and handled the stallion better. I supposed I'd become too accustomed to my beloved mare Carys' easy-going nature and grown a bit complacent.

I stood up with a groan and checked myself over for any injuries that might require some attention. Once I was satisfied that bruises were all I'd sustained

I surveyed the ground around me. Off to the right was a long, narrow building that looked to be a stable, made of wattle and daub. Ahead of me was the stone chapel I'd seen from a distance, and to the left of that was another cluster of wattle and daub buildings that I assumed had been living quarters.

My hand rested on the grip of my dagger as I methodically looked over each building, searching for any threats. When I saw none, I relaxed a bit and did another, slower scan, simply looking for any signs of habitation. Again, I saw nothing. It looked as though this place had been abandoned for years.

The thatch roofs of the buildings had caved in and were rotting away. Tall weeds grew inside the openings of those buildings I could see into. An amusing thought of being able to locate the Grail myself and be relaxing by a fire with it by the time Gawain and the others showed up crossed my mind and I smiled.

I checked on the stallion again, who had stopped running by now and returned to me, though he stopped a few feet away. I suppose he was finally feeling comfortable at least having me nearby. I walked over to him, scanned the area one more time, then gently removed the bit from his mouth.

"Go ahead and relax, boy," I told the horse, speaking softly. "We'll likely be here awhile."

I tucked the bit into my belt, then after a moment, decided I may as well begin looking through the building I had determined was the stable. Not that I expected to find anything valuable or useful there, but it never hurt to be thorough. So I walked over to the building, which predictably smelled of rotting thatch and slowly shifted debris around with my foot until I'd searched from one end of the structure to the other. As I expected, I found nothing except the cracked and broken end of a wooden staff, which had probably been the handle of a pitchfork or some other such tool.

As I searched, I kept getting a nagging feeling that I was being watched. I stopped periodically and turned around, scanning the black, empty windows and doorways of the other buildings that were within my line of sight, but I never saw anything, other than the black stallion of course. He was in fact looking at me from time to time, and once, even came over to me, seemingly out of curiosity. I gave him a pat on his neck, which he tolerated for a moment before scooting away.

From the stables, I walked over to the cluster of other buildings. A deep well had been dug out in an area I thought somewhat resembled a courtyard. I peered down into it, saw that it held water, and continued on with my search. As I expected, they were in a poor state. Next, I walked up to what I assumed was the chapel. A door was still mounted on its hinges, though it was splintered and broken. I pushed it open and stepped inside.

Enough of the roof remained intact that, except for a spot where sunlight streamed through a hole in the center, the rest of the interior appeared as black as night. What bit of the chapel that was immediately visible was a few benches and the wooden beams of the floorboards. Off to my right, I heard water splashing. I turned to look in that direction, and once my eyes adjusted to the dark, I gasped in surprise. In the far end of the chapel, a woman with long, wet, blond hair was squatting beside a bucket full of water, with her back to me. She wore nothing but a threadbare linen shift which clung wetly to her, and her clothing was draped over a nearby broken wooden bench.

Upon my entry, she spun around with a startled yelp and fell over backwards onto the floor. She started up at me, wide-eyed.

"Who are you?" We both exclaimed in unison.

Chapter Eighteen

THE WOMAN MADE NO effort to cover herself. I suppose she was simply as surprised to see me as I was to see her. I came to my senses quickly, and spun around to put my back to her, feeling my face burning from embarrassment.

"I'm Peredur, of Caer Gurcoc. I apologize for uh, intruding upon you like this. Who are you?" I asked again.

Behind me, the woman giggled. "I am Angharad. I come from a village not far from here. I like to visit this place from time to time. It's peaceful here. And I gather herbs to sell at home."

"Peaceful?" I echoed and thought about the skeletons I'd seen at the gate. "This place is a desolate, abandoned fortress."

I heard the rustle of fabric, and water dripping on the floorboards, as if someone were wringing out a wet cloth.

"Yes. It is now. I used to live here as a little girl though, back when a few monks and Christian Picts lived here. I have fond memories of this place."

As she was speaking, I removed my helmet and padded cap, and ran my fingers through my sweaty hair. Her explanation puzzled me. On the surface, her statement sounded reasonable, but too much about it also sounded... off.

"How did you get here? Did you bring food and water with you? Traveling gear?" I asked her, still staring at the wall, and resisting the urge to turn around.

"I came by boat. There's a trail up the side of the cliff, if you know where to look. I have food and mead with me. Enough to share with you, if you're needing something."

Before I could utter a word, my stomach growled loudly. I'd not eaten since early that morning after all, and now it was so late in the afternoon that the sun was beginning to set.

Angharad heard the noise as well, and laughed again.

"I have bread and cheese in a basket over against the wall. It's a bit stale, but it's still good food," she said and I heard her pad over to stand behind me. A combination of feeling uncomfortable with any stranger standing right behind me and assuming that she'd dressed herself caused me to turn around and then immediately look up at the rotting thatch roof when I realized that she definitely had not.

Angharad snickered at my reaction. "Why, Peredur of Caer Gurcoc," she teased. "You're not afraid of women, are you?"

I cleared my throat, and did my best to control my embarrassment. "Afraid? No. But you're, ah, indecent."

"I am as God made me," she said dismissively. "There's surely nothing indecent about that, is there? Anyway, my clothes are drying. I hate wearing wet things."

As badly as I wanted to look at her, warning bells were also going off in my head. Even assuming she was some barbarian, she was being too bold, too fast. And what if Gemma ever found out I'd been in a room, alone, with a woman while she was undressed? It certainly wouldn't matter to her if the woman was a barbarian and didn't have the same sense of modesty as civilized, Christian folk ought to have.

"Well, you can keep staring at the ceiling if you'd like, but while my clothes dry, I'm going to eat," the woman said, and I heard the boards creak from her weight as she walked to the far end of the room, then smelled the aroma of the food as she pulled it out of her pack. "You're welcome to join me, or not," she said around a mouthful of food.

God's blood but I was hungry! If she had no modesty, why should I fight so hard to respect it? I began to rationalize in my head. As I considered joining her, if only for a quick bite of that food, my eyes wandered from the ceiling and back over to the opposite end of the chapel from where the blond barbarian woman sat. Then my brows furrowed and I squinted into the darkness, looking closer at the floor. Maybe it was my imagination, but it looked like there was a doorway built into it. I stared harder, and took a step forward to take a better look when, behind me I heard a sigh, then something slid across the floor toward me. I looked down and saw a wineskin near my feet.

"There I'm covered again," Angharad said, sounding a little petulant. "Have a drink with me. Tell me about yourself. I told you why I'm here. What about you? I never see anyone out here."

I bent down and picked up the skin, pulled the stopper out and sniffed. The mead did smell good, and I was thirsty so I tried a bit, and winced. It was sack mead, I realized; mead made with a higher ratio of honey to water than was normal. It was sweeter, and more potent than the regular stuff. I risked a glance over at her and saw that she had indeed put her shift back on at least, to my relief. She also had her own wineskin and was taking pulls from it in between bits of food, but if the mead was affecting her, she gave no indication of it. Angharad came over and sat down at a bench nearby, and wordlessly offered me a chunk of bread that she tore from a small loaf. I took it gratefully but remained standing.

"I came here looking for something. A lost Christian relic," I told the woman in between bites of the bread. She was correct, it was a bit hard but still tasted good.

"Oh? You came all the way up here, by yourself?" she asked.

"Yes, though not entirely by choice," I admitted, and told her how I'd become separated from my group the previous morning.

She chuckled at my story and leaned toward me, with one arm resting on the back of the bench. This caused her shift to tighten in places, and I squirmed in my seat, looking away from her, and back towards the dark corner of the building where I'd been looking earlier. It was growing even darker, as the sun went down. If I didn't investigate this building soon, it would be too dark to do so before morning.

I walked over to the corner and began moving dirt and rotted clumps of thatch out of the way.

"What's so interesting about that floor?" The blond woman asked.

I kept at my work, trying to pinpoint the outline of the doorway I was becoming more and more sure was there. I also noticed something else that suddenly got my attention. The dirt in this area didn't look as old as it did in other places. I frowned, trying to understand why.

"I think there's a door or something here," I mused. "But this dirt looks wrong..." my voice trailed off and I glanced casually at the blond woman, who was giving me an overly bored look.

"I've been here for days. I was about ready to go back to my village. Come on back to the bench and sit with me. Tell me about your home, Caer Gurcoc you said? I've never heard of it," she said.

I chuckled. "No, I wouldn't expect you have."

A thought hit me then and I glanced past the woman and over to her dress, which she still hadn't put back on over her shift. Her clothes were dirty. Sure, it was possible they'd only gotten that way from her traveling. But a young woman deciding to come out here by herself didn't sound right to me. Adding that with her story of having lived here as a child and things simply weren't adding up. These buildings looked too run-down to have been in use only ten or fifteen years ago, though it was possible.

An uneasy feeling came over me, and a verse from King Solomon's Proverbs popped into my head then. "With much seductive speech she persuades him; with her smooth talk she compels him. All at once he follows her, as an ox goes to the slaughter..."

After a bit more work, I had the corner cleared enough to confirm my suspicions. "That is a door built into the floor," I declared.

"Probably just a cellar to keep food in. And it's probably infested with hordes of rats," Angharad said with a shudder.

I ignored her and bent down, running my fingers along the edges of the door. There was no latch that I could see, or handle of any kind, so I pulled out my dagger and dug into the seam. Soon enough, I was able to slip the blade into it and pried carefully at it, half afraid I would break or bend my dagger. The door slowly creaked open, and cool air wafted up from the depths below, along with a faintly musty odor.

Stairs, carved out of the earth led down into the space, and I peered down, but wasn't surprised to see that it was too dark to make out anything, so I pushed the door all the way open, then scrounged around for a board from one of the broken benches. I pulled out my striker and flint, and a handful of rotted thatching and strode outside. The sun had all but set now, and only a faint orange glow lit the western horizon.

Angharad came out to watch me as I worked to get a small fire started. She'd finally thrown her cloak around her shoulders, though still, oddly, she still hadn't put her dress on over her shift, I noticed.

"Careful with that," she cautioned me. "One errant spark and this place will burn down around us."

"Just… making a torch," I acknowledged her as a spark from my striker finally lit the handful of thatch. I stuck the board I'd found into the small fire, and it lit. The piece of wood, by itself, was a poor torch of course, but it would do for now. I wanted to take a look in that cellar, or whatever was under the chapel. Now was as good a time as any, the way I figured.

With the glow of my feeble torch in hand, I carefully descended the steps with mounting excitement. I knew I shouldn't expect anything, but I couldn't help it. Maybe I would find the Grail in the next few moments! I had a general idea of what I was looking for. Gawain had told us it was a limestone cup. At the time that it had been obtained by his family, it had been stored in an old, ornate chest to keep the cup safe from breaking, as limestone was known to do.

The room was barely more than a cave, from what I could tell as I slowly walked around. A few wooden shelves lined the walls, which had also been supported by timber, though bare dirt and rock was visible behind the beams. The same was true of the ceiling, I observed, which was also barely high enough for me to fully stand upright. The room was small, no more than about ten feet wide and twenty feet in length. At the far end was a large statue of a cross, carved out of stone. It had intricate knotwork decorating the interior, and a nimbus where the two beams of the cross met.

I moved over to it, and noticed another statue beside it. It was smaller and had been knocked over onto its side. Like the cross, this one, carved into the image of a bearded and robed man, was also stone. At first, I assumed it was a representation of Jesus, until I looked closer, and the light of my torch shone on an inscription.

"Pelagius," I murmured, reading the Latin inscription. I thought hard back to my lessons. The name was familiar. He'd been a Brittonic Christian scholar of some sort who died during the reign of the Western Roman Emperor Honorius, as I recalled. He had some disagreement with the Holy Church, in Rome, in regards to whether mankind had truly free will, were considered sinful from the moment of birth or not, and a few other matters. His teachings had become quite popular around the turn of the previous century, then the Church had deemed them heretical, and apparently excommunicated him. They even sent Bishop Germanus, the man who brought the Grail here, to Britain, to ensure that the clergy here weren't endorsing Pelagianism.

"Guess they missed a spot," I mused, looking at the statue.

I looked around a bit more, but saw nothing that looked like the Grail, or anything that could contain it, so after one last look at the statues, I headed back up the steps and out of the cellar.

Angharad was where I'd left her, on a bench near the cellar door. Only now she was laying down, wrapped up in a blanket, and using her rolled-up dress as a pillow. Her eyes were closed, so I quietly walked past her and out of the chapel. Once outside, I checked on the stallion who seemed to still be enjoying himself, then I strolled over to one of the other buildings near to the chapel. This one had a stone foundation and then was built up with wattle and daub. It had clearly been living quarters, and had bed frames, furniture and other items inside. Something small scurried away from me when I stepped inside. Shreds of cloth, chewed up wooden utensils, and other things littered the floor, along with rat droppings.

I was loathe to sleep in such a place, but it was too cold and windy to sleep outside, and I didn't trust that blond woman enough to sleep in the same building as her, so I pushed some stuff aside, made myself as comfortable as I could, and went to sleep in a corner of the building facing the doorway.

***

The sound of a woman calling my name snapped me out of my slumber and I yawned as I slowly came to my senses. Birds sang in the distance, and something skittered about, much closer than I'd prefer. I stood up and stretched, groaning at the stiffness in my muscles from having slept curled up in a ball from the night's chill, and the hard-packed dirt of the floor. I yawned and walked over to the chapel, where Angharad stood, looking around. She jumped a little when she saw me emerge.

"Finally wearing your dress, I see," I commented.

"It got cold." Angharad grinned at me and shrugged. "I'm practical like that."

"Glad to hear it," I remarked, with a half-smile, then asked, "So, how much longer do you figure to be here?"

"How long do you plan on being here?" She responded. "You've no food, no water, not even a blanket."

"Oh, I'm not worried about that," I waved a dismissive hand. "My cymbrogi should be arriving sometime today. They'll have my belongings."

"To search for that relic you mentioned," she nodded. "Is it valuable, then?"

I regarded her for a moment, then responded carefully. "It would be, to certain people. To many, it would be an utterly worthless cup. And after five hundred years, if whoever handled it wasn't careful, it might break."

"Five hundred years?" Angharad asked in surprise.

I nodded. "Give or take, yes."

We talked a bit while she shared some of her food and more of that strong sack mead she'd brought along. As we ate, I wrestled with whether or not to continue searching for the Grail, or wait for my friends to arrive. In the end, I decided that there weren't that many buildings here, and that it would be amusing if I could already have the Grail in hand by the time they appeared, which I estimated would be some time that afternoon.

Angharad expressed concern that I would fall down some hole and break my leg, or get swarmed by rats, adders, or other such things, but I was determined to continue my search. I began with the ground-level buildings, since the sun was up. I reasoned that I would need a torch to check any sub-level rooms I found no matter when I happened to search them, so I may as well make use of the sun while I had it.

I started with the chapel itself. There was a small, stone dais, where a statue may have once stood, but it was gone now. Unlike the one below, the cross here must have been valuable enough to have been carted off by someone. It took about an hour of carefully moving benches, pieces of benches, and checking floorboards to be satisfied that the Grail wasn't in the chapel. So much for the obvious place.

Though I hoped I didn't see it, I also kept my eye out for broken crates, or pieces of chiseled limestone. That did make me wonder though, if the legend about its miraculous abilities were true. If it broke, would it still have its powers? What if it broke in half for example? Could both pieces be taken to different places and each be capable of causing miracles? Or what if I found it in a hundred pieces? Or — what if the Grail would lose any miraculous powers if it were chipped or cracked at all, assuming it had any to begin with? All of these questions went through my mind as I meticulously searched first the chapel, then the living quarters where I slept the previous night. There, I found some shards of pottery that I'd first thought were limestone, and my heart caught in my throat until I held a large fragment up to the light and examined it more closely. I sighed with relief upon realizing that it was merely clay and tossed it aside.

There was one other building to check. It was longer, like the stables in the southeast section of the headland. One portion of it, I saw, was a kitchen. The rest of it also looked like living quarters. Unlike the one I'd slept in; these were clearly for lower status people.

"Even within the Church, some men are more equal than others," I commented wryly to myself. Unlike the two or three bed frames I'd found in the previous structure, this one had a row of bunk beds, and they were crowded together. It also had a dirt floor, and the walls were entirely wattle and daub. As with the others, the thatched roof had collapsed in places, scattering large clumps of rotten straw into the interior. On the whole however, the scant furniture within this place was in better condition than the others, probably because whoever came through this place didn't find as much worth looting here.

Then I noticed a large, ink-stained desk, up against the back wall. I cocked my head, looking at it. Something about it looked wrong. Another moment later and I realized what. Either it was facing the wrong way, or it was the most poorly designed desk ever made, as there was no hollow space under the table for someone's legs.

I got to one end and pushed hard at the desk. It was large and sturdy and only moved a little bit. I pushed again and again, and after a moment, I got the desk moved far enough away from the wall to see that it was indeed hiding something. A shiver of excitement ran through me as I wiped dust off my hands and onto the hem of my tunic. Before me was the gaping hole of yet another cellar. Though the floor of the building as a whole was simply hard-packed earth, stones had been used around the edge. Like the entryway in the chapel, it was about three feet by five feet, and led down into the blackness below by way of an earthen stairway.

I turned around to go fetch my torch from the previous night and jumped to see Angharad standing scarcely two feet behind me. The first thing I noticed was that she was regarding me with a wild, intense expression. Eyes wide, teeth gritted. As if in slow-motion, I saw her right hand coming up with a knife, thrusting toward me!

Without a single conscious thought, I brought my left arm up, deflecting her knife out of alignment with my chest. Instead, it sliced harmlessly into the padded tunic I wore. In the same instant, my right hand came up in a fist and struck her in the jaw. She let go of her knife and flew backwards, landing hard onto the floor.

I bent down and snatched up the dagger with my left hand, resting my right on the pommel of my own.

"God's blood!" I swore. "What was that for?"

Angharad pushed herself up the floor and onto her elbows, blinking slowly.

"I'm sorry. I had to," she mumbled, still clearly dazed.

"You had to?" I echoed in disbelief. "You had to try and stab me in the back? Why?"

She raised her hand up toward me, and I clasped her wrist and pulled her back up to her feet. She looked up at me, being a few inches shorter than I, with a sorrowful expression that put me on guard immediately. Her eyes welled up with tears.

"A man took me from my home, brought me here, and told me I must kill you, or he would kill my parents," she sniffled.

Well now, that certainly wasn't an answer I expected, and I wasn't sure how to respond to it.

"Who?" I demanded.

She shook her head. "I don't know his name. He came riding up to my village two nights ago, seized me, and rode off before anyone could react. He brought me here and told me to expect you."

Tears leaked down her face as she talked, and my hand fell away from my dagger. I thrust her dagger into my belt as well.

"Would the man happen to be about my age, my size, and have short, dark hair?" I asked.

"Just so," she agreed.

I was still weighing the likely truth of her story when I caught her hand slowly inching toward my belt. Instantly, I slapped it away, then backhanded her across her face. She staggered back but didn't go down this time. Instead, she lunged at me, her hands reaching like claws for my face!

"Knock it off! I don't want to hurt you," I protested, sidestepping out of her way. Her hands swept past me and she turned, trying to kick me between my legs, but I'd learned to block that kind of attack long ago, tussling with my brother, Lamorac. I rotated my hips sideways and took a step forward, blocking her kick, then I grabbed her arm and shoulder and shoved her against the wall with her hand pinned to her back.

"Enough!" I snapped at her.

She squirmed and struggled, but to no avail. After a few more moments, she stopped trying to fight me.

"Why don't we start again? I'm guessing you are here on Medraut's bidding, but you came here willingly, that about right?" I demanded.

Angharad glared defiantly at me over her shoulder, but pressed her lips shut.

I rolled my eyes and huffed, "Suit yourself." I forced both of her hands behind her and held them against the small of her back. With my other hand, I pulled off her long, leather belt and bound her hands, then searched her quickly for any additional weapons. I found none.

With Angharad secure, I pulled out the stick I'd used as a torch the night before, started a fire, and lit it.

"All right, now let's go check out that cellar, together," I said as I pushed her toward the steps. She began walking down and I pulled my dagger. A feeling of danger settled over me, and I scanned the cellar as we descended, holding the burning stick high overhead so the flames wouldn't interfere with my night vision. I knew very little of Medraut, but I didn't think for a moment that he would send this woman after me by herself. That meant that he was likely somewhere here on this rock with me. In fact, he had probably been up here since before I arrived, just like Angharad.

We descended the stairs and entered a much larger chamber than the one that had been under the chapel. How much bigger was impossible to say, thanks to the meager light of my torch.

"What now, Peredur?" the blond woman asked loudly, sounding annoyed.

I winced at the volume of her voice, though I suppose I wasn't exactly being stealthy anyway, what with the torch in my hand.

"Just... keep moving," I told her, though my words faltered as the light of my torch caught the faint silhouette of a figure in a checkered red cloak.

Well, crap. That didn't take long to go sideways, I thought with a grimace, and pointed my torch toward the figure. As I expected, it was Medraut.

"Hello, Peredur," Medraut said, taking a step toward me. "I see you met Angharad... and lived," he sneered and looked over at the young woman.

Even in the dim light of my torch, I could see him plainly. He wore his scaled armor, and the helm with the eerie-looking facemask.

"Tell me something, would you? You've been eyeballing me and acting strangely ever since the first night we met back at mine and my brother's camp. Why?" Medraut demanded.

My mind raced as I considered how best to respond. I knew he was good with a bow, but I'd seen very little of Medraut's skill with a sword. But even if he wasn't that good, I only had a pair of daggers. And if I said something to set him off, how would Angharad react? I had a feeling she would get involved, which would put me at yet another disadvantage. Could I talk my way out of this?

"I don't know what you're talking about." I shrugged. "I think you're imagining things. And what are you doing here, anyway? Why would you put this woman up to try to kill me?"

I hoped by throwing so many questions at him, it would put him on the defensive, and give me a bit more time to think my way out of this mess.

Medraut chuckled. "See, this is what I mean. You're terrible at hiding your emotions, Peredur. I see the fear on you plain as day. You are clearly, deeply suspicious of me. You have been this entire time. What I don't get is why."

It hit me then. This man was smart. He knew it, and I knew it. But it bothered him that I had been on to him from the moment we first met. He didn't know that Gemma and I had spied on him back at Caer Amon.

"Maybe you're more transparent than you think you are," I prodded him.

Medraut scoffed. "Transparent about *what*? What have I done to earn your suspicion? I invited you into my camp, saw that you and your betrothed were fed and taken care of, then helped rescue your friends from the Fisher King."

He was inching closer to me, I noticed, and I eased back, towards the stairs. Medraut was only about ten feet in front of me, close enough to thrust a blade into me in the span of a heartbeat, if he were quick enough. How far behind me were the stairs? Six feet maybe? I wished I could turn around, but if I did, it would probably cost me my life.

My mouth was dry and my heart was pounding. My gut told me that Medraut was likely the most dangerous man I'd ever faced. I kept Angharad between Medraut and me, though it felt like I was using her as a shield, a notion that disgusted me. She'd already shown that she was willing to attack me, and I could not afford to have an enemy to my front and rear.

"You're the man funding the Fisher King's rebellion!" I blurted out. "My cymbrogi all know it, Myrddin knows it, and by now, so does your brother."

I had the satisfaction of seeing Medraut stiffen, then he cocked his head in a sort of contemplative gesture. I could see nothing of his face thanks to that annoying metallic mask, however.

"No," he said after a moment. "I don't think they do. They certainly didn't know anything before you left to come here, and there's nothing you could have learned and then told Gawain since your departure that would have given him cause to believe you..."

Medraut's voice trailed off, then he nodded. "Ah," he said slowly. "You must have heard something at Caer Amon. Whatever you heard or saw wasn't enough to go on that you could tell my family about."

"Oh they know," I tried to bluff. "You'll find out for yourself when you return home. You should probably get used to a place like this." I gestured to the gloom around us.

Medraut wasn't fooled. He shook his head and it seemed that I could hear the smile in his smug tone. "Nobody but you, and maybe your betrothed, know anything of my plans, either with the Fisher King, or of anything else, I think. I'm sorry you had to learn things you shouldn't have," he said, and to my surprise, he actually did sound at least mildly regretful. "For what it's worth, I've nothing against you Peredur. Under other circumstances, maybe might have been friends."

He gave no warning, no visual cue that he was about to attack. I sensed it coming nonetheless and shoved Angharad into him. They both stumbled away. I spun and raced up the stairs, taking them two at a time. Behind me, I heard Medraut snarling and swearing in pursuit!

Chapter Nineteen

BURNING PAIN SHOT THROUGH my left calf from, I learned later, Medraut slashing me with his sword as I fled. The instant I was back at ground level I grabbed a broken chair and flung it down the stairs. Medraut had no way to dodge left or right, so he ducked his head, twisted to the side, and the chair smashed into him. He staggered back a couple steps with a loud grunt, followed by a string of profanities and threats. I grabbed another one and threw it at him too as he emerged, but he was ready for that, and while it still knocked him back a bit, he batted it aside with his sword and off-hand.

I scrambled outside, drew my dagger as well as the one I'd taken from Angharad, then leapt to the side of the doorway and pressed myself up against the wall. Hot on my heels, Medraut raced outside, then skidded to a halt, whipping his head left and right. I was on him instantly, thrusting at him with both daggers, but his bloody armor held, and both blades were deflected. He stumbled forward off-balance from the impact of my blows however, and I kept at him, stabbing and slashing high and low. I knew I had to keep on him because the moment he was able to get some distance from me; I would be at a serious disadvantage.

His scale armor prevented any cuts or thrusts I made to his torso from getting through, but soon, his right leg and left arm were bleeding. He howled at me through the faceplate of his helmet and kicked me in the shin. My leg gave out and I lost balance. He used that moment to attack, and brought his sword down, aiming for my collarbone. I threw myself to the side, rolled, and sprang back to my feet with my blades up and ready.

Medraut's left arm was stained red, so I knew I'd cut him deep, but now he was in a stronger position. I tried to slip inside his guard several times, but each time, Medraut either sidestepped, or stopped me in my tracks with a thrust or cut of his sword. All the while, my attention was forced to divide between Medraut and the building we'd come from as well because at any time, I expected Angharad to emerge as well. Then I would have two opponents to deal with. A part of me wished I'd ended her when I first disarmed her. Most men probably would have. I didn't have time for regrets now though. Medraut thrust at my face with his sword and when I weaved to the side, he brought his blade down in a slash against my chest. The padded tunic I wore took the brunt of his attack, so instead of my torso being cut open, only my tunic ripped.

As soon as he completed his swing, I darted in and cut his arm holding the blade. I drew blood, but that didn't do me a lot of good since his next move was to pull out his own dagger in a reverse grip. He slashed at my face and I leapt backward, but I was too slow. I felt his blade tear through my cheek and nick my forehead, followed instantly by a white-hot burning sensation. Blood got in my eye and I had to fight off the panicked thought that he might have just ruined my eye for good!

I braced myself for the follow-up attack I was sure would follow, but Medraut held back, and simply flipped his knife so that he held it in a more conventional grip now, as I held mine. We stared at each other and circled. Both of us were cut and bloody now, both wary of the other. I finally caught a glimpse of Angharad coming out from the stairway. She was bloody too. If I had to guess, I'd say that one of the chairs I'd thrown down the stairs must have tagged her, along with Medraut, as they were attempting to chase me. To my surprise, she didn't come to Medraut's aid, but instead rushed past us and headed towards the gate, apparently choosing to flee rather than fight. That was something, at least.

The red-garbed prince lunged at me in the brief moment when my eyes flicked past him to track Angharad. I leapt backward and swiped desperately at his blade with my dagger. My parry knocked his sword out of alignment with my chest, but I wasn't quick enough to escape unscathed altogether. Instead, his blade cut through my right thigh. I cursed in pain, then cursed some more as I frantically dodged, parried, and backed away as the bastard tried to take advantage of my injured thigh with a series of thrusts at seemingly every part of my body. The only thing that saved me at this point was my padded tunic, but it was quickly becoming shredded. I received minor cuts to my forearms and lower thighs where my light armor failed to protect me sufficiently.

My training with the Red Dragons, and particularly the likes of Decurion Owain, truly paid off when, in one crucial moment, Medraut made another thrust at my chest. I managed to slip out of alignment with his blade, then trapped his right arm against my side with my left arm. He stabbed at me with the dagger in his left hand but I caught his wrist. Before he could break out of my hold, I slammed my helmeted head into his faceplate.

Medraut howled and cursed and threw me back, then he staggered away from me. He'd dropped his own dagger, and his left hand slid up to his face. I saw blood leaking from underneath his mask and chuckled, weakly.

"Bet that leaves a mark," I spat.

I attempted to circle around behind him and maybe, finally, slip through his armor with one of my daggers. He was too quick however, and spun around, slashing at my stomach. This time, the blade got through my padded tunic and cut into my stomach. I jumped back, cursing in pain and fright. My heel caught on a rock and I fell back, landing hard on my rump. Medraut immediately leaped forward and thrust his sword down at me, but I rolled away. He swiped at me as I did, and I felt the blade smack against my back. Thankfully, the back of my tunic hadn't been torn up the way the front and the sleeves had been, so the sword cut didn't get through.

Desperate to create space, I hurled Angharad's dagger at him, and it smacked off his helmet before falling to the ground. He paused to scoop it up. I swore. Yes, throwing the dagger had bought me the time I needed to scramble back to my feet, but now I was down to one dagger, and Medraut had both his sword and Angharad's dagger. His own was somewhere in the grass, a dozen feet or more behind him. I glanced around, looking for somewhere I could go to even things up. I saw a clod of dirt, scooped it up, and threw it at Medraut's face. His faceplate deflected most of it, but some got through the eye sockets. He swore and stepped back, pawing at his face, for all the good that did. I took a chance and rushed him. My shoulder slammed into his thigh as my hands reached around and behind his ankles. He went down hard and lost his grip on his sword.

His free hand shot out and latched onto my throat while his other hand, holding the dagger, swung at my head. The pommel struck me in the forehead with a loud '*clang*' as it smashed into my helm and I reeled away, breaking his grip on my throat in the process. My vision darkened for a moment. He reversed the grip of the dagger and stabbed at me, but my arms reflexively shot out and grabbed his arm. The blade halted a hair from my nose!

I wrenched his arm sideways and he tumbled away, only to spring back up into a crouch, flipping the knife back around, ready for thrusting. I, on the other hand, was still down on one knee and in a bad position. I glanced down, looking for a weapon, then caught movement out of the corner of my eye. I risked a quick look, and felt a profound sense of shock and relief flood into me.

Impossibly, racing towards us for all he was worth, came Gilbert!

Medraut cocked back his arm, preparing for his attack, but he paused, apparently reading the expression on my face. He spun around, but he was too slow, and Gilbert slammed into him with his shield, causing Medraut to go flying onto his back with a loud "Ooomf!" In the process, his dagger went flying. He sprang back up to his feet as quick as a cat, and to my shock, when Gilbert swung down at him with his axe, Medraut darted in, grabbed the wooden handle in his left hand and Gilbert's forearm in his right. Then he thrust his shoulder under the Frisian's armpit and hurled him onto the ground. In the process, Medraut managed to plant his knee onto Gilbert's chest and twist the axe from his hand. He raised it overhead, meaning to chop down at Gilbert.

I dove at him and tackled him to the ground. We rolled around punching each other. As my helm was open-faced, I got the worst of that exchange, and quickly found myself on the ground, unable to do anything more than keep my forearms up close to my head in an attempt to ward off his blows as he straddled me. Then I felt him lifted off of me and when I looked, I saw that Gilbert had wrapped his arms around Medraut's neck from behind, and dragged him off of me, then he wrapped his legs tight around the prince's waist.

Medraut's wheezes and gagging sounds were music to my ears, and I got painfully to my feet before scooping up his sword from the ground.

"Hold him, Gib!" I barked through bleeding, swollen lips. I stood over the prince and raised the sword, intent on ramming it through his eye socket.

"Stay your hand!" Gawain's voice came as sharp and loud as any battle-field commander's.

I turned, and saw Gawain and his three men, Marcus, and Tor all running toward me. Marcus, I noticed, was carrying Angharad over his shoulder. That was strange, but I didn't have time to address that in the moment.

"You don't understand!" I protested. "He's the one who's been funding the Fisher King. And he and that... wench there tried to kill me in order to get the Grail before we could!"

Gawain glared at me and shook his head as he stomped forward. "You," he barked at Gilbert, "Let go of my brother. You," he said, looking at me, "Stop talking." He grabbed me by my tunic and pulled me away from Medraut, who lay on the ground, still gasping for breath.

Gilbert released his choke hold on Medraut and kicked him away, after I gave him a nod to follow Gawain's order. Medraut rolled to his stomach and lay there, panting hoarsely as he caught his breath.

"He's right, Prince Gawain," Gemma chipped in, breathing heavily from the run. Naturally, she followed the group up, if at a safe distance. "Per and I saw your brother meeting with Garwlwyd, the Fisher King, the night we escaped Caer Amon. Then I saw him try to stab Myrddin in the back when you lot rescued him and the others."

"She... lies..." Medraut coughed as he sat up and pulled his helmet off. To my satisfaction, his face was battered and bloodied, just as I imagined mine was.

Gawain frowned, and looked around at the ruins surrounding us, then back down at his brother. "Then why were you here, little brother?"

Medraut shrugged weakly. "I changed my mind about not coming to help search for the Grail. Then Peredur saw me and attacked me. He wanted the Grail for himself."

"Liar!" Gilbert snarled, and he balled his fists up, ready to resume the fight. I darted in between him however and held him back.

"Is Angharad alive?" I asked, gesturing over to Marcus, who'd dropped the blond woman onto the ground at some point.

"She is," he grunted. "Pain in the arse, this one. When we showed up at the gatehouse down there, she'd barred it with debris. She told us that she was alone here and asked us to go away. But we'd seen you fighting Medraut from further back. Well, we didn't know it was him from that distance, just some warrior. So we hacked our way through the gatehouse. She waited until I passed, then the little witch jumped on my back and tried to take my dagger, so I belted her."

As if by magic, at that moment, the young woman stirred and moaned. Her hand went to her jaw and she slowly sat up.

"Oh look," he said. "She's finally waking up."

"Gawain, you should separate her from your brother and interrogate her," I spoke up.

He looked from me, to his brother, to Angharad, then gestured to his men. "Take her over to the chapel over there. Be alert, but don't get rough with her," he ordered.

They nodded, helped her to her feet, and took her away.

"Gemma, can you see to my brother and Peredur here?" Gawain asked.

Gemma's eyes narrowed as she regarded Gawain. "I will take care of each and every cut, scratch and scrape on my betrothed, first. *Then*, if I am not too tired, hungry, or angry, I will take a look at your brother."

A flash of too many emotions for me to single any one out showed on Gawain's face at that declaration, but she was already walking past him and up to me. The hard expression on her face softened instantly as she looked me up and down.

"You look terrible, Per," she said.

"I feel a bit terrible," I admitted, and that was God's truth! I hurt everywhere and felt a bit lightheaded. Even as she came up to me, right then my strength gave out, and I nearly collapsed. She and Gilbert quickly got under my arms to support me, and half aided, half dragged me over to the side of the big barracks-like building. It could have been my imagination, in my semi-conscious state, but I thought I saw Gilbert kick Medraut as we walked past him. The last thing I remember hearing before I lost consciousness was Marcus laughing, then swearing.

***

I woke up to the sensation of a wet cloth being run across my face. As my eyes fluttered open, memories of my fight with Medraut, and of Gawain, Gemma, and the others rushing up and ending the fight flooded into me.

I opened my eyes and blinked as the faces of my friend came into focus. So my eye hadn't been permanently damaged, I noted in relief. Then I saw the worried, solemn expressions on the faces of Gemma, Gilbert, Tor, and Marcus hovering over me.

"Will I live?" I asked, feeling a rising sense of dread welling up.

Gemma smiled radiantly then. "Of course. You suffered a number of injuries, but they're all minor. You passed out. I stitched you up."

I took that information in, then noticed Gilbert. The scar from his own recent injury was still livid and frightful.

"Tell me I don't look as ugly as Gib, at least," I groaned. My mouth was dry and I was terribly thirsty. On top of that, my numerous wounds were throbbing with pain.

The men around me laughed, though more from relief than anything, I suspect.

"Sorry, my friend, but you were and always shall be uglier than me," Gilbert grinned. "Now you'll have a new scar, too. And it's not even as fearsome as mine."

I looked over at Gemma.

"You'll have a scar," she confirmed, and gently traced a line along the side of my head, across my eye and cheek, down to my jaw. "And more elsewhere. But no need to worry. We've already had that discussion, I believe." Her lips curled into a playful smile and her eyes twinkled with amusement.

I smiled back, remembering that conversation at Caer Lleon. It already felt like a lifetime ago.

Then I frowned as a thought hit me. "What about Medraut?"

"He'll live too. More's the pity," Gilbert replied. "Gawain did question the woman though. It took a bit of persuasion, but she admitted that she had been paid by Medraut to come here with him before even we left. She was to distract you however she could if possible, and to kill you if the opportunity arose while he searched for something valuable."

Tor scoffed. "Medraut didn't even tell the woman what he was looking for, or why."

"I'd guess she's been working for him long before this," I mused as my mind raced to fill in missing details. "He wouldn't have grabbed some random woman from Din Pendyrlaw to do his bidding. And of course, Medraut didn't tell her any more than he had to. It's safer for both of them that way."

"She was paid to distract you, was she?" Gemma asked with a raised eyebrow. "And weren't you alone with her for a while before we got here..." Her voice trailed off and I could practically see the wheels turning in her head as she studied me.

"Relax," I reassured her. "She did try, but I resisted her. If I hadn't, I wouldn't have come upon Medraut and fought him. You'd have found just the two of us here on the grounds."

"Let's be honest," Tor added. "Our Peredur is too innocent to fall for her wiles. She probably scared him witless."

Gilbert and Marcus joined in with Tor and had a good laugh at my expense. I wasn't sure how I felt, noticing that even Gemma was amused by Tor's remark.

"Hmm. I think I'd still like to question the little tart myself, for a bit," Gemma grumbled.

I sighed and took her hand, then kissed it. "I promise, I never considered straying from you."

Gemma blushed, then smiled the sweetest smile I'd ever seen on a woman, then she leaned down and kissed me.

For a few moments, my pain was completely forgotten. This time, it wasn't a quick peck like the one or two times we'd kissed before. We kissed longingly and passionately and I felt her cool hands gently cradle my face. I didn't even notice when Gilbert and the others walked out of the ruined building.

I slowly lifted my arms and wrapped them around her as we kissed, and right then, I felt like I gained an entirely new understanding of King Solomon's Song of Songs. I pulled her closer, hungrily, and felt her body pressed up against mine as I lay on the dirty floor. But before we could go any further, I heard a throat clearing loudly.

We broke away from our embrace, and I looked over to see Gawain, standing at the doorway, pointedly not looking at us.

"We uh, need to talk, Peredur. Preferably sooner rather than later," the prince said, sounding a bit sheepish.

"We can talk now," I sighed. "My lady was only making sure my injuries had been seen to."

Gemma giggled and sat back.

Gawain stepped inside and took a knee beside me. "You'll be alright, I assume?" I noticed his gaze was fixed on the cut across my face.

"He will," Gemma assured, then added cooly, "No thanks to your brother."

Gawain flinched as though he'd been struck. "Yes... that's what we need to discuss," he admitted.

"As a nobleman of Caer Gurcoc and one of Tribune Arthur's men, I claim Medraut as my prisoner. His life is mine," I blurted, surprising myself almost as much as Gemma and Gawain.

"I think King Leudon might argue that point," he began, but I shook my head, and propped myself up on my elbows, ignoring the pain. I'd said what I did on impulse, and after a moment of reflection, I wasn't sure I actually could claim him as my prisoner. But, I hated the idea that he might go free of punishment after all that had transpired, and so stuck to my position.

"He started a rebellion against your father. That was your own business. But he specifically then instructed his lapdog to assault my comrades, kill some of them, and imprison the rest of us. We were on a peaceful mission! That made him our problem now, as much as yours. Gilbert and I defeated him as an enemy combatant. He is my prisoner to do with as I see fit, and I'll bring this up to Tribune Arthur when he arrives if you choose to contest the matter," I stated firmly, meeting Gawain's gaze.

Gawain ran a hand through his wavy blond hair and blew out a long breath.

"You aren't wrong, though I could argue that actual possession of the prisoner matters quite a bit. And you don't hold him. My men do."

"We could change that, very fast," Gilbert growled from behind him.

Gawain spun around in surprise and found my three cymbrogi surrounding us. Marcus had his arms folded across his large chest, but Gilbert and Tor both had theirs resting on their weapons. Gawain's own group were still some distance off, watching over Medraut and Angharad. He was alone and surrounded by my comrades.

I felt the tension ramp up as my companions calmly stared Gawain down.

"What would you do with him if I agreed to this?" Gawain asked, still looking warily from me to my companions.

I considered the question. A part of me really wanted to execute the bastard. I had a weird feeling that if I let him live, he would only go on to cause further mischief down the road. On the other hand, forcing the issue and executing Medraut, a prince of the Gododdin, would likely not sit well with them, no matter the cause. If the rumors we'd heard about the Saxons preparing for some sort of campaign were true, we would probably need their help soon. The idea of simply turning Medraut over to Gawain was also unconscionable after everything he'd done.

"I'll return him to you," I said at last, "But I demand a ransom for him."

"Name it," Gawain replied.

"I want his squamata, that scale armor," I decided, upon glancing over at the shredded light armor I'd been wearing during my fight with Medraut. "Then, when we return to Din Pendyrlaw, my friends here and I all get new helmets, shields, and they get swords and armor of their choosing. Quality kit," I stressed.

"Done," Gawain said after a moment. Out of the corner of my eye I saw my companions' faces split into huge grins. Gilbert rubbed his hands together in glee.

"Did you happen to find the Grail?" He finally asked.

"I did not, though I have an idea of where it could be, if it's here."

I held my hand up to Gawain, and with a bit of effort, he helped me to my feet, against the mild protests of Gemma, who felt I should remain lying down for at least the rest of the day. I admit, I hurt all over, but I gritted my teeth and endured it. I did, however, allow Gemma to give me a wineskin from our provisions. That sated my thirst and took a little of the edge off my pain.

While Gawain's men kept watch on Medraut and Angharad in the small quarters beside the chapel, my companions and I, along with Gawain, made torches, proper ones this time, not just sticks lit on fire at one end, and I led them over to the chapel and down into the small cellar. A shiver went down my spine when, with the better light, I saw a skeleton in one corner of the room, still wearing the tattered remains of a green, checkered dress. I assumed this one was likely a Christian Picti woman who'd been here when the place was overrun however many years ago.

I showed the other men the stone cross, and the smaller statue of Pelagius, which was much easier to see now, with five torches lighting the room.

"Can you lads move that cross away from the wall?" I asked them.

They crowded around the tall, heavy carving and with grunts and gasps, the cross was slowly pushed away from the wall.

"Look at the wall, there where the cross was," I said and pointed.

They looked and saw what I did. A portion of the otherwise smooth, hard-packed earth was caved in.

"It looks to me like someone dug out a portion of the wall, then filled it back in," Gawain said.

Tor and Gilbert bent down and clawed at the wall, and the outline of a box soon emerged. They dug faster, and eventually pulled out a wooden chest, bound with metal strips. The pair carefully cleaned the dirt from it, exposing the clasps that held it shut while Marcus, Gawain, and I watched them in growing excitement.

Rust made the clasps a bit hard to work, but once Gilbert worked the tip of his knife into it, the box was opened and we all eagerly crowded around to see what was in it with baited breath. The lid opening with a rusty squeak was the only sound in the cellar, beyond the flames of our torches burning.

Then we saw it. Resting in a wad of wool cloth and padded with straw was a large cup, appearing to have been chiseled out of limestone. It was relatively simple in its design, though not ugly by any means. Could this cup have actually been held in the very hands of Jesus Himself?

"Is this the Grail?" Gilbert finally asked, echoing my own thoughts. There was a touch of awe in his voice as he looked from it the rest of us.

"It matches the descriptions we have," Gawain said breathily, looking down at the cup with wonder. "I can't imagine two such goblets being in this place and kept so carefully."

"The monks who lived here must have hidden it, when they came under attack," I speculated.

"What happens if we touch it?" Tor asked, still holding the wooden box.

"Don't," Gawain said. "Let's close the box back up, get it back south, and then we need to get it to the Fisher King. At all costs, we must keep it safe and intact. The last thing we need is someone breaking it because they wanted to see if drinking from it would give them eternal life, or suddenly enable them to grow a full beard or something," he joked.

"Wait, why did you all look at me?" I glared at my companions, who broke out into muted snickers. "Oh sod off," I grumbled, and slowly climbed up the stairs out of the cellar.

As the rest followed me up, I felt a gush of relief and immense satisfaction. We'd done it. We'd retrieved the Grail, and it was intact. Hopefully, with it we could end Garwlwyd's rebellion peacefully. I smiled to myself, remembering that two months ago, when this whole journey had begun, all my mission had been to be a member of Myrddin's bodyguard in what was supposed to have been a simple mission to secure a treaty with King Domangart Reti.

A short while later, our gear was brought up from the boat and Gemma prepared food for us, with Marcus' help, over a nice fire. Off to one side, Angharad and Medraut sat sullenly together, under guard. I had the immense satisfaction of watching Gawain help Medraut out of his armor and turn it over to me. I couldn't resist making a small show of holding it up and examining it as I accepted it.

"I'll have to make sure I wash it first, before I put it on," I observed with a sideways look at Medraut. "It's quite bloodstained."

"Yes, you did bleed on it quite a bit," the sullen prince bit back.

I didn't feel a need to respond, for at that moment Gemma handed me a wooden bowl with some good wheat porridge, as well as a chunk of bread. I all but forgot about Medraut as the two of us sat down to eat. After the scant bit of food I'd had for the past two days, the porridge was absolutely heavenly, and the cheese I ate with the bread more than made up for its staleness.

We camped on the headland that night, then early the next morning, we loaded back up into the boat. I had originally hoped to ride the black stallion back south, for I could likely have made a tidy sum of coin from him in Din Eidyn, assuming the village elder would have sold it to me at a good price. After my fight with Medraut however, I was in poor condition to ride on my own and would need to take it easy for several days at the very least, a couple of weeks preferably. Everyone else would be needed on the oars. The stallion would likely find his own way home in due time. In the end, we simply removed the stallion's tack, stowed it in our boats, and left. Gawain and his men took Medraut's boat, and my men and I continued our journey in the boat we'd sailed north in.

The weather was mercifully calm, and we made it back to Din Pendyrlaw two days later, with a brief stop at the Pict village to apologize to the village elder for losing his horse.

"If he doesn't show up, or you can't find him in a few days, feel free to travel south and I'll reimburse you from my father's stables. Or if you can find him and want to sell him, you can also come south and I'll give you a good price for him," Gawain told the old man. The Pict smiled and nodded and promised to send some people north to look for the stallion.

Upon reaching Din Pendyrlaw, Gawain instructed my comrades and I to settle back into the barracks we'd stayed at previously. He and his three men then escorted Medraut and Angharad into the great hall and left us on our own.

"What do you think will happen to them?" Gemma asked me, as we all watched them leave.

"Angharad will probably be executed or put into slavery," I replied. "It's anyone's guess what they'll do with Medraut. He's a prince, but Gawain is the oldest, and apparently King Leudon has a third son, Gareth, though he's only a child. Either way, that makes Medraut a bit expendable. I'd say he could face anything from execution to exile to nothing at all," I shrugged.

A short time later, a servant came to us from the great hall with instructions that we were to come with him to the armory, prompting excited cheers from my companions. We all returned the lower quality, simple armor we'd borrowed for our trip north, then immediately began scouring the armory.

"You lot are acting like women at market day they way you're scrutinizing and inspecting every little thing," Gemma cackled with amusement as she watched us.

"This is a rare opportunity," I protested, as I examined a segmented helm that had caught my eye. It was iron, though some areas, like the decorative nasal and reinforced brow were brass. It had an attached neck plate, and large cheek guards that fully protected my jaw and nearly overlapped at the chin when I tried it on and was delighted to discover that it fit.

I turned to Gemma with a grin and she studied me, then nodded with approval.

"Yes, yes. You look very pretty, Per," she teased. "It brings out the green of your eyes and hides that silly beard of yours."

I scratched at the stubble on my jaw a bit sheepishly and moved on to look at the shields.

Marcus chose a helm more in the style that the Romans used to wear. Like mine, his had a neck and cheek plates, though the crown of his helm was more rounded and made from a single piece of iron, as opposed to the more cone-shaped helm I chose. His also sported a metal fin that ran from front to back. Tor chose a similar helmet as Marcus, though his had a brass finish across the entire surface, and didn't include a nasal like ours did.

Gilbert also selected a segmented helm. He couldn't find any with the mask-like pieces that were common among Saxon helms, to nobody's surprise, but the helm he chose did have an ornamental boar mounted on the crown, which he liked. Though his helm at least had a nasal, it didn't include the neck or cheek plates that ours did. Instead, the lip of the helm extended down to just below his ears.

Shields were easy. We each got nice large, oval shields that had been built with a center grip. These however, also had straps on either side that gave us the option to attach to our forearm. We selected shields that were unpainted, so we could have them done up later in the red and white designs favored by our numerus.

Finally came armor. I of course already had Medraut's red leather-trimmed, scale armor, though I did take the opportunity to select a leather subarmalis to wear underneath as a layer of padding. Tor also chose a coat of scaled armor, which had the same brass finish as the helm he'd picked out. Gilbert and Marcus chose long-sleeved coats of mail.

"It's good to see we finally found armor that fits you," Gilbert said with a grin as he made a show of eyeing Marcus up and down.

"Go bugger yourself, little man," Marcus growled, as he rotated his arms and torso around, testing the fit of the coat.

I smiled to myself, noting that between the padded tunic he wore, combined with the coat of mail over that, Marcus did indeed look quite large. I knew from experience though that he was quite strong, if not on the same level of Galhault. But then, I wasn't sure anyone in all of Britain was his equal in terms of raw strength, and that included Arthur.

Lastly, each of my comrades selected a new sword and dagger. I only needed a replacement dagger, since the sword I'd taken from the dead rebel suited me nicely as an upgrade to my worn and nicked spatha. That would be displayed in a place of honor in my home, some day. Gilbert had his precious seax, and the axe I'd acquired for him at Caer Amon, but he still selected a sword to be slung from a baldric like the rest of us did.

"Got enough weapons, Gib?" Tor asked.

"No," Gilbert said immediately. "I still need a spear."

We all did, in fact, I realized, so once we picked out the rest of our kit, we each selected spears from a rack, then walked back to the barracks. Tor kept looking over his helm and scale armor with the most pleased look on his face that I'd ever seen. Gilbert and Marcus shoved and punched each other and laughed at how well their new armor absorbed the blows.

"You men," Gemma sighed in wonder at our antics. "You're behaving like… children who just got new toys."

"And the best part is, we got it all for free!" Tor grinned happily.

"Speak for yourself," I said. "Gib and I had to fight tooth and nail to earn all this. Where were the rest of you while we were fighting Medraut, anyway?"

"That blond woman who was working with him blocked the gate," Marcus explained. "She piled a bunch of broken timbers and other debris across the entryway. That slowed us down."

"Didn't seem to stop Gib," I pointed out.

"I climbed over. We saw you and Medraut fighting as we approached the gatehouse. It looked like you needed help, so while the others cleared the path, I decided to climb over. It was quicker."

"Glad you did," I admitted.

"Me too," Gilbert quipped, then he scooped up a rock and threw it at Marcus' broad back. It hit him between his shoulders and smacked off the mail. "Don't ding up my new armor," Marcus complained. This only caused Gilbert further amusement.

"I think we need to pick up some practice swords so we can break in our new armor properly once we get back to the barracks," I mused.

"Oh no you don't," Gemma scolded me. "Remember how many bloody times Tewdrig and I had to stitch you up two years ago when you kept reopening that wound to your side? We are not going through that again, here. You are going to rest and let your wounds heal properly this time."

"Yes, my lady," I said, feeling thoroughly chastened, and tried to ignore the snickering of my companions.

"You too, Gilbert. I had to stitch you up as well," Gemma said, turning her withering gaze to him.

He flinched and raised his hands placatingly, or tried to, given that one arm had a shield strapped to it and he carried a tall spear in his hand.

"I'll be careful, Medicus," he said, though the glint in his eye suggested otherwise.

Chapter Twenty

Three days after our arrival to Din Pendrylaw, Gawain showed up to the barracks and had me round up my companions for a meeting at a single, long table.

"My father wishes us to travel south to the main road and greet Arthur upon his arrival. We're to travel with him to Din Eidyn, where Father will meet us with an army. Together, we'll march on Caer Amon and either persuade the Fisher King to surrender or destroy him and his rebels."

"Wait, King Leudon is joining us this time?" I asked, surprised.

"Yes?" Gawain answered, puzzled by my question.

"I mean, he didn't join us personally when King Drest's Picts invaded." I shrugged. "I assumed he wasn't the kind of king who went to war himself."

I thought about how that sounded after I said that, followed immediately by an acute awareness of who I was speaking to, and cringed inwardly. As I feared, Gawain bristled at my remark and fixed me with a hard stare.

"My father absolutely is the kind of king who leads his army to war, when he deems it appropriate and necessary. He did not accompany Guinnion and Arthur to the border wall and fight against Drest for two particular reasons. One — we weren't sure that the Picts wouldn't slip around Arthur and Guinnion's forces and attack either Din Eidyn or Pendyrlaw while it was weak, so we had to keep troops in reserve. Two — we have to keep a close eye on the Angles to our south."

Gawain's voice rose as he grew more heated. "The Angles launch cattle and slave raids any chance their spies tip them off that we aren't paying attention. Meanwhile, our own spies tell us that there's so many Angles that have moved in and colonized the east coast that within the kingdom of Bryneich, Anglian is heard more commonly than Brythonic and the kingdom is increasingly being referred to as 'Bernicia'. And everything south of that is thoroughly conquered, either by the Angles or the Saxons. Gododdin will be next to fall if we don't maintain our vigilance."

"And that's why the Red Dragons exist," Gilbert said. "To see to it that no more kingdoms in Britain fall to them."

Gawain smiled sadly. "The Red Dragons can't be everywhere at once, and Arthur is one man. His aid is a double-edged sword, too. Look at what happened here. We accepted his help against Drest, and now our neighbors, and even some of the nobles here, question whether King Leudon is strong enough to hold this kingdom. The moment we're perceived as too weak, the Picts or the Angles will come for us."

"Well, the Picts at least have already tried, and got their arses kicked for their effort. Maybe once we sort out Garwlwyd, we should make a quick trip north and deal with any Picts we find, too," I said in an effort to ease the tension.

Gawain leaned back in his chair and sighed heavily, then nodded. "If they don't attack us first, we might just do that. In the meantime, we need to take the rest of the day to pack our gear and get south. I'll be coming with you, along with a few of my men."

"I trust Medraut won't be one of them," Marcus muttered, but not quietly enough. Gawain heard him and turned to regard the big man.

"No, my brother will not be coming with us to link up with Arthur. He will probably be by King Leudon's side however, when we face the Fisher King and attempt to negotiate with him. That's all that needs to be said on that matter," he said flatly.

Marcus looked ready to continue the conversation, but I kicked him under the table and the only thing that came out of his mouth was a muffled grunt. I saw the logic to bringing Medraut for that. He'd been the one who put Garwlwyd up to the rebellion after all. If the Fisher King saw him side by side with Gawain and the King, and they made it clear that he would be getting no more support from Medraut, that might destroy his resolve then and there.

"We'll be ready to go. Leaving at first light?" I asked.

Gawain nodded, then stood up and left the room.

***

The two-day ride to the southern border of Gododdin, specifically to a gap between the Rivers Clud and Tuedd, was uneventful, though that shouldn't be surprising. As lawless as Britain had become, a dozen well-armed and armored mounted men tended to be left alone a bit more than other folk. We set up camp in a wooded area overlooking the Roman road — the same road I recall riding north on with the Red Dragons two years ago.

We killed time in the time-honored way that soldiers do. We played dice, told stories, Marcus bragged about some of his conquests, while Gilbert took every opportunity to tease him, and me, and Tor, and anyone else who gave him an opening. We also sparred some. Gawain was a truly gifted fighter. He soundly whipped me, then Tor, then Tor and I together. Marcus's brute strength gave him some trouble, but as Gawain was faster and in overall better condition, he just had to wear Marcus down by fighting defensively until the bigger man was winded, then Gawain counter-attacked with feints and making good use of both the stick he used as a sword, as well as his shield.

Gilbert gave Gawain some trouble, particularly when he decided to discard his shield and use two sticks, to simulate his sword and axe.

"You do realize that's a very risky pairing to make in battle, right?" Gawain huffed as he frantically worked to block Gilbert's flurry of attacks from both sticks.

Gilbert grinned as he and Gawain circled. "Yes," he acknowledged. "But it's pretty useful for one-on-one fights, like this one!" As he said this, he feinted to Gawain's left, causing the prince to shift his shield in that direction, then Gilbert deftly leaped in the other direction and made high and low attacks with his sticks.

Gawain was quick enough to block the high attack, aimed at his head, but Gilbert's second attack smacked him in his hip. Gawain cursed, then chuckled in appreciation.

"Well done, Gilbert. You're bloody fast!"

Gilbert grinned and bowed.

"Don't compliment the Saxon turd too much, sir. You'll give him a bigger head than he already has," Marcus grunted.

That was how our days went for the better part of a week when one afternoon, while Tor was draining his bladder, happening to be facing south, he spotted the Red Dragons.

"I can see the column," he called out, and was so excited to share the news that he turned around before he'd even finished pulling his trousers up.

"Oh come on man," Marcus groaned, holding his hand out to block Tor from his vision.

Gilbert of course got a good laugh and made a vulgar joke at Tor's expense. The rest of us packed up our few belongings, and watched the long column of riders slowly approach.

"You've met Tribune Arthur before, right?" I asked Gawain.

"I have, at least once. Remember when the Red Dragons stopped by Din Pendyrlaw to pick up new recruits and supplies for your trip south after dealing with Drest?"

I nodded.

"I was there, as were my brothers and sister. It's possible he's traveled north before, but I would have been too young to remember."

We waited for an hour before the lead riders were close enough to call out to. They were the scouts deployed around the column to prevent ambushes. A trio of men rode up to us. I glanced to my left and right and smiled, noting that there were other groups of riders flanking us, some two hundred paces off. One of the three approaching us raised his right hand in greeting. The man was of a bit paler complexion than most, and his face was sprinkled with freckles. He also had a short, coppery red beard

"I'm Rhun, under the command of Tribune Arthur..." his voice trailed off as we recognized each other at the same time.

"Rhun!" I exclaimed with a laugh.

"Peredur?" Rhun said in disbelief. "What in Hell are you doing here?" He looked over my companions, and his eyes widened further when he saw Gilbert, grinning away. "You lot were supposed to be prisoners! We came north to rescue you."

"Well, sorry to inconvenience you. We decided to rescue ourselves," I laughed. I rarely saw Rhun ever since we'd been assigned to different turmae following our training together, nearly three years ago.

"You left some rebels for us at least, I hope. Surely we didn't ride all the bloody way up here for nothing," Rhun complained in his familiar Gaelic accent.

"And maybe some Picts to fight," Marcus added.

"Again?" Rhun asked, startled.

"How many men did you come with? Arthur's with you, right?" Tor asked.

"Is your brother with you?" I asked nearly at the same time.

Rhun looked from Tor to me and raised his hands. "Whoa, whoa," he laughed. "Yes, Peredur, Ewan's here. He's in the group on our right flank. Taran, of course the Tribune came. So did Cai, and even Bedwyr. There's about two hundred and... sixty of us," Rhun answered. "Not counting a few servants who brought extra mounts and other light logistical support, of course."

"Glad to hear that," Gawain chipped in, inserting himself into our reunion. "I'm Prince Gawain of the Gododdin, here to meet with your tribune and escort your column the rest of the way north."

Rhun straightened up and nodded respectfully to Gawain. "Tribune Arthur will be along shortly, sir, or you can accompany me back to the column and I'll take you to him."

"I'll wait here for him. I would appreciate it if you could pass on to him that we're here though," Gawain replied.

Rhun dipped his head again, then he and his two companions rode away back toward the column.

He returned with three other men trailing him. I picked out Arthur straight away in his red-plumed helmet, crimson cloak, and ornate scale armor. The taller one to his right was Cai, and the shorter, stocky man to his left was Castellan Bedwyr. It occurred to me that I could have identified each of them by their beards alone. Arthur's was short, well-groomed, and blond, Cai's was similar, but dark brown, more like my own hair color, and Bedwyr's thick beard was a dirty blond color, but was becoming more white than anything.

"Lads! You escaped! I should have expected that," Arthur laughed as he rode up to us. "And here we came all this way to free you. Even Bedwyr finally left the fort."

"Bloody right I did," Bedwyr boomed. "Can't let an insult to the honor of the Red Dragons go unanswered."

We grinned up at him.

"Gawain, good to see you again, too," Arthur said, turning to the prince. "You've grown up a bit."

"I'm twenty years old this fall. I can't have changed that much since you last saw me. Must be the beard," Gawain smiled.

"Is that what you call that thing?" Cai said, making a show of peering at the prince's face.

"It's just too blond for you to see properly," Gawain grunted. "Or maybe you can't see too well in your old age."

"I'm twenty-eight. Only a boy like you would consider me old," Cai countered.

"Both of you sound like children to me," Bedwyr scoffed.

"That's because you're so old you probably started your career in the Roman legions," Cai teased.

"And yet, old and one-handed, I could still kick your arse," Bedwyr said, waiving the stump of his right arm towards Cai in emphasis.

"In your most wine-sodden dreams, old man" Cai grinned.

I shared glances with Tor and Gilbert, delighted beyond measure to see that even the likes of Arthur and his inner circle could behave no differently than we did, when they were of a mood.

Arthur cleared his throat then. "Gentlemen, as amusing as this reunion is, we have two hundred and seventy-nine men waiting on us, and we still have a long ride ahead of us, I'd guess." He looked at Gawain questioningly.

Gawain instantly became serious. "Indeed. My father said I should escort you to Din Eidyn, where he and additional troops will meet us. From there we can plan our assault on the Fisher King at Caer Amon."

Arthur cocked his head. "The Fisher King... Garwlwyd, correct?"

"Yes sir," Gawain confirmed.

"I remember him, from Guinnion's Fort," Arthur said, then his gaze became unfocused for a moment as he stared off into the distance. "He won't fight us there," he surprised us by saying at last.

"He's fortified the place considerably over the past year. And he's already defended it twice against our own forces," Gawain argued.

"No offense, Gawain, but he knew he could win then. When he sees our banners, or even hears of our approach, he'll abandon the fort," Arthur said.

From any other man, that statement would sound like a boast. Arthur made it a statement of simple fact.

"How could you know that? And why would he do that? Do you imagine this man is so frightened of you?"

"Frightened? No. But he is cunning, and he'll want to play to his army's strengths rather than ours. Our men excel at fighting conventionally. His men excel at fighting in the woods, in the old ways of our ancestors. The messengers who reported to me at Caer Lleon said he and his men are rumored to be cinbin, correct?"

"Yes, but..." Gawain started to protest.

"He'll abandon the fort and try to fight us in the woods, on ground of his choosing," Arthur spoke softly, almost more to himself it seemed, than for our benefit. "Come," he said, snapping out of his introspection. "Let's not keep the column waiting on us any longer. Gawain, lead the way. Peredur, you and your companions can ride with us. Brief me up on the way."

He paused and looked around. "Where's your wife, Maithgemm?"

Beside me, Gilbert did his best to keep from laughing.

I felt my ears and cheeks getting hot and had to clear my voice. "She's uh, I mean we're not married yet, Tribune," I clarified. "We're still only betrothed. And for this little trip, I thought it best to let her stay at Din Pendyrlaw. She'll join King Leudon and meet us at Din Eidyn."

"Ah. My mistake," Arthur smiled warmly at me. "I am glad to hear that she is safe as well though."

I thanked him, and we rode over to the long column of cavalry. Soon enough we were riding northward again, and Arthur's interrogation began. I told him about everything that had unfolded over the past six weeks, from the day we landed on the shores of Dyfed to the present. Occasionally, Arthur asked for Tor, Marcus, or Gilbert's input, and here or there Cai or Bedwyr asked a question.

We rode and talked for the rest of the day, made camp shortly before nightfall, and resumed our journey the following morning. To my delight, I learned that my former decurion, Owain, was in the column. He and his new turma were all from Alt Clut and so had only to ride east to join the Red Dragons the day before they reached Gododdin's borders. Cornelius, though not originally from Alt Clut, had decided to follow Owain there anyway, in order to continue serving as his duplarius. That night at camp, I joined them at their fire. It felt strange that I'd only been separated from his turma for a couple months, but so much had already changed. Most of the faces were unknown to me. Owain was the same gruff commander he'd always been, though his usual grim expression broke into a surprisingly joyful one when he told me that his wife, back in Alt Clut, had given birth to a son — his third now. Gilbert and I toasted to that and congratulated him.

Cornelius too, had news to share. He held up his left hand for us to see.

"Duplarius, you got married!" Gilbert exclaimed. "About time you settled down in your old age."

The grin Cornelius had worn slipped, and his upheld left hand flipped Gilbert the middle finger. "I'm thirty-one. Sod off, whelp."

We laughed, and after toasting to his good fortune as well, I pressed him for details. Cornelius revealed that he had met and married a young woman in Alt Clut. She was a baker's daughter, and so her bride price wasn't unreasonably high. "I used some of my savings to buy a bit of land in Alt Clut, and her father provided us with a nice dowry of half a dozen sheep," our duplarius announced happily.

We shared another celebratory drink, then later I also discovered that Owain had brought my beautiful mare, Carys, up north with them, along with a few other spare mounts. I'm not sure who was happier at our reunion between the two of us, for I spent considerable time brushing and petting her, and she nuzzled and nipped at me.

The next afternoon we reached Din Eidyn. It was a nice, mostly cloudless day as we rode up, and I admired the beautiful hills and groves of trees surrounding us. One, to our right, stood out. It was as imposing as the rocky hill that Din Eidyn had been built upon. Gawain saw me looking at it and pointed at it.

"That's Mount Agned. It used to have an important hillfort built atop it, back when our ancestors, the Votadini, were still living as tribesmen and raiding Romans. They only started coming together in the past few generations," Gawain mused. "Too many external threats for our people to keep living as they had."

"Impressive," I acknowledged. "Even without any wooden walls left, the earthworks and the hill itself would make bloody good defensive ground."

"It would indeed," Gawain agreed.

He had to leave us a short time later, and as we'd done on our last visit here, the Red Dragons set up our tents just outside the walls of the hillfort, against a particularly steep, rocky slope on the western side. We generally relaxed and tended to our kit while Arthur and his decurions went up to the great hall to hold their war council with King Leudon. Gemma found me there, and we enjoyed each other's company, discussing how the upcoming battle with the Fisher King would likely go, and dreaming of the future. We only parted, reluctantly, as the sun began to set and it would be improper for her to stay within the camp.

I prayed that night, as I often did, for God to keep me and my comrades safe in the battle that the next day would likely bring, and of course I also prayed for victory.

Chapter Twenty-One

As so often happens on our isle, particularly here in the north, clouds rolled in during the night, and we were inconvenienced by a light rain as we were woken up, broke down our camp, and prepared to ride the few miles east to Caer Amon. I was surprised to find that Arthur didn't assign me back into Owain's turma, or any of the others in fact. Instead, he told me to simply fall in with his own turma. I didn't think much of this as Gilbert, Tor, and Marcus were also instructed to ride along with me.

We didn't expect the Fisher King to make his stand there, as Arthur had explained the day before, but Gawain and his men who had functionally become another turma of the Red Dragons overnight were tasked with providing a screen for our column nonetheless. And it was a large column. Our two hundred and sixty-four men rode two abreast along the road, while King Leudon led his own small mounted force of another fifty or so men, with a thousand levied infantry marching four across. Our servants and supply carts stayed back at Din Eidyn. Just in case Garwlwyd decided to surprise us by fighting from the walls of Caer Amon, King Leudon's levies included nearly a hundred archers, and double that number in slingers, who could also fight in a shieldwall if needed. Only a skeleton garrison was left to man the walls of Din Eidyn.

As we approached the fortified town and the two rivers that converged in the area, fog enveloped us, putting everyone on edge. The column halted at two hundred paces from the outer walls. The archers and infantry were brought up and arrayed into battle formation and the archers strung their bows in preparation for battle. Gawain and his men warily approached the shadowy gatehouse while the rest of us watched, tense, having no idea what to expect. The bothersome rain was forgotten as watched a group of horsemen dismount, approach the gate and call out. Nothing happened. From our vantage point further back, it didn't appear to me that anybody was manning the walls or the gatehouse at all. Gawain rode back to us, spoke to Arthur, and then a short while later a pair of men with axes were brought up and they methodically hacked at the large wooden door of the gatehouse.

Once the axemen made a hole big enough, one of them slipped through and fully opened the gate from the inside. Gawain and the rest of his men filed through, gripping their shields and with swords drawn. Time dragged on, and I'm sure I wasn't alone in straining to catch a glimpse of hostile activity on the far side of those low walls or cocking my head to try and hear the telltale sounds of combat over the cursed patter of raindrops hitting my helmet, among everything else. But nothing happened.

Finally, one of Gawain's men rode back out of the gate. His shield was slung behind him and his sword back in its scabbard. He waved at us and called out "All clear!"

I heard several sighs of relief, to include one of my own, as I made the sign of the cross in thanks to God.

"Alright men, let's do a quick search of the town, then we'll pick up the Fisher King's trail and pursue him," Arthur told us. "There's enough of us, so I want us back on the road in an hour. Two at most. Look for rebels, stockpiles of weapons or precious metals that the rebels might have hidden in case they are able to return."

"Sanddev," Arthur said, turning to one of his men. "Go tell Prince Gawain that I need him and his men to scout the outskirts of the fort, please. Garwlwyd left here with his entire force, probably recently, so finding his tracks, or someone who saw his men leave shouldn't be too hard. My guess is that he left out of the smaller gate on the north side of the town. If Gawain doesn't find tracks heading west, they probably took boats and crossed the Firth."

"Yes, Tribune," the man said and galloped away.

We swept through the town in a methodical manner, beginning with the smattering of roundhouses and shops along the outer wall. The levy infantry checked the few homes outside the walls and the surrounding area. Most of them had been abandoned, though a few people, mostly older couples, hadn't been so afraid of our approach that they'd been willing to abandon their homes.

One old man with a raspy voice stood defiantly looking at me and Gilbert from the doorway of his home. "I lived here since before Leudon made himself our king. When that cinbin fellow they call the Fisher King came and killed the garrison up there at the fort, I stayed here! A lot of my neighbors, people I've known for years, abandoned the town out of fear. Now you lot have come and a few more of my neighbors left, along with all the new folk who came in as part of the Fisher King's band. Well, I'll not leave! This is my home. You can kill me or leave me be. I'm too old to care much either way."

Gilbert laughed. "We'll not bother you, grandfather. We're only here hunting for Garwlwyd's rebels. When did they leave?"

"Last night," the old man answered. "If you look, you'll find food still sitting at the table of a lot of these homes. A rider came through here yesterday morning. Galloped straight through town, nearly rode a couple of people down. He sped up to the fort, and next thing I know, the whole place is in an uproar with people packing their things to leave."

We thanked him, did a quick peek into his house to confirm that he was the only resident, and left. The rest of our search turned up very little, though we did find a freshly dug hole behind one empty home. Gilbert pulled out a wooden chest from the hole and flipped open the lid. Inside, we saw an assortment of coins, a few silver rings, and an ornate brooch with gems on it.

"Looks like we found someone's stockpile," I mused.

"Their loss, our gain," Gilbert shrugged with a grin. He moved to scoop out a handful of the treasure.

"Don't even think about it," I said. "We'll get our share. *Later.*"

Gilbert sighed heavily and dropped the coins back into chest before closing it back up, fixing me with a morose look. We lifted the chest out of the ground and brought it to a collection point in town where other small stockpiles were being gathered.

Some of the finer pieces would be returned to their owners if they could be found. Much of the treasure would go to King Leudon, as it had come from rebels who'd been pillaging his people. A portion, however, would be claimed by the Red Dragons, and distributed among us. We might only get a handful of silver per man at the end of it all, along with a few extra looted weapons, but this could add up rather nicely. Over time, the plunder from battle and from sacking even small towns like this one had seen Gilbert amass his own small treasure horde. Occasionally, as a reward for exceptional service, Arthur himself gave out rings or other small silver or copper items to his men.

A commotion went up from within the fort, and while we finished going through the homes surrounding the fort, we waited to find out what had happened. It didn't take long. An excited soldier who'd been helping clear the shops and homes within the fort itself climbed up on the wall and shouted down to one of his friends outside the wall what they'd found. From there, word spread like wildfire and soon we all heard the news. Galhault's turma had gone into one storeroom and found a huge stockpile of old silver and even some gold coins, along with the usual assortment of buckles, brooches, jewelry and the like. The biggest treasure of all though was a large, gold-plated cauldron encrusted with gems. When I heard that, I grinned, remembering the cauldron I'd seen in those pagan ceremonies Garwlwyd had participated in. Today was becoming quite the payoff!

We finished searching the fort in two hours, and by the time we were done, we had a nice pile of all manner of loot to be divided up later. Gawain's men also found indications that the Fisher King's men had vacated the fort from the north gate and marched west. A group of servants from Leudon's court were left to oversee the loot as it was loaded up onto wagons to be transported to Din Eidyn and the value assessed. A small detachment of the king's men, as well as a few Red Dragons were left behind as a security detail. The rest of us formed back up on the road, the archers unstrung their bows to protect the strings from the rain, and in short order we too were on the road west in pursuit of the rebels. We rode in two files, led by Arthur and his turma, followed by the other four turmae that had come north. Behind them rode a few support personnel, to include our medicus Tewdrig, and Gemma, in the capacity as his assistant. Behind them came King Leudon and his levies.

An average infantryman can march at four miles an hour, and travel twenty-five miles a day, give or take. Horses can travel forty miles a day on long journeys with little effort, sixty if they need to, and will be able to rest later. So even with a lead of several hours, it didn't take us long to catch up to the rebels, though the need to cross the river just west of Caer Amon slowed us down. It had slowed Garwlwyd's forces down too, after all. As close to the Firth as we were, the fog refused to lift, even after the rain finally ceased. Our visibility was reduced to less than thirty paces before everything was reduced to vague outlines.

About two miles west of Caer Amon, we came upon an abandoned village that appeared to have been pillaged. It wasn't that uncommon of a sight, though the fog made the broken-down doors and burned-out roofs look a bit more forlorn and unsettling than normal. I wondered if it had been Garwlwyd's rebels or Leudon's men who'd destroyed it, and if the occupants had been able to flee, or if their bones lay scattered about. I made the sign of the cross, in case there were any restless souls roaming about.

We were riding along, struggling to make out our surroundings, when cries of "Enemy contact!" echoed all around us from Gawain's men ahead of us.

The warning cries of enemy contact were followed immediately by the whizzing sound of sling stones being hurled at us. Thankfully, the rebels were as hampered as we were by the fog, and many of the missiles harmlessly splattered into the wet, muddy ground around us or flew over our heads. Too many found their mark though, and the grunts and cries of pain from men and horses rippled throughout our column.

Beside me, one man screamed, and toppled to the ground, impaled by a short spear. Another, not far away, had his horse collapse from under him with an arrow protruding from its neck. Looking around, I faintly saw shapes in the fog, moving about. I blinked and looked harder. A shiver of fear rippled through me as I beheld what looked like dog-headed cinbin moving about, unleashing javelins, arrows, and sling stones at us. The charging figures yelped and howled as they came on, further enhancing their inhuman appearance.

In my head, I knew they were but men, wearing the skins of beasts precisely to make themselves appear more frightening. That didn't help when I looked upon them for myself, and I instinctively hunched behind my shield, not unlike a child reflexively pulling a blanket up to ward against mysterious shadows in their bedroom, I have to admit.

"Form a herringbone," Arthur ordered, and the command was echoed by the other decurions throughout the column. Just like the shape made by the bones of herring, the two files of our column faced outward with spears at the ready.

"Turmae, charge!" Arthur bellowed, once we'd formed up. Our cornicern raised his horn to his lips and sounded the call to charge.

"Last Hope!" we roared our battle cry as we spurred our horses forward in all directions. Instinctively, we kept close to our dragon banners, so even though our column charged outward in several directions, we did so by turma, rather than purely as individuals. Arthur led us straight ahead, while the four turmae behind us each split off left or right, so that we formed a loose, horseshoe-like battleline into which our wagons could occupy, along with the infantry.

We had no way of knowing for sure how many enemies surrounded us, but remaining in a tightly grouped formation, surrounded, was an intolerable situation. Better for us to charge into them, and force them on the defensive. In the distance, I heard the sounds of the horns of King Leudon's infantry responding to the battle unfolding ahead of them.

The fog proved to be as suitable for masking our movements as theirs, and as we rode into them in a widening crescent, I was thrilled to see the brass-headed dragon banners of our turma flying above us, almost as though they were living things. Fear was replaced by a savage lust for battle. Garwlwyd presented himself and his men as wolves, but we were dragons!

I slew the first rebel I came upon as he was nocking an arrow, running him through with my spear. Another rebel charged me as I drew my sword. I spurred my beloved Carys forward and she slammed into the man, throwing him to the ground. I leaned over and stabbed him as he attempted to rise.

To my right, Gilbert shouted triumphantly as he rode down yet another rebel. Two arrows stuck out of his shield. All around me was the most chaotic battle I had ever been in. There were no battle lines, no shieldwalls, just men on horseback riding to and fro, fighting men on foot as the fog revealed them. Spears were thrown every which way, and more than once the rebels attempted to group up into formation. There were too few of them, and we swarmed around them with ease, cutting them down by riding into their exposed flanks and rear. Here and there I saw a frightened horse gallop past riderless, and once I saw a wolfskin-garbed rebel on horseback. From the stallion's equipment, I knew he was one of ours. I growled, intent on charging him, but Marcus beat me to it.

He galloped at the rebel, roaring a challenge. The man fought gamely, parrying desperately with his axe, but he was outmatched, and struggled to both control his stolen horse and fend off Marcus. Marcus slammed the rim of his shield into the rebel's head, followed by a thrust of his blade into the man's unarmored chest.

Behind us, the infantry came up. They had managed to stay in tight shield-walls, guided by banners and horns, with their officers riding back and forth and maintaining order. Here and there, small groups detached from formation in order to break into one of the abandoned homes that rebels were using as cover, killed them, then returned to the shieldwall. Further back, I presumed, was King Leudon and his retinue, acting as our reserve force.

I felt something smack hard into my right side. I looked down in time to see an arrow falling to the ground. In spite of the situation, I found myself giggling a little. My new armor had done such a good job, the arrow had simply bounced off the rows of iron scales that protected me.

I quickly scanning my surroundings I spotted the archer. He was already drawing back another arrow. I spurred Carys into a gallop and held my shield out. A moment later, I felt the impact and saw an arrowhead had punched through the back by a few inches. Then I was on the archer, who had tried to run away. He wasn't faster than Carys though, and I cut him down, then wheeled around and rejoined Arthur's turma as they reformed.

The rebels gradually fell back and finally managed to form into a shieldwall that the Red Dragons couldn't simply break through head on. Because of their proximity to the Firth behind them, we didn't have the space needed to ride around to their rear, either. That's where King Leudon's infantry came into play. While their formations methodically converged on and surrounded the rebels in a half-circle, ranks of archers and slingers formed up behind them.

The rain let up, and the fog was finally beginning to thin as the sun rose to its zenith, as the archers and slingers loosed volleys over the heads of their comrades in front of them. A mounted officer, having a slightly elevated position, acted as an observer to guide them onto their targets more accurately. In short order, rebels began dropping left and right to the projectiles being rained down on them.

We swept across the field, never venturing too far from our core of infantry until at last, only the one large pocket of the enemy remained. There were more of them than I expected — two or three hundred perhaps. They stood tightly packed, knee deep in water along the shores of the Firth where we'd driven them. Red Dragons closed in around them, encircling them as best as we could. There was still a healthy distance of about thirty feet between each group. In the space between our forces, the speckled sand of the riverbank was spattered with blood and fallen men. In the front and center of the group was Garwlwyd himself, bloodied and battered, but he still stood proud among his men.

Further out in the water I saw the shapes of men in boats and figured I understood what was going on. We'd come upon the Fisher King's force as he was attempting to ferry them to the far side. He must have kept a lot of extra boats stashed here at this old village, I guessed.

All this flashed through my mind in a few moments, and my attention was snapped back to the rebels when Cai, in the front rank of our men, held up his empty right hand.

"Garwlwyd," Cai, called out, and I was startled to hear the sorrow in his voice. "We fought together two years ago. Your men fought bravely here today. Surrender now and spare them, I beg you. Don't make us kill you all."

Maybe it was sweat, but from where I was, it almost seemed that a tear rolled down the Vicarius' eye. Looking around, I saw the same expression on many other men's faces as well. This had indeed been a fight few of us had wanted.

"What would you have us do, hang by our necks outside of Leudon's walls?" The Fisher King spat.

"We came to end this conflict *peacefully*, not to do battle," Cai shook his head. "You don't have to die."

Just then, Arthur, accompanied by King Leudon, Gawain and Medraut, pushed forward to stand beside Cai. That got a reaction from Garwlwyd all right! He stared in shock, then in fury at Medraut, who was conspicuously unarmored and unarmed.

"You!" He hissed. "Have you betrayed me then?"

"Yes," Medraut sighed. "Though not exactly by choice, if it's any conso-lation. I am Medraut, a son of King Leudon. He's come to offer you terms of surrender."

Garwlwyd's eyes went wide and his mouth hung open, dumb-founded. His sword, which had been held at the ready, slowly dropped to his side. Gawain stepped forward then, with a familiar wood chest in his arms.

"My errant son offered you the Grail to defy my authority," King Leudon said. "I have been told of your grievances caused by my tax collector, whom you and your men murdered. Mistakes were made... I now offer you the use of the Grail, though it will remain in the possession of my priest. We will entreat God to restore the fish, and your own injured body. In return, your men will lay down their arms and leave this land and go with Arthur to the southern kingdoms."

"So God may bring the fish back to the river, but my men and I will not be permitted to reap the benefit. Makes the gesture a bit pointless, does it not?" Garwlwyd growled.

If King Leudon was offended by Garwlwyd's blunt, disrespectful tone, he ignored it. "Any of your family members who did not take up arms here may stay and continue to go about their lives. The same holds true for those people who supported your rebellion by providing aid and comfort, but who did not take up arms directly. They too will be allowed to continue living in peace. If you surrender now."

"There's land in Gwent or Gwynedd that your men can resettle in," Arthur added. "It wouldn't be the first time in recent history that a group of men of the Gododdin came south to settle and made themselves useful."

Garwlwyd looked around at the men beside him. I recognized Brynn, and his son Dylan in the small crowd. They nodded, though they looked almost as dazed as their leader, their 'Fisher King' did.

"I accept your terms," the rough, gray-bearded rebel leader finally said with a bow.

"Splendid. Now then —" King Leudon began, but he was cut off by someone pushing through the mass of our men crying "Make way! Let me through! I must speak with the King!"

The man's voice sounded familiar, though I couldn't place why until he made it up to the front. It was the old retired spymaster who owned the alehouse at Caer Lleon.

"Damon?" Arthur called out in surprise and confusion. "What are you doing here, old man?"

"Urgent news," another man huffed, coming to stand beside Damon. I recognized Ector Artorius, a former commander of the Red Dragons, and Cai's father. He was a bit shorter than average, but made up for that by still being a powerfully-built man, despite being in his fifties.

"Ector? You're both here? What's going on?" Arthur asked as his eyebrows rose so high they practically disappeared beneath the rim of his helm.

Both men, who normally looked very neat, now looked rough, a bit haggard, and had a heavy stubble on their jaws. I suspected that their horses were even worse off.

"Things have been happening that you needed to be aware of. I didn't want to rely on my messengers, so I came myself. Ector insisted on coming with me. Most immediately, are you aware of the Pict warband south of here? We spotted their campfires as we were riding north to come find you a bit before dawn. We'd hoped to link up with you yesterday, but this damned weather slowed us down."

"Picts?" Arthur exclaimed. Now everyone looked alarmed.

"We've been focused on these rebels. Where exactly were they? How many?" King Leudon demanded.

"Hundreds," Ector replied. "A few miles south of here. We'd thought at first that they were your force. We got within a dozen paces of their sentry line, realized our mistake, and slipped away."

"You two came alone, father?" Cai asked. "All the way up here?"

"Don't be silly, boy, of course not," Ector scoffed. "We rounded up a dozen mercenaries first."

Damon and Ector shared pensive looks before the older man looked over to Arthur and King Leudon. "There's no easy way to say this, but the Saxons are pushing west again. They've already attacked and seized the lands north of that island, Vectis... Vecta... Anyway, the king of Gwent put together an army and tried to stop them... he failed." Damon and Ector both looked grim as he reported the news.

"How bad is it?" Arthur asked, having to clear his throat.

"Bad," Damon replied, looking around. "They've been driving off, killing or enslaving everyone in their path. Our people were scrambling to put together a response last we heard. That was two weeks ago. I don't think much of their chances though," he admitted.

A sense of shock hit me nearly as palpably as if I'd been bashed by a shield. It seemed too terrible to imagine! I looked around as my shock gave way to horror and grief. I wasn't alone. Around me, I saw slack jaws, and more than one man had tears streaming down their faces.

"So many?" Medraut asked, scowling. "Surely the Saxons can't muster the kind of numbers to fight on that scale? Who are you, anyway?"

Damon gave the young man a withering look.

"Child, I'm a man who's been matching wits with some of the most devious minds in the world since probably before your father was born," he snapped. "Don't you dare question my word again."

Medraut shut his mouth and edged away, looking a bit sheepish.

"W-which Saxons are leading this campaign?" Cai asked hoarsely. "Cerdic?"

"Cerdic and Cynric are leading the West Saxons, yes. But they aren't alone," Damon admitted. "Cymen's South Saxons have joined them. Banners bearing the horse motif of Hengist's grandson, Octa of Cant, have been spotted along with the white dragons of the other Saxon lords.

Gasps of shock and cries of outrage and denial rippled through the ranks at Damon's pronouncement.

"Are they tightening their grasp on that territory, or pushing further west?" Bedwyr asked after a few moments.

"Hard to say what they've been doing while we've been on the road," Damon said, shrugging wearily. "My guess is that with the size of the army they've mustered, they won't stop at those marshlands. If they continue on the course they started on by the time Ector and I left, I'd guess Caer Badon will be next."

I looked over to Gilbert, whose face had turned ashen, and put a hand on his shoulder to steady him. "*Myn famylje*" he moaned quietly.

For his part, Arthur looked absolutely furious over the news Damon and Ector had brought. His face was nearly crimson and his hands had tightened into fists. He looked up towards the sky and let out a long, slow breath.

"Decurion Drystan," he barked out abruptly.

"Tribune!" Drystan responded.

"Gather up the wounded at a safe location where they can receive care. See to the dead, get the wounded moving towards Din Eidyn. Garwlwyd, designate one fifth of your men to do the same. King Leudon, I would advise you to do likewise," Arthur said.

I noticed with a little amusement, in spite of the circumstances, that Arthur's tone all but made his *advice* to the king sound very much like an order, which spoke volumes as to the nature of Arthur's true level of authority. Even more interesting was that both Garwlwyd and King Leudon nodded along with Decurion Drystan. The only difference was that while Drystan left to carry out his assigned task himself, Garwlwyd and King Leudon each called up someone else to get it done.

Arthur eyed the two, along with Cai and Bedwyr. "Our first order of business must be to deal with those blue-painted bastards. This time, we show them no mercy," he said in a tone that sent chills down my spine. I'd seen Arthur annoyed, and, I thought, angry before. Now I realized I had not — not until this moment. I almost pitied those Picts.

"We are going to kill every one of those whoresons, then ride south as fast as we can and rally the free Britons to confront the Saxons," Arthur continued. "King Leudon, Garwlwyd, I need you both to muster as many men as you can and get them south to Caer Lleon. How soon can you make that happen?"

"I need a few days to let my men gather their families and get supplies... we left most of what we had at Caer Amon," Garwlwyd said ruefully. "Between the blessing of the Grail, and a new home awaiting us in Gwent, I think my men will be up for another fight."

"My army is already assembled, as you can see," King Leudon said with a gesture around us. "I'll send my sons, Gawain and Medraut with you, along with the bulk of my mounted contingent. I must remain here with some of my army to protect my kingdom, but I can spare a thousand men to march south as soon as I can gather supplies for their journey. Give me... two weeks?"

"One," Arthur countered flatly.

A look of annoyance flashed across the king's face, but he nodded in agreement with Arthur.

"It's settled then. Now, let's get our men ready." Arthur said. He turned his horse around to the rest of us, raised his bloody sword, known to us as Caledfwlch, and bellowed for all to hear.

"Men! The Picts have broken their word and come south, again! More than that, they desecrated the graves of our brothers who died defending this land at Guinnion's Fort! Now a warband of these swine have taken advantage of this unfortunate conflict with Garwlwyd and moved around south to get behind us and are even now within striking distance of Din Eidyn! Will you tolerate this?"

"No!" Many of us cried out loudly in response.

"We must slaughter these barbarians to the last man for what they have done!" Arthur continued. "Once we have annihilated them, we will ride back south and confront the Saxons. For their transgressions against our kin, we will rain down such wrath upon them, our vengeance will be remembered for a thousand years! Are you with me?"

This time the response was deafening as every man present, both northern and southern Britons roared in approval.

We raised our spears and swords into the air and a chant began.

"Arthur! Arthur! Arthur!"

When we finally quieted down, Arthur lowered his sword and called out, "Form up and get ready to ride, my dragons! And you, wolves of Caledonia," Arthur said nodding to Garwlwyd's men. "We have some barbarians to kill!"

And just like that, our fight with Garwlwyd was over, and his men were cymbrogi again, thank God. We were united against a common enemy. The shock and dismay over the news that Damon and Ector had delivered transformed into cold fury and a thirst for blood such as I, at least, had never experienced before, and rarely experienced since.

Epilogue

Caer Gurcoc, Isle of Mona. 549 A.D.

Enid, Rhys, and Cadoc stared wide-eyed at Peredur as he finished his tale.

"So that's how you got that scar," breathed Cadoc in a hushed tone, reaching out with a small finger and delicately tracing the white line that ran across his grandfather's cheek jaw.

Peredur nodded slowly.

"That's the first thing you have to say, after a story like that?" Enid asked in exasperation, then turned her attention to her grandfather. "What happened with you and Gemma? When did you finally marry her?"

"Who said I ended up marrying her?" Peredur asked with a twinkle in his eye. "Have some patience. I haven't got to that part of the story yet!"

"Grandmother, what's your name?" Enid called out, staring defiantly at Peredur.

"If you don't remember, why should I tell you now? As far as you're concerned, my name is apparently *Grandmother*," Peredur's wife grumbled from where she was stirring a pot of porridge over a fire.

"Fine, I'll ask Mother later," Enid huffed.

"What happened with the Picti bastards?" Rhys asked, drawing a giggle from Cadoc.

Peredur cocked a bushy eyebrow at his grandson. "I may have to watch what I say around you boys," he mused, then looked out of the small window that lit up the dining area of the large room.

"It's getting late. I imagine your mother will want you three home soon."

"Ooooh grandfather," the boys whined together. "You can't end the story like this!"

"Don't say things like that to him," Peredur's wife chortled girlishly. "You'll only make him want to do exactly that."

"Isn't it unusual, having to fight two different armies one after the other?" Enid surprised Peredur by asking.

"It is... and it isn't," the old man answered, scratching his jaw. "In regions where there's only two factions likely to feel the urge to fight each other, it would be very rare. But here, unfortunately, we have several factions, all trying to take over. Best time to attack an enemy is when they're weak. So, plenty of armies have attacked their enemies if they're experiencing famine, plague... or have recently fought a battle against a different enemy. Or if their enemy's army is simply not present. That's what Drest did, as well as the Saxons. Arthur's done it too," Peredur chuckled.

"That doesn't seem fair," Cadoc muttered.

"It's not," Peredur agreed. "Life isn't fair. Neither is war. In fact, if you're fighting an enemy fairly, you're not doing it right."

"What happened with... Modred? Rhys asked, scrunching up his brow as he tried to recall the name.

"Medraut," Peredur corrected, then sighed. He and his wife shared ruthful glances as Peredur reached over and grabbed his goblet, then he took a large sip of mead.

"Well," he finally said. "He came with us to Caer Lleon."

"His name is carved on this table, like yours and other cymbrogi you mentioned," Rhys pointed out. "I guess he behaved himself after you fought him?"

Peredur's eyes lost focus as he stared out of the window. He shook his head and grimaced. "No, he did not. But just like the Battle of Mount Agned against the Picts, that is definitely a story for another day."

The boys sighed in disappointment and Enid frowned a little.

Peredur finished his mead, then stood up, wincing at the flash of pain in his back and knees, which popped audibly. "Let's not make your mother angry now. She might not let you come visit so often if you take advantage of her generosity," he said. "Best you get on home to your parents now."

The children stood as well, hugged their grandparents tightly and wished the two good night. Then trudged out of the door. Peredur's wife came over with a bowl of porridge in her hands.

"Time to eat, before you get busy with something or other and forget, dear," she said.

Peredur smiled lovingly and he took the bowl, then looked out of the window, watching the three children walking away. "It's not going to be pleasant, telling them about Medraut and Arthur," he said heavily.

"It's been over ten years," his wife said, resting her head on his shoulder.

"I know," Peredur said, and his voice choked up. "And it still hurts, every time I remember what happened. It feels like it could have been yesterday."

"Well, eat your porridge and I'll think of something to take your mind off it," his wife said and kissed him on the cheek, then walked away.

Peredur smiled a little as he watched her go, then stared over at his armor stand while he finished his food. Finally, his gaze settled down to the large, round wooden table that dominated the room, and memories flooded into him. He recalled times when he was much younger and standing beside Arthur, Cai, Bedwyr, Drystan, Gawain, and others, all crowding around that same table. They were all alive again, and laughing as they talked, and ate, and drank. The old man traced the names of Arthur and then Medraut. Resolutely, he finished his bowl of fine, wheat porridge, downed the rest of his mead, then headed towards the bedroom after his wife.

Author's Note

As with the first story of Peredur, Beyond the Wall, there's very little in the way of known history from which I could draw on while writing this novel. Some of the people mentioned here are considered "semi-legendary", some are probably historical and are even found in genealogical records, along with the dates in which they lived. Of course, the historicity of Arthur himself is widely debated. Beyond that, the 6th-century writings of Gildas, and those of Bede, two centuries later, provide a good idea of what life in Britain as a whole may have been like in this period. I hope I have fairly represented Britain, and the various peoples who inhabited it in this period, within the context of the times in which they lived. That was certainly one of my goals here.

The first battle of this story, "The Battle of the City of the Legion" is the ninth of twelve battles the 9th-century Welsh writer Nennius claimed Arthur fought in the capacity of Dux Bellorum. Historians generally agree that the modern cities of Caerleon, Chester, and York are the strongest candidates for this battle, though none can be proven to be so as of the time I wrote this book in 2025. For my story, I decided that the city of Chester made the most sense geographically, within the context of the time period.

The Wolves of Caledonia was heavily influenced by the early medieval Welsh stories found in the Pa Gur, and the Welsh Triads. These texts provided the narrative of Arthur, Cai, and Bedwyr fighting Garwlwyd, the leader of an army of cinbin, which seem to essentially be werewolves, in a battle of Tryfrwyd. Some historians have suggested a link between this battle with the Battle of the

Tribruit, first mentioned by Nennius in his History of the Britons as Arthur's tenth battle. By comparing the etymology of both Tryfrwyd and Tribruit, there is some thought within the historical community that this battle likely occurred in the vicinity of the Firth of Forth, as I have portrayed in this novel. Other sources of inspiration, particularly regarding the character of Peredur/Percival come from Chrétien de Troyes tale of Percival, the Story of the Grail, and Book 6 of Thomas Malory's The Death of Arthur, which I have done to help keep the story familiar, and because they were fun additions.

Overall, I have tried to write a story that is historically authentic, relatively faithful to established Arthurian lore, and even more importantly, entertaining. If you, reader, agree that I have met these goals, I would greatly appreciate a rating and/or review on Amazon or Audible. It helps me out more than you can imagine!

Thank you for reading my novel.

Acknowledgements

My thanks to J.F. Holmes and the Cannon Publishing "Gun Crew" for their support, assistance, and for giving me the opportunity to write as part of the team.

I would also like to thank James Mace of Legionary Books for his mentorship, encouragement, and for offering insights that helped shape this work and improve its historical accuracy.

Samantha Houston, along with several others, deserves thanks as well for providing technical feedback and for serving as enthusiastic test readers.

Glossary of Important People

Arthur (AR-thur): the son of Riothamus "Uther" the Pendragon. Arthur is a noble and lord of Din Tagel, in the kingdom of Dumnonia. He is also the Prefect of the Red Dragons Cavalry, and frequently the Dux Bellorum (field commander) in battles he is involved with where troops from other kingdoms are present.

Bedwyr (BED-wir): the One-Handed: the Castellan of Caer Lleon, and a decurion of his own turma.

Brynn (BRIN): a long-time friend and second-in-command to Garwlwyd

Cai (KAI): the son of Ector Gaius Artorius and foster brother of Arthur. He is the Vicarius and Second in Command/ the Executive Officer of the Red Dragons Cavalry.

Cadoc (KAH-dok): one of Peredur's grandchildren.

Cadwal: a member of Peredur's contubernium.

Cornelius (kor-NEHL-ius): a duplarius within Owain's turma.

Damon: A Greek man who had lived in Rome but left for Britain shortly before it was sacked in 476. He entered the service of Vortigern until his death at the hands of Ambrosius Aurelianus and Uther, then went to work for them.

Domangart Reti (DOH-man-gart REH-ti): a king of Dal Riata of the early 6th century, following the death of his father, King Fergus Mor.

Drest II (DREST): a prominent king of the Picts of the early 6th century.

Drystan (DRIS-tan): one of Arthur's decurions. Drystan (based on Tristan) is from Cair Wisc (Exeter, UK).

Ector Gaius Artorius (EK-tor GAI-us ar-TOR-ee-us): former Vicarius of the Red Dragons while it was under the command of "Uther" the Pendragon. He is Cai's father, and Arthur's mentor and foster father. He is from Caer Londin.

Enid (EH-nid): the oldest of Peredur's grandchildren.

Euron: a member of Peredur's contubernium

Ewan (YOO-an): a former fellow recruit in Peredur's training turma. He is Rhun's younger brother.

Galhault (GAL-holt): one of Arthur's decurions. Galhault (based on Galehaut) is from the island of Guernsey (Sarnia), off the coast of Gaul/Frankia (France).

Garwlwyd (GAR-oo-loo-eed): a former Penteulu of Gododdin, turned rebel leader. Garwlwyd, whose name translates to "Rough Gray" is named as the leader of an army of Cinbin in the Pa Gur. For my story, I have merged his character with that of the fictional "Fisher King" often featured in later medieval Arthurian tales.

Gilbert (also known as Gib): a member of Peredur's contubernium within Owain's turma. Gilbert is of Frisian descent, and is from Cair Badon (Bath, England).

Leudon (LAY-oo-don): Gododdin's king in the early 6th century. He is married to Arthur's half-sister, Morgause

Maithgemm (Gemma) (MATH-gemm): a runaway slave of Gaelic father and Pict mother. She is from western Caledonia (Scotland).

Marcus (MAR-kus): a member of Peredur's contubernium within Owain's turma.

Morcant (MOR-kant): one of Arthur's decurions.

Myrddin Wylt (the Wild) (MIR-thin WILT): an all-around wise man and bard (based on Merlin) who was a former advisor to Uther, and current advisor to Arthur.

Owain (OH-wine): Owain, a noble of Alt Clut, is one of Arthur's decurions.

Peredur (PER-eh-door): the youngest son of Lord Pelinor in Cair Gurcoc, on the island of Mona (Anglesey, UK). He is a member of Owain's turma.

Quintus (KWIN-tus): a member of Peredur's contubernium within Owain's turma.

Rhun (RHIN): a fellow Red Dragon and former fellow recruit in Peredur's training turma. He is Ewan's older brother.

Rhydderch (HRU-thairk): one of Arthur's decurions.

Rhys (REES): one of Peredur's grandchildren.

Sawyl (SOW-ul): one of Owain's two decanii.

Sextus Brocius (SEX-tus BROH-see-us): a merchant who accompanies the Red Dragons and acts as their primary armorer.

Taran (also known as Tor): a member of Peredur's contubernium. Taran is from Mona, like Peredur and bears a striking resemblance to him.

Tewdrig (TEYOO-drig): the middle-aged medicus (doctor) of the Red Dragons Cavalry.

Titus (TIE-tus): one of Arthur's decurions.

Tyree (TIE-ree): a duplarius in one of Arthur's turmae.

Ythel: a member of Peredur's contubernium.

Glossary of Important Locations

Alt Clut (AHLT KLOOT)

Modern Location: Modern-day Dumbarton, Scotland.

Significance: Alt Clut was a powerful fortress and the center of the Kingdom of Alt Clut in the 6th century, ruled by the Brittonic-speaking peoples in the Clyde Valley. It was a key stronghold for resisting the Picts and Anglo-Saxons, playing a critical role in defending the western Britons during this period.

Antonine Wall (AN-toh-neen)

Modern Location: Stretching across central Scotland from the Firth of Forth to the Firth of Clyde.

Significance: Built by the Romans in the mid-2nd century, the Antonine Wall marked the northernmost frontier of the Roman Empire in Britain for a brief period.

Caledonia (KAL-eh-DOH-nee-ah)

Modern Location: Roughly corresponds to present-day Scotland.

Significance: Caledonia was the Roman name for the land north of their empire, home to the fierce, independent tribes, most notably the Picts. Roman attempts to conquer Caledonia were unsuccessful, and it remained a largely unconquered region beyond Roman control, marked by its resistance to Roman occupation.

Caer Amon (KIRE AH-mon)

Modern Location: Cramond, a village and archaeological site at the mouth of the River Almond, just northwest of Edinburgh.

Significance: Originally the Roman fort Alaterva, Cramond was later known by the Brittonic name Caer Amon, meaning "Fort of the Almond [River]." The name reflects its position at the mouth of the River Almond (Afon Amon in Brittonic).

Caer Ligion (KAI-er LIG-yon)

Modern Location: Chester, on the River Dee (Dyfrdwy in Welsh), Cheshire, England.

Significance: Built during the early days of the Roman occupation of Britain and known as Deva, it housed the Roman Legion II Adiutrix, then later the XX Legion Valeria Victrix. The fort's name then became Deva Victrix. After Rome's withdrawal, it remained a strategic stronghold on the frontier of Powys between Britons and incoming Anglo-Saxons. This city is a strong candidate for the city Nennius, writing in the early 9th century, named as Cair Legion/Caer Ligion- the City of the Legion, and the site of Arthur's ninth of twelve credited battles.

Caer Ligualid (KAI-er LEE-gwa-lid)

Modern Location: Carlisle, near the Scottish border in northwest England.

Significance: An important Roman settlement and military site that remained significant in the early medieval period. It was part of the kingdom of Rheged, a major Brittonic power in northern Britain during the 5th and 6th centuries.

Caer Lleon (KAI-er HLEE-on)

Modern Location: Caerleon, near Newport, Wales.

Significance: This site was well established by native Britons even before the Romans built up a significant legionary fortress, which they called Isca Augusta. It remained a major power center after the Roman withdrawal from Britain. It is sometimes associated with the legendary King Arthur and his court as a contender for the fictional city of Camelot.

Dal Riata (DAHL REE-ah-tah)

Modern Location: Spanned parts of modern-day western Scotland and north-eastern Ireland.

Significance: In the 6th century, Dal Riata was an emerging Gaelic kingdom that straddled the Irish Sea, with settlements in both Ireland and western Scotland. It played an important role in early Gaelic expansion, and its kings helped shape the early political landscape of both Scotland and Ireland.

Din Eidyn (DIN AY-din)

Modern Location: Modern-day Edinburgh, Scotland.

Significance: Din Eidyn was a major hillfort in the kingdom of Gododdin during the 6th century. It was a center of power for the Brittonic-speaking peoples of the region.

Din Pendyrlaw (DIN pen-DUR-law)

Modern Location: Traprain Law, East Lothian, Scotland.

Significance: Din Pendyrlaw, now known as Traprain Law, was the primary stronghold of the Votadini tribe in the early medieval period, including the 6th century. It was a key power center in southern Scotland, acting as both a defensive fort and a trading hub.

Din Tagel (DIN TA-gel)

Modern Location: Modern-day Tintagel, Cornwall, England.

Significance: Din Tagel, commonly associated with Tintagel Castle, was a coastal fortress and settlement in the 6th century. It held significant strategic and symbolic importance in the kingdom of Dumnonia. Though much of its later fame comes from its association with Arthurian legend, in the 6th century it was a vital defensive position controlling access to the southwestern coast of Britain.

Dumnonia (DUHM-noh-nee-ah)

Modern Location: Modern-day Devon and Cornwall in southwest England.

Significance: In the 6th century, Dumnonia was one of the most prominent Brittonic kingdoms resisting Anglo-Saxon expansion. It was a bastion of Romano-British culture, and its rulers maintained control over a significant portion of southwestern Britain during this period.

Dun Foithear (DOON FOY-er)

Modern Location: Dunnottar Castle, on the northeastern coast of Scotland, just south of Stonehaven.

Significance: A Gaelic name meaning "Fort of the Slope" or "Fort of the Terrace." The site occupies a dramatic rocky headland with steep cliffs on three sides and has evidence of early medieval occupation. A chapel at Dunnottar is said to have been founded by St Ninian in the 5th century, though that is unconfirmed.

Dyfed (DUH-ved)

Modern Location: Southwest Wales, corresponding to modern Pembrokeshire and Carmarthenshire.

Significance: Dyfed was a small but strategically significant kingdom in the 6th century, established by Irish settlers who had gained control of the area. It maintained strong connections with Ireland and was involved in regional politics with other Welsh and Irish kingdoms.

Glywysing (GLU-wiss-ing)

Modern Location: South Wales, corresponding to modern-day Glamorgan.

Significance: In the 6th century, Glywysing was a smaller Brittonic kingdom located to the west of Gwent. It was often closely associated with its neighbors, sometimes forming alliances with Gwent, and was known for its coastal defenses against raiders from Ireland and the Anglo-Saxons.

Gododdin (goh-DOTH-in)

Modern Location: The region around modern-day Edinburgh, Scotland.

Significance: The kingdom of Gododdin was one of the major Brittonic kingdoms of the north in the 6th century.

Gwent (GWENT)

Modern Location: Southeast Wales, corresponding to modern Monmouthshire and parts of Glamorgan.

Significance: Gwent was an important Brittonic kingdom in the 6th century, known for its strategic position along the Severn estuary, allowing it to engage in trade and conflict with both neighboring Brittonic kingdoms and the expanding Anglo-Saxons. It was a key center of power in early medieval Wales.

Gwynedd (GWIN-eth)

Modern Location: Northwest Wales, corresponding to modern Gwynedd and Anglesey.

Significance: By the 6th century, Gwynedd had become a dominant Welsh kingdom, playing a key role in resisting the Irish raids and consolidating power over northwestern Wales. Its rulers, such as Maelgwn Gwynedd, were instrumental in shaping early medieval Welsh politics and culture.

Guinnion's Fort (WEN-yon's Fort)

Modern Location: Uncertain; some traditions place it in northern England or southern Scotland, though its exact site is lost.

Significance: Cited in *Historia Brittonum* (9th c.) as the location of one of Arthur's battles, where he is said to have borne the image of the Virgin Mary on his shield. Its precise identification is debated, but it is often treated as one of the legendary sites tied to Arthur's campaigns against the Saxons and Picts.

Hibernia (hi-BUR-nee-ah)

Modern Location: Modern-day Ireland.

Significance: Hibernia was the Roman name for Ireland, a land they never successfully invaded. In the 6th century, Ireland was a land of powerful petty kingdoms, known for its warrior elite and increasingly for its growing Christian monastic tradition, which would soon become a major cultural force across the British Isles.

Powys (POW-iss)

Modern Location: Mid-Wales.

Significance: Powys was a major Brittonic kingdom in the 6th century, controlling central Wales and parts of modern-day Shropshire. Its rulers played a significant role in defending against Anglo-Saxon encroachment, particularly from the Kingdom of Mercia.

Rheged (REH-ged)

Modern Location: Modern day Cumbria and possibly parts of southern Scotland.

Significance: In the 6th century, Rheged was one of the most powerful Brittonic kingdoms in northern Britain. Under rulers like Urien Rheged, it played a central role in military campaigns against the Angles and Picts, and its kings are celebrated in early Welsh poetry.

Glossary of Terms

Castellan

Definition: The governor or keeper of a castle, responsible for its defense and
the surrounding land.

Singular: Castellan /ˈkæs.tə.lən/

Plural: Castellans /ˈkæs.tə.lənz/

Pronunciation: KAS-tuh-luhn

Chi Rho

Definition: A Christian symbol made by superimposing the first two letters of
the Greek word for Christ (ΧΡΙΣΤΟΣ), representing Christ.

Singular: Chi Rho /ˌkaɪ ˈroʊ/

Plural: Chi Rhos /ˌkaɪ ˈroʊz/

Pronunciation: KAI roh

Contubernium

Definition: A unit of eight soldiers in the Roman army who shared a tent and
were the smallest organized group.

Singular: Contubernium /ˌkɒn.tuˈbɜː.ni.əm/

Plural: Contubernia /ˌkɒn.tuˈbɜː.ni.ə/

Pronunciation: kon-too-BER-nee-um (singular), kon-too-BER-nee-ah (plural)

Cymbrog

Definition: A Welsh term meaning "fellow countryman" or "comrade-in-arms." It was historically used to describe someone who shared a close bond, particularly in the context of warriors fighting for the same homeland or cause.

Singular: Cymbrog /ˈkʌm.brɒg/

Plural: Cymbrogi /kʌmˈbrɒ.gi/

Pronunciation: KUHM-brog (singular), KUHM-broh-gee (plural)

Decanus

Definition: A leader of men in the Roman army, often commanding a contubernium.

Singular: Decanus /dɪˈkeɪ.nəs/

Plural: Decani /dɪˈkeɪ.niː/

Pronunciation: deh-KAY-nus (singular), deh-KAY-nee (plural)

Decurion

Definition: A Roman officer in charge of a turma, typically a cavalry unit of about thirty men.

Singular: Decurion /dɪˈkjʊə.rɪ.ən/

Plural: Decurions /dɪˈkjʊə.rɪ.ənz/

Pronunciation: dih-KYOOR-ee-uhn

Duplarius

Definition: A soldier in the Roman army who received double pay, usually due to a promotion or distinction in service.

Singular: Duplarius

Plural: Duplares

Pronunciation: doo-PLAH-ree-us (singular)

Dux Bellorum

Definition: A Latin term meaning "leader of wars" or "war leader." Historically, this title was used to refer to a military leader or commander, often in the context of late Roman or early medieval Britain, who held significant authority over other military forces, but it was not necessarily a formal rank.

Singular: Dux Bellorum /dʊks bɛˈlɔː.rʊm/

Plural: Ducēs Bellorum /ˈduː.keɪs bɛˈlɔː.rʊm/

Pronunciation: DOOKS bel-LOH-room (singular), DOO-kays bel-LOH-room (plural)

Levy

Definition: A term referring to the act of raising or gathering troops, typically by conscription, or the imposition of taxes, often for military purposes. Historically, a levy was a compulsory draft for military service or a collection of resources by a governing authority.

Singular: Levy /ˈlɛ.vi/

Plural: Levies /ˈlɛ.viːz/

Pronunciation: LEH-vee (singular), LEH-veez (plural)

Pace

Definition: The Roman pace (passus) was a unit of measurement equal to roughly 4.9 feet (1.48 meters). Five thousand paces made one Roman mile. A pace represents the distance covered in two natural steps by an adult man.

For added context, a spear could be thrown accurately and with force at a distance of roughly ten to twenty paces. A sling could be used effectively against individual targets at about twenty to forty paces, and at roughly double that distance when loosing volleys into a mass of troops. Bows of the sixth century, in Britain, were effective against individual targets at about thirty to fifty paces, and at roughly double that range when shooting into dense formations.

Penteulu

Definition: A Welsh term meaning "chief of the household," specifically referring to the leader of a warband or personal guard. The penteulu was responsible for the king's or lord's warriors and acted as their commander in battle.

Singular: Penteulu /pɛnˈteɪ.li/

Plural: Penteulu (the plural form remains the same)

Pronunciation: pen-TAY-lee (singular and plural)

Plumbata

Definition: A type of throwing dart used by Roman infantry, featuring a lead weight to give it extra momentum.

Singular: Plumbata /plʌmˈbɑː.tə/

Plural: Plumbatae /plʌmˈbɑː.teɪ/

Pronunciation: plum-BAH-tuh (singular), plum-BAH-tay (plural)

Seax

Definition: A short sword or large knife used by the Saxons, commonly employed for combat and utility purposes.

Singular: Seax /sæks/

Plural: Seaxes /ˈsæks.ɪz/

Pronunciation: SAX (singular), SAX-es (plural)

Tribune

Definition: A Roman military officer rank, equivalent to a senior commander of a cavalry unit or legion. Historically, this title referred to a high-ranking official, often leading a cohort or, in later periods, specialized units like cavalry.

Singular: Tribunus /triˈbjuː.nəs/

Plural: Tribuni /triˈbjuː.niː/

Pronunciation: tri-BYOO-nus (singular), tri-BYOO-nee (plural)

Turma

Definition: A Roman cavalry unit composed of around 30 men, commanded
by a decurion.

Singular: Turma /ˈtʊər.mə/

Plural: Turmae /ˈtʊər.maɪ/

Pronunciation: TUR-mah (singular), TUR-my (plural)

Vicarius

Definition: A Roman administrative and military rank, meaning "deputy" or
"substitute," often used to denote someone acting as second-in-command.

Singular: Vicarius /vɪˈkaː.rɪ.us/

Plural: Vicarii /vɪˈkaː.rɪ.iː/

Pronunciation: vi-KAR-ee-us (singular), vi-KAR-ee-ee (plural)

Wealh

Definition: An Old English term used by Anglo-Saxons to describe a native
Briton, meaning "foreigner" or "slave."

Singular: Wealh /wælk/

Plural: Wealas /ˈwæl.əs/

Pronunciation: WAL-k (singular), WAL-uhs (plural)

About the Author

Jason Kyle was born in California and grew up across the United States as the son of an Air Force servicemember. He joined the Army after high school and deployed to Iraq in March 2003 as a Combat Engineer. Over the years, he completed two more deployments to Iraq as a Cavalry Scout, and earned a bachelor's degree in history before finally retiring from the Army in May 2025. He is the author of Beyond the Wall (February 2025), the first book in this trilogy about Peredur/Percival, and a fantasy novel based on the Miniatures Tabletop Game Warlord by Reaper Miniatures called The Apprentice Mage (Aug. 2025).

Jason currently lives in Idaho with his son and their dog and is working on many more Arthurian books as well as other stories.

More from Cannon Publishing

Join the Crew!

Sign up for our newsletter for the latest news on new releases and more.

Follow our authors at their Amazon Pages!

Shane Gries (Dragon Finalist)

Lucas Marcum

Al Hagan

James Copley

Jason Kyle

G. Scott Huggins

Michael Morton

Charles Hackney

Jon LaForce

Jason Weiser

Kal Spriggs

Brian Gifford

Charli Cox

Dan Kemp

Jonathan Shuerger

J.R. Wise

Steven Vickers

David Hensley

Irregular Scout Team One

In July of 2016 a plague swept the world, and the civilization collapsed and fell. For a lone National Guard sergeant, a veteran of the wars overseas who had settled down to a new life, the nightmare began on a hot summer evening at the barricades. Orders and chaos, gunfire and being overrun, his unit dwindles away in the face of the infected. Months later, living in the ruins, the thud of helicopter rotors followed by a crash and the rescue of a downed pilot leads Sergeant First Class Nick Agostine back into the arms of the US military. From his experience comes the idea of teams, military and civilians experienced in dealing with the undead and barbarism of the wilds. The first Irregular Scout Team leads the way for Task Force Liberty to advance down the Mohawk Valley in Upstate NY, making contact with survivors and clearing out the infected with stealth and firepower.

Volume 1

Volume 2

Volume 3: Civil War

Volume 4: Bad Company

Volume 5: End of Days

The Line

When the world descends into chaos and anarchy with an unbelievably swift plague, turning victims into ravenous maniacs, the soldiers of America's storied 1st Infantry are asked to hold the line. From the brutal streets of urban combat to the bloodied, desperate defense on the plains of Kansas, they fight a war against an unrelenting enemy who used to be their fellow citizens. As civilization falls, can they hold the line?

The Thin Dead Line
Dead Storm Rising
The Big Dead One

Fallen Empire

What's a soldier to do when the war is over? When he's only known conflict his whole life? Since time immemorial the solution has been to find another war, this time for pay. Whoever has the credits and wins the high bid gets the experienced fighter. Sometimes, though, the credits aren't enough to cover the price. Empires rise, but Empires also fall. The Terran Union has spent five centuries under the control of the alien Grausians, like a barbarian tribe under the thumb of Rome. Now, after almost two decades of civil war and succession struggles, the formerly subject races have settled back in their ancient territories to lick their wounds and re-arm, leaving hundreds of settled planets to exist in a political vacuum. Into that space steps the free companies, mercenary units that fight for gold, honor, power and glory. Veterans who can't get the wars out of their souls, new recruits looking for adventure, corporations with their own agenda. Join us in a 27th Century that echoes history.

The Irish Brigade

Overrun

Silent Violence

Doom Company

From Book 1: Sandy Decker had a problem. Well, multiple problems. Some good, some bad. Some pretty bad. The good problem is that she was up a whole bunch of credits and the title to an Azelia class yacht called Vagabond King. That was the good problem. The bad problem was that she was in debt to Daresh An-Jaska, Former Princeps in the Golden Legion, Grausian exile, and the biggest gangster in the sector. Not a money debt but a favor debt, one that she paid principle on doing favors in return. Dirty deeds that never seemed to pay enough, of course. That was until yesterday, when she found a line she couldn't cross.

Today, faced with a brutal and violent death at the hands of Jaska, Sandy did what any good former spy would do. She told a story and sold a secret. Operation Marconi and the missing Terran Union battleship *U.S.S. Resolute*. Now it's good news, bad news.

The good news: Jaska bought the story.

The bad news: Jaska didn't trust Sandy as far as she can throw a grat. So the mob boss put 'controls' in place to ensure her compliance. The kind that blew your head off if you didn't do the job.

Now all Sandy and the crew of the Vagabond have to do is follow a decade old trail to the *Resolute*, salvage the mission package for Operation Marconi, and find the objective—a secret location where the Old Empire produced their greatest weapon.

Vagabonds: A Fallen Empire Novel

Athenaeum, Inc

The Professor has problems, and not just what decades of soldiering did to his back and his knees. His boss just died, leaving him as CEO of the extremely discreet intelligence contractor Athenaeum, Incorporated. His old buddy the Operations Director is a highly skilled Army Ranger veteran but his finance chief is slightly unhinged and spends her money on highly inappropriate work outfits. The surviving old men on the Board of Directors are stuck in the 1970s. Running Athenaeum out of an old Cold War bunker and keeping their roster of experts together is expensive, but the government contracts are drying up or going to bigger, flashier corporate players.

Door Number Three

Doubling Down

Off World

When nuclear war erupts on Earth, the American colony in the Alpha Centauri system is left stranded. As the new day dawns, a furious attack by the native inhabitants threatens to overwhelm the colony's defenses. It's left to the thin red line of the US Army's 9th Regiment to stem the tide and ensure humanity's survival in this harsh new world. From two time Dragon Finalist and author of the best selling series "Irregular Scout Team One" and "Invasion" comes a new tale that tells of the struggle for survival on a brutal planet.

Offworld: Ragnarok
Offworld: Expeditions

Cannon Fodder: Tales From the Gun Crew

Fifteen stories from Cannon Publishing Authors, each taking from the universes of their novels to bring you perspectives and deepen their world. From 27th century mercenaries fighting on distant planets and young soldiers riding with Arthur to defeat Saxon hordes, to enchanted weapons dealing damage in hands of Fae, we bring you the best of Science Fiction and Fantasy!

Valkyrie

Humanity engages in a desperate struggle with an alien species for this side of the Orion Arm. Space ships die in instantaneous bursts of light and turn into vapor, but on the ground Marines scream and lie wounded in the mud and blood, praying for the Valkyries to come save them. They aren't wishing for death and a Nordic goddess to take them to Valhalla, the wounded are praying for the men and women of the '348th Field Hospital MEDEVAC to dive through fire and hell to come save them. Because they know that ...Valkyries never die!

Valkyrie

Valkyrie: Rebellion

Valkyrie: Attrition

High Caliber Awards

The Cannon High Caliber Awards are an annual contest for new writers. In it we ask them to submit a novella length story of Science Fiction, Military or Fantasy genre to challenge their skills.

2024

2025

The Wishkiller Saga

While on patrol Captain Aethal Paaling discovers evidence that an ancient terror has reached the rich soil of his home: the Lotus, a prolific growth whose addictive leaves devour their victims from within turning their hosts into horrible, terrifyingly violent mockeries of humanity. Created at the dawn of history by the twisted power of a godly relic called the Well, the return of the Lotus may be a harbinger of even more horrors to come. Carrying the fatal news to the capital, Aethal discovers that even in the face of death itself, the Lords Paramount of Verlaen will fight to keep their secrets and their power. With only the guidance of his legendary Greater Rifle and the aid of the Pheonix Lancers, the soldier must find his way through the halls of a forgotten holy order and into deep dens of crime seeking answers. He must find the truth as quickly as he can, because the Lotus may have already taken root among those he loves... and fighting it may cost him everything, including his soul.

A Cold and Mortal Spring
War of the Shattered Moon

Hexen

When nine out of ten people in the world have died in a brutal plague, what do those who remain do to pick up the pieces? Does the creed, "Duty, Honor, Country" have a place any more if there's no country left? On his way across the devastated remains of Texas, Marine Corps veteran and survivor Eric Marten rescues a young woman from a vicious attack by men who have turned into savages. As Dani slowly learns to trust him, they try to stay alive in the deathlands that America has become, using all their wits to survive a post-apocalyptic nightmare.

90% Death Rate: A Post Apocalyptic Thriller
Angel of Death: A Post Apocalyptic Thriller
The Bloody Princess: A Post Apocalyptic Thriller
The Devil's Pitchfork

Hell Train

A single train carries what might be the last vestige of civilization through a hellish nightmare. A few hundred alive out of millions, lights going out all across what was once America as the possessed arose from the dead and murdered the living. A few hundred survivors travel across the country in an armored train, seeking some place to shelter in a fallen world. All that remains is a dystopian nightmare marked by rains of blood, impossible horrors, and portals to Hell opening in the skies.US Army Captain Jack Zamora is responsible for their safety, a self-imposed burden that wears on him every day. Fighting off undead, protecting the survivors, keeping the train running and supplied as his team desperately plans their next moves. Starvation and disease threaten. but it gets worse, because the ancient gods have sent their emissaries, horrific beings of myth and legend that walk the Earth. Things that can drain a man's very life essence or even that of an entire city.

Hell Train: All Aboard

Sometimes a hero isn't what you expect, and the one you need comes from the castaways of society. Nearly broken and at the end of his rope, former decorated scout pilot and prisoner of war, Red has finally accepted the inevitable. He and his kin have no future in the Human Confederation of Worlds, being gene mods and barely human themselves. With the help of his friend he flees Terra for adventure and fortune out in the reaches of the galaxy. Along the way he's dragged back into conflict that calls on all his piloting skills and he learns the deeper meaning of Kin, as his crew becomes his family.

Path to Freedom: The Path, Book One

Invasion

More than a decade after the Confederated Earth Forces were defeated, their commanding general, a boyhood protegee, lives in exile and disgrace. His life on an isolated farm is forever changed when two strangers show up at his homestead, and the war comes crashing back down on him. The problem though, remains the same. How do you fight an enemy that is technologically superior and holds the high ground?

Invasion: Resistance

Invasion: Day of Battle

Invasion: Total War

Cannon Publishing
Military Sci-Fi / Fantasy
Anthology
Spring 2019
J.F. Holmes
T. Allen Diaz
Barry Ireland
Jason Cordova
Kevin Steverson
Lucas Marcum
Yakov Merkin
...and more

Fifteen classic Science Fiction stories from both masters of the craft and up and coming new writers! A tyrannical United Nations pulls the strings of its colony worlds, ruling with an iron fist. Corporate interests take precedence, and brushfire rebellions smolder on the edges. One system, home to the only alien species yet discovered, with human allies throws off the yoke and calls itself Independence.

Feedback from the slight pressure of a hand closing sends a powerful mechanical arm smashing into an opponent. A neural link hurls blustering plasma fire from your suit's shoulder mounted cannon. Your reactor levels scream with overload as return fire smashes into your armor, and damage alarms wail while you hurl your twenty ton body sideways for cover. You're a Mecha, a mechanical fighting machine with a human pilot. The guy that the infantry curse at in training and pray for in combat. The machine that the last hopes of your people ride on. The construct that strikes fear deep into alien hearts as they hear your turbines power up. The one able to pass through hell and come out the other side victorious, or die trying.

In the near future, massive empires rule the stars, and west of the Reach, they are battling for control of new systems. In the no-mans land between the front lines, Captain Nate Meric and the crew of the privateer Lexington fight for prize money, and loyalty to their ship and their friends. Beneath it all, though, runs a hidden dream. To see America restored, and take her rightful place among the stars.

Brian Corel, former slave, gladiator, ex-fiance to an Empress, exiled Captain of the Taland Royal Guard and now owner of the frigate *Widowmaker,* does the best he can to balance the lives of his crew with his own desire to live life as a free man. Skirting the border between being a privateer and an outright pirate, Corel stumbles into a war with a religious cult intent on corrupting the kingdom of an old friend and has to set things right while grieving over his lost love. Along the way he signs a dragon into his crew and has to risk everything to rescue his brother from the grasp of a demon that has destroyed an entire continent.

Chosen by the Sword

There are some things a PhD doesn't prepare you for, like running two feet of steel through the guts of a flesh-eating monster straight out of a nightmare, while ducking razor sharp claws. Or having the sword critique your fighting style while you do it. Dave Howard had a problem. Last week, he was out looking for a teaching job in the middle of a wrecked job market. This week he was neck deep in green blood and hellfire. Dragged into it by the very sword, his grandfathers' mysterious possessed blade, that was now walking him through hacking up a ghoul without getting his own head cut off. This wasn't exactly what he had gone to school for, and the University he had just taken a job with seemed to be anything BUT an academic institution. More like some kind of monster hunting bunch of weirdo nerds. Maybe his degree in Personality Psychology might be useful there, at least. The fighting though ... as he dodged another swipe of claws and awkwardly tried to follow the instructions the sword was screaming at him, he shot back at it, "Hell, I'm Canadian! Swordplay isn't in my cultural DNA!"

Beyond the Wall: A Novel of Post-Roman Britain

The legions are but a memory, the glory of Rome only a shadow of crumbling ruins and broken walls. A darkening tide of barbarism was washing across Britain's shores and the lights of civilization were slowly flickering out into darkness, only kept burning by the legendary Red Dragons cavalry unit. Led by their Tribune, Arthur, who serves no kingdom but goes where the fight is hardest and most crucial, they wage desperate battles to keep back the tide. The Red Dragons ride the length of Britannia to fight the invading Saxons, Scoti and Picts, wherever they show, from across the seas or down from the Highlands. At sixteen years old Peredur of Gwynedd has listened all his life to the stories of his father Pelinor fighting with Ambrosius Aurelianus. When word comes that his older brother has been slain in battle with the Saxons, his desire for revenge leads him to follow in his father's footsteps as a warrior, becoming a cavalryman with the Red Dragons. Along the way he may either find himself a warrior and leader worthy of Arthur or be left lying forgotten in the dust of history.

Hell's Bells: War & Love Downrange

Two souls collide in the middle of a deadly war.

Sergeant Sylvie Lyons of Her Majesty's Royal Engineers wishes she'd listened to her grandda's advice and stayed away from the military.

USMC Sergeant Hondo Cassidy wants nothing more in life than being a Marine and fighting. Hondo and Sylvie find themselves thrown together when his artillerymen are assigned to provide security for her engineers deep in the desert of Afghanistan.. Amidst death, destruction, cultural misunderstanding and the inevitable that happens when you mix an all male unit of Marines with an engineer unit that is mostly female, Sylvie and Hondo find in each other a reason to live. That is, if they can survive.

Semper Die

The dead rose expecting a feast. What they got was a firefight.

Sergeant Alex Slaughter and the Marines of Alpha Squad were on a routine training exercise near Quantico when everything went silent. No comms. No command. No clue.

What they find when they return to base is worse than anything they trained for: a bioweapon has unleashed a zombie virus that has shattered civilization, and now they must survive the Collapse.

But as the squad pushes deeper into hostile territory—through the death-choked streets of Arlington and into the rot-stained corridors beneath D.C.—they discover that the undead aren't the only threat. Desperate survivors, rogue military units, and darker truths buried beneath the weight of secrecy will test their loyalty, their mission, and their very humanity.

Written by USMC veteran Jonathan Shuerger and set in J.F. Holmes's brutal and unrelenting Irregular Scout Team One universe, Semper Die delivers pulse-pounding action, authentic military detail, and a terrifying vision of what happens when duty and apocalypse collide.

Lock. Load. Semper Fi. Semper Die.

Semper Die

Espirit De Corpse

Troll Hunter

In a world ravaged by endless war between humans and trolls, Gabriel Cullen, a grizzled hunter gifted with the rare ability to track by scent, is captured by the very creatures he hunts.

Bound both by his captors' chains and by an ancient prophecy, Cullen glimpses a chance to end centuries of bloodshed—if he can trust the trolls who butchered his kin. When a sinister force from the deep dark threatens both sides, and even trolls tremble at its approach, the tracker is forced to question everything he believes.

Unaware of her father's changes in hearts, his daughter, Isabo, a fierce warrior driven by duty and vengeance, vows to rescue him, leading an army that wields a devastating new weapon to crush the troll clans. Yet her quest risks igniting a deadlier war. As Cullen allies with a young troll warrior and a blind shaman to confront a demonic evil from a forgotten age, both father and daughter face wrenching choices between peace and betrayal.

In a land where hope is fragile and blood stains every blade, their sacrifices will forge a new world—or shatter it forever. Troll Hunter is a raw, gripping saga of loyalty, loss, and the brutal cost of survival.

More From the Fae Wars

Get the full series!

Onslaught

What would you do if America and the world were invaded tomorrow by a relentless and brutal enemy? In an alternate 2015, a US Army Special Forces Team, part of the legendary black ops unit "Delta", is in midtown Manhattan to take out a Chinese spy and his handlers, sending a message short of outright conflict. All goes smoothly until they find themselves in a full blown shooting war through the canyons of the City. Portals from another world have opened in Central Park, making a way for figures out of historical nightmare to invade. The Fae, creatures banished from Earth thousands of years ago and now only part of our legends, have returned with Dragon fire, spell and sword to conquer and take revenge. The first volume of The Fae Wars covers Team Three, G squadron, Special Forces Detachment (Delta) as they fight their way off Manhattan and then join the defense of the refugees as the Fae assault the bridges. The fabled 69th Infantry puts up an epic fight against superior weaponry and then the war descends into the asymmetric hell that the Delta Operators know so well. Along the way they find new allies and old powers that come to their aid.

The Fall

For the first time in two hundred years an enemy has stepped foot on American soil and war has come to our cities. The US military is rocked back on its heels and driven into a fighting retreat as each defense line falls. The foe is unstoppable and ... Fae. Creatures from a legendary past who have come to reclaim the Earth in the name of magic and revenge. In the hills of Pennsylvania a ragtag, devastated army prepares to make a last stand against dragon fire capable of melting an Abrams tank and wizardry that stops fifth generation fighter jets in mid-air. Inevitably it comes down to shining steel verses human will, and Sergeant Oliva Acevedo transforms from a hospital clerk to a hardened fighter. Volume Two of the best selling "Fae Wars" follows the fighting retreat of the US Army as the Fae establish control of a shattered America.

Futures Past

Two thousand years ago the Fae were banished from Earth and they've spent that time plotting return and revenge. When their portals open around the world and start crushing the human's military with spell encased steel and dragon fire, it becomes a massive struggle between technology and magic. When the Fae Invasion hammers the West Coast, Captain James Powers and his California Army National Guard artillery battery is caught on its way home from Annual Training. In a running battle the unit is smashed by combat with orcs and elves, leaving their commander struggling to keep his people together and alive. Along the way a dying priest with a strange ability to see the future manipulates people and events to bring Captain Powers to his true calling as a Seer. As they run and fight, the humans gain new allies, Fea tinkerers who love all things mechanical and hate the elves. With their help they begin to take the war to the enemy in a brutal mayhem of ambush and assassination. Book Three of the Fae Wars series following the bestselling "Onslaught" (set in NY City) and "The Fall" (Pennsylvania)

Tales From the Occupation: A Fae Wars Anthology

Wars end, enemies are defeated and territories are conquered and the combatants have to return to a life changed. America and the rest of humanity have fallen to the Fae, ancient mortal enemies of mankind. After building their strength for two thousand years, the Elves have claimed their vengeance and now rule Earth with an iron fist and dragon fire. Down but not out, a human resistance is building, but first daily life needs to be lived. An anthology of stories exploring life during the Occupation in the best-selling Fae Wars universe.

Insurgent

Wars come and wars go. Eventually even the most belligerent of combatants will arrive at some kind of living arrangement, either through exhaustion or slaughter. Kill enough, down to the last child, and there will be no more war ... until the next one, of course.

In August 2015, the war started, portals opening up between their world and ours, allowing the Fae to return to our (or their) home world in blood, fire and magic. Conventional forces fought back as well as they could, but the invasion had been planned to hit us in the middle of our civilization. America's military was scattered overseas or concentrated in large bases that were quickly overwhelmed by forces that were dropped right in the middle of their units. The fighting was brutal and horrific, magic overwhelming technology. It took six weeks, and the President surrendered to spare the civilian population. A puppet government was put in place and the Fae started to divide the conquered lands into principalities run by their Great Houses, slowly turning America into a land of feudal slavery. Thing is, though, the Fae had lived in their exile for thousands of years, fighting wars among themselves and against various races that populated their new home. Pitched battles where there was a clear-cut winner and loser. They had never fought an insurgency and had no idea how bloody it could get. Major David Kincaid. United States Army 1st Special Forces Operational Detachment–Delta, soldier of a defeated but unbroken nation, was going to show them. If, that is, he can keep the faith. The follow up novel to the bestselling "Fae Wars: Onslaught" by J.F. Holmes.

Ghost

There are wars, and then there's War. The all-encompassing thing that is fought on many levels, and with many kinds of weapons, many kinds of warriors. Even ghosts.

Alex was no one, a man just trying to get by at his paperwork job at the new Homeland Security. A man grieving for his wife, who had died in the Invasion. Someone just trying to keep his head down while the elves appointed him to do the paperwork of putting their boots on the necks of a conquered American people. Thing is, even a nobody paper shuffling clerk has a weapon, one that had lit the fires of revolution in America hundreds of years ago. His mind, and his words. The internet was still up and running, somehow and someway, and Alex takes to his keyboard. Inspired by his hero Patrick Henry, soon the words of the "Ghost" start inciting attacks on the Fae and the District of Columbia rings with explosions, gunshots and cries of Freedom. The Resistance notices, and Alex is soon assigned a bodyguard and a handler, an ex-police officer who is running from her own hidden past. Together they work to keep the flame of resistance alive and escape from the tightening net of the Fae. The consequences are, as always, Liberty or Death.

Northwest Front

Fae Wars returns on a new front as war rages in the Pacific Northwest!

Corporal Erik Doherty isn't some kind of special operations super soldier; he's just an infantry grunt trying to get by in what was once the United States Army, now an enforcement arm of the Fae overlords. When orders come down from a chain of command more interested in boot licking their new masters than protecting American citizens, he has to make the choice. To serve and live, or run and die? Ashleigh Greene is a teenage girl with a price on her head, the Fae looking for retribution for the killing of one of their nobles. As her hometown burns behind her, she flees into the mist shrouded forests of the Pacific Northwest, her family killed by dragon fire and her world destroyed. On separate paths, each human comes face to face with a haunting legend that has lived for thousands of years. One that has been waiting, watching, and hating the old enemy that has finally returned. Together, they bring war to the Fae in a battle for honor and revenge. Book seven in the best-selling Fae Wars series!

Vendetta

The echoes of the Fae Invasion have died out in the Midwest when a new thunder rumbles across the plains. Tukor, former warband leader of the Red Arrow Clan, now rides with a motorcycle club of humans and orcs against his former masters. It's hard to tell which challenges Tukor more though; being the new chief of all the orcs in the free city of Wichita Falls, Texas, or being engaged to the tough and lovely human woman Misty.

Throw in an elven duke that's still pissed at Tukor for murdering his sons, a motorcycle club that'll follow the chief to hell and back, and a newly arrived orc matron determined to prove Tukor and Misty wrong about their future. The Fae occupation of the Midwest just got way more bloody.

Featuring orcs on choppers, magic ammo and a whole crew of Army SpecOps, the tale of Tukor and Misty is a front seat view of the occupation in the Southwest that no one expected, least of all Tukor himself.

Relics of Empire

In a world shattered by elven conquest, where magic crackles and dragons soar, the Navajo Nation stands as a defiant refuge. Living there is Ben Yazzie, a battle scarred Marine veteran who wants no more war—until a brutal encounter with elven oppressors at a remote gas station ignites a spark of rebellion. Alongside Maria Hernandez, a grieving widow fueled by vengeance, and a band of unlikely allies, Ben is thrust into a fight against an empire wielding arcane power and ruthless ambition.

As ancient ley lines awaken, unleashing chaos across the American Southwest, Ben uncovers a legacy of resistance tied to his ancestors and a mysterious relic from a forgotten era. Magic surges and the earth itself stirs, forcing Ben to embrace his destiny as the Coyote, the elusive and mysterious warrior leading a desperate stand against an otherworldly tyranny.

From the dusty trails of Arizona to the neon-lit chaos of Las Vegas, *The Fae Wars: Relics of Empire* is a pulse-pounding tale of courage, sacrifice, and defiance against overwhelming odds. Will the old ways and a warrior's heart be enough to reclaim a shattered land?

The rebellion begins here.

Harley's War

In the tale of years, counting from the day the Fae returned to Earth, the war was done in six weeks. Fighting stuttered on for two years afterward, as the Great Houses assumed control and built human society into their liking. Or ignored it. The shock troops and great armies of the King were withdrawn, to leave the conquerors, the conquistadors, to send back tribute to the Old World.

The Event, when the Demon Core made its presence known on this world, changed the nature of everything, allowing t he magical Paths of the Way to be accessed by Humans on the level of what they had known of old, before the closing of the portals in 528 CE.

However, throughout the ages between that date and the Event, despite the closing the Ways by the Magus Concilium, there have always been wild magic users. Some haunt humanities legends as heroes, some paid a high price and were burned at the stake. When the Fae returned and our technology failed, they were often the fire that kept our resistance burning. Hereafter is the tale Harely Osman, the woman who was to become famous as The Dragon Rider throughout the war-torn lands of a defeated county.

~ Major James Bognaski, Unit Historian, United States Army Mage Corps
Excerpt from "Spelljammer: The Corps Monthly"
Issue #271, Vol 1, August, 2046

More Tales From the Occupation

Life is hard. Under the bootheels of an oppressor who cares nothing about human life? Almost impossible. Thing is, though, when you put the boot on the neck of Americans, they tend to get a little pissed off and a lot worked up. Doesn't matter if they face overwhelming odds, heavy firepower or bewildering magic. They're going to resist, to the death.

The Fae have won, and they're trying to do their best to beat that spirit of independence out of their ancient enemy, humanity. In a lot of places, people are just trying to survive, but here, there and everywhere someone, somehow, will stand up and say, "Not me. Never."

Eight tales of ordinary people, and some not so ordinary, fighting a war that they may never see the end of but never giving up.

<u>Authors</u>

John Holmes

J.F. Holmes is a retired Army Senior Noncommissioned Officer, having served for 22 years in both the Regular Army and Army National Guard. During that time, he served as everything from an artillery section leader to a member of a Division level planning staff, with tours in Cuba and Iraq, as well as responding to the terrorists attacks in NYC on 9-11.

From 2010 to 2014 he wrote the immensely popular military cartoon strip, "Power Point Ranger", poking fun at military life in the tradition of Beetle Bailey and Willy & Joe.

His books range from Military Sci-Fi to Space Opera to Detective to Fantasy, with a lot in between, and in 2017 two are finalists for the prestigious Dragon Awards.

In 2018, he launched Cannon Publishing, www.cannonpublishing.us specializing in military science fiction, fantasy and thrillers, with an emphasis on works from up and coming authors.

Lucas Marcum

Lucas Marcum is a critical care nurse practitioner and an officer in the US Army Reserve. When he's not working, or performing his reserve duties, he can be found hiking, reading, attempting to perfect his soft pretzel recipe and spending time with his family.

James Copley

James Copley is a former Non-Commissioned Officer of the U.S. Army, having served over twenty-one years in both Active and Reserve/Guard units, variously trained as Infantry, Communications, and Ordnance specialties before finally retiring from the Army National Guard in 2016. During his service, he deployed four separate times, twice to Iraq and twice to Afghanistan.

He is currently working as a software engineer in Central California with his wife, two children, and two dogs. Reading was his number one passion from a very young age, and more recently he decided to try writing his own. Feel free to join him on his writing journey!

Charli Cox

Charli Cox is a best-selling Military Sci-Fi and Horror Comedy author. She also writes Sci-Fi, Alternate History, and Military Fantasy stories.

If you enjoyed Fae Wars: Northwest Front and want to see more stories about Ash and "Gunny," Cannon Publishing has you covered. Burnt Mountain and Sasquatch will be coming to your Kindle later in 2025. Also, please be sure to leave a review!

Representing #teamandmore, Charli's first published short story is in The Phoenix Initiative: First Missions from Chris Kennedy Publishing. She has stories in Bureau 42 and Express Elevator to Hell, also from CKP.

Look for Whistles of the Wendigo, an Alternate History/Military Fantasy novel set in the Joint Task Force 13 universe from Three Ravens Publishing, due to release soon.

Charli's previous experience has been as a Realtor, HVAC Business Manager, IT Office Manager, and freelance bookkeeper. Professional skills such as drafting strongly worded emails transition surprisingly well into writing fiction.

An animal lover and #boymom, she lives in SW Oregon with her Leg husband, two sons, an Arabian mare, and two Husky mixes who think they are hooman.

Learn more about Charli and sign up for her newsletter on her website. Hang out with her on Facebook, Instagram, and/or TikTok.

Jason Weiser

Mr. Weiser has been a government contractor for the last eleven years, and before that, a writer working odd jobs trying to get by. He has a BA in History from CUNY Brooklyn. Mr. Weiser released his first novel in 2025, with Cannon Publishing, but before that, released a short story in their 2018 Spring Military Sci Fi Anthology.

Mr. Weiser is also an avid wargamer and has been published quite a bit in the hobby, having most recently run "Military Miniature" magazine as it's editor in chief from 2021-2023. Before that, he wrote for EpochXperience (a division of SJR Research) as a contributing writer for their blog on wargaming and military history topics from 2020 to 2021.

He also wrote two scenario books on Cold War wargaming topics, "Red Star, Burning Streets" and "Red Star, White Lights".

Mr. Weiser encourages all his fans to visit Cannon Publishing at their website

Brian Gifford

A military veteran with more than 25 years of service in the U.S. Air Force and Army (in an order that would surprise you!), Brian is a lifelong science fiction and fantasy nerd of the highest order. A student of the hard sciences and the arcane arts of cybersecurity and IT alike, Brian has spent a lifetime accumulating his unique view of the world, which he now insists on sharing with everyone else. He is a husband in awe of the magnificence that is his wife and the proud father of three awesome sons, and looks forward to retiring from the military in the near future to focus on his family and his writing.

ML McIntosh

ML McIntosh is a part time rock star, part time vengeful essence of femme wrath. She works the always shift in unapologetic science fiction, dream fiction and urban fantasy. Follow her Instagram @ml_mcintosh and stay weird.

www.ingramcontent.com/pod-product-compliance
Lightning Source LLC
Chambersburg PA
CBHW070312310726
48976CB00005B/1683